At the King's Command

The Mowbray Chronicles - Book 1

Mette Holm

Second edition with new title in 2021. Previously published with the title Blood of the Unicorn in 2019.

ISBN-13: 978-87-971343-4-4

DEDICATION

to my husband and my parents who never seized to support me. And to all the wonderful women and men who inspired me to keep going.

History is a gift too rarely given.

ACKNOWLEDGMENTS

Let the herald sound his trumpet for Steve, my resilient and persistent editor, for showing me the light of a well-written book and saving me from the plight of 'first book syndrome'.

A grand hurrah to my many beta-readers, for sparking new ideas and pointing out hopeless flaws in the original plot. Without you, no one would ever finish this book with a sense of true insight - or knowing who said what half of the time.

Raise a glass to the wonderful women on my workaways who took a few ideas and ran away with them, making the final version just as bloody and sinister as I could have ever hoped for.

A standing ovation to my proof-reader to whom I owe much more than meagre words can ever say.

I sweep a curtsey to my graphic designer for designing a stellar cover that made all my dreams come true.

And finally, a salute to my husband for sheer determination and perseverance in the face of all my cries and hues - there is always a place on the dais for you. I love you.

GALLERY OF CHARACTERS

HOUSE MOWBRAY

John Mowbray
Baron of Mowbray
✝1368

married

Elizabeth Mowbray
✝1368

Children:

- Margaret
  b. 1361
  m. 1380
  Sir Reginald de Lucy
- Joan
  b. 1363
  m. 1382
  Sir Thomas Grey
- Eleanor
  b. 1364
  m. 1385
  Baron John de Welles
- John
  b. 1365
  ✝1383
- Thomas
  b. 1367
  m.1383
  Elizabeth le Strange
  ✝ 1383
  m. 1384
  Elizabeth FitzAlan
- Argyle
  b. 1368

HOUSE PLANTAGENET

Edward III
✝1377

- Edward ✝1376
  The Black Prince
  - b. 1367
    Richard II

    m. 1382
    Anne of Bohemia
- John of Gaunt
  Duke of Lancaster
  - b. 1367
    Henry of
    Bolingbroke
- Edmund of Langley
  Duke of York
- Thomas of Woodstock
  Duke of Gloucester

OTHER KEY CHARACTERS

Blanche Wake, Baroness of Liddell [aunt to the Mowbray children, also known as Blanche of Lancaster]

La Fontaine [Knight]

Lockley [in the employ of John of Gaunt]

Sir Coxcombe [Knight]

Stephen Smith [Squire/Soldier]

Edward Warden [Master of Arms]

Abbas [Turk]

Najeelah [Turk]

Thomas Holland, Duke of Surrey [nephew to King Richard]

John Holland, Earl of Huntingdon [half-brother of King Richard]

Edmund Holland, Earl of Kent [half-brother of King Richard]

John Beaufort, Earl of Somerset [half-brother of Henry of Bolingbroke]

Thomas Beaufort, Duke of Exeter [half-brother of Henry of Bolingbroke]

Richard FitzAlan, Earl of Arundel [father-in-law to Thomas Mowbray]

Thomas de Beauchamp, Earl of Warwick [grandfather in law to Thomas Mowbray]

George [Page]

Prologue

Spring 1368 — Nottingham

Her hair still clung to her skull, wet and sticky with the exertions of childbirth. Her lips were blue, and her empty eyes stared up at the canopy. Beneath her limp body, the sheets were soaked in blood.

The birth was supposed to be like all the others, yet now, the two midwives stood staring at the woman's pale face. In a corner, a maid with her face turned away held a whimpering little bundle.

'Have you summoned the nurse?' The older midwife's voice was husky with emotion.

The young woman turned from the bed, her plain woollen dress grazing the rushes, and waved at a girl who opened the door and slipped into the gloom of the hall with gratitude painted plainly on her face. The maid cleared her throat and shuffled her feet; a tiny hand escaped the bundle and waved aimlessly at the stuffy room.

'Open the shutters.' The older woman pushed her grey hair back under her cap and wiped her forehead with a trembling hand. 'She feels naught, and M'lord's not here. We need a change of air.'

'It went so fast.'

The older woman sought to soothe her young assistant. 'Unfortunately, it isn't uncommon, m'dear. The fever took her 'fore the child was even born. There was naught to be done. 'Tis the lot of a woman. We must take comfort in the healthy babe.'

A servant opened the door a little, but he stayed outside in the corridor. Tradition and religion equally demanded that a woman should live in seclusion during the last months of her pregnancy and until six weeks after the birth of a child. No man was to set foot in her chambers during this time.

'Any message for M'lord?' the servant enquired.

'M'lady did not survive the birth.' The midwife's voice took on a sad ring.

The servant paled. 'The child?'

'He'll be fine if the wet-nurse'll get here soon.'

The young woman opened the last shutter, the wood clanged hollow against the stone wall as the open windows let in gushes of fresh air.

The servant shot both women a doubtful look. 'Ought you do this?'

'The room no longer houses a woman in labour.' The old woman shook her head slowly, pointing towards the bed. 'Best you summon a physician and make the necessary arrangements.'

'I shall announce that the house is now in mourning over the loss of its mistress.' The servant hung his head and quietly closed the door behind him. The newborn whimpered.

Elizabeth Mowbray would never know her son.

Summer 1368 — near Constantinople

John Mowbray fell clumsily onto the low stool; inside the tent the air was completely stale. Noises from the camp made their way through the sliver where the tent flaps met, a reminder that life went on right outside, while his own world had come crashing down just seconds before. John lowered his head to his chest, hands shaking. The messenger did not move; he just stared vacantly into the air. Time seemed to have stopped.

After a while, the messenger cleared his throat. 'Any message to send back, M'lord?'

'No.' John's voice was thick and hoarse, his head still sunken. With a heavy, tired hand, he sent the messenger away.

He let a hollow, rasping breath escape, struggling to accept what had happened so many leagues away. John had married Elizabeth for her family connections as much as for herself, yet their marriage had been happy and love had grown gradually. Still it was not until this moment when he felt his heart being ripped from his chest that he knew how deeply he had loved her. How deeply he still loved her.

Shouting and commotion outside the tent dragged him back to the present. Had only a minute passed, or had it been hours? John got off the low stool with a groan, his legs stiff; in two steps, he was at the opening of the tent and threw the flaps aside.

Outside, the camp was dissolving before his very eyes. Soldiers were scrambling in all directions, squires struggling to get to the horses. Arrows rained down on the human sea from all directions. Soldiers fell screaming to the ground, cut off in mid-run. A squire, his eyes mad with fear, came running towards John's tent. One moment, John looked directly into the poor boy's wide, sky-blue eyes, the next, one of those eyes exploded as an arrow hit its mark, spraying blood and flesh across the youthful face. He fell backwards a few feet from the tent opening, his hands stretched out as if he was reaching for heaven.

Alas, my young friend, there is no Heaven, John thought sadly, but his instincts were stronger than his sorrow and, within a few seconds, he had grabbed his shield and sword. His last thoughts went to England, to his children and his beloved, dead wife. Then John stepped over the squire's body into the blinding sunlight.

For Elizabeth …

February 1370 — Nottingham

The chubby, almost two-year-old boy tottered across the floor with determination, drawing lines in the rushes with his little shoes. He clearly enjoyed his family's admiring comments. With a happy grin, he fell into the arms of his eldest sister who immediately pulled him from the floor, kissed his nose and swung him into the air. The child, like his youngest sister, took after their mother, his hair blonde and eyes blue. The four others had the characteristic dark brown hair and grey eyes of their father. But all shared the same charming smile.

Behind them, the door opened, and a servant entered. 13 year-old Margaret turned; annoyed to be disturbed during the one time a day when all the family was together. Since their mother's unexpected and untimely death during childbirth, Margaret had been running the household and minding her brothers and sisters; a task she did not take lightly.

'What?' Margaret snapped at the servant before noticing that his face was white and his hands shaking.

Joan gave a startled blink. As the middle sister, she often felt slighted and forgotten - she had felt the loss of their mother more keenly than the rest, at least if anyone ever asked her. Which hardly ever happened.

'A message ... from M'lord's squire.' The servant's voice shook almost as badly as his hands, which were grasping a piece of paper.

Margaret nodded to her oldest brother John who snatched the note from the servant and gave the servant leave with a gesture far more adult than his five years.

'Hand it over.' Margaret put down her youngest brother and reached for the dirty piece of paper. It had clearly been underway for quite some time, and she shrugged in wonder at the sight of a broken seal.

'Who it from?' Thomas, who could not quite speak in full sentences yet, came tumbling out from under a table. He had a habit of hiding whenever he got the chance, scaring the servants half to death, always popping up when they least expected it. His behaviour had led to many broken cups and frayed nerves.

'Father?' Margaret's voice laid bare her confusion.

They had not had a single word from their father since before their mother had died. She read the hastily scrawled note with increasing horror.

'What is it?' Eleanor asked. 'Say it! You may be the oldest, but I am 8 now. You cannot keep things from me - from us.' She pointed to the other children, and John nodded.

One look between Margaret and Joan exchanged a hundred unsaid words. Margaret made to send the younger children from the room, but Eleanor resolutely grabbed Thomas by the hand and pouted. Stubborn as an ass, their mother had always said of Eleanor. In the middle of the floor, little Argyle stumbled and squealed. Thomas broke free and went to his brother's aid.

The four eldest children gathered by the large fireplace, as the only one, Margaret stood as tall as the mantelpiece where she put the note down and gave the others a serious look. 'Our father is dead. It seems he died just months after mother. His forces were attacked by the Turks at Constantinople - very few survived.' Her tone was calm, but her eyes betrayed her emotions.

Eleanor and John looked from their eldest sister to Joan who was crying openly but made no sound. In the background, Argyle squealed again, and Margaret turned just in time to see Thomas hide something behind his back. That boy was an impossible troublemaker, would he ever outgrow that?

Margaret straightened her back, summoned a servant and asked him to gather the household in the great hall.

She gave her brothers and sisters a serious look, then turned her attention to John. 'As the eldest son, it is now your job to ensure the future of this family.' Margaret said this with great formality and then turned towards the door. 'But I shall announce father's death to the household. After all, you are only five.'

John looked after his sister and, in that moment, his eyes took on a serious gleam that would never leave again. For a time, Thomas forgot his mischief and even accepted Joan scooping him up. Eleanor struggled to lift plump, little Argyle from the floor. In a group headed by John, the children followed Margaret.

As they walked into the hall, Eleanor gave Joan a worried look. 'What shall bccomc of us now?'

Spring 1392 — London

On the soaked ground lay a battered shield. The prancing unicorn emblazoning it was spattered in blood.

He was dead … How could that be?

ℵ ℵ ℵ ℵ

Part 1
Chivalry

CHAPTER 1

29 July 1381 — Nottingham

Argyle's feet pounded on the worn stone stairs; he seemed to have lost all control of his body and he could feel goose bumps up and down his arms. Down and down he went ever faster. Clapping his hands together, he leapt two steps at a time. Finally … it is finally my turn, he thought.

As his feet made contact with the wooden floorboards, he was almost completely out of breath - still, he managed to skip down the hall, smiling until his cheeks hurt. Argyle's older brothers and sisters always craved attention and got it. But not today. This was his day - and what a glorious day to set off on his very own adventure!

Since daybreak, the sun had warmed the house and surrounding lands, enticing the entire household outside. At one point Argyle had actually thought that the others had completely forgotten that today was *his* day. Everyone was busy doing chores; Joan was in the dairy overseeing the daily production of butter and tasting the cheese, John was in the stables tending to his new horse, and Thomas was probably hiding in the library even though he was supposed to be helping John.

Only Eleanor seemed as excited as Argyle was. 'I truly cannot believe that you, the baby, will be the second one of us to leave,' she sighed with envy. 'Why you anyway? Why not John or Thomas? They are far older and stronger than you!'

Eleanor shot him an impertinent look and Argyle made a face at his sister. 'Don't be silly. They already know what they are destined for. John is knighted and heir to father's estate, he is probably just waiting to be old enough to establish his own household. And Thomas will be appointed a position at court when he comes of age.'

'I suppose that they will do alright.' Eleanor peeked out of the window scratching her nose, a habit of hers when she felt overlooked or cheated out of something. 'But what about the rest of us?'

He tickled her side, making her squeal and run for cover behind a big chair.

'Well, *you* are to be married off to some important courtier or other and you will make plenty of babies. Girls must, you know.' Argyle added an important air to the latter and earned a disapproving look from Eleanor.

He was right of course; even Eleanor could not escape the tradition among the children of nobility that their marriages should make powerful alliances with other great noble houses. His sisters were almost guaranteed to marry well - where rank and title were concerned at any rate.

As children of the fourth Baron of Mowbray, it fell to the head of the family, the court - and in the end the King - to ensure that they made suitable matches. It had turned out that their parents had already been making prosperous alliances for their children before their unexpected deaths some 13 years ago.

To everyone's surprise, the family had gained a royal decree announcing the betrothal of Margaret to Sir Reginald de Lucy of Woodcroft. And so, Margaret pulled the wool over everyone's eyes when she was wedded and lead to her new husband's estates only weeks after the children had been turned over as wards to their aunt Blanche.

Though petrified, Margaret had found some solace and entertainment in her younger sister Joan's pouting when it was announced that Margaret - the least attractive of the girls - was promised to a young nobleman who was quickly making a name for himself at court. Amidst her new and unfamiliar situation, Margaret probably still clung to this fact.

The other children had scant news from her, but the short letters from her seethed with deprivation and melancholy. While her husband was courteous and respectable, Margaret had been far from ready for marriage, and she clearly disliked her role as a married woman.

Within the next few years, Argyle's eldest brother John would take his rightful place at the old family estate. An event that would most likely be swiftly followed by him finding a bride to ensure the Mowbray succession. As it stood, Thomas was next in line to inherit the title and lands and was destined for a career at court. As the youngest, Argyle had little prospect of wealth and inheritance, and to remedy this, aunt Blanche had declared that Argyle would serve as squire to a great knight. He thought it was an exquisite plan - by far better than the responsibilities his brothers would shoulder.

'I am bound for adventure. Meeting knights and fighting great battles, that is my destiny!' Argyle would brag this when anyone bothered to ask him. They would nod solemnly and tell him how brave he was; apparently serving king and country was something rather extraordinary.

Argyle enjoyed feeling extraordinary. When visitors came by, the guests always showed John and Thomas the most interest and, at times, even Joan and Eleanor, who were not yet married, would claim attention too. A wide range of important men would visit aunt Blanche who had taken on the task of arranging prosperous marriages for the two remaining girls. But no one ever took much notice of Argyle.

The noblemen would bring their sons who expected to be entertained by the boys and would pine after Joan when she entered the room bedecked in jewels and fine clothing. Some of them looked more at Eleanor, though; Argyle thought that was because she was by far the prettiest.

But no one would watch Joan or speak to John and Thomas today because this was Argyle's day. For months, he had practiced being dignified and slightly unimpressed, but now that the day had finally come, he had forgotten all his rehearsed airs. Argyle could hardly contain himself, let alone find anything sensible to do until the important guests arrived.

'Argyle!' Aunt Blanche's authoritative voice cut through the heavy summer air. 'Get down here this instance, boy. They are already in the courtyard.'

'Yes, Aunt.' Argyle ran even faster.

Along the narrow stone corridor, down another set of stairs, his hands were tingling at the touch of stone. Out of breath, Argyle stopped just inches from aunt Blanche's billowing skirt and she looked him up and down with a critical gaze.

'Your shirt,' she said, her voice had a slightly tired ring to it, and Argyle quickly tucked his shirt into his breeches.

The servants threw open the massive doors, and aunt Blanche swept down the stairs to receive her guests. John was holding the horse of one of the many riders, while Thomas strolled down the corridor from the library whistling a merry tune. Argyle paused in the doorway taking in the scenery of the courtyard; there were so many men and horses.

'Ready? This is your moment, you know. Make sure you do not ruin it.' Thomas nudged Argyle and then bellowed with laughter, as he ducked when Argyle made a swing for him. 'I cannot imagine that they will take kindly to you beating your older brother.'

Aunt Blanche summoned him with a commanding wave. 'Now, here he is, Sire. I am confident he will meet your expectations.'

Argyle scrambled out to stand beside aunt Blanche and he stared up at one of the largest men he had ever set eyes on. The knight was still on his horse, towering high above, his head emblazoned by the sun, which made it impossible for Argyle to make out the man's features. He had to leap back when the man got off his horse in a flourish, landing elegantly on the courtyard cobbles, kicking up dust around his leather boots. Some of that dust settled on the bottom of his long dark blue cloak, giving the edge of the fabric a dull, brown colour.

With a steady look, the knight bowed deeply to aunt Blanche; when he looked up again, his dark blue eyes shot a humorous glance at Argyle. Then he straightened his back and offered aunt Blanche his arm.

'I am confident that we will make a fine knight of him.' His voice was deep and comfortably booming.

Aunt Blanche smiled. 'There is much to work with, I am sure.'

Argyle gave his ancient aunt a bewildered look. Was she blushing?

Just as Argyle made to speak, the two adults turned and headed for the house. Over the shoulder, the knight added. 'See to my horse and my men.'

This task usually fell to John, but Argyle asked the stable boys to take care of the horses, and one of the maids to make that the knight's retinue was fed. While the courtyard went into a state of busy flurry, Argyle was left feeling quite lost in the middle of it all.

'You are supposed to go with them.' John had appeared next to him, smiling calmly. Although only three years his senior, John was almost a head higher than Argyle, and now he mussed Argyle's blonde hair and pushed him gently on the back. 'Off you go. We know what we're about here.'

Argyle nearly tripped over his own feet in his vigour to catch up with aunt Blanche and the large knight. They had already descended into the shadows of the great doors, but he could hear their faint conversation and his aunt's tingling laughter.

Argyle found them in the front room, their backs to him, looking out over the flower garden. It was his aunt's pride - a veritable sea of colours spreading out before them. Argyle briefly wondered if it was on purpose that his aunt had invited their guest at this particular time.

The knight's voice reached his ears as he approached. '… reminds me of myself at his age. Not quite as alone in the world, but still …'

Just then, aunt Blanche caught Argyle's reflection in the window, she touched the knight's arm and they both turned around. 'Argyle, come meet Sir Edmund La Fontaine.'

Aunt Blanche beckoned Argyle closer, so he hurried over to the large man and bowed deeply.

La Fontaine nodded courteously. 'It is a pleasure to make your acquaintance, Argyle. I have heard so much about you, and now that I lay eyes upon you, I feel reassured. Are you ready to become my squire?'

'Oh yes Sire. I have been practicing, just as aunt Blanche has promised.' Argyle tripped over his words and noticed aunt Blanche arching her eyebrows at his familiar mention of her in the presence of a stranger. 'Well, that is to say … Yes, Sire.'

Argyle shot a sideways glance at La Fontaine who appeared not to have noticed Argyle's little slip. 'Good. We shall rest here for a few days if your Aunt will have us. The area is pretty and charming, and my men need the break. This will give us time to settle the final details and perhaps for my men to hunt a little game?'

La Fontaine looked at aunt Blanche who nodded her agreement, and the knight turned back to Argyle, smiling. 'Once we are done, you will come with me to London. We are requested at court.'

Argyle stared in awe. He had never imagined that he would be going to London right away - to court! Of course aunt Blanche had told Argyle that La Fontaine was a great friend to the young king who often relied on the seasoned knight for advice. It was just that Argyle had never imagined that he would get to go to court, too - and so soon!

ജ ഇ ജ ഇ

The great hall was full to the bursting with La Fontaine's retinue and the regular household having to rub shoulders to make room for everybody. The many people were seated according to their rank, the least important men sat at the tables furthest away from the dais and the enormous roaring fires. Back there, the guests would catch a draft every time the door to the hall opened, which it frequently did, and this night, Argyle envied them; the air in the hall was stifling hot and he could feel drops of sweat coursing down his spine, slowly soaking his shirt.

Closer to the dais the more prominent figures of La Fontaine's retinue, as well as certain members of aunt Blanche's family were seated at the massive, trestle tables. The most prominent family members and friends as well as La Fontaine's closest companions sat closest to the dais.

Everywhere dogs were feasting on the leftovers from the tables, occasionally fighting over a choice bone or piece of meat, their growling mingling with the noise from the guests.

The family and La Fontaine sat by the heavy oak table on the dais. Usually, John would sit to the left of aunt Blanche, but today that particular honour fell to Argyle, although he was very uncomfortable with that part of the arrangement. Argyle constantly felt like his older brothers and sisters were watching to see if he made a mistake. But when he looked at Joan, she listened demurely with her head tilted ever so slightly, apparently engulfed in her companion's tales, and John was busy attacking a particularly savoury dish. Even Margaret had shown up with her husband and a large entourage in tow. All of this made the evening extra special.

'Do not keep me at bay any longer, La Fontaine. What news from court?' Aunt Blanche sent another dish to a few distinguished supper guests close to the dais, who nodded in return before selecting choice pieces of meat.

'His Grace was successful in stomping out the shocking peasants' revolt. A sinful movement if ever there was one, though I cannot deny that they might have had some cause of complaint.' La Fontaine smiled, when aunt Blanche raised her eyebrows in a saying manner. 'They made it as far as London. The King was barricaded in the Tower, but for all his well meaning counsellors, he chose to meet the peasant leaders.'

La Fontaine raised his glass and nodded at aunt Blanche, who sipped her wine.

'Why put himself in such danger?' she asked.

Argyle had to strain his ears to hear their hushed conversation. He gently leaned towards his aunt while reaching for a piece of pie. The thick, salty crust was hard as rock but the filling was burning hot and filled with succulent pieces of leek, onion and rabbit. Argyle broke the lid with a sharp crack that earned him a stern look from his aunt before she turned her attention back to La Fontaine.

Argyle pierced a piece of rabbit and once again leaned towards his aunt's large oak chair.

'His Grace probably thought it was high time he came into his own as King of England,' the knight pondered out loud, reaching for another leg of duck. 'I have to say, Lady Blanche, your duck hunt has been particularly successful this year.'

'Oh yes, although I always ask our gamekeeper to make sure the flock is never thinned too much. It provides entertainment for our guests, you see. And of course you will see the game, when you hunt here yourself the next couple of days.' Aunt Blanche favoured him with a tiny smile.

The jewels around her neck glistened when she moved, and Argyle could have sworn that the old lady looked years younger, engulfed in the flickering light from the dripping candles and open fires.

'I am more than happy to accept and go out once or twice before setting off for London,' La Fontaine said. 'But you asked about court. While many of his advisors were happy to stay safely locked in the Tower, watching London turn to ashes, his Grace had a different idea. In the end, they had to surrender to the King's command and open the Tower portcullis and gates. From the Tower, the King made for Smithfield with a few select advisors and the Mayor of London, ready to hear the peasants' demands.' La Fontaine smacked his lips happily. 'The King's meeting with the leaders was not an unlimited success. Several of his companions got into a clamour with the leaders, and the Mayor managed to slay the leader Tyler in the confusion. Naturally, the King was immediately engulfed in turmoil when the peasants set out to repay the courtesy.'

Breathless, aunt Blanche raised her eyebrows. 'Why would anyone do such a thing?'

'The Mayor was ever a rash man, but his inherent suspicions did him credit to some extent this time. I do not think the mob would be easily appeased, even if the King had already agreed to most of their demands in a decree sent out before that fateful day in Smithfield. However, what transpired must have been planned - Tyler fell right in front of the King's horse.'

Aunt Blanche let out a gasp.

'The King rode his horse directly at the mob, while they shot their arrows, and said to them 'I shall be your Captain, leader and true King!' Then he turned to the Mayor and asked him to leave Smithfield while still in possession of his good health and head. In truth, it fell to the Mayor to fetch the city militia, though they were not needed by then,' La Fontaine smirked.

Aunt Blanche nodded thoughtfully. 'What a truly regal act, and yet so rash - even you must acknowledge this, Sire?'

'Gladly … But you do not question the King's intention,' La Fontaine reached for another baked apple. 'I am sure his Grace merely did what he truly believed God demanded of him. He is a true heir to the legend of King Arthur! At 14, few are afraid of death, this too is true of our King, who made a serious play for the kind of regent he is destined to become in time.'

Aunt Blanche narrowed her eyes. 'Do you truly believe this, La Fontaine?'

'You liar!' Thomas threw a cushion at Argyle, which fortunately missed its mark when Argyle ducked out of the way.

'Hey now,' John said mildly while he pulled the bedding away to make room for his brothers and himself.

A single torch lighted the chamber; the fire already banked up for the night. The shutters were closed, but John opened one to let the warm summer breeze stir the stale air in the room. He turned to his two younger brothers.

Argyle stood with balled fists starring indignant at Thomas. He felt tears of injustice rise and blinked them away angrily. 'Oh no, it is not a lie!'

In his usual stoic manner, John played intermediary. 'Come to bed, both of you and no more fighting.'

Argyle failed to suppress the urge to go on with his story. 'La Fontaine told Aunt Blanche. The peasants had come all the way to London to kill the King, but he could not be beaten. In stead he stood right in the middle of the peasants. And he was so mad at the Mayor of London for killing the leader!'

Argyle saw his brothers ogling in wonderment and encouraged by their reactions he continued. 'The silly mayor was close to losing his own head, but the King bid him leave Smithfield before any such thing happened. King Richard was not afraid of them at all. He does not fear death; a King does not need to. God watches over him.'

Thomas and John looked at Argyle in awe and exchanged surprised glances. Now that was quite a story.

John folded his hands behind his neck. 'He will be a great King.'

'He cannot become something he already is.' Argyle yawned and pulled a blanket up to his chin.

'That may well be … but even a king can lose his life,' Thomas whispered his thoughts into the darkness once he felt sure the other two had fallen asleep. Argyle closed his eyes, his back already turned to his tiresome brother and let sleep wrap its soothing arms around him.

ဢ ဣ ဢ ဣ

CHAPTER 2

18 August 1381 — Westminster

It felt like stepping into a fairy story. Every room was lit by more candles than Argyle had ever seen before, which left the rooms smelling strongly of a mix of honey and stale wax. Whenever a door opened or closed, the candles would flicker and wax would drip into the rushes, making lavender and herbs stick to the massive wooden floors.

La Fontaine negotiated the many corridors and rooms with ease, greeting those familiar to him by way of a nod or brief salute. Occasionally he would stop to exchange a few words in hushed tones with some courtier or other. On these occasions, Argyle took in as much as he could before being ushered on further into the royal apartments.

Brightly coloured tapestries lent warmth to the massive stone walls and silver and gold thread glistened in the flickering lights. Many window arches were crowded with courtiers and ladies wearing beautiful garments showing off their wealth and prosperity. Pearls and gemstone inlays decorated their gowns and tall, conical hats, streaming lengths of silk in all the colours of the rainbow towered on their heads. The men sported wide belts adorned with gold and mother of pearl that hung low on their hips, on top of their tunics and doublets, their heads adorned with long colourful liripipes or small hats with large feathers, a few even favoured elaborate chaperons.

The greatest experience was yet to come, for that afternoon, they would attend the King. La Fontaine made it sound like the most natural thing, but even Argyle knew it was a great honour and to make sure, he fit in, Argyle had dressed in his finest clothes, the only ones not stained by the dust of travelling from Lancashire to court, which was currently residing in the Tower of London.

'Come along, squire.'

La Fontaine's large hand completely covered Argyle's shoulder, as the knight drew him through the mass of courtiers. Anyone wanting to make a petition to the King was in the outer reception chamber; the further into the Tower they got, the fewer people crowded the rooms. In these rooms, it was clear that anyone present was specially selected and warranted great respect. Argyle gaped when they entered the inner apartments.

'Sire, who is that young man?'

Following Argyle's discreet nod, La Fontaine frowned slightly. 'The King's cousin; Bolingbroke.'

Before he could elaborate, a courtier gestured to La Fontaine, who took part in a game of hazard for a while. When he grew bored of the game, he began working his way around the room, flirting with the ladies he knew and laughing loudly with some of the other courtiers. La Fontaine introduced Argyle to more people than he would ever remember the names of, so Argyle made sure to study their faces, so that he would know them again at a later time. He only spoke when asked a direct question and kept close to La Fontaine at all times.

A page resplendent in the royal livery made his way over to them. He whispered a message in La Fontaine's ear and by a simple gesture, bade them follow.

'This is it, boy. Most Englishmen can scarcely dream to meet the King, yet you are asked all the way into the throne room.' La Fontaine turned towards the page. Argyle swallowed hard and followed the knight towards the massive, oak doors at the end of the room.

On a dais high above the floor was an elaborate, empty oak throne.

'La Fontaine! Finally, you see fit to tend your duties and visit your King at court,' the voice rang out from behind them.

La Fontaine bowed with an extravagant flourish bringing his head very close to the stone floor. Argyle immediately mimicked him, tottering for an instant, only just managing to keep to his feet. Argyle stared into the rushes, the scent of herbs and lavender strong in his nose.

'Your Grace.'

The King touched La Fontaine's shoulder. 'Do get up, La Fontaine, your presence bestows great joy upon your King. It truly has been too long.'

In three long strides, the King reached the dais, he gestured La Fontaine to join him.

La Fontaine cleared his throat and reached for Argyle. 'Your Grace, may I present my squire, Argyle Mowbray.'

Argyle stood but fought to keep his eyes firmly fixed on the floor. He felt the King take a step toward him and held his breath, daring to look up a little.

The King half-smiled and gave a measured nod. 'Welcome, young Mowbray. Your father was an extraordinary knight and a great defender of England. It may be some time before you can offer England the same services - but you will, young Mowbray, you will. Your brother Thomas has done well since he came to our court.'

'Indeed, your Grace. Once I had met young Thomas, I became convinced that he would serve you with great fervour and make quite a career for himself, if guided by your skilful courtiers,' La Fontaine said.

The King laughed heartily, and clapped his hands together. 'How I have missed your experienced voice among my counsellors. Have you heard about my recent success?'

The King sauntered up the steps to the throne and threw himself lazily into it, one leg dangling over the armrest the other stretching towards the four steps rising from the floor. He commanded the room with ease. La Fontaine dropped unceremoniously onto a low stool on the topmost step underlining his close relationship with the King.

'Of course, your Grace. Rumour has spread across the kingdom. You have acted with great valour. A true King Arthur of Camelot,' La Fontaine remarked with an admiring nod.

Argyle had heard that more than anything the King aspired to bring England back to its former glory, and an extra wide smile had broken on his face, when La Fontaine mentioned King Arthur. To the King there was no greater hero than Arthur and he worshipped the knight's code of chivalry with a passion that bordered on obsession at times. The King seemed determined to restore chivalry to England and, at the same time, end the war with the French. Something his grandfather would never have considered a possibility - even for a moment.

La Fontaine scratched his cheek. 'Your subjects gobble it up, but was it so very wise to meet the rebels in such an open place as Smithfield?'

'You sound like my stuffy advisers! Of course your King makes nothing but wise decisions. God himself bade me meet the leaders of the peasant revolt to end England's sufferings. I listened to Tyler and judged that they were entitled to some small concessions!' The King was bursting with pride.

'Naturally, I could not make too many allowances, but some were required. Why else would I sign that letter of freedom? If only we had not had to slay Tyler, everyone could have left Smithfield alive.' The King's voice had darkened, but the next moment his face lit up in a bright smile. 'You should have been there, La Fontaine! In my time of need, God spoke to me! He bid me ride out to meet my subjects, for all to see that I am truly God's rightful, anointed Regent. If anyone, you will understand that a King must be at the forefront.'

The King stared intensely at La Fontaine who was quick to answer with a smile. 'You were in that place acting on behalf of God, your Grace. If He bade you speak to the rebellious masses, then naturally you did the right thing.'

The King leaned back nodding contently. He waved Argyle further from the throne. 'Boy, leave us to speak alone. There is a fine view from yonder window.'

Argyle rushed to meet the order.

Their conversation seemed to go on forever, and Argyle soon began feeling bored. The view of the Tower's many small courtyards and stone buildings was truly grand, but to him it was uninteresting. Instead, he looked around the King's reception chamber with increasing curiosity.

All manner of comforts were on display here. Soft cushions and low chairs, music instruments, writing desks and richly decorated tapestries all made the room warm and welcoming. At the back of the room near the thick doors, guards in the King's livery stood watch and pages came and went through hidden side doors. They provided wine and little dishes of sweetmeats and fruit, first served to the King and then offered to La Fontaine and some even to Argyle.

As he popped another small, sweet treat into his mouth, Argyle began feeling a little more comfortable amidst all of the lustre and splendour of the King's young court.

1 September 1381 — London

'In a week, the King will celebrate a decision of great political consequence.' La Fontaine was seated in a comfortable chair; Argyle was standing in front of him. 'We are invited to dine with him - or at least as close as the King can make out without offending others. It is a great honour.'

'We?' Argyle looked intently at the knight, who nodded, smiling.

'Why of course! You are my chosen squire, and you will wait on me. The King knows how important it is for a squire never to be far from his knight.' La Fontaine looked Argyle up and down. 'But you simply cannot participate in that attire. It may do for the audience chamber but not a night dining with some of England's finest families.'

'But Sire, it is all I have!'

The clothes, that had been some of his finest at Aunt Blanche's household, apparently did not do in the splendour of court. Argyle was suddenly ashamed of his clothing although he was not entirely sure why.

'Then we must change your situation. Come along, it is past time you see a little more of what London has to offer.'

La Fontaine summoned a servant and declared that he and Argyle would be going to the tailor to make sure, La Fontaine's squire was adequately equipped for court. As the servant went to fetch La Fontaine's cloak, the knight tied his purse to his belt and slid a small dagger inside his sleeve.

'You can never be too careful in London,' La Fontaine remarked, when he noticed Argyle's curious expression. 'And out into London we must go!'

ꕤ ꕤ

As soon as they stepped into London's narrow, dusty and filthy streets, the city's smells assaulted Argyle's senses. The knight noticed his discomfort and laughed.

'Aye, London may be our capital, but it is a far cry from the clean country air to which you are accustomed! Best you get used to the stench, it is the only way to truly become part of court,' La Fontaine said with a wry smile.

As La Fontaine strode ahead, Argyle had to half run to keep up. It was hard to stay close to the knight with all these people bustling about him, and it was not long before Argyle felt completely lost. Was this really the glorious capital he had longed to visit?

An ox carriage blocked the increasingly narrow street further ahead, where two tradesmen were engaged in a heated discussion of who had right of way. Argyle was pushed against a wall and watched with wide eyes.

'Come along, boy, we have to turn down here,' La Fontaine's booming voice reached Argyle from across the noisy street and he was relieved to see La Fontaine pointing down a narrow, almost empty alley. They walked past several shops before finally stopping before a timber-framed house.

A tailor stood in the doorway spreading his arms wide. 'Sire, back at last.'

Standing aside, the tailor ushered them through the open door. Inside the dark room, yard upon yard of fabric were piled high on shelves and floor. Argyle saw silks in every colour, silver threaded lace and even a roll of cloth of gold, glittering on the top of one of the many shelves. The air was dry and stuffy, even though the room was clean and the windows open.

Turning towards the tailor, La Fontaine said. ''Tis true, Romaine, however this time it is my squire who is in need of finery. The clothes must be finished this week as we are asked to dine with the King this coming Saturday. I trust you to make it happen, Romaine. Measure young Argyle Mowbray here for his new clothes and help him select the right fabrics, I shall be back within the hour.'

As he turned to go, La Fontaine's huge frame seemed to take up most of the door. He looked down at Argyle. 'Romaine may be French, but he is also the finest tailor in London.' La Fontaine winked. 'He will make provision for you, Argyle.'

Before Argyle could say anything, the knight was gone.

'Well, young Mowbray, shall we get started?' Romaine said.

Argyle was measured for hose, a shirt and a doublet and soon the tailor had rolled out several bundles of brightly coloured fabrics on the counter. Romaine had Argyle feel the different kinds of fabrics while they began discussing the specific details of his new wardrobe.

'Best to avoid certain colours, young Mowbray. Some, because they are for his Grace's own household, others for the significance they carry. Why not combine La Fontaine's colours with your own? That ought to prove a good solution.'

'My colours? I do not have any?'

The tailor chuckled. 'The colours of your house. As I recall, house Mowbray is red and white, n'est pas?'

'Oh ... Why yes, quite right! And La Fontaine's are green and blue.' Argyle smiled to himself. Of course, he should boast both houses, as he was now both a part of La Fontaine's household and a member of a noble family. Argyle liked the idea of not looking like anyone else at the forthcoming celebrations.

When La Fontaine returned an hour later, the tailor had all the measurements for Argyle's clothes ready, and they had also carefully chosen appropriate fabrics and colours. The knight then personally chose a slim belt with a large buckle and put it on top of the pile of fabric.

'You are ready for an evening dining with the King at court!' La Fontaine slid a pouch of silver coins across the counter. 'Romaine, please deliver the clothes to my house in exactly six days.'

'Certainly, Sire, it will be my pleasure,' Romaine smiled and followed them to the door, holding it open for them. Together, La Fontaine and Argyle stepped back into the hustle and bustle that was London.

ꟷ ꟷ ꟷ ꟷ

8 September 1381 — London

Once more, Argyle straightened his clothes and gave himself a critical look. The tailor had certainly made good on his promises. Argyle was very proud of his new clothes and several of La Fontaine's entourage had said nice things about both the colours and fabrics.

The festivities were about to begin when La Fontaine and Argyle entered the vast banquet hall. Even though Argyle was now used to both the court and the many rooms and hallways of the Tower, this was altogether something else.

To get to the palace, they had sailed on a richly decorated barge up the Thames from La Fontaine's townhouse, which was right on the riverbank. As they moored by the pier, two of the Kings guards had been ready to greet them. The walk through the beautiful gardens, where the leaves shone in all of autumn's golden colours and the last roses stubbornly bloomed in the many beds, could not have prepared Argyle for the sight that met him when the high hedges lining the gravel paths finally gave way to a large open space from which the castle was revealed in all its glory.

'Oh …' Argyle was unable to stifle a little outburst.

La Fontaine gave him a mild, indulgent smile and then led the way through the glistening grand hall. The doors to the King's private chambers were still closed, and the hall had been lined with tables and trestles. On the dais, the King's vast throne presided beneath a cloth canopy of state. The room was dressed with all anyone could possibly want, and every table had large, solid gold candelabra set with sturdy wax candles giving off the faint, comfortable scent of honey.

'We should make our rounds,' La Fontaine said, heading into the crowd. He greeted his friends, the energetic Robert de Vere, the Bishop of Norwich Henry le Despenser and the young, enigmatic Michael de la

Pole with great joy. Argyle had to work hard to keep up with his master while bowing courteously here and there - and it seemed, everywhere.

Several courtiers nodded at Argyle as if they already recognised him and it made him feel a little more at ease. The court of England was quite an ordeal, especially to a boy of just 13 and when Argyle looked round the hall packed with people, he could hardly imagine how they would all be seated without being squashed shoulder to shoulder.

'His Grace, King Richard II of England.'

The hall instantly fell silent and all eyes turned to the massive oak doors now thrown wide open, with the young King in the centre. He slowly took in the room, and wherever his eyes rested, his guests bowed or curtsied deeply. The King stepped into the room and clapped his hands together. Hundreds of servants appeared with brimming trays and flacons full of wine. The guests hurried to their seats at the long, massive tables.

One table stood out. It was placed directly below the dais and was not occupied by the King's closest family or the country's most important noblemen, as Argyle had expected. Instead, it was reserved for the King's closest friends - the group of young men La Fontaine had been speaking to before. Most of them could scarcely claim a single title, making them, in the eyes of the nobility, poor company for a young King. This was where La Fontaine took his seat after first pointing out one of the squires' tables to Argyle.

He picked a seat at the table where he could keep a watchful eye on the knight. If he needed anything other than food and drink, it was Argyle's task to ensure La Fontaine's every request was fulfilled.

The King was seated comfortably on his throne, sending select dishes around the room after he had taken the first helping. All the prominent members of the English nobility were greeted, but he focused his attentions on the table below his dais.

When the last of the many dishes were finished, the King stood. The room once more fell quiet, as the King raised his glass to the room. 'It is my great pleasure and honour to announce my upcoming marriage to Princess Anne of Bohemia.'

His announcement was met with a collective intake of breath and then quickly followed by spontaneous applause and cheers from around the hall. Some of the King's closest companions quickly raised their glasses to toast the King on his match.

However, the King's uncles merely nodded at him and then exchanged meaningful glances. Princess Anne was the daughter of the Holy Roman Emperor, and rumoured to be a beautiful woman from a highly fertile line, all of which should have suited the nobles. It was of course high time the King ensured his succession - and yet for some reason, not all of the guests looked pleased at the announcement.

At the squires' table the conversation spurred a wave of hurried comments.

'That was some news!'

'I wonder when the bride will get to England?'

'Finally!'

'What took so long?!'

'My Lord was just saying the other day that the King ought to marry an English girl.'

'Princess Anne? Has anyone seen her portrait?'

'I hope she brings beautiful ladies in waiting!'

'Just what the court needs!'

Argyle, still new to his position, stayed silent and looked around in awe. Apparently, all the other squires had something to say about the King's impending marriage, though for himself, he had had no idea the King was not yet married, or that he had planned to be soon. In all fairness, the King was still just 14, and to Argyle this suggested ample time for such things - but the rest of the court seemed to think differently.

From the corner of his eye, Argyle saw La Fontaine waving discreetly at him.

As soon as La Fontaine had congratulated the King on this most prosperous union, La Fontaine and Argyle left the festivities. Argyle wondered why they could not stay and enjoy the evening and the good news.

'You do not wish to stay, Sire?' Argyle asked as they walked out of the great hall.

'I think that will do for the time being. Certainly it is splendid news, and yet I worry that not everyone in England will be pleased. There are those, who would rather the King marry someone else. Then again,' La Fontaine remarked, 'he has hardly to ask permission - even from his uncles.'

This silenced Argyle on the topic, although he could not help but wonder who might object to a King marrying a Princess. However, he dared not broach the subject again, and so the trip back on the barge was carried out in silence, the knight apparently contemplating something to which Argyle was not privy.

When they got back to La Fontaine's London house, he asked Argyle to inform the men and make ready for departure in two days' time. They would leave the city two days later; according to La Fontaine it was high time to return to his Hampshire estate of Beauworth.

ཐ ཐ ཐ ཐ

CHAPTER 3

10 January 1382 — Beauworth

Since arriving at La Fontaine's estates in Hampshire shortly before Michaelmas, Argyle could not remember going to bed at night without new bruises. Apparently that came with training to be a knight.

Before joining the household, he had never wondered how soldiers and knights came to be. Certainly, Argyle had never imagined that as a squire, he would be expected to hold a sword and ride with a lance like a true soldier. Still, he felt stronger than ever before and found he slept exceedingly well after long days of hard training even in sleet and frost.

This morning, the sun bounced off the powder of new snow, sparkling like silver. Argyle opened the shutters and his chamber window. He loved the icy winter wind sneaking in through the window and wrapping its cold fingers around his body and sending joyful chills down his spine.

With a happy shudder, he pulled on his wool breeches and raked through his belongings to retrieve an extra pair of gloves. The ones from yesterday still hung dripping before the hearth where the fire had all but gone out.

The day's training session was rough as always, but Argyle and the other young men still enjoyed it. The cold seemed to induce an extra desire to try harder. Several of La Fontaine's officers were yelling orders, overseeing their training or replacing the straw men on the shooting range. Their breath turned white every time they called a parry or charge.

Argyle wiped perspiration off his forehead; it still amazed him how it was possible to sweat in the midst of winter. He was circling another trainee in the melee, when he noticed La Fontaine appearing near the tilting course. Just then, a soldier yelled the command to switch weapons. The entire group walked towards the tilting course, laughing and swinging at each other with the broad side of their blunted swords.

Argyle made sure he was within earshot of La Fontaine and Edward Warden, the master at arms.

'How are they doing? How is Mowbray doing?'

'There's much to work with, Sire,' Edward Warden said tersely.

Argyle heard La Fontaine laugh. Warden spat and shaded his eyes from the low sun with a gloved hand.

'That was what Lady Blanche promised when I took on the boy. Neither more nor less,' La Fontaine conceded.

'The boy is not without skill, but he needs to grow up,' Warden said. 'He'll come into his talent in time.'

La Fontaine stepped back as a young man on a lively red mare came thundering by. Argyle pulled out a mace with blunted ends and tested it by swinging it lightly in one hand. Some of the other men had turned for the stables but he stayed near La Fontaine and Edward Warden.

'Aye, but a talent for what, I wonder?' La Fontaine said. 'I am pleased though. It would be a shameful thing to spend this much time and effort on him, if he never amounts to more than a decent squire.'

'I should wonder you hadn't already sent him packing to Lady Wake if that be the case, M'lord.'

La Fontaine nodded. 'Send Mowbray to me when practice is over for the day.'

As La Fontaine turned, Argyle ducked out of sight and walked back to the training grounds.

'Do you miss your family, Argyle?'

Argyle reached for the pitcher of mulled, spiced wine and poured La Fontaine a cup. 'Sire?'

'Much time has passed since last you saw your brothers and sisters. Mayhap you would like to visit?' La Fontaine accepted the cup and motioned to Argyle to pour another.

Balancing the cup in his hand, Argyle sat on a low stool opposite the knight, both were facing the fire. 'I suppose, I do. Although to be fair, so much is going on I hardly have time to think of them. For any longer period of time at least.'

La Fontaine tried to hide a smile. 'Now, I asked you here because I have received an invitation.' He paused for effect, but kept his eyes on the dancing flames. 'The King has announced his wedding is to be on the 20th of this month. I received the message a few days ago and plan to go to London in three days time.'

Argyle looked at the knight with equal amounts of anticipation and concern.

'With the letter there was a brief message from your brother, Thomas.' La Fontaine held out a small scrap of paper for Argyle.

Upon reading the message made out in Thomas' characteristically spiked writing, Argyle looked up, wonder in his eyes. 'Thomas is inviting me to visit?'

'If I was to bring you to the festivities, you would meet at least two members of your family,' La Fontaine smiled. 'In fact, I have good cause to believe the entire Mowbray family will participate in the wedding. As your eldest brother has taken his rightful place at your father's estates and is in want of a suitable bride, he must journey to court to gain the King's acceptance. I have it on good authority that he will even have a prominent role in the ceremony.'

Argyle stared at La Fontaine. 'Me, a guest at the King's wedding?'

'Why of course. You will see your family - and our nation's new Queen.' La Fontaine held out his cup to Argyle. 'I believe this warrants a second helping.'

'But Sire, do you truly believe Thomas will have time to see me? And that the others will be there?'

La Fontaine leaned back and drank deep from the steaming cup. 'Certainly. It was your brother's idea to ask you join to me.'

As Argyle's cup hung limply a few inches from his mouth, La Fontaine smiled at him. 'You cannot have thought, John had forgotten about you?'

Argyle smiled at himself. Of course John would not have forgotten him; he had thought of Thomas, when La Fontaine had mentioned his brother. Now he was even more eager to visit London once more.

ꙮ ꙮ ꙮ ꙮ

CHAPTER 4

26 April 1393 — Amiens, France

Argyle had spent many a day in the saddle letting memories wash over him. This last one of La Fontaine mentioning his brother John was pulling slowly back into oblivion, when Argyle heard the familiar command for the riders to stop. For a moment, he let La Fontaine's kind smile stay in his mind's eye and then he dismounted. Looking around, Argyle saw the haggard faces of men who were longing for a good night's rest, some decent food and perhaps even a little female company.

Bolingbroke had left behind much of his entourage on his frantic journey back from the Holy Land to England, leaving it up to his half-brother John Beaufort to pose as him as to not draw attention to his sudden return. The country seemed to be breaking apart, the King restored to his former ways and many nobles were sent packing either abroad or to their houses to stay there indefinitely under house arrest.

Determined to rein the King in once more, Bolingbroke had decided to pack and go as soon as word reached his camp outside Jerusalem. He had picked a few knights and ordered them to bring only their most seasoned soldiers. The rest must make their way home as best they could.

England held on to a brittle truce with the French and letting their court know that England was on the brink of a civil war could prove disastrous. Surely, the French would wallow in the knowledge that the English King's cousin was on a rampant ride back to avoid disaster in England. Bolingbroke's choice of Beaufort to take his place was perhaps not altogether a bad idea. Beaufort would be spending lavishly and travelling slowly back to England, while Bolingbroke hoped to slip quietly back onto English soil.

Argyle knew he had been selected not for his experience - which was lacking at best - nor his own soldiers, but rather because Bolingbroke once again felt unsure of Argyle's loyalties. The same could be said for his sometime friend Stephen, one of the unfortunate leftovers from the missing knight Lockley's retinue.

As the party rode north, the nights quickly turned from cool to cold leaving the tents clammy and uncomfortable. As they were always packed in a hurry, the tents soon took on a mouldy smell. Most nights, the riders went without heaters to make sure the camp could be broken down swiftly in the morning.

The next day, the drizzle of spring rain woke Argyle. The camp was quiet, with only a few squires preparing food for the party before another day's relentless ride.

As the caravan was preparing to depart, Bolingbroke summoned Argyle for the first time in weeks.

'Sir Argyle. What do you make of this?' Bolingbroke thrust a note into Argyle's hand and resumed his pacing from one side of the tent to the other. Argyle recognised the distinct handwriting.

'This is from my brother?'

'Yes, yes, but that is not important. What do you make of the content?' Bolingbroke asked.

Argyle quickly read the short message. 'That your first reports were correct. But surely the King has no need for a private army, he has only to call for the lords of the land to rally to his cause?'

Bolingbroke snorted at this. 'Nonsense.'

'My Lord?'

'The lords of the land are lucky to still be alive!' Bolingbroke exclaimed. 'Certainly this is more proof that my cousin is losing his bearings. He may be anointed by God - but he is not God!'

Argyle kept quiet. Clearly, Bolingbroke was looking for some kind of proof that Argyle had known all along. Once again he faced the consequences of having a scheming brother at the heart of the royal court as well as his own actions in Jerusalem.

'How long have you known?' Bolingbroke demanded.

'Known, my Lord?' Argyle asked.

'Do not play the fool with me. Your brother in the midst, his allegiance always a question, you must have heard from him!' Bolingbroke insisted.

'I have not, my Lord,' Argyle said. 'Thomas and I are estranged at best. Since my departure I have had but one letter and it contained no news of interest to anyone, including me.'

'This I am to believe? Do you think me as stupid as La Fontaine?' Bolingbroke turned and faced Argyle. Even though he was a head shorter than Argyle, Bolingbroke was a formidable man and his fury seemed to make him grow taller.

'No, my Lord,' Argyle sighed. 'Thomas finds me difficult and believes I am not to be trusted. While his allegiance is questioned often, Thomas thinks himself a man of action and I one of hesitance. He has long since decided I am useless.'

Bolingbroke stopped to bark a laugh at this; then continued his pacing. 'Very well. You called out Lockley - and he disappeared. Now I have need of loyal men, and I find myself dragging you along. Lockley was not a clever man, but he was loyal to a fault. You appear to be neither. Remind me why I have not yet disposed of you?'

'I should not presume to know,' Argyle said wearily.

'Nor I …' Bolingbroke paused and scratched his chin. 'Pack and be ready to ride before the sun rises above the horizon. I will be in England before June come hell or high water!'

Argyle bowed and left Bolingbroke's tent.

Thomas kept meddling in the most unfortunate way, and Argyle briefly considered writing to his brother to ask he kept out of the dealings at court and then thought the better of it.

For now, let Thomas think Bolingbroke's caravan was slowly returning to England.

ꕤ ꕤ

2 May 1393 — Calais

When the weary men finally reached Calais, they found the port closed by a rare late spring storm, with most of the ships moored up and not a single captain willing to accept the task of sailing across the black surging sea.

Argyle leaned heavily against the battlement, squinting against the raging storm. It seemed that lately nothing had gone quite according to plan. Providing he had had one to begin with.

Argyle pulled his cloak closer together against the increasing chill. On a clear day he should be able, at least he thought so, to make out the English coast, but not in this weather. Upon their arrival the day before, they had heard that the port of Calais had been engulfed in storm and thick fog for more than a fortnight, the weather showing no sign of waning.

Still, Argyle felt somewhat reassured; he had all the answers he needed, but one. What initially seemed a poorly devised plan had worked far better than he had ever imagined. Not that he was famous for his imagination. According to Thomas that had been beaten out of him while training to be a knight. Argyle was more tempted to believe that he and his brother simply did not share the same notion of what imagination was.

The thought of Thomas stirred up all manner of emotions, none of which Argyle was very pleased about. He had not yet made up his mind if Thomas was blameless or not. Nor was he likely to do so. That would be in the hands of the King. After all, Argyle was sent to make a very simple discovery. And now he believed he had achieved his goal. The rest was not for him to say. Still he could not but wonder …

Behind him a door creaked open and a shadow emerged.

'M'lord. It is cold and neither man nor beast'll be out in such a night.'

'I was entrusted to keep watch, and so I shall.' Recognising the voice, Argyle smiled a little while turning from the blurred view to face his old friend, Stephen Smith.

'I believe all the others wanted was for you to leave the hall. Not even M'lord Bolingbroke would have meant for you to be out here all night.' Stephen approached the battlement gingerly.

Argyle knew Stephen had little love for castle walls and even less for the dark.

'Never you mind what the others wanted,' Argyle said. 'Here I am, still in one piece and not alone at all.'

'Who's with you?' Stephen asked.

'My memories. They may be muddled by time and prejudice, but they are as vivid as ever.'

'Ah …' Stephen did not pursue the notion.

If Argyle was truly devoid of any imagination, he had found his match and master in Stephen. Although, when Argyle considered what the young man had been privy to as a boy, he did not blame Stephen his ardent desire never to open the door to childhood memories in his mind.

Argyle motioned for Stephen to come closer to the small fire a few paces from the battlement. 'It is but a little warmer than in the face of a storm, but it serves me just fine.'

Stephen smiled at Argyle's peculiar idea of just fine. No one would be able to get in or out of port while the gale was this strong. However, the port had plenty of other diversions to offer, all far more enticing than setting sail in the unruly weather.

Stephen joined Argyle - happy to get away from the great dark chasm just inches from the battlement. 'You and I've different views about just fine.'

'I suppose. What news from home?'

It was well-known that Stephen always had some titbit or other to tell; how he came about them, Argyle neither knew nor cared to know. Stephen sniffled. 'The King's slowly turning back to his old ways. The court's stirring to support Woodstock. The nobles were never happy that the King filled his council with hangers-on.'

'This is hardly news.' Argyle stirred the small fire and threw on a few more split logs. It hissed angrily and set about devouring the damp wood.

'And what'd you expect?' Stephen sounded exasperated.

'I could not tell you. Albeit I will concede, I am surprised that Woodstock has risen so high in the King's good graces once more,' Argyle admitted.

Stephen chewed his lower lip thoughtfully. 'I'm not entirely sure it's anything to do with good graces.'

'Go on.'

'Well, you know that La Fontaine's death was a shock to the King,' Stephen said, holding his hands close to the flames for warmth. 'And the loss of another babe only made the grief deeper. And that Woodstock never strayed far from power. Some say the King's just given up. That he's happy to let Woodstock rule. They call him a puppet King.'

Argyle frowned, aware that Stephen's thoughts were dangerous and that the situation was worse than he had thought. The two men stood quietly watching the small flickering flames for a while. The gale screamed all around them. Rain began falling, first lightly then heavily, splattering on the stone parapets and engulfing the battlements in a thick, whirling wet curtain.

'I'm going back inside. You should come too; there's no need to stand watch on a night like this. Oh, to be home to see the budding trees and sprouting fields. Wouldn't that be a sight for sore eyes?' Stephen left without waiting for either reply or response.

Argyle felt his leather gloves go soggy and the rain soak his cloak and boots; it would not be much longer before the pitiful fire would go out, drowned by the pelting rain. Perhaps he should go in. He could keep watch over the port from one of the small turrets. Yet he could not move.

The King a puppet and Woodstock in command? All of this had an eerie familiar ring to it he did not like. It would certainly please Bolingbroke, with whom he was trying to get back to England.

Finally, the storm got so fierce that Argyle had to seek refuge inside one of the parapets. He closed the small rickety door on the rain and hails, shook his cloak and took of his soaked gloves.

Since their departure from the Holy Land, Argyle had been treated as an outcast. For all his secrecy and cunning, in the end everyone had known that Argyle had not joined the pilgrimage for the same reasons as they had. While they had sought salvation, honour and glory, he had sought the truth and a murderer to present to the King of England. Bolingbroke had made sure they knew Argyle's true mission and had even requested they assist him in his search. While some had done so gladly, others had been reluctant.

Then in the midst of it all, someone had torn his life apart. Argyle could not even say if it was himself or the wretched Lockley, who had certainly done all he could to slander and tarnish Argyle's name. If only the others knew what Lockley truly was.

But the greatest pain was not to be dragged across the world towards England, he found that the piece of his heart - and quite possibly more than that - he had left behind in Jerusalem hurt more than all the rest. But it was done, and probably done for the best. He would not ruin his life taking unnecessary risks, even if this meant that Argyle was further from Heaven than ever before.

Resting before the hearth, Argyle closed his eyes. His memories whisked him back to a clear, crisp January day, where scores of men, women and children had crowded the streets of London, which were decorated by the guilds in the royal colours. He could even hear the humming excitement that had filled the air and held everyone spellbound. All of them waiting for one person - someone to bring joy to England.

CHAPTER 5

20 January 1382 — Westminster

Princess Anne of Bohemia had arrived with her vast entourage of family, soldiers, knights, ladies in waiting and all manner of spectators.

She was followed closely by a whole host of guests from her father's kingdom as well as ambassadors, envoys and diplomats from most of the continent. Everyone had brought their own retinue, and as a result, a city already filthy and smelly only seemed even more so when the number of people in it had almost doubled over night. Every bed in London was taken, some holding two or more occupants.

Today, the King would marry Princess Anne of Bohemia and all of London was out to celebrate.

The couple were the very image of virtue and gallantry. The bride, dressed in the blue, red and white of the House of Luxembourg, her head and neck bedazzled in white pearls and gems, had floated down the aisle towards her expectant groom. As she reached the alter steps, the Princess curtsied in one fluent motion, sending her and all her ladies gracefully dipping to the floor like a bouquet of exquisite flowers.

The Princess alone raised her eyes to look at her groom.

The King exuded youth, beauty and confidence. Dressed in cloth of gold lavishly decorated with gemstones, he sparkled in the rays of a rare winter sun struggling to get through the tall, slender church windows in Westminster Abbey.

For a moment, the King held his future wife's gaze; then he offered the Princess his hand and raised her from the floor. Everyone turned towards the bishop of London who, in a melodious voice, began the mass.

ꟾ ꟾ ꟾ ꟾ

'Who was that man next to the King?' Argyle was racking his brain, trying to decide where he had seen the young man before.

The guests were making their way out of the vast church. Several side doors were opened making it easier for the wedding guests to get from the church to the festivities in the Tower.

'The King's cousin, Bolingbroke. You may have seen him last time we visited court.' La Fontaine stepped aside as a group of bustling noblemen pushed to get through the large church doors. He pulled Argyle out into the pale January sunshine. The horizon was slowly turning dark, a grey warning that snow was coming.

'They were close as children although I should say they are estranged now,' La Fontaine continued. 'Until his Grace has produced an heir, Bolingbroke is next in line to the throne; something his father never seizes to remind the King. His position entitles him to a place at the King's side.'

In his usual easy fashion, La Fontaine weaved through the crowd, which was slowly dissolving. Further ahead, Argyle heard cheering as the King and Queen of England showed themselves for the first time to the people of London. The procession from Westminster to the Tower was already underway, Argyle's brother John playing a key part as one of the almoners, and a banquet awaited hundreds of guests once the royal couple arrived.

Argyle nodded, he remembered now. 'He looks older than the King. Why is he not King?'

Argyle's naivety made La Fontaine try to conceal a smile. 'His Grace is the son of the Black Prince. Bolingbroke is the son of King Edward III's younger son, John of Gaunt. When the Black Prince died before King Edward, the succession passed to the Prince's heir.' La Fontaine paused to contemplate a sudden outburst further ahead in the crowd and then dismissed it.

'However, this is not a topic for discussion. Especially as your questions suggest we have a mortal King.' Sternness had crept into La Fontaine's voice and Argyle winced. He knew as much. It simply had not occurred to him that a question of succession could be conceived as treason. Guiltily he looked at the people around them.

La Fontaine considered him for a while. 'Do not fear. No one heard you - except me - and if they did, I believe we could avoid catastrophe. But be sure never to mention it at court.'

'No Sire, I never shall.' Argyle felt a surge of relief.

Together La Fontaine and Argyle made their way to the Tower and the extravagant wedding celebrations. Soon, thoughts of what the feast would bring and if he would see his family pushed away his concerns.

When Argyle had arrived in London with La Fontaine and the rest of the retinue, a letter from his sister Joan had waited for him. She had briefly commented that she, along with John and Eleanor were invited to participate. Thomas would also be there by way of his position working for the Chamberlain.

Argyle imagined that his own relationship with Thomas was somewhat similar to that of the King and Bolingbroke. Perhaps not always the best of friends, they were kin, and he had missed all his family since leaving Epworth to serve La Fontaine.

'Sire, do you think, I might be able to see Thomas?' Argyle asked.

'I should not wonder. And if not, there are your other family members to visit.'

The thought cheered Argyle up immensely. This was true. John and his sisters resided in the family home on the outskirts of London and if nothing else, he would visit them there, before they returned to Lincolnshire.

Thomas now lived at court, but Argyle believed he might get a chance to see him before La Fontaine would return to Beauworth. Whenever that might be.

21 January 1382 — Smithfield

'I wish he would not fight.' La Fontaine held out his arms for Argyle to remove the breastplate that was strapped tight around his shoulders. He shook his arms, once the straps were opened and removed the shoulder protection. 'After all, it is the Queen's coronation, he should let the King shine.'

'Sire?'

La Fontaine looked as if he was deciding what to say, when the King entered the tent, his thick cloak lined with ermine and fox fur.

'How could you let him?!' The King's cheeks were blooming red in his white face.

La Fontaine bowed low to the King. 'You made the tourney open to all contestants, your Grace, surely you must have known …'

'MUST!' Spittle flew from the King's mouth and Argyle shrunk back into the shadows. 'I must do nothing! If I had my way, he would be commanded to leave the tourney at once, but Gaunt …'

The King's fists were white, his golden rings glittering in the light from the fire, he looked ready to strike, but La Fontaine stepped over the heap of chainmail on the floor and put a hand on the King's shoulder. 'I know that this is not what you envisioned, your Grace, but perhaps it will all turn out for the best. If I meet your cousin in the tourney, I shall easily unseat him. And never forget that some of the finest knights are riding, he will not steal the show.'

'She cannot see … not already,' the King said, his voice childish and cross. 'Anne must love ME! If she sees him win - what if she will not love me, but him?!'

'Your Queen is not easily charmed, I think, and I am sure, she will love only you,' La Fontaine signalled for Argyle to bring forth wine and fruit. He scrambled to meet the command. 'She understands her role, you have nothing to fear.'

The King drank deep from the cup. 'She has already commented that she thinks he looks like an ogre.'

La Fontaine laughed, a little dutifully Argyle thought, and filled the King's cup once more. 'Then we must make certain she never changes her mind about that and she will not when you are always with her. I recognise true devotion when I see it and she is already devoted to you, your Grace.'

'Yes, she is,' the King smiled and helped himself to some pickled plumbs, leaving greasy finger marks on his cup. 'For all that I love the legends of King Arthur and his knights, I simply cannot understand why everything must always be settled with swords and lances! But then it is tradition I suppose …'

'Men who are not as eloquent and peace-loving as you know only how to speak with their hands and swords, your Grace,' La Fontaine said. 'You have so much more to offer than any of us.'

Argyle saw how the King relaxed and began to smile, his face handsome and charming once more. It was extraordinary how his mood dictated his appearance, Argyle thought, how easily he turned from lamb to wolf and back again.

'I saw your brother's name on the lists,' the King said to Argyle. 'Is he any good? Could he unseat my cousin?'

'I … I have only seen Thomas tilt a few times … your Grace,' Argyle stammered. 'He … I believe he can hold his own …'

La Fontaine shot Argyle a sharp look and he stopped talking immediately. This was obviously dangerous territory, although Argyle could not imagine why. After all, the King could not ride in any tourney and risk his life when he was just married and had no heir to his throne. And then again, would a new wife not expect her husband to be a valiant knight, riding out to defend her honour, even if it was all for show?

'Not quite enough to beat Henry,' the King huffed. 'You could, La Fontaine, I know it! I must think of some way to make sure you will meet him.'

'Your Grace.' La Fontaine bowed low before the King. 'It would be my honour to win the tourney in your name and claim victory for your fair bride.'

'Yes … I will have nothing to fear from you. Anne knows what a great friend you are and that you are loyal only to me.' The King gestured for another cup of wine. 'But why must he joust? He is only 14 and my uncle has no other heirs … Perhaps I can convince him that

Henry should not joust and that it is too dangerous. What if something was to happen to him?'

Argyle noticed a strange glimmer in the King's eyes as he looked into the cup of wine, the shadow of a smile playing in the corner of his mouth. La Fontaine must have noticed it too. 'Surely they have already discussed it.'

'I think not!' the King flared up. 'He is as headstrong as any I know! I am sure Gaunt is displeased that he has written himself on the list without first asking permission! And have you seen his armour?'

La Fontaine laughed. 'Yes, your Grace, I have.'

'Roses!' The King exclaimed throwing out his arms, wine sloshing everywhere. 'Silver roses! I am only surprised he did not order the suit made entirely from gold!'

'Perhaps there was none to be had,' La Fontaine said. 'You have been very lavish with your presents to the Queen, there cannot be any more gold left in London.'

'She deserves it! Is she not the most beautiful woman you have ever seen, La Fontaine?'

'She most certainly is!' La Fontaine toasted the King. 'And how could she not be, when she has married the most handsome prince in Christendom?'

'King!' The King paused ever so slightly before he laughed and returned the toast. 'But you must not call her Queen until she is crowned tomorrow. I have been planning the coronation for months; it will be the most exquisite event ever to take place in London. And her crown! I designed it myself, picking out every stone and every inlay, it has to be perfect, it has to fit her perfectly!'

La Fontaine looked past the King at Argyle. 'I cannot wait to see her.'

'She will do it all alone, she will go before the nobles and the clergy, she will sit in state on the throne and I shall be in the corner to see it all,' the King said. 'I shall be watching to see that all is done as I commanded. All will bow to her, all but me.'

La Fontaine kept smiling and the King seemed to take it as silent agreement, but Argyle wondered if it would all go according to plan. As with many large ceremonies, there was much that could go wrong and the King seemed somehow to be overly focused on details. He hoped the ceremony would live up to the King's expectations and that the Queen would too.

'Make sure you knock Henry off his horse, if you get to meet him!' the King said as he left the room.

'Yes your Grace.' La Fontaine waited for the door to close before he turned towards Argyle. 'How good is your brother?'

'Uhm … honestly I could not say,' Argyle began. 'He showed great promise when we were younger, as did we all, but I know not how much he has trained since I went away.'

'As much promise as you?'

Argyle felt warmth crawl up his neck and his cheeks burn. 'Yes.'

'Good! Then it proves to be an event to remember.' La Fontaine took his wool gown from Argyle and pulled it on. 'I have seen Bolingbroke joust a couple of times, he sits his horse very well and knows how to handle his lance, if he keeps it up, no one will be a match to him.'

'Not even you?'

'No, not even I. My skills are good, but I am more a soldier than a tourney rider,' La Fontaine said. 'I think there is merit in both, but I am far better in battle than in the field. There is less grace to bringing a lance to battle than there is to joust, and I for one like that better. But the King has commanded I join the list and so I shall. If I am lucky, I shall be the only one still seated in the saddle when the tourney is over.'

Lucky, Argyle thought, I have seen you in the saddle and luck has nothing to do with it. Every squire and soldier in La Fontaine's household secretly dreamed of having the same skills and abilities on a horse that La Fontaine had; it looked so easy when he rode the tilts or wielded a sword one-handed while forcing his horse forward at a thundering pace.

Argyle only hoped Thomas would not have to come up against either Bolingbroke or La Fontaine, he might be good and even show promise, but against two of the finest jousters in the country, Thomas could have little hope of succeeding.

ᘓᘐ ᘓᘐ

22 January 1382 — Smithfield

'You shall ride against your brother,' La Fontaine smiled.

Argyle felt his heart falter. He had looked forward to seeing the joust, not riding in it himself, and certainly not against his own brother. 'But how?'

'Wearing armour and mounted on a horse, I suspect.' Swinging his sword arm lazily, La Fontaine weighed the sword, pausing to balance it every so often. 'The King desires a spectacle, and he believes it will be quite a show if you begin the tourney riding against your brother. You have nothing to fear.'

Besides Thomas' wrath and the ridicule of the crowd, Argyle thought looking at La Fontaine to decide whether he was joking or not, but he looked sombre and serious.

'I have had so little training,' Argyle tried to escape what felt like his doom. 'Thomas has jousted for years - well longer than me anyway and he has trained with Bolingbroke, I know that for a fact.' Argyle heard the high pitch of his own voice and cringed, he sounded like a silly child.

'Nevertheless, the King has decided that the two of you will open the tourney,' La Fontaine said. 'I hear rumours that the Queen is quite excited.'

'She does not even know me!'

'No, but the King has told her of your brother and she thinks it very charming that two brothers of such an even age should also be matched in the field at her coronation.'

The finality of La Fontaine's words was unmistakable; whether Argyle wanted to ride or not the decision was already made for him. 'I have never ridden in a tourney before.' He made one last feeble attempt.

'You have to start some time but not to worry, nobody expects much of you - except me - and everyone knows the real jousting will be done by those more seasoned. Thomas is getting an easy start, I agree, and that is not to say anything of your skills, but he will soon be unsaddled by a better man.' La Fontaine put down his sword and grabbed Argyle around the shoulder. 'You will do fine. No one expects you to win, but I know you can hold your own and that should be enough for you.'

'I would rather squire you than ride against Thomas.'

'I shall be right there, cheering you on. Forget about Thomas, you are about to be one of the youngest men to ever ride a royal tourney, you will be even younger than Bolingbroke!' La Fontaine put a little force into his hold on Argyle's shoulder. 'Just imagine that! It will not matter how you fare, what will matter is that you will best the King's own cousin on age alone!'

Argyle smiled dutifully, but his heart felt cold and beat very strangely. He could feel sweat trickling down his spine and his palms go moist. Even if he was the youngest man ever to ride in a tourney, he might also be the youngest man ever to be unsaddled by his brother at the very first turn. What a story that would be!

'Best get some rest, tomorrow is a big day and the King will not allow any of us to fail him!' La Fontaine patted Argyle heavily on the back. 'Make sure my armour is ready - and your own too - before you turn in, there will be little time between your first turn and mine, so we must be up at dawn to make sure we are ready when the bell tolls.'

'Yes, Sire.' Argyle began picking up pieces of armour, trying to ignore how sick he suddenly felt, his belly was a big knot and his head was whirling with images of Thomas' lance striking true and knocking his head clean off on the first turn.

ꕤ ꕤ

23 January 1382 — Smithfield

'Thomas Mowbray and the squire Argyle Mowbray!' the royal herald announced to the rumbling sea of people gathered by the tourney grounds.

Argyle looked around and saw La Fontaine standing to one side, most of his armour already on, his dark blue cloak billowing slightly in the rippling January wind, revealing a little of its grey lining. He looked knightly and proud, but Argyle also thought La Fontaine looked concerned. At the opposite end of the field, Thomas was seated on a great chestnut destrier, he was wearing the familiar Mowbray colours proudly, his armour of wrought silver with red inlay glittering in the dull light. He held his helmet in one hand and the reigns loosely in the other, sitting easily in the wooden saddle.

Argyle looked down at his own horse, adjusting the reigns. Suddenly his gauntleted hand was clumsy and heavy, the chainmail bit into his armpit, and he thought the straps holding the armour together were much too tight. He had left his cloak of dark blue wool lined with red by his four lances, it would prove hard to stay in the saddle for all four; he knew full well the skill of Thomas, and he would be hard pressed to stay seated even for two lances.

The King stood and the crowd hushed. 'This is a rare moment when two of my most beloved servants - brothers nonetheless - ride the first turn of the Queen's tournament!' He beckoned Argyle and Thomas forward and Thomas immediately spurred his horse into a short canter, looking calm and in his element.

La Fontaine nodded ever so slightly when Argyle turned nervously towards him before spurring his horse on to join his brother in the centre of the field for the obligatory royal greeting.

The Queen stood beside the King, both of them magnificent in crimson and cloth of gold, her head adorned with the newly commissioned crown that the King had designed himself. She smiled at Thomas first and then Argyle.

'Two brothers, I cannot choose.' Her voice was melodious with a sharp hint of her native tongue. 'I shall favour you both!' The Queen claimed, and the crowd roared as she tied a piece of crimson silk first on Argyle's lance and then on Thomas'.

Argyle looked over at his brother, who never looked back, but bowed his head gracefully.

'I ride for your honour, my Queen!' Thomas' voice rang clear across the cheering crowd, but Argyle did not know what to say, so he simply bowed his head and touched the lance to his chest making the Queen smile and the King applaud before sending the opponents back to their camps.

Clear across the field he could make out Thomas on his steed, but not his face, mist was still crawling along the wet sand of the field, and the low sun was in his eyes. Thomas slammed down his visor, and Argyle followed suit thinking how different they must look; Thomas in his sparkling armour, his crest on his shield and breastplate, and Argyle in a plain suit of armour with nothing adorning it or his wooden shield. He looked once more at La Fontaine who motioned quickly for Argyle to focus on the joust, he turned his head just in time to see the herald lower his arm and Thomas spur his horse into a thundering gallop.

Argyle let instinct take over, driving his horse forward and lowering his lance half a second after Thomas. He felt Thomas' lance strike along the shield, sending rays of pain up his arm but the shield held and his own lance graced Thomas' shoulder the tip splitting upon the impact. Thomas stayed seated. The crowd cheered making Argyle's courage swell.

Turning at the opposite end of the field, Argyle let his horse trot back to get his second lance. He had held his own! When he passed Thomas, he pushed his visor up and shot Argyle a dark, angry stare, clearly he was furious that he could not unseat a squire, and Argyle knew Thomas would never forget this moment.

'Well done!' La Fontaine roared when Argyle threw down his lance and took the second one. 'He rides well, your brother, but if you aim for his breastplate, he will not be able to take the blow!'

Argyle nodded, he knew Thomas always flinched when someone rode straight for his body, but he was less certain he would be able to hit true without unseating himself in the process.

'THE CHEST!' La Fontaine roared as Argyle spurred his horse for the second round, Thomas barrelling down the field, his destrier spraying sand at every hoof-beat. Even though the visor hid Thomas' face, Argyle knew that whatever brotherly leniency he might have thought to administer was gone; Thomas meant to win this joust.

This time, Thomas lowered his lance last, clearly aiming for Argyle's head. He flinched, turning a little in the saddle and loosing his balance when his lance dove and hit Thomas' armoured leg. Thomas' lance hit Argyle's shoulder so hard he heard bone crunching as he fell sideways and focused on rolling away from his horse.

The crowd roared and screamed, the sound echoing inside Argyle's helmet, ringing in his ears. He felt a sharp twinge of pain when one of the royal guards grabbed his arm to pull him up. Thomas was smiling at the crowd, waving his helmet in his hand and making as lavish a bow as possible in a full suit of armour at the Queen. She in return smiled, her hand grabbing the King's tightly. Argyle grunted when he tried to remove his helmet with his left hand before finally succeeding in pulling it off. For just a moment, he thought the King looked angry, but then he smiled.

'Lord Mowbray takes the first win!' the herald proclaimed, and the crowd howled when Thomas put his heavy armoured arm around Argyle and smiled.

'Smile brother, you just had a fine first joust before the entire royal court!' Thomas put force into his grasp and Argyle winced. 'Smile!'

The sand was being raked when Argyle walked back towards La Fontaine, one of the Beauworth stable boys had fetched and calmed down Argyle's horse and was rubbing it with a bundle of straw.

La Fontaine pushed Argyle inside the tent. 'What the HELL was he thinking?!'

'Sire?'

'Riding his lance like that! He could have killed you!' La Fontaine paced the tent. 'Aiming for your head - good thinking to turn when you did! I would have been a squire short - and he a brother!'

Argyle pulled off his left gauntlet, his eyes watering at the pain in his shoulder before trying to unstrap his shoulder armour, but the plate was badly dented and seemed to dig into his flesh.

'It was not a joust of war!'

Finally understanding La Fontaine's anger, Argyle sat heavily on a low stool, his vision blackening when another squire pulled off his armour, he bit down so hard that his mouth was flooding with an iron taste when finally the last straps were loosened and the armour removed.

'He could not lose before the court,' Argyle said, a little surprised he would defend his brother's actions. 'It was nothing to me, I never wanted the match, but to Thomas - his life is here, he had to prove himself.'

'By trying to kill his own brother?' La Fontaine offered a cup of wine. 'It is one thing to want to impress the King, in the end Thomas would have unseated you, I am sure …'

Argyle winced at La Fontaine's words; he liked to think he was a little better at jousting than that, but La Fontaine saw his face and smiled. 'Clearly, he has had much more practice at jousting than you. I train all of you to be soldiers, you are far better with a sword, I'll wager! But yes, he would have unseated you, even if he had not aimed for your head. I swear by God, if I meet him in this tourney, I shall make an example of him!'

Secretly, Argyle hoped someone else would unseat Thomas before it came to that.

La Fontaine broke every opponent in the tourney without much effort. Thomas crumbled before John Holland's aggressive attacks, falling from his horse and narrowly avoiding being trampled when Holland's horse reared and stomped about.

In his silver armour, Bolingbroke stole the show, his opponents falling out of their saddles at a rate that made more than one knight wonder if his glittering suit simply blinded them. La Fontaine roared with laughter when Argyle retold the banter between Sir Peter Courtenay and Robert de Vere, in which the latter had said that should he face Bolingbroke, he would close his eyes and trust his nose to smell out the roses on Bolingbroke's armour.

'Yes! He must surely try to do that,' La Fontaine said drying his eyes. 'I think very few would be able to unseat Bolingbroke; he is on fine form and one of the most able riders I have ever seen. I knew as much but to see him joust is something else.'

'But you can unseat him!'

'Hopefully, it will not come to that.' La Fontaine stretched, rolling his shoulders. 'Go and see who is left on the list, we must be coming to a close soon!'

Argyle dragged his feet going back to the tent after hearing the two names of the last joust and Thomas appeared, his right hand bandaged.

'Damned Holland! He rode too hard at me!'

'And you at me.'

Thomas looked down at his feet for just a moment. 'Not at all, my aim was off.'

'If you say so, but it does not matter, you would have won anyway,' Argyle said. 'I have had little practice in the saddle since I joined La Fontaine's household, and you were always a better horseman than I.'

Thomas seemed pleased with the praise. 'In a mélee you would defeat me any day. Thank God the King wanted a joust!'

Argyle laughed and Thomas worked his wrist, glancing at Argyle's shoulder. 'Not hurt too bad, I hope?'

'I will heal, I always do.'

Nodding, Thomas stopped. 'Did you see who is last on the list?'

'Yes.'

'You are going there now?'

'Yes,' Argyle said, noticing a slight change in Thomas' expression. To anyone not familiar with the two brothers it would be nothing, but Argyle knew that Thomas was worried.

'Tell him not to win.'

Before Argyle could argue, Thomas walked off, hugging his wrist tightly and looking down. But I cannot tell him that, Argyle thought, if I tell him that he will wonder why. Pushing through the tent flap, he bit his lip.

'Well?'

'You and Bolingbroke.'

La Fontaine stopped for the briefest of moments, then shrugged and signalled for Argyle to take over strapping in the breastplate and securing the armour on his shins. When he had donned his gauntlets, La Fontaine reached for his helmet, the only ornamental piece of his armour, a plume of feathers dyed a deep dark blue, swaying off the top of it.

'In battle, this kind of helmet is useless,' La Fontaine said. 'But the King gave it to me as a gift and I always wear it - for luck … and to please him.'

Argyle fretted over the cloak until La Fontaine stopped him. 'Not to worry, Argyle, I shall win.'

That is what I worry about although I do not know why, or how to say it, Argyle thought and smiled bravely. 'Of course, Sire.'

'Bolingbroke is one of the best in a joust, but I have more experience. That will serve me well today, I think - and I have promised the King to win for him, so I shall.'

'Is it wise, Sire?' The words were out before Argyle could stop himself.

'Wise? Probably not, but I am honour bound to the King and even Bolingbroke understands that.' La Fontaine adjusted his elbow piece. 'Why do you ask?'

The question was lightly asked, but Argyle knew better than to confess. 'I know the King was furious that Bolingbroke would ride in this tourney, and I know why you want to win for the King and Queen, but …'

'But you worry about the greater cause?' La Fontaine asked and Argyle nodded. 'The cousins have their own problems to contend with for certain, but they are naught to me, I merely do what the King asks of me. I should have thought you had little interest in politics.'

'I have none!'

'Nor do I, unless I am asked to and then my interest is always that of the King. A word to the wise; should you ever find yourself in a position where you are asked an opinion about anything political, you have two choices. Be honest - or support the King.' La Fontaine walked towards the fading sunlight, a few snowflakes dancing in the entrance of the tent. 'This time, I support the King.'

Argyle fell in behind La Fontaine's broad frame, feeling the light snow cool his brow.

La Fontaine and Bolingbroke greeted each other before the royal pavilion, where the King and Queen were now packed in furs and blankets to keep warm in the increasing cold. The sun was touching the horizon and all around the field, torches had been lit to ensure that the last two duellists could see each other. The flames added an air of supernatural mystery to the afternoon, bathing parts of the field in gold and leaving other parts increasingly dark.

'Before us stand two of the greatest jousters in the country!' the King said loudly. 'My beloved cousin Lord Bolingbroke and my good friend Sir La Fontaine! You are both a credit to this country and to us!'

The two competitors bowed their heads at the King and Queen before greeting each other coldly; Bolingbroke offering a forced smile and La Fontaine inclining his head at his superior - in every sense but on the field, Argyle hoped.

La Fontaine's armour screamed a little, when he reached for his first lance. 'Heavy, cold and dirty work ahead, Argyle!' he announced before slamming down his visor and turning the massive grey destrier, Noble, towards the field.

At the opposite end, Bolingbroke sat heavily on his fair steed, it's mane almost silver in the increasing darkness. Bolingbroke looked resplendent in his golden armour with the wrought silver roses and red and white inlay. He had changed from his silver armour, and the message he was sending was clear; while the King might sit his throne, here was the heir to the largest fortune in England.

Argyle hoped the Queen could see past Bolingbroke's blatant boasting and would know to cheer when the King did. Argyle sniffed and pulled his cloak tighter against the increasing wind that was kicking up snowflakes, which were swirling in the crisp air.

'READY THE HORSES!' the herald shouted and then he lowered his hand.

La Fontaine spurred Noble on, the big horse breaking into a gallop that made the ground tremble. Bolingbroke pressed his horse on lowering his lance at just the right time and impacting with La Fontaine's iconic shield. Argyle heard the capped tips splinter on the hardened wooden shields and saw Bolingbroke sway slightly in the saddle before straightening and halting his horse.

Cantering back to collect his second lance, La Fontaine pushed up his visor. 'This will be a great match! If I fall, I shall not regret it, he is a fine horseman!'

Argyle forced a smile and held out the lance.

Two more rounds made light work of the lances, which lay in splinters all around the field, but both riders were still in their saddles when the last round was called. Argyle crossed himself and said a short prayer; Thomas' words were still ringing in his ears, but Argyle could not see La Fontaine losing, after all he had nearly unseated Bolingbroke in the first turn and after rattling him in the second and third too, La Fontaine looked more the winner than the loser.

The herald signalled for the opponents to ride, La Fontaine leaning slightly backwards when Noble kicked up the frozen sand and snow, jumping forward. Bolingbroke's horse reared before lunging forward, Bolingbroke wobbling slightly in the saddle. His lance looked a little unsteady when he lowered it, while La Fontaine's lance seemed to float completely smoothly through the air.

Argyle squinted against the swirling snow, the flickering shadows from the torches played on charging knights adding to the otherworldly feeling of the final turn.

The lances crashed into armour and shields, splinters flying about the field, Bolingbroke cringed in the saddle and had to throw away his lance to grab the pommel tight, but he kept his seat. La Fontaine too threw his lance away, but he had not moved in the saddle and still sat proud. Noble snorted and kicked the sand when La Fontaine drew the reigns in tight and cantered back towards the royal pavilion.

'A DRAW!' the herald announced and the crowd held its breath when the King rose.

Holding out his arms, his red cloak billowing, the King looked at both riders. 'WE DECLARE BOTH CONTESTANTS WINNERS!'

The crowd went into a mad frenzy, applauding, shouting and stomping their feet, the nobles of the land rising to congratulate Gaunt on his son's magnificent talents and cheering the King and Queen in their royal pavilion.

The Queen swept a curtsey to Bolingbroke and La Fontaine and waved at the crowd when she heard her name being chanted. The King looked fit to burst with pride and even smiled thinly at his cousin before patting Noble's neck while he waited for the noise to die down.

'We declare the tourney over!' The King took the Queen's hand. 'THE WINNERS WILL SIT AT OUR TABLE TONIGHT!'

Argyle thought the crowd would never stop cheering, but the snow and wind which was fast turning into a blizzard forced the spectators from the grounds and back into their warm houses. La Fontaine left Noble with one of the stable boys and let Argyle take off his armour.

'What a final turn!'

'Yes,' La Fontaine said. 'For a moment, I thought he would fall.'

Argyle thought he heard concern in La Fontaine's voice, but dismissed the idea. 'So did I, so did everyone!'

La Fontaine laughed. 'I am pleased that we both won and that the King did not demand another turn. The lances were growing very heavy.'

'You could have gone on, Sire, I am sure of it,' Argyle said.

'Yes, but to what end?' La Fontaine pulled on his grey woollen gown and tied his belt around his waist. 'No one could say that either of us did not do our best.'

What an odd thing to say. Argyle wondered if La Fontaine had really done his best, or if he had let victory slip between his gauntlets.

CHAPTER 6

18 March 1383 — Beauworth

Argyle looked at the narrow black band around his right arm. John had passed away a few weeks ago. He died unwed and without issue, although Argyle did not know why his eldest brother had not married to produce an heir.

Rumours surfaced at court that John had never really cared about women, but they were quickly scotched by Thomas. Upon John's death, Thomas inherited the title of Baron of Mowbray and Seagrave, which suited him splendidly, although he was not pleased with losing the title of Earl of Nottingham.

In a letter to Argyle, Thomas had announced that John had been buried in Whitefriars in London. He had not thought to invite Argyle; most likely thinking it was not worth the bother. He did profess that Margaret had scolded him and that Joan and Eleanor were in a temper as they had not been invited either. Thomas quickly went on to boast about his prospects of advancing at court, including his intention of marrying.

His recent advancement had made Thomas into one of England's most suitable bachelors and he had set his eye firmly on his prize. In his letter, he confessed he had already asked for the King's permission to marry the nine-year-old heiress Elizabeth le Strange, granddaughter to the Earl of Warwick. Thomas relayed ecstatically that the King had happily given his blessing, and had even agreed that he could wed the girl although she was years from being of a marrying age.

Argyle was fairly confident that Thomas had primarily showed an interest in Elizabeth due to her father's extensive estate and the fact that she was the immediate heir. Much could be said of Thomas, but he was never one to sniff at personal gain.

Early Tuesday morning, a messenger arrived with another message from Thomas. True to form, he had not been sluggish. Only weeks after his appointment, Thomas had married Elizabeth at a hastily arranged ceremony performed by the Bishop of London. At least her father could take pride in the fact that his son-in-law was now the Earl of Nottingham.

Argyle shook his head in disbelief just as La Fontaine came through the door followed by his master of arms, Edward Warden. La Fontaine noticed the note in Argyle's hand. 'Any news?'

'Yes, Sire. My brother Thomas is married to lady Elizabeth le Strange.'

'I say. What a suitable match for little Lady Strange - and your brother for that matter. It must have warmed many a heart.' La Fontaine raised an eyebrow and shot him a sly smile. The sarcasm was unmistakable.

Many of the King's favourites were less than taken with Thomas, who had a tendency to cross most of those he met. While the other nobles acknowledged his ambitious actions as suitable, there were those among the King's favourites who felt he posed a threat. Most of them were from less renowned families than Thomas', but La Fontaine seemed not to worry; after all he had taken on Thomas' own brother.

Now La Fontaine opened the door to the great hall. 'Come along Argyle. We must toast your brother's happiness.'

'Thank you, Sire. He has brought great honour to our family,' Argyle conceded.

They crossed the room together and La Fontaine put a fatherly arm around Argyle's shoulder. 'May his marriage be long and happy!'

Perhaps the little, virtuous Lady Strange was just the price that would settle Thomas' appetite, Argyle thought. Especially if in five years' time when Lady Strange came of age, she would bestow an heir upon Thomas.

ꟷ

15 September 1383 — Beauworth

'The first buck hunt of the season!' Argyle jeered at a couple of other squires.

The woods were dressed in the golden foliage of autumn. After several weeks of pouring rain and leaden clouds the sun had finally come out. Spider webs sparkled in the bushes when the sun's rays pierced the dew. After the uncommonly raw and chilly mornings of late August, September was on its best behaviour.

The sun sent the mist away as the riders made their way from the cobbled courtyard through the arched gate and clattered over the drawbridge.

There was nothing worse than being forced to train combat and tilts in the pouring rain. Just as there was nothing better than riding out for a day of hunting on a sunny September morning. Argyle had great plans to take down his first buck before sunset. Last year, he had come so close - this year, he meant to get it.

All amusement aside, the hunt was sorely called for. The larders needed to be replenished before winter. The peasants had worked the fields, harvesting through July after an unseasonably hot summer that had ripened the grain much faster than expected. However, the meat had been scarce. Slaughtered lamb and pig now hung to mature or lay in the great salt vats. Fish were brought in by the cask; the fishermen did not care about the weather, but hunting was best kept for good weather.

Just the day before, La Fontaine's brother in arms, Sir Coxcombe, had come through the castle gate bringing a large retainer with him. While La Fontaine had greeted him with a wide smile, the whole house bustled to find room for all of them, including several of Coxcombe's squires. Now, Argyle shared his chamber with the youth Stephen Smith, who rode up next to him.

'How's the hunt in these parts?'

'There ought be plenty of birds and game for everyone,' Argyle said.

Stephen gripped his reins harder, his dapple-grey snorted quietly. 'It has been so long since I was last on a hunt. Sir Coxcombe has been moving about quite a lot this past year.'

A couple of minutes went by before Stephen spoke again. 'There's trouble in the realm, but you'll know that.'

'Trouble?' Argyle was careful to keep his voice level.

Stephen shot Argyle a sideways glance. 'Oh, perhaps the news hasn't come down south?'

'No, it has,' Argyle admitted. 'And yet, it has not deterred La Fontaine.'

Stephen slumped a little in the saddle. 'Coxcombe doesn't possess much land. Until recently, we stayed just outside London.'

Behind them a rider clicked his tongue. Several of the horses fell into a trot; up ahead the dogs ran beside the master of the hunt, tongues already lolling. The pages still on ponies had to motion their mounts into a canter to follow troop with the big hunters.

'Not to worry,' Argyle smiled. 'There is plenty of room here for most of you. If you do well today, I am sure there will be more days like this.'

Argyle patted his horse's neck and Stephen looked at him in gratitude, just as the master of the hunt signalled the gallop. Argyle took the opportunity to spur his horse on, leaving Stephen and his dapple-grey behind. The dogs were loosed and the whole party took off into the woods.

Once the party returned home, Argyle received an unexpected letter from Thomas. In it, he briefly announced that Lady Strange had died. He did not proffer more details, merely declared that he was once more on the lookout for a wife. In an unusually speculative undertone, Thomas lamented that this time he would prefer one who might immediately bestow upon him the family he so anxiously desired.

The surprise prevented Argyle from regretting the buck that got away, and he climbed the stairs deep in thought. He wondered what might have happened to Lady Strange, the poor girl had not yet turned ten years of age. It must have been arduous for Thomas too, having lost his claim to the Baron's lands along with the girl. The marriage was not made for love, but then few aristocrat matches were. Perhaps this was why Thomas had not sounded too distraught in his note, after all the two had spent very little time together, and Lady Strange was only a few years out of the nursery while Thomas was almost a man grown.

Stephen entered their shared room, his boots muddy and the smell of horses and autumn on his clothes. 'Where did you get to?'

'I had a message from my brother,' Argyle said.

'Something good?' Stephen asked and then checked himself when he saw Argyle's frown. 'Or perhaps not … I didn't mean to pry.'

'You were not to know. My brother wrote to tell me, he has lost his wife.' Stephen looked crestfallen and Argyle quickly continued. 'She was just a girl, they were formally wed but she was years from being a woman. He married her without asking any of us to the wedding, so I have never met her, and now I never will.'

Stephen nodded gravely. 'That's bad news to be sure.'

'Yes, although now I find myself unable to feel anything but a little regret on my brother's behalf,' Argyle smiled sadly. 'Now what does that say about me?'

'It's hard to feel sad for someone you've never met. But it serves you credit that you'd feel for your brother,' Stephen said, smiling a little.

'I suppose so, and yet I feel foolish for wanting to be sad for a girl I have never met. Even though I know the marriage was not made for love,' Argyle said.

'Not for love?' Stephen looked baffled.

'Oh, my brother is the Lord Mowbray, Earl of Nottingham,' Argyle added by way of explanation.

'So your lot doesn't marry for love?' Stephen wondered.

'Well, some do, but most learn to love each other, I guess.' Argyle realised he had never really given the matter much thought. It seemed an extreme luxury to marry for love, and much more reasonable to marry for alliance and securing fortunes. 'Did your parents marry for love?' he asked Stephen.

'I think so. Though in the end, the love ran out,' Stephen said and looked away.

'Now I am sorry to pry.' Argyle felt he had overstepped the newfound confidence with Stephen. 'Please forgive me.'

Stephen looked back at Argyle. 'There's nothing to forgive, you're no more a mind reader than I.' Stephen rubbed his freckled nose. 'I think my mum loved me, but I don't think my dad did. They'd many children, but only three of us survived childhood. I guess that takes a toll on a family, on a marriage. And then my dad left to join the great revolt and marched with Wat Tyler.'

'Wat Tyler?!' Argyle exclaimed. 'The man that made the peasants rise against the King?'

Stephen looked bewildered. 'No, he's the one who inspired the peasants to save the King.'

'Save the King?!'

'Yes, they wanted the bad advisors turned away and the King to deal directly with his people,' Stephen said matter-of-factly. 'My dad was at Smithfield the day the King met Tyler. And he saw that bad mayor kill Tyler. My dad even strung his bow, but didn't loose a single arrow 'cause the King rode to his people and saved them.'

Argyle nodded, he had heard this story when La Fontaine had come to Nottingham to fetch him, although it sounded a little different told from the peasants' point of view. 'I know, La Fontaine told my aunt about it. You are lucky to have such a father!'

Stephen's face darkened. 'Luck's nothing to do with it. Oh, my dad liked to tell his story, but mainly in the tavern 'fore he came home to beat me, my sisters and my mum.'

Argyle stared at his new friend. 'Beat you?'

'For a man who claimed to have met the King, to've been in the great revolt and ridden beside Wat Tyler, my dad was not the same when he came back. He's always angry and rough, a drunkard who'd come home in a foul mood. He'd take it out on us every chance he got!' Stephen scowled. 'He sent me away the moment I grew too big for him to handle. Last I saw my family was the night he'd been beating my mum within an inch of her life. I punched him so hard in the face, he lost some teeth. Sweet Lord, the blood gushed from his nose and mouth, but the look of surprise in his face, I'll never forget it!'

'You hit your own father?' Argyle whispered.

'Yes! And I'd do it again any day.' Stephen flushed from anger. 'He knew, of course, he knew, he couldn't have me under his roof no more, it'd be the end of his tyranny. So the very next morning, he sent me away, my mum peering from behind his shoulder, her face black and blue, one eye closed entirely, her rattling breath the only sound in the cottage. He thrust my few belongings into my arms and shoved me out the door. I never even got to say goodbye to my sisters!' Stephen hung his head.

'But you could write to them? Tell them you are well? In the service of a noble knight?' Argyle asked.

Stephen laughed, the sound harsh and cold. 'Write? To who? My dad can't read, nor can my mum or sisters. I can only read and write a little, 'cause Sir Alan insists we spend time in the classroom when I'd much rather be on the training field. Even if I did know what to write, who'd read it to them?'

Argyle had never considered that there were people in England that did not know how to read and write. He tried to think of something clever to say but failed, he had no idea what it must be like to grow up with a father that beat you, or with a father at all for that matter.

In the end, Stephen spoke again. 'Please, don't tell anyone. You're the first one I've told, and I'd rather no one else knows. Sir Alan thinks my family died from the Black Death – won't change nothing to say different.'

Stephen's pleading look silenced Argyle on the subject, he nodded and threw a piece of cloth to Stephen, who took it and rubbed his face gruffly, wiping the angry tears from his eyes.

'Your secret is safe with me,' Argyle promised.

CHAPTER 7

5 April 1384 — London

Argyle leaned forward and patted the gelding. Its neck was slick with sweat from the day's long ride. He admitted to himself that he had pushed the beast unnecessarily, but he had wanted to make good time.

Since Thomas' first and highly unexpected marriage to Lady Strange that had been completed without family participation, Margaret had scolded Thomas to such a degree that he dared not venture into a second marriage without inviting the family. As Thomas was now to take vows with a new wife, Margaret had twisted his arm, forcing him to have a ceremony complete with feasts and guests.

Leaving all of the arrangements to Eleanor, Thomas had probably thought to thwart his as yet unwed sister, but she had taken to the preparations as a fish to water. Sending out formal invitations, she had made sure to include the entire family and most of the nobles in the country. The setting was to be Thomas' London house in Dowgate, and Eleanor had been lavish in all her endeavours.

'M'lord, I can take your horse?' A young stable boy looked up at Argyle, who smiled benevolently at the boy not bothering to correct his mistake of calling him a lord.

The clamour of the busy courtyard had not gone unnoticed in the house, the doors now opening wide to reveal two of his sisters. They flew down the stairs to greet him. 'Argyle, you came!'

Eleanor was first, breathless from running. Her headpiece was askew, but in her usual fashion, she cared little for looking composed. Argyle picked Eleanor up and swung her around, ending with a warm embrace before putting her down gently. She pushed her headpiece back in place and grinned at him.

'Little brother.' Joan came towards him with open arms, smiling sweetly and heavy with child. She shot Eleanor a quick, reproachful glance for her childish behaviour that was completely ignored.

'Joan, it has been too long.' Argyle took in the sight of Joan's big belly.

'Indeed. If Thomas had his way, we would never have met at all,' Joan said and then returned to her usual state of serenity. Argyle gave her a quick, soft hug and looked round.

'Are there any flowers left in London?' he asked.

'No!' Eleanor laughed. 'And if there are, it is only because I have kept a few by, in case some of these need changing. I had to make up for his first marriage. No flowers, no guests, no dinners. Honestly, he might as well not have married at all!'

Joan slid up to Argyle's side and locked arms with him. 'Eleanor is living out her own marriage in advance.'

'Not true!' Eleanor huffed. 'I believe Thomas will soon settle mine, but until then I intend to make this a marriage we can all be proud of. After all, Elizabeth has been married before. I need this to exceed any memory she has of her previous wedding.'

Eleanor was already halfway up the stairs, dividing the busy courtyard much like Moses divided the Red Sea in the Bible, as she went. Joan tugged at Argyle and they followed in a leisurely pace.

'I have missed you all,' Argyle said.

'I have missed you!' Joan exclaimed. 'I enjoy my life in the country with Sir Thomas and the children, but sometimes I feel so far from all the excitement. By God, we are closer to the Scots than I like and the north is such a cold, harsh place.'

Passing through the hall and into the sitting room, Argyle eased Joan into a chair and plumped an extra cushion for her back. Eleanor came in from the adjacent room.

'Is it really wise to be bustling about in your condition?' Eleanor asked Joan, who just smiled.

'I find it helps the child birth faster.'

'Do not say that, not even in jest,' Eleanor said reproaching.

'Oh, let me live a little, I have already given birth to two healthy children,' Joan said. 'I need no advice, thank you.'

Eleanor gave Argyle a pleading look, but he backed away laughing. 'Do not drag me into this, I have no knowledge of women's ways.'

'Isn't it high time you did, brother?' Eleanor said with a mischievous smile.

Argyle waved his hands disarmingly. 'We are celebrating Thomas' wedding, not mine. I should say no one of consequence is looking to wed a lowly soldier, dear sister.'

As if on cue, Thomas appeared in the doorway, holding a pile of papers. 'Certainly not. I have tried to find you a suitable wife, brother, but without success.'

Eleanor made a face; Joan simply ignored Thomas, leaving Argyle to greet his brother. 'Congratulations on your wedding, Thomas.'

'Yes, yes. I am fortunate. Elizabeth Arundel is a good match. Her father is a great man and I am happy to be part of his family - as he is to be part of mine,' Thomas said before leaving the room again, the papers in his hand fluttering.

Joan rolled her eyes and placed a hand at her back, easing the ache that came with being pregnant. 'You should think he was marrying the father, not the daughter the way he speaks of the Arundels.'

'In a sense he is, Joan,' Eleanor said. 'This is a highly attractive match on both sides.'

'I for one cannot see what he could possible see in Elizabeth. She is pale and pasty!' Joan rebutted in a haughty tone.

'She is proven fertile and our brother wants a family,' Eleanor said but Joan was not letting it go.

'Our brother wants a dynasty.'

Argyle decided to plead for a truce. 'Whatever he wants, Thomas is going to have a new wife, and we should welcome her into our family.'

Eleanor left her place at the window, tracing her finger over the back of a chair along the way and finally stopping before Argyle. As she looked up into his face, he felt like he was looking into a mirror. Unlike the rest of their brothers and sisters with their dark hair and grey eyes, Argyle and Eleanor were fair-haired and blue-eyed.

Squeezing Argyle's arm lightly, Eleanor smiled. 'Yes, we will little brother. Neither of us could ever deny you anything.'

'I tried once, you were about 4,' Joan sighed. 'You screamed so loudly, I immediately gave in.'

Argyle bent to kiss Joan's hand then grazed Eleanor's hair and made for the door.

'Tonight, we dine *en famillie*,' Eleanor called after him. 'Margaret should be here by then.'

ꕥ ꕥ ꕥ ꕥ

'How can it be that all of you were here before me?' Margaret surveyed her brothers and sisters with an air of slight dissatisfaction. Eleanor smiled at her comment and sent the tray of sweetmeats around the table once more.

'No thank you, Eleanor, I cannot take any more sweets.' Thomas patted his stomach. 'Eleanor took it upon herself to come early and make the final arrangements. Joan has been in London these last few weeks as Sir Thomas was requested to attend court. I did not think, she should travel more than absolutely necessary in her state.'

Thomas looked around the room and smirked at Argyle. 'I cannot tell you, how Argyle came to be here before you. Although to be sure, his horse did need a rest after the trip.'

'The reason is simple, upon hearing your news I rushed to get here lest I miss another Mowbray wedding,' Argyle said with a smile. Eleanor tutted at the snide remark and Thomas shot him a sour look, while Joan inclined her head ever so slightly to acknowledge the truth of it.

'Well, I cannot believe you did not have time to visit me all this while, but were happy to rush here. Sir Reginald might not be often called to court, but you could make an effort,' Margaret said to no one in particular and received little more than a few mumblings in return.

Eleanor switched the topic. 'We are all excited to meet Elizabeth tomorrow, Thomas. Is she much changed since I saw her last?'

'She ought be, she was a mere girl when she married her first husband,' Thomas said. 'Now she has grown to womanhood.'

'Will you stay in the city after the wedding or whisk her away to Nottingham?' Eleanor pressed.

'She will travel there herself and establish her dominion,' Thomas said. 'I shall follow in due course, when the King sees fit to release me.'

Joan scrutinised her brother. 'If I did not know better, I should say you are not keen on the match, brother?'

'I could not ask for a more suitable wife!' Thomas emphasised.

'A wife already bedded.' Margaret scrunched up her nose and looked at Thomas. 'You went straight from a nursery to a widow! Honestly, I do not know which is worse.'

'We cannot all hope for the same bliss bestowed on you, dear Margaret,' Argyle said before Thomas had time to make a spiteful response.

Waving for the servants to clear the table, Eleanor rose and beckoned them all into the adjacent room. 'Here we can speak without prying ears.'

Eleanor settled on a chair near the hearth, Thomas sitting next to her, completely ignoring Margaret. Insulted, she retired to a chair at the far side of the room.

Joan leaned heavily on a table and yawned overtly. 'I think, I must retire if I am to be worth anything tomorrow. Carrying a child is tiresome work, do you not agree Margaret?' This was Joan's olive branch and Margaret quickly grabbed it.

'Indeed, I was so very tired when I carried Walter. He is a dear little one, but I always fret when I am away from him. Oh Thomas, I do wish you would have let me bring him.'

Joan rolled her eyes before closing the door behind her; everyone knew that it was Sir Reginald who did not like to travel with the child. It was bothersome, and Margaret would have demanded more breaks than there were miles to London.

Once more Eleanor prevented a heated debate. 'How did you come to settle on Elizabeth, Thomas?'

'The King suggested her. Lord Arundel had approached him asking for advice on a new marriage, and he believed I might be more fortuitous in this match than I was with Lady Strange.' Thomas stroked his sharp chin, pausing perhaps not for the first time to contemplate his luck.

'From Warwick to Arundel, I dare say you could not have done much better,' Eleanor said.

'His Grace did apologise for offering a widow and not a virgin, but I am satisfied in his choice.'

Argyle handed wine around, then settled in a windowsill overlooking the riverbank. 'I, for one, am simply happy to attend your wedding, Thomas. We may not see much of each other, and I prefer the occasions to be happy ones.'

Thomas acknowledged this remark with a half smile, and then rose to make a toast. 'To marriage! May it soothe us all in the end. I wanted to tell all of you together, but perhaps it is better announced now: Eleanor you will wed next year. The Baron de Welles has accepted my proposal on your behalf.'

'Oh, Thomas!'

Disregarding Thomas' usual distaste for affection, Eleanor threw her arms around his neck and kissed his cheek. Argyle smiled and offered his sister a warm embrace, only Margaret stayed in her seat.

She pursed her lips and mustered her most civil voice. 'What a great match, sister. Congratulations.'

'Thank you, what a surprise!' Eleanor's smile lit up her face. 'I know you mentioned him earlier, but when I heard no more, I did not think the King had accepted. Nor de Welles!'

'And why would he not? You are among the finest ladies in the country, naturally you should not settle for less than a Baron.' Thomas basked in her admiration and even went as far as shaking Argyle's hands gruffly before he went to stand behind Margaret's chair, gripping the high back tightly. 'That leaves only you, Argyle. If only you would make something of yourself and soon.'

'I shall try, Thomas. For now I am happy to celebrate your and our dear sister's good fortunes.'

Thomas was somewhat appeased by this and Margaret bit her lip trying to hide her extreme displeasure at being so firmly put in her place by Eleanor's match.

Margaret rose and straightened her gown. 'Now if you will excuse me, I too am very tired. The journey was long.'

'I shall join you, sister. Preparing for a wedding is quite an ordeal.' Eleanor stood and laced her fingers into Margaret's, forcefully dragging her from the room before she could argue with the offer.

Argyle took Eleanor's seat near the fire, contemplating the pulsing embers. The room had gone instantly quiet when the sisters had retired. Thomas sat in Margaret's vacant seat, blatantly demonstrating the distance between the two. 'My condition is not contagious,' Argyle said.

'I am well aware,' Thomas said. 'How can it be that you are not yet knighted? Of course, I have not asked the King, having just recently secured the match for Eleanor I do not wish to seem impertinent.'

'I have not yet proven myself. These are peaceful times, and I am after all a soldier now,' Argyle tried to avoid a long lesson from Thomas. 'In time I shall come into my own.'

'In time - we have no time,' Thomas grumbled. 'We must secure the best matches in the kingdom before all the heiresses are swallowed up by lesser families.'

Argyle turned from the embers to face his brother. Half hidden in the dark, it was difficult to make out what mood Thomas was in.

'I shall speak to La Fontaine when I return.'

'A peace offering, brother?' Thomas said.

'What would you have me do?' Argyle asked. 'I cannot force his hand, no more than you can force the King's.'

Thomas leaned forward with a dangerous glint in his eyes. 'There are always ways to get what one desires.'

CHAPTER 8

3 May 1393 — Calais

Argyle was lost in his memories of the words he had exchanged with Thomas the night before his wedding. It seemed a lifetime ago. Argyle remembered his sisters at the wedding, happy, dancing and chatting and Thomas at high table with his new wife, gracefully accepting congratulations and presents. The cheering guests eating and drinking till their hearts' content.

Argyle had danced with all his sisters, careful not to bump Joan about too much. It would not do if she went into early labour in the middle of the wedding. Argyle smiled at the memory. How glittering it had been, warm and almost homely, and Thomas had been in his element, his hands on another noble's daughter. Then Argyle sighed, it was these ties to some of the most established English magnates that had, in time, led Thomas down a dark path from which there was surely little chance of his returning unscathed.

Argyle's head snapped back at a loud crunching sound outside the turret. He got up, fed the fire to keep it going and then opened the door against the relentless wind. In the distance a shrieking sound plunged into the dark.

Well below the battlement, the ships moored in Calais' natural harbour bounced about in a restless sea. Yet he could see more than before, the rain was finally letting up. There had been days on this journey, when Argyle had wondered why he had accepted the undertaking in the first place. Although he never complained of his prolonged stint as a squire to what was, in the eyes of most others, little more than a jumped up nobody, he had at times felt that the real reason he had not been awarded a knighthood sooner had more to do with Thomas' misdeeds than anything else.

Even so to this day, Argyle could not say whether Thomas was truly guilty of all the slander he had heard at court - or if he simply had a knack for landing himself in the thick of things. If nothing else, these last few days had proved to Argyle that all men were capable of double-dealings. Even people he had trusted blindly seemed suddenly to have sides he had not previously noticed - or perhaps his mind was playing tricks on him. Not all memories were good ones.

The creaking sound returned, and Argyle was strangely relieved to see that it was one of the galleys, which had been pushed right up over its mooring and onto the harbour itself.

'Sir Argyle, my Lord wishes to have a private word,' someone called to him.

Argyle sighed and turned for the door. It was ajar and whoever had spoken was already gone. This was no weather for man or beast to be out in. From of the corner of his eye, he saw a shadow slink away from sight. He squinted and made to follow it.

'Now, Sir Argyle!' the insistent voice called him back.

Bolingbroke did not like to be kept waiting. No doubt they would have another battle of wills before this night was over. Looking one last time for any sign of the shadow, Argyle retraced his steps to the tower door.

At the end of the narrow staircase another door stood ajar. Mumbling voices reached his ears; a warm orange glow invited his cold body into the room.

'What took you so long?' Bolingbroke stood in the centre of the room, screening the long trestle table behind him. A few servants were clearing the table hurriedly, one of them dropping a large roll of parchment that made for the open hearth. 'Fool! Get that out of here, now!'

Argyle stopped a few paces inside the room. 'You summoned me, my Lord?'

'Quite right. More disconcerting news has reached me since we last spoke,' Bolingbroke said. 'Now I want the truth from you.'

'What truth might that be?'

'Why, the real reason you came, of course!' Bolingbroke sat down on the edge of the table.

'You know this. I came on behalf of the King to root out the man who killed La Fontaine. It is my misfortune that Lockley disappeared in Jerusalem, but I cannot help to think, he is also making his way back to England right now. As for any other suspicions, I have said all I can. I suspect your spies have filled you in as to my movements in Jerusalem,' Argyle said poignantly.

The fire crackled and spat in the corner of the room, casting contorted shapes along the uneven stonewalls. The fortress held little comforts as it was, and Bolingbroke had quickly seized the only room worth having. Looking at Bolingbroke's haggard and worried face, Argyle did not begrudge him a little sanctuary; he only hoped to find salvation for himself as well - and soon, if it could be helped.

'I am sure you are still hiding something from me.' Bolingbroke rested his hands on the table, looking as if he could pounce at any moment. 'Very well, we have plenty of time to play at guesswork. I shall go first: You came in part for the reasons you have already claimed. In part, I suspect, to keep me from returning to England. That might explain your frequent visits to a certain house in Jerusalem. How am I doing so far?'

'To what end would I keep you from England, my Lord?'

Bolingbroke smiled without humour. 'I should think because the King has ordered you to do so.'

Argyle held his tongue. Whatever came next, he would have to take his lead from Bolingbroke.

'Nothing to add to this? Well, then I shall venture to assume that I am correct in my speculations.'

'I know nothing of any plans - if the King should prove to have any. I was as shocked to learn of his mustering a private army as you were.' Argyle kept his voice level.

'Is that so?' Bolingbroke snarled. 'I should think that since you managed to lose Lockley, you would be eager to seek my cousin's favour by keeping the one person from returning who would have the power to confront the King.' Bolingbroke narrowed his eyes, reached for the mug of ale and took a hearty swig. Droplets ran down his stubbled chin. Bolingbroke wiped his mouth on his sleeve, never once breaking eye contact with Argyle. 'Come now, Sir Argyle. Do not disappoint.'

'My Lord, I gave you a full account in Jerusalem of my reason for travelling with you,' Argyle said. 'I have nothing further to add to this. I could not tell you about it at first because I was told to trust no one. I shall have to make my peace with the fact that Lockley disappeared. You have openly admitted that you had spies follow me wherever I went in Jerusalem, which means you know that I did nothing and spoke to no one about any other plans. And I knew nothing of the King's plans to increase his private army that you have not told me yourself or that was not known before we departed.'

'You do realise that on this journey, you are as good as my prisoner?'

When Argyle did not answer, Bolingbroke's eyes narrowed. 'I wonder … did my cousin decide you might be of some other use than merely to prevent my return? Could it be he wanted you to rid the kingdom of me - for good?'

'No such order ever passed between the King and I,' Argyle said through gritted teeth. 'You have little cause to trust me, I know this well enough, but I was not given any such task as you suggest.'

'How am I to know you are not yourself a member of the White Hart?' Bolingbroke asked.

Argyle fought to master his temper. Since La Fontaine's death he had slowly come to view the royal family in a new light, one that shone mercilessly at their distrusting nature. 'I am no archer, nor do I hail from Chester.'

'No that I will allow.' Bolingbroke leaned back in his chair. 'Your talents with a longbow are wanting at best although your skills with a sword are another matter … But now that I know Richard has decided to expand his army to include knights from across the realm, it makes all the difference, would you not say? I know the King does not trust me, that he believes me to be his enemy. It would make perfect sense that he would send a mercenary on my pilgrimage.'

Argyle waited in silence.

'I will throw you in a dark, cold cell to live out your days in if I find out that you have been holding a knife to my throat this whole time,' Bolingbroke said.

Argyle shrugged. 'If that had been my mission, I have had ample opportunity to slit your throat. But I have not. I quickly learned you could not have been involved in La Fontaine's death. Since my departure from England, I have not heard from the King. He has no reason to suspect you of anything and so no reason to change my orders.' Argyle marvelled at his easy way of telling half-truths to Bolingbroke without wavering.

Bolingbroke took this in. Clearly, he was far from satisfied but then he switched tactics. 'Then explain your furious ride into Jerusalem before we set off. If you think your weak explanation that morning had satisfied my thoughts about your loyalty, you are a bigger fool than I can imagine. And knowing your brother, the Mowbrays are not in the habit of being fools.'

Argyle's mind darkened at the memory. 'It is of little consequence now.'

Bolingbroke snorted. 'I shall be the judge of that, Sir Argyle.'

'Very well, I went to say goodbye to the lady, as you might well know,' Argyle said coldly. 'She was not present and I went away immediately, surely your spies will have told you that too.'

'They only told me you rushed to Abbas' house, spoke briefly with a maid and returned in a foul mood,' Bolingbroke said. 'You could easily have given or indeed received an order or message from whoever you were working for. I will have the truth from you, you mark my words.'

Argyle felt his blood boil and struggled to keep his voice neutral. 'You already have the truth. There was no message, only a fool standing outside a door. Be content with that, my Lord.'

'You are prepared to swear upon your own life and that of your entire family that you had no other cause to continue on the journey than the pursuit of Lockley?' Bolingbroke asked. 'That you return with me on my orders and not that of the King? That you have not deliberately dragged out our return? That my men will not wake one morning to find my throat slit, as you put it, and you gone?'

'Yes, my Lord, I will swear to that. As to my discoveries about Lockely, I shall relay them to the King. I will clear your name entirely. My return is at your command, not the King's. Your throat is quite safe.' Argyle eyed Bolingbroke wearily for a little while before gesturing to the window where the wind screamed at the panes furiously driving water into any crack it could find. 'Even you cannot think that I have any power over this strange storm.'

Bolingbroke snorted at this and then released Argyle to return to his solitude on the rampart. Behind him Bolingbroke's companions returned to the warm room. All save one.

As Argyle stomped up the narrow stone stairs he saw nothing at all. He tried to think the situation through, tried to find another way of convincing Bolingbroke that he was not an assassin or a spy, but all he could think of was a different conversation long ago, when Argyle was just a squire, eager to prove himself to the world.

CHAPTER 9

18 May 1385 — Beauworth

'I have been summoned to assist the King in his endeavour to oust French garrisons from Scotland. This is a mighty responsibility and I am eager to prove myself and earn the favour of the King.'

Argyle smoothed the letter on the wooden table, tracing the grain beneath the paper, frowning at his brother's earnest wording. This was not like Thomas; granted, Argyle knew a little about warfare, but Thomas had never seemed very keen to risk his life on a battlefield; in the jousting field of a tourney he was a great champion, but never battle hungry. Yet here it was, proof that Thomas would once more race Argyle to the finish and win.

Argyle leaned back and peered out the window. Little droplets coursed lazily down the panes; it had been raining steadily for over a week. Most of the farmers had been lucky to plant their seeds in time and only a few now had to force their ploughs through the wet, greasy earth, their oxen sloshing along hanging their heads.

La Fontaine had received word from court and with it came this letter. Argyle sighed. If his brother should do battle before him, he would never hear the end of it. He bit his lip absently, fingering the edge of the letter when the door creaked.

'Mowbray. M'lord is assembling the household.'

ꕥ ꕥ

The hall rumbled with the voices of the gathered men. Argyle noticed La Fontaine standing to one side, discussing something with Edward Warden. They nodded at each other and Edward Warden slid quietly from the room.

'I have received word from the King!' La Fontaine announced. The noise died down, everyone turning towards La Fontaine. 'We have been summoned to partake in a great endeavour. We are to march for Scotland and root out the French garrisons there, once and for all. The King wishes to eliminate the Scots as his enemy and conquer what his grandfather could not!'

The hall erupted in cheers for the King and general acknowledgements of agreement flew about the room. La Fontaine had a large retinue stationed on his lands and his many soldiers were itching for a battle.

La Fontaine held up his hands. 'Come June we march for London.'

Argyle smiled, he would get to see his brother and wage a war alongside him. For once, Thomas would not outdo him.

ꕥ ꕥ

21 June 1385 — Carlisle

The King stood before his army in all his splendour. When the sun broke through the clouds his armour glittered and the wind moving his long, crimson cloak. He was wearing his battle-helmet adorned with a gold crown and behind him, his standards fluttered in the summer breeze. It had been some time since Argyle had last seen the King and, as ever, he marvelled at the majestic power that seemed to surge around him.

Before the King stood four men, their backs turned to the crowd. Never one to miss an opportunity for drama and theatrics, he had the men go down on one knee - one by one he touched each man's shoulder with his sword.

'My Lord Langley, we raise you from Earl of Cambridge to Duke of York.'

'My Lord Woodstock, we raise you from Earl of Buckingham to Duke of Gloucester.'

'My Lord de la Pole, we raise you to Earl of Suffolk.'

'My Lord de Vere, we raise you to Marquis of Dublin.'

The army cheered as the men rose with their new titles. It was a glorious spectacle and a benevolent act before waging a war; this would surely bring luck and success to the army.

As the crowd dispersed, Argyle fell into step with La Fontaine who looked worried. 'The King was most generous today.'

'Sire?' Argyle gave La Fontaine a puzzled look.

'Perhaps you did not notice that he raised his personal friend to Marquis?' La Fontaine continued. 'He is now on par with the King's royal uncles.'

'And this is bad news?'

La Fontaine smiled slightly and slapped Argyle on the shoulder. 'It may mean nothing at all.'

When he saw Argyle's creased brow, La Fontaine continued. 'I do not complain to be the King's friend, but sometimes he makes it difficult for us to do our duty. To advise him as we might, if he were … Well, if he were more like the Kings before him.'

'Like his grandfather Edward?' Argyle asked.

'Yes, or his father, the Black Prince. Now he would have made a fine King! I fought with him in France, you know, not long before his untimely death.'

Argyle pondered this a little. 'Sire, why was he called the Black Prince?'

'His armour was black,' La Fontaine said. 'Some say it was because he always rode a black destrier, others that it was for his personality. But I never saw anything but an amiable, young man, who would have been the pride of England. He also rode under a black standard. Any or all of these may be the cause of his nickname.'

'How did you come to meet him?' This was the first time, La Fontaine had mentioned knowing anyone other than the King, and Argyle was curious to know more.

'Ah yes … How indeed? I was part of a large retinue of soldiers fighting under the standard of the Duke of Lancaster. We were successful for some time raiding the south-western duchies, before finally giving battle to the French outside Poitiers.' La Fontaine looked up at the sky. 'We joined forces with the Black Prince and it was his great knowledge of strategy and tactics that secured our splendid victory.'

'Is the King much like his father?' Argyle asked.

La Fontaine smiled a little sadly. 'Some say so.' And then he silenced Argyle with a gesture before he could ask any more questions.

23 July 1385 — Dryburgh Abbey

Although the Scots were clearly just as opposed to English rule as they had been in the past, the King and his advisers had believed they would give battle once the English army marched across the border. It had been weeks now, and the Scots had proven almost impossible to find in the rugged northern landscape.

The Scots lords had taken to the hills, sending small raiding parties to attack the stretched out English army. The King had abandoned the idea of clearing a road through the dense forests and rugged terrain, which had served his grandfather well when he had invaded Wales. The rocky Scottish land had proven too difficult by far to carve a road into, and now many of the seasoned soldiers were grumbling about poor strategy and a lack of clear leadership. They felt vulnerable marching only two and two, easy prey for the Scottish warriors' guerrilla tactics. The general displeasure in the army began to disrupt the usual line of command. As the men were spread out thinly and weaving their way in unknown territory it was easy for any disgruntled men to simply abandon the cause.

Once clear of the woods and mountains, the army marched through field upon field of burned crops, leaving them with no chance of foraging along the way and feed the men; displeasure became more and more obvious not only among the soldiers but also among the commanders.

Argyle was rubbing down his horse late one afternoon when a rider arrived, careering past the long line of tethered horses, stopping right in front of the King's massive royal tent. A soldier snatched a scrap of paper from the messenger's hand and pushed through the tent flaps.

Only a few moments later, a roaring outburst sent a jolt through the horses and men.

Argyle left his horse and crept closer, slipping from tree to tree to get close to the royal tent. Behind the tree closest to the King's tent, he paused taking measure of the situation. He was not one to eavesdrop, but then again …

'They did not call my grandfather the Hammer of the Scots for nothing! And I shall finish, what he started!' The King burst through the opening in the tent and stalked off with a few of his household knights following close behind at a half trot in order to keep up. Argyle frowned slinking back into the shadows.

Next, Thomas emerged, looking carefully around before making his way towards the main camp. Argyle decided to intercept Thomas. 'Brother!'

Thomas jumped, choking a yelp. Then he hissed. 'What are you doing here?'

'Tending to the horses. I was about to turn to camp when the messenger arrived.'

'Well then you had better make for camp!' Thomas looked furious but Argyle persisted. 'What was in the message?'

'Would that I knew.' Thomas paused for a moment, looking around to make sure the two of them were alone. Apparently satisfied, he grabbed Argyle's arm and pulled him close. 'The King did not care to share his information, but I would hazard a guess that he has had bad news from further south.'

'How so?'

'He is a stubborn fool,' Thomas spat. 'He should listen to his advisors. After all, most of them have seen war, some of them even served with his own father and grandfather. They have fought the Scots before and they warned him that the Scots lords were wily. But he is determined to emulate his grandfather - the Hammer of Scots - what a joke!'

Argyle pulled away from this brother, this was no way to speak of the King. Argyle gave Thomas an angry stare; but in the increasing darkness his brother's face seemed carved in stone. 'You disagree?'

'I know very little about the goings on in the King's tent,' Argyle admitted, still shocked by Thomas' treasonous outburst.

'Then who are you to judge?' Thomas snapped. 'He listens to no one, not even Gaunt! He will make the same mistakes as his grandfather, and who is going to question his actions if not his uncles? You mark my words, there will be repercussions.'

ஐ ஐ

The next morning, La Fontaine summoned his men. The King's standard was unfurling as La Fontaine informed them what had happened in the south. 'The Scots have burned Carlisle.'

The men mumbled among themselves and exchanged worried looks. More than a few looked like they would rather turn south at once and see if they could not root out the Scots and force them to fight. Most of the soldiers were weary of the fruitless marching, their swords thirsty for blood.

'We are to march on Edinburgh!' La Fontaine's booming voice cut across the disquiet. 'The King commands that if it is burning they want, then they will get it! Where better to make our mark than to burn their beloved capital?'

His speech made several men cheer loudly and most nod in agreement. A few simply stood there waiting for their orders. Whether they agreed or not, they could do little other than what they were told.

Argyle wondered what they might find once they reached Edinburgh. If the Scots would burn their own crops, what was to stop them burning their own cities? What if Thomas was right, and the King was on a mission that would never succeed? Argyle simply could not see how burning a city would spur the Scots to give battle, when marching through their lands had not, but then the King would know, he would have God on his side, and he would know.

ஐ ஐ

8 August 1385 — Edinburgh

Edinburgh was intact when the starving English army reached the city walls - clearly the Scots had decided that it was not in any danger, or that it could be built anew if it came to that.

Argyle had waited outside the King's tent for hours, trying not to eavesdrop as tempers and voices rose and discord broke out between the King and his advisors. At one point, Argyle could have sworn he heard metal scratching against scabbards as if someone was drawing a sword. When La Fontaine had finally emerged from the tent, he was deep in thought and clearly angry.

That evening, Argyle and La Fontaine stood before the walled city. La Fontaine looked left and right as if trying to decide how to best proceed with the King's orders. Edinburgh was not an easy city to take; the road leading up to the city was steep, and the stronghold was nestled in the rocky hillside and heavily fortified with thick walls. There were only two ways to get in: the main road or from the seaside. Without ships, the English army was left with just one course to take.

'Burn the city,' La Fontaine sighed. 'I wish that his Grace should change his orders. Sacking it is one thing that will give the men new reason to fight and keep morale high, but burning it … is folly.'

Argyle eyed La Fontaine. 'Sire, should you speak thus?'

'I will speak any way I choose, and I have already told the King what I think of his plans.' La Fontaine seemed dispirited his face dark and closed.

As the two of them turned to walk back to the camp, La Fontaine turned his head and spat. 'This will end badly, you mark my words. I understand why the King does not want to go from Edinburgh without making a clear and undeniable statement, but burning the city when there are none but women and children left is the wrong kind of statement.'

'And what would you do?' Argyle felt curiosity mingle with anger. 'If this is the King's command, surely …'

'Surely it must be the right thing to do, yes. That is what we are all lead to believe, and yet none of his advisors think it is the right thing.

His uncles are in uproar, even Gaunt who is well-versed in the art of warfare. If this had been in the time of the King's father, we would perhaps have gone about it differently.' La Fontaine stepped off the stomped down path cutting through the thick undergrowth. 'I wish his Majesty would see reason.'

Argyle swallowed some of his anger trying hard to remember that he was speaking to his master, not to an equal. 'And what reason would that be?'

'That it is better to sack a city, plundering its residents but leaving them alive than it is to burn every last soul in there. Poor bastards.' La Fontaine leaned against a tree, something in his manner was forced and he looked extremely uncomfortable.

'The Scots are our enemy, Sire!' Argyle was seething at La Fontaine's reluctance. 'The Scots and the French, and the people in that city too! I believe the King is right, and even if I did not, it is his command that we burn the city.'

La Fontaine grabbed the hilt of his sword, his leather glove squeaking as he tightened his grip. 'If the King cared as much for chivalry as he lets on, he would know that a knight does not burn innocents. Women and children are innocents, they did not choose this war, they do not even know who we are. To them, we are strangers forcing ourselves on their lands. They would gladly let their possessions go to live another day.'

'I cannot believe you!' Argyle was trembling with anger, he felt the veins at his temples throb and he took a warning step closer to La Fontaine, who merely eyed him. 'What kind of soldier are you to doubt your King's command? What kind of a friend?'

At Argyle's last words, La Fontaine started and grabbed Argyle by the wrist. He squeezed tight enough for Argyle's eyes to water. 'I fear I have been too lenient with you! You are overstepping your position. I am the kind of soldier and friend who fears what will happen, when we return to England with nothing to show for all our efforts than a city of burned women and children. I am the kind of friend who knows what is truly at stake for a young King. Never doubt my loyalty to the King! Or my love for him!' La Fontaine let go of Argyle, who rubbed his wrist, which was raw and sore to the touch.

'Then how can you disagree with our orders?' Argyle asked submissively.

'I am not alone in my concerns. Your brother and most of the council feel as I do - that burning the city is not right. Even now, I assume the King's uncles are hard at work trying to dissuade him. We are risking the lives of 14,000 English soldiers the longer we stay here.' La Fontaine pointed towards the city. 'This may be the only way in - but it is also the only way out. We have no ships and I'll wager the Scots did not leave a fleet for us to commandeer if they return to find us burning their capital.'

Argyle frowned, he had not thought that far. 'But Sire, surely if the Scots have just burned Carlisle they are days away from us?'

'Days?' La Fontaine snorted. 'We are in their land, they know it like the back of their hand and I am certain they did not march all their men to Carlisle. Have you not felt watched as we have marched?'

'No. And the King has had scouts out roaming the hills and woods this whole time. He would know!' Argyle felt exasperated with La Fontaine, why would he not see reason? That the King was right in his command. 'You sound like an old and frightened man!'

La Fontaine gritted his teeth. 'And you are too like the King - rash and unchecked!' Argyle felt pride swell within at the thought of being like the King; he even felt an inch taller when La Fontaine continued. 'There are larger forces afoot in our realm than can be controlled - even by the King. If he chooses unwisely once more, I am not sure any of us will return unscathed.'

La Fontaine's words deflated Argyle's staunch belief in the King's decision, but before he could ask La Fontaine what he meant, a company of soldiers emerged on the road. Pushing past Argyle, La Fontaine hit him on the shoulder and the impact seemed to linger long after La Fontaine had stomped angrily back to his tent, closing the flaps tightly against the relentless Scottish rain.

Little did Argyle know how close he had come that day to having the screams of burning and dying people within the city walls haunt him for the rest of his life. But in the end, the King was persuaded by his counsellors to leave Edinburg unscathed. The King was furious at his defeat to an enemy that never even showed itself and the march back to England left the army even more tired, starved and dejected.

ꕥ ꕥ ꕥ ꕥ

3 September 1385 — Westminster

Failure! That one word kept circling in Argyle's mind. The entire campaign had been a failure.

All those soldiers itching for a fight, ready to retaliate for Carlisle, ready to root out the Scots' French allies who had been aiding the Scots in resisting becoming part of the English realm. Almost all of the soldiers returned home with nothing to show for their efforts but haggard faces and worn boots.

By pure chance, some soldiers had fallen upon a small group of Scots warriors who had fought bravely and killed almost an entire English company of soldiers. But on the whole, the entire venture had been an utter disaster.

This morning, La Fontaine's men would march for Hampshire. Argyle was waiting near the great doors for La Fontaine to emerge and call his men to order. Instead another man threw open the doors, the hinges creaking and screaming.

Gaunt stomped across the courtyard, yelling for a horse, his face red and his eyes shining with malice. Gloucester and York came after him, trying to reach their brother before he could mount his horse. Argyle could see more commotion through the crack of the doors still swinging dangerously.

'NO!' Argyle jumped at Gaunt's booming voice and turned to see Gaunt mount his destrier, waving one hand angrily. 'I have suffered enough insults. You make your own choices, but I shall not stay in a country where my advice is not wanted.'

Gaunt turned his horse with a fierce tug on the reins and galloped out the courtyard. His retinue scrambled to follow suit, knights bellowing for the men to fall in outside the portcullis, squires running for their lives to pack the remains of Gaunt's camp onto carts and horses.

In the tumult, Argyle spotted La Fontaine striding towards him. 'Are the men ready?'

'Yes, Sire. What …'

'None of our concern. Perhaps a few egos were bruised, but that is naught to us.' La Fontaine brushed Argyle aside, grabbed the reins and swung himself into the wooden saddle that was padded with subtle leather, the high pommel shiny from years of wear. 'Make sure everything is packed before you ride out.'

Argyle acknowledged the order with a nod. What on earth had happened in there? Then he shook his head; he would know in time if it was of any consequence.

Turning towards the camp, Argyle nearly toppled Thomas, who quickly snatched his arm and dragged him towards an archway. 'A word, brother.'

'I cannot speak now, I am to secure the baggage train,' Argyle argued.

'It will keep, I am sure.'

Reluctantly, Argyle followed his brother into a small, abandoned courtyard. He could hear the clatter of horses being led out, and could only hope his tardy return to camp went unnoticed.

'What?' Argyle asked irritably.

'I could ask the same of you. What did *your* knight say?' The snide remark was almost more than Argyle could bear. He shrugged to release his brother's grasp, then glowered as Thomas tightened his grip. 'Well?'

'He said it was nothing to concern myself with.'

'Did he? Well he would. He does not see, what the rest of us do. Too damn loyal for his own good. Or perhaps he is the wiser one - I find myself not quite knowing what to think these days.' Thomas barked a laugh. He released Argyle and leaned on the warm stonewall. 'The campaign was a disaster, everyone knows that.'

'Because the Scots would not give battle?'

'Yes and no,' Thomas said. 'If only they had given battle, perhaps the situation would not be as sinister as it is. Mayhap many matters could have been avoided.'

Argyle was curious, what exactly was that supposed to mean? Nonetheless, he was thrown by Thomas' next question. 'How old are you now?'

'17 - you know that.'

Thomas nodded. 'And I 18, like the King.'

'What of it?' Argyle felt close to losing his temper.

'Although you have been groomed for battle - do you think you are a master strategist? Would you try to give battle without consulting those more seasoned in warfare?'

Argyle pondered this a little; this was not an answer to give lightly. In the end, he shook his head.

'Nor I,' Thomas said. 'Yet it seems, if you are King, you do not need any advice from those who have fought battles before. Nor from those who have fought the Scots and French before. All you need is a flock of followers to cheer you on, no matter how inane your ideas are.'

Argyle felt his breath catch; Thomas was speaking treason.

Thomas drew Argyle close, his eyes were cold and angry. 'And your knight did all but nothing. Remember that when the day of reckoning dawns.'

Before Argyle had a chance to respond, Thomas turned on his heel and vanished back into the confusion of the great courtyard, leaving Argyle astounded.

Thomas' parting words had an ominous feel to them. Argyle knew that La Fontaine had tried to advise the King and that he had most likely succeeded, when Edinburgh was saved from the flames. He even knew that Thomas and La Fontaine had agreed on that point. What was Thomas playing at?

೨ ೧ ೨ ೧

CHAPTER 10

10 September 1386 — Nottingham

It was years since aunt Blanche had died at the ripe old age of 75. She had been buried at a ceremony that would have pleased the old lady immensely. A burial worthy of a Lancaster. And she would not have settled for less.

Argyle was reminded of her as soon as he entered the hall. On the right, several portraits of the family stared benevolently down on the visitors, in pride of place on the left were the portraits of his parents and aunt Blanche. How she would have revelled on this day. He sighed lightly and made his way into the great hall.

The preparations for Eleanor's wedding were in their final stages. Servants wound their way around each other while decorating the grand hall with fresh flowers, arranging tables and trestles for the guests. Argyle could not make out any family members amidst the hustle and bustle and he soon learned that no one recognised him from childhood. Many of the servants were new; the old ones had retired or left during the temporary passing of estate and lands while the children were wards of their aunt.

He beckoned at a servant. 'Where might I find the Earl?'

'The family is gathered in the living room. Shall I lead the way?'

'Thank you, I will find it myself.' Argyle walked the length of the hall and opened the living room door. 'Thomas, Eleanor … Joan?'

Once the initial loud and gleeful greetings were over, the four paused and eyed each other. It was more than two years since they had been together for Thomas' wedding. Today, Thomas looked far from pleased, although his wife was with child and he should at least be satisfied in that.

'Brother. Good to see you. I have arranged a room for you facing the courtyard,' Thomas said.

'Thank you.' Argyle briefly wondered at Thomas' strange, stiff manner, then he turned to Eleanor. 'The house is alive with activities, you certainly understand how to keep the servants busy, Eleanor. And Thomas, how kind of you to host our sister's marriage.'

Argyle hugged Eleanor before turning to Joan. 'How is Sir Thomas treating you? Have you brought the children?'

Shortly after, Thomas sent their two sisters away, letting on that the seamstress would soon arrive with the dresses. He turned from Argyle and went to sit in a chair to the right of the fireplace.

'John de Welles,' Argyle said. 'Our sister is finally to be a Baroness. That would have pleased both aunt Blanche and our parents, I am sure.'

'You do not know how hard I had to work to secure the match,' Thomas said. 'There were those at court who did not think our Eleanor was right for de Welles. But what do they know of such matters?'

The piercing tone made Argyle frown. He tried to lighten the mood. 'And yet they are to be wed tomorrow, as you proclaimed the night before your own wedding. It serves you credit, brother. A cup of wine perhaps?' He made for the pitcher.

'You do know how to wait on somebody.' Thomas' voice was cold. 'Still a soldier, brother. Are you not bored of it?'

Argyle knew Thomas was deliberately trying to bait him. 'La Fontaine has taught me much and more. In time, I will be a knight. But for now, I have no complaints.'

Argyle made his way to the window with two full cups and handed one to Thomas. Reluctantly, Thomas joined him by the window and ran a finger around the rim of his cup.

'But enough of that. How is life at court these days?' Argyle asked.

'A fine place to make my career,' Thomas said. 'The King has decided to make me Earl Marshal to reward my efforts in the war on the Scots. It is truly a great honour.' No joy seeped into Thomas' toneless voice.

'Congratulations.' Argyle tried to hide his surprise.

'Thank you, brother.' A thin smile ran across Thomas' face. 'Now, you have travelled a great length; do not let me detain you. No doubt, you will want to be well rested for the festivities tomorrow. If John de Welles and our darling sister had their way, we would be celebrating for weeks on end. As it is, they will have to make do with two days celebrating under my roof. They can continue once they arrive at the Baron's estate.'

Even as he said this, Thomas opened the door and left Argyle contemplating the gardens and wondering why the King would reward anyone for the fiasco in Scotland. Especially Thomas, who had, by his own admission, achieved very little and given almost no advice to the King's liking.

8 October 1387 — Beauworth

It was nearly two years since Thomas had received the title of Earl Marshal, he now had an heir in the nursery and another in the cradle, and Argyle's darling sister Eleanor had already given her husband his first male heir.

Of late, rumours had surfaced that the King had lost his grip on power over the country and the realm was governed by Woodstock, the Duke of Gloucester and the King's own uncle. And still, Argyle could hardly believe his own eyes. The letter from Thomas had arrived late last night, and Argyle had decided to wait until after breakfast to read it. Now he regretted reading it at all.

Trust in Thomas to always be industrious, but to publicly go against his King that was news Argyle found extremely hard to digest. Like a dog licking an open, festering wound, Argyle read his brother's letter once more, trying to find some sign that Thomas had not gone mad.

- Dear brother, I wanted you to know that I am helping the other great lords of this land root out the vermin that has long pestered the court and the King. I trust that once our work is done, the King and indeed the country will be much happier and better served than is currently the case. You too should be pleased, I am ensuring that our family help stem the tide of upstarts and poor counsel and that the law of the land be placed firmly into the hands in which it belongs - first and foremost in the hands of the King and his uncles. I hope to gain a little for myself as well, and am working tirelessly to once more become one of the King's trusted counsellors. For the time being, the King resists our demands, but I have no doubt that he will change his mind once he is back at court. As soon as can be, I pray and believe that our King shall be delivered and that the law of the land will be restored. When this happens, know that I will always welcome you at court, regardless of where you are currently residing - and with whom. - Thomas

Argyle groaned and slammed his hand down hard on the table, his drinking cup toppling over and spilling what little ale was left in it.

'What is this?' La Fontaine appeared in the doorway.

'Nothing, Sire,' Argyle said quickly, shoving Thomas' letter under a pile of paper.

La Fontaine looked seriously at Argyle. 'Then you are treating your table very harshly if it is nothing. What will you do to the poor table the day it is something?'

Argyle smiled despite the dire circumstances. 'I have just had a letter from my brother.'

'Ah … well that is always a cause for pleasure,' La Fontaine said with a slanted smile.

'He is saying that the King is surrounded by bad advisors.'

'Nothing new there,' La Fontaine replied, walking over to take in the view of the fields from the small window. 'What kind of bad advisors is it this time?'

'Your kind,' Argyle said grudgingly.

La Fontaine turned his back on the view. 'And what do you think?'

'I think my brother needs to come down from his high horse. Before someone pushes him down.' Argyle sat down heavily on his bed, the sheets still crumbled from a restless night. 'He says that the Lords of the land are going to …'

'Yes?' La Fontaine asked.

'Never mind, it will not come to pass, I am sure. The King is surrounded by the advisors he himself has appointed, why would anyone try to change that?' Argyle wondered out loud.

La Fontaine sat down at the edge of Argyle's table, careful to avoid the little lake of ale. 'Because many egos have been bruised over the years.'

'In Scotland?' Argyle asked.

'That was just the last time.' La Fontaine seemed to weigh his words before continuing. 'What else does your brother write?'

'Nothing much. He claims he is helping restore peace to the land and hopes to promote our family in the process and that, once the deed is done, England and the King will be much happier than today.' Argyle ran his hand through his thick, blonde hair. 'Surely you do not believe him, Sire?'

'I believe that Gaunt leaving may prove to be the worst thing ever to happen to England. I had little love for the man, God knows, but he kept the King and all the nobles of the land in check. Now they are all free to do as they please,' La Fontaine said.

'But surely, the King …'

La Fontaine waved dismissively. 'The King does not always know what is happening right under his nose. Do not for a moment doubt my loyalty to our King, I know you did in Scotland and I understand why - but know that I am devoted to him, although he is young and sometimes rash.'

Argyle nodded, he still remembered every word of their argument in Scotland before the walls of Edinburg. La Fontaine got up, shaking his right hand, which had landed in the ale lake when he pushed off the table. 'Clean this up. Then go and meet the rest of the men on the training field.'

'Oh, and think no more on your brother's letter,' La Fontaine said as he reached the door. 'I am going to London soon, and when I do, I shall enquire as to the facts of the matter. The King is our sovereign and I doubt very much that the nobles will try to topple him, whatever their personal grievances.'

Argyle nodded gravely, for all of La Fontaine's reassurances, he could not shake an ominous feeling that something was going wrong. Whether it was because Gaunt had left the country, as La Fontaine suggested, and the nobles were free to act as they please, or whether it was just his knowledge of Thomas' immense ambition, Argyle could not say. However, guessing and speculating would achieve nothing for the time being. Perhaps a day of training was just what he needed.

ꕥ ꕥ

9 November 1387 — Beauworth

La Fontaine clearly brought shocking news with him after a brief visit at court. He had returned with a worried frown on his face and for days, he had lived secluded in his study. When finally he reappeared on the training grounds, La Fontaine was grim-faced and snapped at the soldiers and new recruits alike.

That night, Argyle broke several unwritten rules of the household and knocked on the door of La Fontaine's private chambers, after yet another meal had been served with the master of the household absent.

Argyle knocked on the door before opening it with great caution. 'Sire?'

In the flickering light from the fireplace, La Fontaine's frame shifted in the great chair to the right of the hearth. Argyle stayed at the threshold not sure whether to venture forward or close the door again.

La Fontaine looked up as if shaking off a bad dream. When he saw Argyle, he gave a limp wave of entry. 'Close the door behind you.'

'Sire …' Argyle stopped mid-sentence, unsure how to best continue. Then he plunged in. 'Sire, everyone is so worried. How did you find court? Why did you come back so soon? What has happened?'

The questions came tumbling out and for a moment, only the fire's low cracking was audible, then the knight spoke. 'How old are you now?'

'19, Sire.'

'I see … And your brother, Thomas? A year older?'

'Yes, Sire.' Argyle was curious what La Fontaine was getting at.

La Fontaine gestured to Argyle to sit on the low stool to the left of the hearth. 'You mean to tell me, you have heard nothing of how Woodstock, his Grace's own uncle, has recruited several noblemen to his cause? That he has joined forces with Henry of Bolingbroke to banish the King's favourites from court? You are completely unaware that Arundel and the Earl of Warwick along with Woodstock have plotted against the King?'

Argyle did not know what to say. He knew what Thomas was up to, but how much he knew, he had kept from La Fontaine, and now he felt he had made a grave mistake.

'Your brother, the Earl Marshal no less, has joined Bolingbroke, Warwick and Woodstock. He is in league with the very men who are attempting to seize control of the crown. The King is in shock! The nobles have turned against him!' La Fontaine snorted. 'They call themselves the Lords Appellant.'

A chill crept up Argyle's back. 'Sire, I swear, I knew nothing.'

Argyle hated lying to La Fontaine but he saw no other way out of it. He had burned Thomas' letter, certain that his brother was just playing a little mischief. But this, this was a different kind of beast all together. Openly defying the King was too much, even for Thomas however coldblooded he might be. Thomas had risen at court due to the King personally elevating his status. Why turn against the one person who had secured Thomas his prosperity and titles?

La Fontaine cleared his throat, dragging Argyle back into the present. 'No matter the circumstances Argyle, we are no longer welcome at court. Woodstock has sent me packing in disgrace.'

'Sire? I do not under…'

'You do not understand!' The knight slammed his palm onto the small table beside his chair and Argyle jumped.

'What is there to understand, boy? Your brother and the nobles have all gone mad!' La Fontaine raged. 'That is the only explanation! It is hardly helpful that for many years, the King has set aside the greatest families in the country and played favourites among those without noble birth; people like me, who are descended from lesser families and have fought our way up the ranks at court either by means of our abilities in battle or our eloquence. If the King had not shown such disdain to his own kind, none of this would have happened. And yet, you knew nothing? Not a word from your own brother about this betrayal?!'

La Fontaine shook a finger angrily at Argyle. 'If you had even the slightest inkling about your brother's plans, you cannot stay here! I am not welcome at court right now, but a time may yet arise, when the King sends for me once more. And I will not bring the brother of a turncoat, should it be proved that you knew of this treachery.'

'Sire, I swear it! What I knew I told you in October.' Argyle's mouth was so dry his answer came out in a hoarse whisper. 'My loyalty is bound to his Grace the King and to you. My brother has told me nothing. Had he chosen to include me in his plotting, I would have told you - I swear it.'

Argyle's eyes burned with hot tears and he blinked them away angrily, this was the punishment for lying to his master - and for what? So that Thomas might be safe? If this was loyalty, Argyle did not care for it. And still something kept Argyle from telling La Fontaine the truth - that he had received a letter, that he had still had it while La Fontaine was in the room, and that the two had agreed that it was nothing because Argyle had not simply handed it over to La Fontaine.

'Very well,' La Fontaine resigned. 'I choose to believe you. But know that if I should uncover proof of your guilt, you will go immediately.'

'Yes, Sire. You shall find no such proof, for none exists. I am but a humble servant of England. Until my death!' Argyle said, choking on the betrayal in his own hollow words.

CHAPTER 11

22 December 1387 — Beauworth

'ENOUGH!'

La Fontaine's voice boomed out and all around him, people scrambled for safety as he pushed his way through the mass of squires, soldiers and would-be knights on the training field. He grabbed Argyle by the collar and threw him into the freshly fallen snow. La Fontaine's one hand was balled into a fist, the other grabbing the hilt of his sword so tight his knuckles were white. He towered above Argyle as one of the legendary giants Argyle had heard of in his bedtime stories.

Startled and shocked, Argyle stared back at him feeling the icy ground hard beneath his body. 'Sire?'

'Walk with me!' La Fontaine's cloak snapped as he turned and stomped towards the house.

The other young men looked from the knight to Argyle and then around at each other. It had been long since they had had such a tasty treat to discuss as the lights burned low in the evening. Argyle got to his feet, his clothes soaked by the snow that had melted away underneath him. His shoulder blades hurt and he felt bruised where a stone had pushed into his side. Argyle was forced to jog to reach La Fontaine although they were all but matched in height by now.

Slightly out of breath Argyle caught up and found his voice. 'What might I have done now, Sire?'

La Fontaine turned towards him, a mixture of anger, but also sorrow, in his cold blue eyes. 'You cannot guess? It is your brother once more. Now ask me, what he has done and tell me, you did not know. Prove to me you are as loyal as you have claimed to be!'

Subdued, Argyle followed La Fontaine up the stairs to his private study. A guard quietly closed the door behind them. By now, La Fontaine was white-hot with rage. 'Ask me!'

'What did Thomas do?'

'All the King's closest confidants have been banished from court! But even that did not satisfy the angry Lords. It is widely said that Thomas helped Woodstock, Warwick, Arundel and Bolingbroke intercept de Vere. It was a mere stroke of good fortune that de Vere managed to escape abroad.' Argyle could feel bile rising in his mouth as La Fontaine continued. 'The King attempted to stall negotiations with Woodstock in order for de Vere to bring reinforcements down from Cheshire. The King sent word to your brother to tell de Vere to march on London immediately; he wanted to raise the army against the nobles of the land. To put it plainly, Woodstock is now in control of the royal army! Courtesy of your brother.'

'Thomas?' Argyle said weakly, as realisation of his brother's betrayal began to dawn. This was much more than what Thomas had hinted at in his letter. This was treason.

'Well, who else! Your brother was the only one privy to the King's command.' La Fontaine sat heavily in his great chair by the hearth and put his head in his hands.

The sudden silence became oppressive. Argyle kept near the door ready to make a run for it if La Fontaine chose to act on his previous threats and send him away. Which was about as likely as could be right now.

Eventually, the knight looked accusingly at Argyle. 'You knew none of this, had not even an inkling? It was carried out by a member of your immediate family; the head of your house no less and you would have me believe you knew nothing?'

Argyle nodded, no words would come. Even to contemplate how far Thomas' ambition had taken him left Argyle feeling sick. He would have never believed that Thomas would defy the King so openly. Argyle wondered, what Thomas would stand to gain, what the other conspirators had promised in return for his betrayal. It had to be a reward great enough to warrant corrupting the Mowbray name.

It seemed to be forever before La Fontaine finally spoke again. 'Very well. The folly of the one should not lead to the demise of the other. Only know that I am watching you even more keenly than before. My household may not be welcome at court just now - but that will change. Once it does, I will not have his Grace suspecting a single action of ours. Mind yourself, Argyle!'

Argyle fled through the now open doors. As soon as they had closed behind him, he turned and ran the length of the hall, then up the stairs taking two steps at a time until he reached his chamber.

Inside, Argyle locked the door, opened a window and giving rein to his emotions, he threw up.

3 May 1393 — Calais

Argyle fought the memory of La Fontaine, looking at him with contempt painted on his distraught and defeated face and his threats that if Argyle was not loyal to his master before anyone else, he would be sent away in disgrace, that he would be a traitor too. Why was it that even now, so many years later, Thomas' shadow continued to loom over him? How could he ever outlive the reputation that Thomas had given the Mowbray name?

Bolingbroke had picked at the same old bone, could Argyle be trusted to be loyal to the King before all others? Argyle shook his head to clear it after his disturbing conversation with Bolingbroke. How could he accuse Argyle of being part of the White Hart? How was he to redeem himself, to clear his name and prove his loyalty?

They were supposed to be across the sea by now. How Argyle longed to set foot on English soil once more. To spur his horse towards London, make his report at court and be off to Beauworth. He had come to regard that place as his true home, much more so than his ancestral home could ever be. After all, Argyle could not remember ever living there for any considerable amount of time. He always felt like a guest, never a resident.

A fat, full moon climbed slowly towards the horizon, sending an eerie light across the glittering wet battlements, hail still piled up in the corners of the parapets and arrow slits.

For some odd reason, the scenery reminded him of an evening a spring night two years ago when the King had summoned him. That evening the moon had been fat and full as well, bathing the castle windows in a pale eerie light. In the confines of his private chambers, the King had laid a plan before Argyle that he could hardly refuse. A plan that had led him to this particular time and place.

Argyle leaned heavily against the wet walls, feeling his shoulders scrape against the stone slabs. Absentmindedly, he ran his fingers down the wall, his fingertips tingling at the touch. Closing his eyes, Argyle slowly slid down the wall, his knees buckling and his cloak dragging him mercilessly down. He breathed in heavily as his mind was suddenly lit by a memory, bright as a bolt of lightning.

CHAPTER 12

25 January 1388 — Beauworth

- What have I done? If only I had known that the other lords would seek to unseat the King, to usurp the throne! Do not believe for a moment that I ever intended to go along with such a scheme. I was shocked and horrified when they suggested this act of treason. I believe even Bolingbroke was put off; he certainly denounced their idea of putting him on the throne instead of our King. Now, all I can do is pray that our side comes out victorious, and that my fellow lords decide to keep the King. I pleaded as much today, but Woodstock and Warwick would not hear of it. I believe my father-in-law might soon have a change of heart, although he stood firmly on the side of Woodstock. I think perhaps he does not dare otherwise. But what can I do? Tell no one! Burn this - Thomas

Argyle blinked at the letter, then threw it into the smouldering flames of the banked fire as if the paper had burned him. What was this treason? How could Thomas imagine that Argyle would not inform La Fontaine? That he would keep it a secret?

Throwing a cloak over his shoulders, Argyle went in search of La Fontaine, nearly trampling down a couple of servants lingering outside his room.

'M'lord, what can we do?' One of the servants asked glancing sideways at the other.

Argyle shook his head in irritation, he had asked not to be called my lord, but no one in this wretched house ever listened to him. 'Nothing, thank you.'

'If you are looking for M'lord La Fontaine, he is out,' the servant said.

'What?' Argyle asked; he had not heard that La Fontaine had any plans for riding out. They were outlawed, exiled from court, banished and confined to La Fontaine's estate, where would he go?

'He rode out this morning early. Ouch!' The servant howled as the other punched him hard in the ribs.

'What is this?' Argyle demanded, and the both of them looked crestfallen.

'We weren't to tell a soul, M'lord. I'm ever so sorry, but you didn't hear it from us. I'm sure it was just to go into town, nuthin' more, he'll be back soon.' The other servant dragged off with his more talkative friend, both of them looking over their shoulder at Argyle.

These days, La Fontaine never went off without an armed escort, so Argyle decided to pursue the subject in the stables. He had made fast friends with several of the stable boys and that would pay off now.

Halfway across the courtyard, Argyle saw a little boy scurry away from the stable doors, running along the side of the stables and around the corner. Argyle made to follow the boy when someone called out. 'Mowbray!'

Argyle raised his hand in salute and went to one of the pens. 'Reggie, where are all the horses?'

Reggie looked concerned. 'You didn't hear? M'lord has taken an escort to London.'

'London?! But we are not to leave the estates?' Argyle pondered out loud hoping to get more information from Reggie.

'Nevert'less, a messenger arrived at dawn, and whatever he brought sent M'lord into a fit. Sent for men and horses so fast some of the other boys missed it all just gettin' dressed,' Reggie said.

'But not you?' Argyle asked.

'Nah, I always sleep in my shirt and breeches, right? Less fleabites that way!' Reggie looked around then lowered his voice in a conspiring way. 'I heard M'lord curse under his breath, sayin' Woodstock or some such.'

'Really?' Argyle said, stepping closer still. 'Did you hear anything else?'

Reggie nodded. 'I 'eard him say to Warden that this is what you get, when you poke the snakes.'

Argyle frowned. 'Snakes?'

'Yes, 'though I couldn't say what that's all about.' Reggie nuzzled the brown mare currently occupying the pen he was supposed to be cleaning out. 'Think it's important, do you?'

'Yes, but I do not know why.'

Reggie smiled. 'That's what's the difference 'tween you and me, you wonder, and I don't.'

'Then maybe you are the smarter one of us,' Argyle said and headed back towards the house.

'Oh, I almost forgot!' Reggie half-shouted after Argyle, who turned around. 'M'lord said, if anyone come askin' to say he don't know when he'll be back. No point in waitin' then is there? He'll be here, when he is.'

'You are some philosopher, Reggie, ever consider becoming a churchman?' Argyle shouted back, and ducked when Reggie threw a dry pile of horseshit at him. 'You missed, and now you have to clean the yard too.'

'Worth it!' Reggie yelled with a grin and Argyle walked back to the house wondering what message could possibly make La Fontaine risk his life and break his exile.

7 February 1388 — Beauworth

The sun crept slowly over the horizon and the treetops shattered the first delicate rays while the clouds got dressed in shades of pink. Last night, the sky had been bloody, an ill omen according to the folklore.

Dressed in only his breeches, Argyle looked through the narrow tower window.

Sighing, he turned, pulled a tunic over his head and opened the door. Outside the household was in uproar.

'What is this?' Argyle stopped a servant in mid run.

'M'lord has just returned with word that Sir Coxcombe is fleeing. Along with many others.'

Argyle let go of the servant's arm. Ever since the King's uncle Woodstock had formed the Lords Appellant, all the King's favourites had become fair game. Still, to have it come to this. He ran across the courtyard to find answers to his many questions.

In the great hall the tense atmosphere felt like a lightning storm waiting to happen. Quietly, Argyle closed the massive door behind him and sought refuge in a dark corner. From this vantage point, he had a good view of most of the hall but was hidden from sight at the same time.

As soon as La Fontaine stepped into the hall, the mumbling stopped. Everyone turned to him. He stood in the middle of the low dais at the far end of the hall, still in his dirty travel cloak, which was dripping from the wet February weather. La Fontaine took in the sight of his household.

'Regrettably, it is my duty to inform you that Thomas of Woodstock has succeeded in a rebellion that has sent the King's most trusted advisors running for their lives! For the time being, Woodstock is controlling the affairs' of the realm.'

The hall broke out in heated protests to his announcement, people gesticulating wildly or simply starring blankly around. Argyle crept further into the shadows. Finally, La Fontaine silenced the room by raising a hand. 'Let us count ourselves lucky that we are only confined to Beauworth and not running for our lives, as most others are. But we must remain here and we must remain loyal to the King. That is all.'

La Fontaine turned on his heel and exited through the small door directly behind the dais, leaving the hall in total confusion.

ꟾ

Later that day, word spread that Coxcombe had asked Woodstock for voluntary exile and permission to leave for France. This had been denied. Upon finding he was no longer safe near London, he had made for Wales, making it across the border just moments before Woodstock's men could arrest him.

Coxcombe had already asked La Fontaine for sanctuary, prepared to risk the ride east if La Fontaine agreed, but he had flatly refused, stating that he had to keep his own household safe. While Coxcombe was sure to understand La Fontaine's decision, he was just as likely to hold a grudge for some time to come. The two had fought side by side in more battles than either cared to remember, and yet in his hour of need, Coxcombe had found his old friend wanting.

According to the gossip, La Fontaine had deliberated a long time, before finally refusing. Several squires still in favour with La Fontaine, came and went at all hours, carrying messages to riders with horses ready to take off at a moment's notice. Argyle, meanwhile, had chosen voluntary confinement in his small tower chamber, knowing he would not be welcome in the knight's presence.

During the next weeks, Argyle wrote several letters to his sisters, pleading for news from court and from their own households. In truth, he was testing the waters to see if any would take him in, should La Fontaine decide that Argyle was disloyal and want him gone.

He waited anxiously, sleeping only a few hours each night and though he was on the training field from dawn till dusk, he could do nothing to relieve the intense knot of fear in his stomach.

ꕥ ꕥ ꕥ ꕥ

Eleanor was the first to send a letter in response to his plea.

- Naturally, you are always welcome in our house, dearest little brother, though I cannot claim to know much of the dealings at court. My husband is very preoccupied with matters of his estate and goes but rarely to London. In these trying times, I confess, I am happy not to be in the midst of court. To that end, I cannot envy our dear brother his position. I hear little from him, and what I do hear is very unnerving.

I am content to be a country wife with a large estate and much to do with children and keeping house. -

She included a lengthy description of how her children were growing and other happy news that she probably thought would soothe him. Sadly it did not.

Two days later, Joan sent a short note most certainly included in a letter from her husband to some knight or other in the county. Like Eleanor, Joan attempted to keep his spirits high, though her message was more brisk and matter-of-fact.

- I cannot imagine any of us should concern ourselves. Our brother is high in favour at court, and though I truly cannot condone his decisions at present, I am sure he has acted in our family's best interests. Sir Thomas is adamant that I offer an open invitation to you. We should be pleased to welcome you into the household. The children speak often of their uncle the knight, though I tell them that you are not yet knighted. I am sure this will happen, though now it may be longer than either of us expect or desire. Do come, dear brother, should the need arise. – With love, Joan

Joan probably knew much and more about life at court, as Sir Thomas was well connected there. He rarely went, claiming gout and frequently taking to his bed as if to prove the truth of his illness. Even so, he was a kind husband to Joan and a good father, a keen royalist and, most of all, a realistic man, who cared more about his family and estate than advancements to be made at court.

Uncharacteristically, Margaret remained silent. If she had received his plea, she had either decided to ignore it, believing it to be a trick, or she simply did not want to help. Giving his eldest sister the benefit of the doubt, Argyle resolved that she would not be so cold. Although Margaret had always felt a little out of step with her brothers and sisters, she had never been anything but kind and generous to him.

Argyle treasured his sisters' offerings but knew in his heart he would only leave if asked to. For better or worse, he belonged at Beauworth with La Fontaine. If only he could be persuaded that Argyle's loyalty was true.

Having resolved in the end not to tell La Fontaine about the second letter from Thomas, Argyle swore to himself never to tell a lie again, even to protect his own family.

26 February 1388 — Beauworth

From gossip and eavesdropping, Argyle had gradually learned of what had transpired back in February. The court had been and still was in turmoil, which to some degree allowed him to think that Thomas could have been pushed to his treasonous acts, as he had proclaimed in his letter.

Apparently, the King had become increasingly difficult to deal with after the failed war on Scotland. The nobles had openly disagreed with what they saw as an oppressive and tyrannical way of leading the land.

When the Lords had finally had their fill, they decided that the King's many favourites were poor counsel for the young and impressionable King. Determined to resolve the situation by any means necessary, had they launched an armed rebellion against the King to end the problems. Their ultimate goal was to remove his friends and restore peace to the land, just as Thomas had written, except that the Lords had gone too far in their efforts. They had purged the court, leaving a trail of blood in their wake. La Fontaine had been right when he said that de Vere had been lucky to escape to France.

Argyle struggled to share the Lords' view. As a soldier in the household of one of the King's favourites, he was disturbed by their rhetoric, and rather feared they would attack La Fontaine's lands. The news was scant at best and much of what he heard was bits and pieces, often speculations of those not entirely in the know. As Argyle no longer trusted Thomas, and felt sure someone in La Fontaine's household kept a vigil eye on his correspondence, he had no way of finding out for himself.

The following Monday, while tending to the horses as an excuse not to enter the main hall while the knight and his household ate, Argyle overheard a couple of the servants talking of the latest news.

'They condemned all of them to death.'

'But they weren't even there!'

'Makes no difference. They hung that Brembre, didn't they? Clearly the Lords can do as they wish. It wasn't enough to replace his counsellors, they wanted to purge the royal household to make sure, it didn't happen again.'

'I still cannot get the image of the Queen begging for a man's life out of my mind.'

'You don't even know what she looks like!'

'I can imagine. And I can imagine what'll happen next.'

'Really?'

'War! The King still has many friends. Of course they'll rise for his cause.'

One of the servants coughed and spat. 'Let us hope it doesn't come to that. It would put our Master right in the path of some of the most powerful men in England.'

As they walked away, their voices drifting towards the summer skies, Argyle straightened from his hunched position beside the horse. Surely, it would not come to war, would it?

6 March 1388 — Beauworth

The next morning, La Fontaine finally summoned Argyle. Reluctantly, Argyle made for La Fontaine's chambers, trying to think of something to say and coming up blank. He had burned the letters from Thomas, he had tried to forget the content and anyway it was too late to admit what he knew.

In the end, Argyle entered La Fontaine's study feeling completely defenceless. 'Sire?'

'I should think you would be interested in the latest news. Or have you already heard? It is truly outrageous!' La Fontaine calmed himself before continuing. 'The Lords have torn apart the royal household! Anyone they thought to be a threat to their power was put on trial. Including the King's beloved tutor. I have it on good authority that the royal couple begged for his life, the Queen on her knees, crying before the Parliament.'

La Fontaine sat down on a low wooden stool near the smouldering hearth. 'All to no avail. The old man vas tried and sentenced to a traitor's death along with a host of the King's household knights. It was a bloodbath.'

Argyle felt a knot of fear in his stomach; what the servants had been speaking of was true. However, La Fontaine's voice brightened a little. 'It may please you to know that towards the end of these trials, your brother began to show doubts, as did Bolingbroke. They must have realised that the Lords had gone too far. I think if they had dared they would indeed have deposed the King. Perhaps even had his head!'

Argyle stared at La Fontaine, feeling the cold hands of fear clawing at his throat. How could La Fontaine speak like this with barely a trace of emotion?

'I should not put it past them,' La Fontaine persisted. 'The Lords have long found the King's friends wanting - perhaps they were even right about some of them. To be sure, his Majesty will not let this rest. He will, without doubt, view Bolingbroke and the rest as his mortal enemies for the rest of his life. The King has never taken kindly to being told what to do, and he is unlikely to start now.'

La Fontaine shrugged and stood up once more. He paced to the window, resting his hands lightly on the windowsill. 'The King has a temper and was raised with a blind belief that God is always on his side. The Lords have merely affirmed this by sparing his life, even if they did take the lives of many others. For now, there is peace. It may be frail and ill-begotten, but there we are.'

La Fontaine looked at Argyle. 'You should know that some say your brother played a dangerous game of double-dealing, pretending to work for both sides loyally. What is true and what is false, I cannot say. But I think it speaks in his favour that he stood up to the other Lords, perhaps even swayed Bolingbroke to keep the King on his throne. Mayhap your brother has redeemed himself somewhat in your view - he has in mine.'

'Sire …'

'No need. I am now convinced you knew nothing.'

Argyle bowed his head; he knew that Thomas had been every bit as guilty as the other Lords. Whatever changed his mind and let him to refuse the Lords' demands, something greater must have been at stake and, knowing Thomas, it was most likely something to do with lands or riches.

'But I implore that you inform me, should you hear from your brother,' La Fontaine's voice cut through Argyle's thoughts. 'Any news from court will be welcome - and you can help secure that.'

As Argyle left the room, he thought about La Fontaine's final words. Until this moment he had thought him a good soldier, even a sound war counsel, yet now he had seen another side of the knight, the deft politician.

Argyle felt sure he would never possess the same skills.

Christmas 1388 — Beauworth

'I have given it much thought and that is my decision.'

'To be true, I am honoured …'

La Fontaine stopped Argyle. 'Are you going to squabble?'

'No Sire, of course not.'

'Well then, there you are! I am confident this is the best decision.' La Fontaine sealed the document and pressed his ring into the hot wax. A servant was ready to grab the paper and take it to the messenger waiting in the courtyard.

'There! With any luck, I shall father many sons and you will have nothing to worry about!' La Fontaine smiled and beckoned Argyle to step around the table. 'Why the long face?! This is my decision. Your aunt was adamant that I make a will and I have put it off for far too long.'

Argyle inclined his head and smiled back. Despite his attempts to change La Fontaine's mind, Argyle was deeply honoured to be chosen as La Fontaine's heir and, at the same time, formally raised to the rank of senior soldier. La Fontaine would no doubt in time find a woman to warm his bed.

'I am sure you will have a son,' Argyle said.

La Fontaine laughed. 'So am I. But it is better to be safe. This at least ensures there is someone to carry on my legacy.'

Argyle expressed his gratitude once more, then excused himself. Walking slowly towards the training grounds, the knight's words rang in his head. 'Better to be safe.'

Suddenly life seemed much more uncertain than it had before and the fact that power now lay with the King's uncle Woodstock, the infamous Duke of Gloucester, did nothing to soothe Argyle's foreboding feeling.

But Woodstock's power was happy tidings to Thomas who was once more excited to have helped clear the court of these 'upstarts' and 'reinstate the nobles to their former rights and glory', as he put it in a letter, Argyle received back in September.

Argyle had spent a long time contemplating his brother's tidings, yet had hesitated to respond. It took a letter from Margaret to finally force a reply. When Thomas had heard nothing from Argyle, he had approached their sister to seek her counsel and in her letter, Margaret forcefully decreed that Argyle take the extended olive branch.

Their initial correspondence was tentative and feeble. Argyle felt unable to congratulate his brother, and Thomas, for his part, kept insisting Argyle found another household. Or better yet that he reconsidered entering the Church.

In every one of his letters, Argyle vigorously declined the idea of a career in the Church, emphasising both his lack of interest in churchly matters and, thanks to La Fontaine, his increasing skills as a soldier. Argyle showed much talent for knighthood and had grown to a size that warranted a new horse and new armour.

Thomas' subsequent silence on the subject of sending money to purchase both horse and armour was answer enough. Thomas would never be content to have a soldier for a brother. Despite having brokered a delicate truce on the subject of Argyle's future, Thomas was not about to give up entirely. Knowing his brother to be stubborn at best, Argyle expected nothing less. Perhaps his newfound title as heir to La Fontaine's estate would appease Thomas, but Argyle did not really believe it would.

CHAPTER 13

4 May 1393 — Calais

If only he had known five years ago how much safer he had been in La Fontaine's care, Argyle might have enjoyed the moment when La Fontaine named him heir to the Beauworth estate and lands. And if only he had known what would happen later, he would have squabbled with La Fontaine, Argyle thought, he would have offered up a better prospect. He would have said no and he would now have been safe in England, not part of this mad journey that had brought with it nothing but deceit and regret.

Argyle's legs were heavy after the long night wandering along the rampart, climbing the stairs of the many turrets and prowling the cobbled courtyard. His cloak and boots were soaked and he felt chilled to the bone.

Leaning over the rampart to survey the harbour once more, Argyle noticed a small fire come to life. It flickered at first; running along a shape that was too far below him to make out. All at once, it seemed to catch on and began burning more brightly.

Argyle squinted to make out what this uneven light was devouring. While the rest of the retinue slowly sprang to life, the light of pre-dawn crept up over the horizon.

The storm had finally died down, leaving Argyle's ears ringing from its nightly screams. Below him, the shutters of narrow windows flew open to let in the cool May air. Someone opened the little harbour gate, and herders were ushering out the few goats and cattle, though Argyle did not think, the poor animals would find anything to eat in the muddy, water swollen fields.

Argyle went back to his makeshift fire, jolting the embers with a few damp logs from the bottom of the pile. Then a call rang up the walls.

'FIRE!'

Argyle rushed to the rampart and saw that the fire below had grown and was slowly making its way towards the dockyard, the moored ships and the provisions storage. It seemed amazing that it could burn on the wet planks. Feet pounded on the stairs in the main keep. More men streamed out of the harbour gate.

'Argyle!' Stephen was out of breath; he had probably scaled the narrow staircase two steps at a time. 'Come quickly.'

Together they ran down the stairs to find the rest of the retinue in uproar. Bolingbroke came barging out, the massive oak doors slamming against the stone, spraying flakes down the stairs. 'Sir Argyle! Smith! Come with me!'

'What is it? If it's the fire, why aren't they just putting it out?' Stephen asked under his breath.

Outside the gate, Bolingbroke pushed his way through the growing crowd on the dockside. Clearly this was no ordinary fire. Several soldiers were attempting to put out the flames that were licking their way towards the storage, hauling up buckets of seawater to throw on the hissing fire. Others were stomping out the source of the fire, the uneven pile that Argyle had spotted a little earlier.

As the sun clawed its way up over the horizon, bathing the harbour in a ghostly light, Argyle stopped dead next to Bolingbroke. Before them on the dockside lay the charred remains of a man.

Stephen stumbled backwards, his hand slapped over his mouth. It was one thing to see men dead on the battlefield or dismembered for a crime, but the corpse before them looked nothing like this. It was maimed, contorted and burned beyond recognition.

'Who is it?' Stephen whispered.

ᘓ ᘕ ᘓ ᘕ

'DAMN!' Argyle burned his hand trying to remove some of the smoking clothes; he cursed himself for not bringing his sword or even his dagger. More soldiers joined to make a chain transporting buckets of water from the harbour to cool off the smouldering corpse.

'Do you think he was burned alive?' Stephen's voice was unnaturally shrill. Several men from the city had run from the sight, crying that this was the Devil's work.

Bolingbroke took charge. 'We must find out if it is one of our men before the town folk return.'

Argyle looked up. 'My Lord?'

'No. If it is one of my men, I demand to know, and I will personally find the culprit,' Bolingbroke declared. 'If it is not, we must leave the body to the crowd and they can make out, who it is. Well, get on with it, Sir Argyle!'

Argyle grabbed the burned cloak once more; this time it yielded, still scorching to the touch. Ignoring the searing pain, Argyle pulled at the charred cloth. A slushy sound revealed that the body's skin had melted into the cloak and was ripping away along with the piece of cloth Argyle was holding on to.

Behind him a man gagged at the sound and several others averted their eyes. Argyle steeled himself, then tugged hard. The cloth ripped and he held a large piece of the cloth, meat clinging to the inside. Argyle threw the cloth aside; it was burned so bad that it was impossible to make out colour or other features that would reveal who was inside and part of it now.

He looked into the pile of flesh, clothes and ashes. The tip of a sword hilt glittered in the cold sunlight. Argyle frowned; the hilt looked strangely familiar.

'Sir Alan!' Stephen staggered backwards once more, slipping on the icy cobbles and only the resourcefulness of a fellow solider prevented him going head first into the harbour.

Bolingbroke stepped forward and pushed the cloth aside, flesh and all. The sound of moist meat letting go of the bones reminded Argyle of a spoon going through a bowl of thick stew. He was revolted to find his mouth watering a little at the sweet, meaty smell of the corpse.

'Get him inside the garrison!' Bolingbroke barked the command then turned, grabbed Argyle by the arm and forced him ahead into the crowd.

In the background, Argyle could make out Stephen's panting breath and several men calling for a makeshift stretcher to move the corpse onto. A crowd was quickly gathering, mothers holding small children back and men pushing forward to get a glimpse of the burned body. They crossed themselves.

'Diable!'

ꕤ ꕤ

'You are sure?'

'Ye … yes,' Stephen stammered as Bolingbroke paced the room.

The cellar walls were wet and the air musty. Coxcombe's contorted body lay on the butcher's table. Someone had found a spare cloak to cover it with, but the shape stood out stark against the folds of the cloth and the smell was palpable.

'And you agree?' Bolingbroke stopped in front of Argyle.

'Yes, my Lord. That is his sword. He never left it out of his sight,' Argyle said.

'A skilled soldier and knight would never have surrendered his sword without a fight. It must be him.' Bolingbroke stared at the body. 'But it is hard to tell, given the state of the corpse. His hair burned away. Someone tried hard to disguise who he was. Why not take the sword if they wanted to mask a crime?'

Argyle had wondered about this since he saw the hilt. So much effort to conceal the identity of the body and the one thing to give it away was lying there right before them, it made no sense.

'Perhaps the act of a madman? Or someone who didn't think to remove the sword before setting the body on fire?' Stephen asked, his voice quivering.

'Could be. But it makes little sense. What enemies did he have?' The second the words left his mouth, Argyle regretted them.

Bolingbroke stopped dead in his tracks and snapped his head around. His eyes crept over Argyle's face. Stephen's eyes bulged as he looked from Bolingbroke to Argyle.

'Yes, what enemies indeed?' Bolingbroke stroked his scruffy beard while scrutinising first Argyle then Stephen. 'Not many, I should wager. Not here at least. Although two come to mind.'

Stephen looked horror-stricken. 'No M'lord! He and I never had words. After a while, he did recognise me, but he never made an enemy of me, nor I of him.'

'Still, he did leave you in England, no word about his escape, no service for you. If someone had done that to me, I would not forgive so easily. And he did know more than most about La Fontaine's misfortune,' Bolingbroke said.

Stubbornly, Argyle refused to take the bait. Yes there had been words and more in the Holy Land, but since then much had happened to reassure him that Coxcombe was but a small pawn in a very large play for power.

'He betrayed a friend. To the death.' Bolingbroke turned his back to the burned body.

'Sir Alan was insignificant,' Argyle said.

Bolingbroke stepped closer to Argyle. 'Indeed?'

Argyle folded his arms across his chest and looked Bolingbroke right in the eye, something the other man did not like, even at the best of times.

'Something to add, Sir Argyle?'

'Nothing to clarify how this came to be,' Argyle said.

'Perhaps he felt remorse and decided to end it all?' Stephen was wringing his hands around a piece of his cloak.

When Bolingbroke looked at him, Stephen shuffled his feet. The floor was dark where he stood, unlike the rest of the floor, which was white with old flour and grime.

'And how did he come to burst into flame?' Bolingbroke asked.

'Suicide's the Devil's work,' Stephen whispered.

'So he burned in the fires of Hell?! I have seen others kill themselves. None of them burned instantly.' Bolingbroke slapped his hand on the butcher's table, sending knives dancing in the air and onto the floor, clattering as they hit the grimy tiles. At the sound, a faint memory slipped away from Argyle.

'Do you think he killed himself, Sir Argyle?' Bolingbroke demanded.

'No, my Lord. I might not have found him a true knight, but I do not think he would risk eternal damnation either.' Argyle knew how devoted Coxcombe had been, never failing to visit a shrine along the way, praying for hours on end at the Holy Sepulchre.

A rough laugh slipped from Bolingbroke. 'Ah, we all risk eternal damnation, no matter how pious we are! Too much killing will make a man immune to redemption, even if our priests claim that God is on our side and that we all can pay our way into Heaven. Still I agree with you, Sir Alan would not have been so desperate. Why, just this evening I had promised him a place in my household.'

Why would Bolingbroke do that? Perhaps he stood to gain the most by ridding himself of a tiresome ally?

'He was murdered then?' Stephen muttered.

'Most likely. Some time between my meeting with him and this morning.' Bolingbroke looked straight at Argyle. 'Between our meeting and this morning. When you were alone on the rampart.'

Stephen gasped and moved away from Argyle, who bit down hard to swallow a sharp response. 'If he left as I entered then yes. Some time between our meeting and this morning.'

'Now, there is a coincidence,' Bolingbroke said coldly.

Argyle nodded curtly and stomped up the cellar stairs. As he escaped into the crisp winter day, he heard Stephen asking Bolingbroke a pointed question. 'How d'you know he was alone, M'lord?'

Once more, Argyle grasped for a whisper of a memory that kept floating just beyond his reach. What had happened that night and why could he not remember all he had done?

He looked down at his burned hand. Was it really the Devil's work?

ꕥ ꕥ ꕥ ꕥ

CHAPTER 14

13 August 1389 — Beauworth

Late in the night, Argyle put down Thomas' latest letter.

Since the King had reclaimed his power in May, his favourites had largely returned to court save a few whom the King, probably to avoid too much trouble with the nobles, had decided would remain in exile. Chief among them his beloved friend de Vere, whose return, Argyle suspected, would have been too much for the nobles to swallow.

At the same time, large parts of the nobility had been busy protecting their own hide or slithering away, returning to their estates and strongholds. The old faction of the court was slowly returning, and Argyle could not imagine that the King was not openly defying the Lords to see, how far he could push them.

A light midnight breeze found its way through the open door, dancing around the chamber. One of the few who remained was Thomas, and his letter clearly communicated an increasing desperation.

- Brother, should you hold any sway with La Fontaine, I besiege you put in a good word for me. I swear upon our bloodline that I am entirely without blame. When the others began discussing the usurping of our anointed King, I immediately turned against the Lords Appellant, as you well know. Surely, you would not now

lay their misdeeds at my door? Surely you remember my letter to you, although you never answered me? Surely family is everything in this cruel world. -

Bolingbroke had left London so quickly that rumours flew far and wide. Allegedly, he had had in mind to simply get rid of his cousin. To this end, Bolingbroke was said to have summoned several of his inner-circle at his father's castle Pontefract and issued an order that anyone who got close to the King would be rewarded handsomely, if the King was to suffer a fatal accident.

Argyle leaned on the windowsill and looked into the night. Here, in the countryside, it was quite possible to forget all about the dealings going on far away at court - until the next messenger came thundering over the drawbridge. He remembered how happy the household had been, when a messenger delivered the joyous news that the King once again held supreme power of England - and that the Queen was with child, the long awaited heir that would hopefully be the deliverance of the royal couple and the end of speculation and turmoil in England.

Although the King had sanctioned that Bolingbroke went on a crusade, the King's cousin was still too close to the throne for comfort. As long as the King had no heir of his own he would have to suffer Bolingbroke as his heir, whether the rumours of his desire to disperse of the King were true or not.

Argyle did not need to read Thomas' last lines again. They were etched into his mind.

- Brother, I besiege you plead my case to La Fontaine, and the King will know that I was ever a loyal subject. What I did was based on falsehood and devious plans of which I knew nothing. I shall do anything to once again be the King's good graces. - Thomas

As soon as Argyle had seen Thomas' letter crumble in the embers of the banked fire, he went in search of La Fontaine to speak to him about Thomas' words. To soothe his own mind if nothing else. All other things aside, Thomas was the head of his family and, as of yet, the only one not summoned to testify in the case of the Lords Appellant.

La Fontaine listened with true concern and then sent Argyle away with the message not to worry about Thomas' situation any more. La Fontaine's opinion was clear. 'A schemer must wear away his own tarnish.'

Argyle was quite certain Thomas did not intend to spend years on end trying to wear away his tarnish. Actually, he still doubted whether Thomas had known more than his letters had expressed. As a true troublemaker from an early age, Thomas had often been led astray and Argyle could not help but wonder if this was the case now. Was his brother really as innocent as he kept insisting upon?

10 December 1389 — Beauworth

It should have come as no surprise, and yet Argyle had the hardest time comprehending how Thomas had recently been appointed Warden of the East Marches towards Scotland.

In a letter, Eleanor revelled in their brother's ability to turn disaster into triumph. She had been at court with her husband and was thrilled by the prospect of their family's latest honour. In a sudden turn of events, the King had awarded Thomas the title just as the court was assembled to witness the ceremonial lighting of the Yule log. While the fire chewed at the massive log, which was to burn for the twelve days of Christmas, the King had risen and ordered Thomas to step forward and kneel before the throne.

Ceremonial sword in hand, the King had hesitated for only the briefest of moments before touching the sword to Thomas' shoulder and announcing his new title. It seemed that even at his darkest hour, Thomas was quick to turn his misdeeds into success. His collection of titles grew steadily.

Although Eleanor was happy, for the first time ever, Argyle found he simply could not rejoice as she did. What he could hope for was peace in England, peace at court and no messengers arriving with letters of any kind suggesting Thomas was up to no good again.

CHAPTER 15

26 July 1392 — London

The smell of dirt and grass threw earthy notes in the vaporising dew of early morning. The horses whinnied and the pennants flapped in the breeze. The air was thick with excitement.

Squires ran among each other and to an outsider it must have looked very disorganised. However, everyone knew exactly where they were going and what they had to do when they got there.

Argyle fell into step with Stephen, as they threaded their way through the sprawling encampment. Over the last couple of weeks the area had grown considerably as knights, hedge knights, tradesmen, bards and fortune hunters had gathered from all corners of the realm. Around the campfires pages, squires and young knights shared stories and mulled wine, all serving to create an atmosphere of friendship.

At the horse pen, Stephen turned left to saddle Coxcombe's horse. Argyle greeted some of the grooms who were on loan from the court stables. It was their task to keep the great number of horses under control. Some way down the line of horses, La Fontaine's dark grey warhorse Noble was tethered. It neighed quietly and lowered its massive head when Argyle held out his hand.

'Do you feel the excitement, boy?' The horse nuzzled Argyle, who fed Noble treats while looking around. The camp was waking up to one final day of training. The tension in the air should have foretold the events that were about to unfold.

In the last training session, Lockley and Coxcombe went head to head in a melee. The two fought with such vigour that the rest of the knights had left the field to let them fight it out by themselves.

Argyle stood at one corner of the enclosure, leaning against a chipped, wooden pole, watching the fight with some concern. This did not look like training to him. This looked like a bloody feud. The knights circled each other, Lockley holding his blunted mace, Coxcombe swinging his sword viciously; crouching every time his opponent charged. So far, Coxcombe seemed on top.

Stephen showed up with a worried expression. 'They're really going at it.'

'A little too hard, I think,' Argyle said. 'Should they have any reason to fight this way? It is only training after all.'

'The heat of battle, mayhap?' Stephen suggested.

Argyle frowned at his friend. A tourney was not battle - it was a show. The training should be about exercise and honing your skills, not a fight that had the rest of the knights leaving the field. Argyle opened his mouth to argue and, just then, Lockley swung his mace with such force that Coxcombe went tumbling over. It would have looked funny if Lockley had not stomped on Coxcombe's arm to make sure he could not retaliate. Coxcombe groaned and let go of his sword, which fell heavily to the ground. Stephen gasped.

Two knights ran to intervene, forcing Lockley away before he could do more harm. Coxcombe got up with difficulty; he was clearly out of breath and his armour's breastplate was badly dented. As Lockley turned away there was malice in his dead grey eyes. Argyle thought. for the briefest moment, that Lockley's mace did not look blunted at all, its spikes were sharp, shining points in the pale afternoon sunlight.

Stephen ran to Coxcombe's side, assisting him in getting out of the breastplate. The release allowed the knight to catch his breath enough to curse wildly. Coxcombe spat after Lockley, who simply kept walking at a steady pace back to his camp, seemingly oblivious to his defeated opponent's words.

Stephen carried the badly dented breastplate past Argyle. 'The blacksmith'll have much to do to get this ready for tomorrow. Sir Coxcombe's first on the lists and he can't fight without proper armour.'

'Especially if he is to meet Lockley,' Argyle said.

'Not on the first round.' Stephen looked relieved. 'Fortunately! I don't know what that was about, but they didn't seem on good terms.'

Argyle agreed silently with Stephen. No, they did not. And that was a curious thing.

27 July 1392 — London

The next day, London was alive with excitement. Commoners and nobility alike were ready to see some of the most famous knights in the land facing each other in the lists, combat and archery. The atmosphere was strung tight as a bowstring. Even so, the first couple of tilts were carried out with very few surprises and Sir Coxcombe easily unsaddled his competition in the second race. La Fontaine was not due to joust until late in the day, leaving Stephen and Argyle free to lounge in the grass close to the track, betting on who would win the other jousts.

'I know La Fontaine will take the prize.' Argyle felt sure of it.

'Well, I think Coxcombe'll beat him.' Stephen ducked as Argyle took a mock swipe at him. They both laughed.

'Honestly, I had never imagined there would be this many participants for the tourney,' Argyle mused and stretched his long legs. The air was dry and dusty, the horses' smell piercing. He was enjoying a moment off.

'I know.' Stephen surveyed the grounds. 'This morning, Sire said that too many strangers've been permitted. He thinks they'll never get done.'

'It is all because many of Bolingbroke's knights decided to turn up with full entourages and plenty of them have joined the lists at the last minute. Though I cannot admit to be dissatisfied, after all it provides us extra time to enjoy the other jousts.' Argyle shaded his eyes from the low set April sun.

'Well, I'll not complain about time off. And here of all places.' Stephen chewed on a straw of grass.

Argyle looked at the many spectators. In one end, they were packed as tight as fish in a barrel. Most of them in plain brown and grey clothes, the women's heads bare or just covered by a thin veil of linen. Children were running around among the adults, their feet bare and dirty. He judged that at least half of them were probably skilled at loosening the strings holding purses on the hips of the more wealthy patrons in that section. Merchants, peasants and other good folk who were lucky enough to get here early were most prominent in the mirage. They were busy laying wagers on the various knights while eating and drinking very modestly.

On the opposite side, the court was shimmering in the sunlight. In the middle, seated under the royal canopy was the King, as ever surrounded by his closest advisors, including the King's uncle Gaunt, who had been persuaded to return to court two years ago, and the Earls of Warwick and Arundel. To one side, the king's other uncle, Woodstock, was listening with feigned interest to his brother Edmund of Langley, the Duke of York, who was renowned for his ability to speak at length about nothing at all.

The beautiful wives of these prominent courtiers looked like rare gems, generously sprinkled around the spectator seats. Gold and jewels flashed and sparkled in the spring sun transforming the right side of the jousting track to a giant treasure trove. The women were in their finest dresses, the men wore long cloaks and covered their hair with liripipes, many of which were studded with precious stones and exotic feathers.

Each time a joust ended, everyone cheered enthusiastically, bags of gold changed hands and several people laughed loudly at their good fortune. Right at the heart of things was the King, nodding at the winners and speaking warmly with the people surrounding him.

The King was seated next to Queen Anne, who, as always, was surrounded by her beautiful, young ladies-in-waiting. Her cool smile and reserved manner was striking in the face of the King's openly easy ways.

Yet it was widely said that the political union had nonetheless bloomed into true romance; a rumour the King often confirmed, leaning lovingly towards his wife or taking her hand in his.

ꟃ ꟃ

Early in the afternoon, the tourney's main attraction began in earnest. The knights put on their heavy armour and lances lowered they raced toward each other, their horses' hooves thundering and sand spraying. As the duels finished, the list of competitors grew shorter. La Fontaine was still on top, and Argyle struggled to conceal his enthusiasm.

Dusk had crept over the range when the two last knights met to joust. Argyle handed La Fontaine his first lance. La Fontaine adjusted his helmet and slammed down the visor. A light breeze toyed with the big dark-blue feather streaming from the top of his tourney helmet. Through two narrow slits, Argyle could just make out La Fontaine's eyes.

'Shield!'

With his shield firmly locked onto his left arm, La Fontaine spurred on his battle horse, Noble, which trotted towards one end of the range. The other end was still empty. The audience stirred impatiently, where was the opponent?

Stephen appeared at Argyle's side just as it began to drizzle. The two exchanged a glance. Argyle was nervous and excited. La Fontaine had been unstoppable in all his jousts and now only one opponent remained. At the other end of the field, Lockley finally appeared on his great, brown gelding. The horse flicked its head while Lockley saluted the King's dais before slamming down his visor and raising his battered shield. The two opponents briefly acknowledged each other with a curt nod.

The Queen raised her handkerchief, silencing the crowd. Argyle almost forgot to breathe, his body taut as a bowstring. Stephen crossed himself absently.

At the exact moment the Queen let go of her handkerchief both riders charged. The lances still pointed directly into the leaden skies, the drizzle turning into fat, full raindrops, drumming on the helmets and armour. Halfway down the field, Lockley lowered his lance, a few seconds later La Fontaine followed suit. Hooves thundered on the hard-packed sand and dirt, where puddles were quickly gathering.

Seconds later, lances struck shields and armour. The crowd roared. The King rose halfway in his seat. Both knights were still in their saddles. To deafening applause the knights turned back towards their own ends, where their squires stood. La Fontaine discarded his broken lance and grabbed the new one, Argyle was holding out.

Once again, the opponents took their positions at opposite ends of the field. The herald signalled the next round and the two charged at each other again. They lowered their lances. At the very last minute, Lockley turned slightly in his saddle and thrust towards La Fontaine, nearly unseating himself to avoid La Fontaine's outstretched lance. The impact sent a wave of excitement through the crowd. The King applauded with fervour and nodded his approval.

Both knights jerked upright, turning their horses to trot back to take their third and final lance. Lockley took his time, running his hand along the horse's neck and nodding at the crowd. La Fontaine seemed to momentarily lose grip of his reins and then he slumped sideways on his horse. So slow it seemed time had frozen, La Fontaine slid out of the saddle and landed with a crash on the wet sand. Confusion spread in the crowd, where some cheered on and others abruptly stopped applauding.

The King rose from his throne. Argyle dropped the last lance he had been holding since La Fontaine charged the second time. His legs carried him over the wet sand before he realised he was running. Up close, he saw a large splinter poking out from La Fontaine's left armpit. The sand surrounding La Fontaine was already stained, scarlet tendrils seeping into the puddles around his lifeless body.

Lockley still mounted on his steed, had turned back and now loomed over his opponent.

On his knees, Argyle saw La Fontaine was still breathing, but it was shallow and gurgling. Blood was bubbling from the corner of his mouth when Argyle removed the helmet. With fumbling hands, he began to remove the armour around the wound. As he reached to draw out the lance splinter that was forced into the gap between La Fontaine's breastplate and shoulder plate, a chain mailed hand stopped him.

Lockley bent over Argyle shooting him a cold, dead stare. 'Remove it and he dies!'

'But ...'

'Boy! You wouldn't want to be the one to kill him, would you? It'll certainly look that way.' Lockely squeezed Argyle's wrist harder. Then Lockley released it and turned, the heels of his armoured boots drilling into the wet, red sand. Argyle heard women screaming and men yelling. They too had spotted the large blood pool, which kept diluting and doubling in size as the rain pelted down over the field.

Finally, more knights stirred and they came splashing through the wet grass, pushing down the wooden railing, which had been hastily erected before the tourney began, carrying away La Fontaine's lifeless body.

Dreamlike, Argyle reached out and picked up La Fontaine's solid shield. On the front a prancing unicorn stood out against a starry black sky. Its white skin was spattered in blood.

CHAPTER 16

28 July 1392 — Westminster

In the pre-dawn, Argyle had been lulled asleep by La Fontaine's rattling breath, which seemed to have steadied itself somewhat. Argyle was dreaming that the knight had survived; they were back at Beauworth, watching a soldier break in a new horse.

A rasping, gurgling sound cut through the pitch black of sleep, wrestling Argyle unkindly from his dream that La Fontaine was saying that of course he would win the tourney, not to worry. Argyle turned towards La Fontaine, mechanically reaching for the cloth in the washbasin next to the cot. When he looked up, La Fontaine was staring back, his eyes sunken into his skull, blank from fever and exertion. Argyle gasped.

'Boy …' La Fontaine's voice was strained and raw. Argyle closed the gap between the bench he had been sitting on and the cot, forgetting about the cloth and grasping for the pitcher of water. His hands shook so bad, when he tried to fill a cup that it slopped all around him, turning the rushes and sand from the jousting field to a muddy mess.

'Sire,' Argyle whispered, bringing the cup to La Fontaine's dry, broken lips and slowly tipping it to let La Fontaine drink. La Fontaine's lips were wetted, but he did not seem to swallow the water, it simply trickled down his chin and seeped into the cloth covering his body. Argyle noticed that the wounded side was red, the cloth wet as if the wound had not closed, but when he reached over, La Fontaine shook his head slowly.

'No … no need to look,' La Fontaine croaked. 'It will not … heal.'

'Sire, do not speak!' Argyle was scared of the force of his own voice. 'I shall get a physician.'

Once more, La Fontaine struggled to shake his head, locking his blank stare on Argyle. 'No. It won't be long now. I feel … You must be watchful.'

Argyle had been struggling to get up, but now La Fontaine grabbed his arm and pulled him close. For a man close to death, La Fontaine had a surprising iron grip. 'Listen to me! You must be watchful. The court is full of dangers … I had not …' La Fontaine's strength left his hand and his head fell down onto the pillow, his breathing gurgling and rattling.

'Sire … What do you mean?' Argyle asked, feeling stupid for not understanding and useless for not sending for help.

'The King …' La Fontaine coughed, his whole body shaking at the effort. Beads of cold sweat trickled down his face, streaking his gaunt cheeks. Argyle could see blood pulsing steadily from the wound in La Fontaine's left armpit.

'The King?' Argyle prompted, suddenly feeling the urgency of La Fontaine's message.

'The King knows … He will ask your help.' La Fontaine once more struggled to get up, his left elbow buckling under his weight, but he kept his head up, his eyes swimming for a moment at the effort. 'You … do not …'

At that moment, the door opened and Argyle recognised the scrawny little physician who had tended to La Fontaine's wound, when they first brought him in. The physician took in the scene for a moment before throwing the door open, yelling for help, for guards, for anything that might help the patient.

Argyle looked back at La Fontaine, his eyes cloudy and blood seeping from his mouth.

'Sire?' Argyle breathed, feeling tears stinging behind his eyelids and not bothering to blink them away. He reached over to grab La Fontaine's limp hand; Argyle could almost feel life slipping from La Fontaine's body.

'Do not trust …' La Fontaine struggled, choking on the blood in his mouth, spitting angrily, his eyes momentarily clear and alert. '… anyone.'

Argyle nodded fervently, he was oblivious to the tumultuous scene behind him, but La Fontaine noticed something and nodded towards the door. 'No one.'

La Fontaine's eyes rolled back, they seemed to sink into his head, his rasping breath catching, gurgling and then stopping. Argyle tried to pull his hand free, but in the grips of death, La Fontaine held on tight for a few seconds longer, before he was delivered by death and his grip loosened. Argyle pulled away, sobbing openly, biting his tongue until it bled to avoid screaming out his pain and despair.

'Mowbray,' The King's voice was all but a whisper, and yet it was so loud in Argyle's head that he spun around balling his fists. The King moved slowly forward, his hand resting on Argyle's shoulder for a moment. 'Is he …?'

Argyle could not speak, not believe that La Fontaine was dead when they had been speaking just moments ago. The King shook him softly and then more fiercely when Argyle did not reply. Finally, Argyle nodded, gasping like a fish dragged from its wet home in a lake to lie dying on the brink.

The King swallowed, his eyes darting around the room, before he turned, stumbling over the small stool where Argyle had sat just a few moments ago. Roaring in anger, pain and grief, the King all but ran from the room, the physician and guards jumping out of his way.

Argyle felt his legs give way and he fell clumsily to the floor, banging the side of his head on one of the legs on the upturned stool. The searing pain felt strangely like relief, the blood trickling from his split eyebrow mixing with his tears. He did not even know if the screams he was hearing were his.

'He is dead,' The scrawny physician announced completely unnecessarily, before turning towards one of the servants. 'Cover him up.'

As the servant made to do as he was bid, Argyle felt a blinding rage surge through his body. He jumped up, barging into the servant, pummelling the surprised man's face, chest and neck, when the servant doubled over, trying to protect himself from this mad attacker.

'Now boy …' the physician tried to interfere and Argyle let go of the servant, lunging for the physician. A guard stepped in just in time, grabbing Argyle by the wrists and pushing him violently back until his shoulders hit the stonewall with a sickening crack. Argyle winced at the pain, but he kept on fighting.

'No one touches him!' Argyle screamed, his vision blotted out by red fury. 'NO ONE!!'

The guard pinned him to the wall but shook his head at the other men in the room, who were looking around at each other not quite sure how to proceed.

'Leave us.'

Argyle turned his head and saw Thomas standing in the doorway, his dark hair a mess, his clothes the same as he had worn yesterday at the tournament, only now they were crumbled and dirty.

Thomas looked around in irritation. 'Have you lost your ears? LEAVE US!' he bellowed.

The men woke from their trance, scrambling to get out of the room, two of them clogging the doorway when they tried to get out at the same time. If not for the churning pain and sorrow, Argyle would have laughed at the scene.

The last to leave was the guard, shooting Thomas a doubtful look before closing the door.

'Argyle …' Thomas' voice trailed off.

Argyle slid down the wall, crying hysterically - as a girl, he thought angrily, but he could not stop himself. Thomas moved close, but rather than slap him or yell at him, Thomas simply sat down next to him and put his arm around Argyle's shoulder.

Once Argyle's crying subsided, Thomas spoke softly. 'I know what he meant to you.' He turned his head to Argyle. 'I may not have understood your bond, but I know … Neither of us had a father, and God knows for all his virtues, John was no more than a toddler when father died, but …'

Argyle swallowed hard and rubbed his face roughly with his sleeve. 'Thomas, there is no need …'

'Yes, there is.' Thomas offered with a slanting smile. 'It cannot have been easy. We just let you go, we became all but strangers. I know … I know I have not been much of a brother. I certainly have not been much of a replacement for a father.'

'You are one year my senior, if you had been more like a father, I would have been scared.' Argyle gave a shaky smile in spite of his raw grief and pain.

'I know, but … I wish we were better friends,' Thomas said simply. 'When you are ready, pull the cloth over his face. You must deliver him unto God.'

Thomas got up slowly, brushing rushes from his clothes and fastening the pin on his cloak. 'Whatever our differences, in many ways I admired La Fontaine. I suspect, aunt Blanche knew what kind of a man he was, since she chose him to be your guardian. I could not have suffered it if she had sent you to a lesser man.'

'Thank you,' Argyle said. They looked at each other for a while before Thomas turned for the door.

'Thomas?' Argyle got up; his shoulders were painful from the rough treatment before, his eyes red and swollen and his temple throbbed. 'I mean it, thank you.'

Thomas waved a slender hand. 'We are a family, whatever anyone else might think. Come and see me later, but first hand over La Fontaine to the church, and get some rest, you look a frightful mess.'

Argyle nodded obediently as Thomas opened the door. 'No one enters this room until my brother allows it,' Thomas ordered the guard outside the door and added with a threatening air. 'And I mean no one!'

When Argyle had said his final goodbye, he let in the friars waiting silently in the hallway. Turning towards the bright July sunlight, Argyle found his path blocked.

'Argyle?' Stephen stepped gingerly forward. 'Argyle … Is he …?'

He could not deal with Stephen just then. In truth, he could not deal with anyone. In the small cold room lay the closest thing he ever had to a father, now as pale as a ghost from the grave. La Fontaine had died trying to warn Argyle, bled out while Argyle had just sat there, and now the friars would wash the body, dress it and prepare La Fontaine for his final journey.

With a deep breath, Argyle angrily blinked away a new torrent of tears. It was just a silly tourney! Not a battlefield. When it was time for La Fontaine to die, it was to have been on the battlefield where he belonged. Tourneys were a show. Not a fight for life and death. Not even when made to look the part. La Fontaine was first and foremost a soldier. He should have been granted a soldier's death.

Stephen nervously cleared his throat. 'I'm sorry … I … Sir Coxcombe's nowhere to be found.'

Argyle stared at his friend with empty eyes making Stephen cringe. What did he want? Could he not fathom that at this very moment nothing mattered but the death of La Fontaine? And so what if Coxcombe had gone? He had probably retreated to his small house on the outskirts of London. What was it to him anyway?

Argyle felt anger surge through his veins. 'And what of it?!!' The quiet corridor threw back a hollow echo of his strained voice.

'It's just … They're saying it was a conspiracy. That Coxcombe helped Lockley win.' Stephen's voice broke. 'I don't know how, I swear. But Coxcombe's gone.'

'How could Coxcombe have helped Lockley? Everyone knows Lockley should have lost! He was cheating! I was right there and I saw him cheat. He turned. He thrust the lance much harder than he ought. He …' Argyle choked up.

'He was free to turn in the saddle. Many of the others did too …' Stephens voice trailed away.

Argyle was white-hot with fury. Oh most assuredly, it was cheating. Cheating that had turned into murder. He shot Stephen a scorching look and his friend shrunk back another step.

'What exactly are you not telling me?' Argyle demanded.

'What? Truly … I don't know anything. What'd you mean?' Stephen looked bewildered.

'If you are my friend, as you like to boast, then tell me the truth!' Argyle spat. 'Where is Coxcombe? What is his link to Lockley?'

'I … they've never met. Well, they've met, but only at tourneys like this. I've never seen Lockley in Coxcombe's house. I swear, I don't even think Lockley knows who Coxcombe is.' Stephen chewed his lower lip, and Argyle let the silence drag out.

'Well, Lord Bolingbroke visited Coxcombe once,' Stephen said hesitantly. 'Back in Warwickshire. But it's so long ago, I couldn't even tell you if Lockley was there or not.'

'I see. Think carefully.'

'I don't remember. And that's the truth.' Stephen's neck and cheeks blushed. Argyle shook his head slowly.

'I'm sorry, Argyle. It's all so …' Stephen shook his head. 'Don't think about what I said, I don't know why I've been such a fool …'

Argyle nodded indifferently. None of it mattered. When again he entered the room, La Fontaine would still lie under a cloth, dead and gone. Argyle squared his shoulders; after all he was the heir of Beauworth, he would be knighted now, he would be in charge. La Fontaine had left him all his earthly possessions. Suddenly the horror of such responsibility threatened to outweigh the raw grief of La Fontaine's demise.

That night, the King signed a royal decree announcing a court in mourning. The rest of the tourney was to be cancelled. Thomas brought the news to Argyle when they met in Thomas' apartments after the King's announcement.

'I assumed, you would be grateful for this gesture.' Thomas brushed invisible dust from his long sleeves and sent his brother a sneaky glance;

gone was his care and dejection from this morning. 'After all, you are now the head of La Fontaine's entire household. Bravo, little brother.'

Argyle shook his head slowly, how could Thomas be so callous? 'What?'

'All your patient waiting has finally paid off,' Thomas said. 'I have to admit; I was about to give up on you. Having never displayed any particular gift for anything or an interest in rising in the estimation of others. And then, with a single thrust of a lance, you are on the cusp of being part of the King's inner circle. You have land and men of your own.'

Argyle stared back at Thomas with a cold, hard look that he obviously chose to ignore.

'As part of the King's closest confidants, it must now be in your own interest to promote your family's happiness,' Thomas pressed on. 'You should not hesitate in choosing a suitable bride. And that name. The Unicorn! You must lay that to rest. You ought to be proud to be a Mowbray and not hide behind such a juvenile alias. I grant you, the King himself did long ago bestow the name upon La Fontaine, but it was when the King was just a boy, but now he is a man and so have you finally become, little brother. Finish this charade and discard of the unicorn. You already have a coat of arms for your use.' Thomas rubbed his hands together in a very unseemly fashion.

'Have you no shame?' Argyle immediately regretted his angry outburst.

Thomas eyed Argyle. 'Most would say I do not. Then they do not know me as you do. Advancement in life is no shame. Nor is it shameful to keep close to the King. If you know what is best for you, you will now begin to play the game, little brother. It may well be our father was a great hero, but he died among infidels far from his beloved England. It may well be that our older brother would have acted quite differently, but he is not here to handle the situation. Perhaps it will serve you best to listen to the advice of the head of your house, for once.'

Argyle gestured disarmingly.

'After all, I have survived much and more at court already,' Thomas said almost as an afterthought.

೩ ೧ ೩ ೧

1 August 1392 — Westminster

'I am convinced La Fontaine's death was no accident. I have pondered and prayed over this for some time, and yesterday, God returned my questions with an answer.' The King looked haggard and tired, his eyes set deep in their sockets, dark circles surrounding them. His mouth was drawn and lines had emerged where before the skin had been smooth and youthful. Clearly, the King was devastated by his friend's sudden death.

Argyle was kneeling before the throne. 'Your Grace?'

'Hmm … Yes, I have come to the decision that something rotten must be rooted out. I am quite sure my beloved cousin Henry knows much and more about this but how do I ask him, when he is miles and miles away. Now, he writes to ask my permission to go on a pilgrimage.' The King laughed harshly. 'He believes a change of scenery and some serene prayer in the Holy Land will be just the thing to lay our dispute to rest, although I think he is just fed up with his lack of results outside Vilnius and unwilling to come home and admit he is not the great soldier, he likes to think he is. Get up, Mowbray.'

Argyle stood still as a statue in the middle of the room while the King prowled the floor restlessly.

'As if I could so easily be convinced of his innocence. Maybe he truly knows nothing, but I very much doubt that. After all, I have known Henry all my life, and while he is a great many things, innocent is not one of them,' the King said.

Argyle nodded along, he did not really know Bolingbroke but from a few times of seeing him at court. La Fontaine had never thought much of him, but had treated him with all the graces befitting the Heir Presumptive.

'I believe that, in due course, I shall have to give my assent to his plans. After all, who can deny a man the chance to become godlier?

Even if I am sure he has some wicked plan in the making.' The King finally stopped pacing and turned to Argyle. 'I want to be assured I have your full allegiance. That you will be ready to take my orders once I decide what to do. That you are as much my man as La Fontaine ever was. You must swear it, and then I will grant my dear friend his final request and bestow his lands and household on you!'

The King's speech hardly warranted an answer from a lowly soldier, even if he was of noble blood, yet Argyle found it necessary to speak. 'Your Grace, I am at your command.'

The King nodded thoughtfully, then waved his hand in dismissal. 'You may go, Mowbray. Know that I shall hold you to your pledge. Until such a time, not a word of the matters we have discussed tonight. To anyone! Especially that brother of yours, he ever acts a dutiful servant, and yet I am never quite convinced.'

Argyle retreated, back to the door, bowing and mulling over the King's words.

'Oh, and Mowbray? I trust you will keep the unicorn?' The King's order was unmistakable.

Argyle did not mind, he had already decided to keep the token bestowed upon his teacher and master, if the King would allow it. Thus, he simply accepted this order by bowing his head submissively and stepped out of the doors.

ꟾ

Once the door was shut tight, he barged into Thomas who was quick to speak. 'Now, now, brother, do not be alarmed.'

Argyle frowned and looked at Thomas with what he hoped was a calm, expressionless face. It clearly had some effect on Thomas, who involuntarily hunched his shoulders. 'I was merely seeking you and was told you were with the King. Naturally, I am curious to know what passed between you. Surely, you will not deny me some information about your conversation with his Grace?'

The question hung limp in the air while Argyle tried to gather his thoughts. 'And what need did you have of me, brother? Since you were seeking me before you knew, I was with the King.'

Thomas immediately coloured at his collar and fingered the crested ring on his left hand. It was obvious he had not sought Argyle out, but had most likely been informed by one of his spies of Argyle's whereabouts. Argyle had no illusions about his brother; he knew full well that Thomas had spies who kept him informed of the comings and goings at court.

'Ah, well yes. The reason I was looking for you is a delicate matter, perhaps not fit for a public room such as this.' Thomas grabbed Argyle by the elbow and drew him into a nearby niche.

In the past, Thomas would have squeezed harder to impose power, but those days were behind them. Argyle stood at least a head taller than his older brother and was broader across the chest and shoulders. Life at court might give you thick skin, but muscles came from hours of drilling on the training course and that Thomas did not have.

Argyle gave Thomas a calm stare. 'Do tell. I cannot begin to guess what might be so delicate you felt you had to come for me personally. It must be serious indeed, as you did not choose to send a servant to fetch me.'

'It is. But before I divulge my information, please dear brother, humour me and tell me, what the King might have you do,' Thomas said in his silver-tongue.

'He merely wished to share the grief of La Fontaine's death with one who was sure to sympathise. It has been a trying time for the royal household, having lost such a great favourite.' Argyle was careful to leave any emotion out of his voice.

'Nothing more?' Thomas sounded disappointed.

'Surely that is no small feat, brother. The King summoning me to share grief was a display of great honour, whatever you might think.'

'Do not think you can cheat me with your honeyed words.' Anger crept into Thomas' voice. 'I begin to suspect you have been far too long at court. You are trying my patience, now I will have the truth, and all of it. What did his Grace want from you?'

'If you must know, it was the King wanting to bestow something on me.' Argyle said. 'La Fontaine had endowed all his lands and his household to me, though it was not his to give. It was originally a gift from the King to his friend, therefore, he needed me to swear a solemn oath to be his faithful servant before he felt comfortable yielding to La Fontaine's final will. I suspect, in due course, he will announce his decision to the court - and you.'

Thomas' eyes turned icy, his temper rising rapidly. He had to steady himself on the sill before going on and his voice shook with the effort. 'I see. Nothing else? No fancy ideas about treachery and foul play, eh? I have it on good authority that the King is quite certain his cousin killed La Fontaine!'

'His Grace did not see fit to reveal his innermost thoughts to me. Why would he? I am a nobody to him.'

'Do not play clever with me, brother,' Thomas spat at him. 'I will have the truth, one way or the other.'

'I think you forget yourself, Thomas! I am no longer dependent on being in your good graces. Our King just released me from any such duty. It will not do to be cross with me. I may be younger than you, but I am no child anymore. As you have been so fond of pointing out to me - I became a man long ago.'

Thomas tried and failed to control his blinding rage. 'Then I think you no longer any brother of mine. Be-gone from my sight. Why I would ever waste time on you! Rest assured that the right people will hear of this!'

As Thomas turned on his heel to leave, Argyle clamped a hand on his shoulder and snarled. 'Oh no, brother. You rest assured that the right people will hear of this. I believe you know much more than will ever be good for you on many a matter. Let it not be connected to La Fontaine's untimely death.'

Thomas shook off Argyle's hand and marched out of the room so fast the rushes crushed and swirled around his supple leather boots. Argyle sighed. It would be a long day of writing letters to his sisters trying to avoid too much trouble. Yet, for the first time, he felt free from the yolk of family duty. And found it agreed with him just splendidly.

5 August 1392 — London

As the afternoon pushed the sun down over the horizon and bathed London in shades of orange, a knock on the door disturbed Argyle in his musings. He sat in La Fontaine's chair, in La Fontaine's study, in La Fontaine's house. Argyle could not think of all of this being now his; he did not feel he owned it, or that he even deserved it. Yet here he was, sitting in the chair that had always been occupied by La Fontaine.

Argyle opened the door to find Stephen standing outside, looking a little lost, his cap neatly folded in his hands, his face solemn.

'Stephen! It is good to see you.' Argyle motioned Stephen inside.

'Thank you.'

Something in Stephen's manner made Argyle pause. He strode to the desk and hastily packed away the letters for his sisters. 'Is something the matter?'

'It's only … Last we spoke …' Stephen stalled again.

'I know, and I have wanted to apologise for some time. Please forgive me. I was not myself at the time, of course it must have been a grave loss to lose your place in Coxcombe's retinue.'

Stephen relaxed a little. 'No, I'm the one to apologise, you'd just lost La Fontaine, I know he's like a father to you. I shouldn't have come to you at a time of grief.' He shook his thick mop of ginger hair and looked a little embarrassed. 'I wondered if you might've a place for me in your household?'

'My word, news travels fast in this place, the King has yet to formally announce that I have inherited La Fontaine's estate and responsibilities.' Argyle invited Stephen to sit by the empty hearth; summer in London required no fire. 'But you are just in time. I am leaving court as soon as possible. I do not believe, it was ever the right place for me.'

'And I can come?'

'Yes, of course. I am ever in need of dedicated and loyal men, no more so …' Argyle stopped himself just in time and feigned a cough. 'A refreshment perhaps?'

Stephen nodded apparently unaware of the stumble, Argyle had narrowly avoided. 'I would be most pleased to welcome you into my household. Have you need of horse or garment before we leave? I warn you, I do not plan to be much in London unless the King commands it.'

'Oh, no, well, I don't have a horse. I still have my old, trusty dapple grey, but I'm afraid that she'd not survive a long journey.' Stephen flushed and looked out the window.

'We shall find you a good steed. If nothing else, La Fontaine always kept a few good horses by, in case any were needed.' Argyle pushed down the lump in his throat with an effort. 'You will be well equipped by the time we leave the city.'

'When? Just so I'm ready.'

Stephen added the latter a little too hastily, but Argyle shrugged it off. It was just a sign that they would have to find a new way to be around each other now he was master and Stephen still a squire.

'In two or three days. I shall know more on the morrow. In the meantime, you may ponder if you feel up to being a real soldier. I am certain you are, but it is your decision of course.'

Argyle smiled at Stephen's surprised face. He felt very good about himself just then.

CHAPTER 17

14 August 1392 — Westminster

As soon as Argyle stepped into the audience chamber, he immediately noticed the King's pale, worried face. A strange and disturbing silence had fallen over the once so lively court. In niches, courtiers huddled in small groups, their voices faint whispers. The slightest rattle of a cloak or dress sent a roar through the room.

Persistent rumours had Queen Anne bedridden once more, which had thrown the court and King into fear of her losing another unborn child. It would be devastating to the couple still grief-stricken by the loss of a close friend.

Argyle bowed deeply when the King beckoned him closer to the throne. He carefully walked towards the dais. In the uncannily quiet room, each step sent a loud crack through the air as his heels crushed the pine rushes on the floor. Somewhere in the shadows a courtier cleared his throat and gave Argyle a condescending glare. The King barked a command and the remaining people were quick to leave. Some dared to look reproachfully at Argyle when he did not follow suit.

'Come closer.' The King's dry voice gave away his grief.

'Your Majesty.'

'Nothing has changed, I am still entirely convinced that La Fontaine did not die by accident nor a stroke of bad luck,' the King said abruptly. 'For that a few too many actions should have occurred quite independently of each other. I highly doubt it was mere coincidence that one of Bolingbroke's favourites was left to joust against my friend!'

The King paused and stroked his chin where day old stubble bore testament to his prolonged struggle. His eyes were still ringed by dark circles and his skin had turned ashen. 'You have sworn loyalty to me, now I ask that you sacrifice yourself for your King.'

Glaring at Argyle, the King sat heavily on the throne, gone was the boyish way of dangling one leg on the armrest. 'I lay it in your hands to discover how all the pieces fit together. Know only that they do fit, on that my mind is firmly made up.'

Argyle suffered the ensuing silence. He had not been asked a question and was still unsure if, upon taking over La Fontaine's estate and service, he was now allowed to address the King without first being commanded to.

'Well. What do you say, boy?!'

Despite the grave situation, Argyle smiled a little. After all, the King was scarce a year older than him. The King seemed to come to the same realisation because he laughed hoarsely then stifled it.

'Your Majesty, I say it is my honour to serve you,' Argyle replied.

'Very good. La Fontaine always bragged how bright you were. Not just of body but of mind too. Now, you must prove him right,' the King said. 'I assign you to follow Bolingbroke, on his quest to find salvation and God in the Holy Land.'

The King paused and mischief briefly shone in his eyes. 'Find some way to join the pilgrimage. Say you are called upon by God to visit the holy city of Jerusalem, or that you wish to see your father's final resting place. No one can know that you are really there to solve the mystery of the Unicorn's death. I cannot aid you; you must make your own provisions. Ask Gaunt, he is organising the pilgrimage, and I know he wishes the party to get underway as soon as can be, Bolingbroke is already on his way from Vilnius to France.'

The King waved away Argyle who bowed again and retreated towards the door, still facing the throne. The more Argyle had thought about it, the more he was likely to agree with the King that it was a touch too strange that Bolingbroke was always lurking in the shadows of any seedy affair. Last time, he had plotted with some of the oldest families in England. This time, one of the King's absolute favourites had died by the hand of one of Bolingbroke's knights. All roads seemed to lead back to Bolingbroke and his followers. Was there perhaps a connection not yet clear to Argyle?

17 August 1392 — Westminster

'What do you mean, you have to LEAVE?' Thomas' shouting was bound to stir his servants and yet, no one came to the door.

'I cannot stay,' Argyle insisted.

The backside of Thomas' hand hit Argyle's cheek before he could react. Instinctively, Argyle stepped back feeling shock and anger flashing across his face. Thomas rubbed his hand, fingering the rings that had been forced askew by the impact.

'You …'

Thomas cut him off. 'Fine! If you must leave then so be it! But know that you are no longer welcome in my house; indeed I shall renounce you as my brother to the whole world. This time you have gone too far!'

'Why?' Argyle forced his hand to stay by his side and not dart up to feel his burning cheek.

'Why? Because you have betrayed me, you have betrayed our family,' Thomas hissed. 'Because I am the head of our family and you did not even think to ask my permission to go. Because I need you here, our sisters need you here and you do not seem to care!'

At Thomas' high-pitched tone, Argyle found his bearings once more. 'What use could you possibly have of me? You have never once expressed any desire to see me, never cared what happened to me. How do you think I felt, when you openly opposed the King? How can you possibly know what my life was like, while you were making useless friends and …'

Thomas lunged, but this time, Argyle was ready for him. He jumped into the attack barging into Thomas' chest. Thomas lost his footing and stumbled, knocking over a chair that clattered into the fireplace, where flames immediately began devouring the embroidered seat, scorching the chair legs. Thomas was breathing heavily, the wind momentarily knocked out of him, but he quickly regained his bearings. Giving Argyle a wide berth, Thomas slid behind his desk, his right hand rummaging around in the piles of papers, knocking over an inkwell.

Argyle shook his left hand, which had bent backwards at the impact with Thomas' big silver belt buckle. Gritting his teeth, Argyle eyed Thomas, who looked increasingly desperate, pushing papers to the floor and never breaking eye contact.

'Looking for this, brother?' Argyle held up a slender dagger.

Thomas' breath caught in his throat before his eyes closed to slits. 'Do not be silly, what use would I have of a knife?'

Argyle threw it into the corner furthest away from Thomas. 'I would not know!'

Brushing back his dark hair, Thomas seemed to reconsider his options now that drawing a knife on his own kin was out of the question. Argyle too assessed the situation; he was far bigger than Thomas and trained for combat where Thomas was trained for a life at court. Although they were both skilled with a sword, Argyle had little doubt that in a struggle he would come out victorious, however, this was neither the time nor the place to be fighting.

'Perhaps you are right, it is time you left.' Thomas also seemed to have come to the conclusion that he would not win a physical struggle.

Argyle inclined his head, reaching for the door.

'Where will you go?' Thomas asked.

Argyle paused, his back turned defiantly to Thomas. 'Anywhere but here.' He pushed the door open and strode down the bright corridor.

18 August 1392 — Westminster

Argyle lingered in front of the massive oak door. In his thoughts, he once more went over what he had come to say. It had to be said just right - and it also felt as if he was walking straight into the lion's den. He felt a trickle of sweat slowly crawl down his spine. Shaking his head to clear his thoughts, he raised his fist to knock just as door was thrown open and Argyle had to sidestep quickly not to be stomped down by a burly man with greying hair. He was fuming with rage and walked straight past Argyle without a single glance. The hand resting on the man's sword hilt squeezed it so tightly his knuckles had turned white.

Argyle looked in through the open door to spot Gaunt standing in the middle of the room. He too seemed infuriated, but concealed it slightly better. When he caught Argyle's eye, his brow creased. 'Yes?'

'My Lord, I have come to join your son's pilgrimage.'

Argyle took a tentative step forward. Gaunt surveyed him for a moment then waved him in. Behind him, the door closed softly. The rushes gave off a sharp scent of pine and in the deep of the gloomy room, a fire crackled, shadows dancing on the walls. Argyle moved a little uncomfortably, knowing he would have to lie to Gaunt in order to achieve his goal.

'I am curious. How have you come to know of my son's pilgrimage?' Gaunt asked.

'Word travels fast at court, my Lord. And I have been making enquiries on the subject.' Argyle hoped he sounded sincere.

Gaunt scratched his cheek where a thick greying beard covered a receding chin. The sign of a feeble soul, some might say, although that was a far cry from the feeling Argyle was left with. Standing close to the King's uncle, it was quite clear they were both made of stern stuff.

'Is that so?' Gaunt motioned for Argyle to take a seat near the fire. Taking a cup, he followed suit, sitting in a formidable chair overflowing with plush cushions. 'The word is true, he is planning a pilgrimage. Henry shall go to the Holy Land and seek solace in the presence of God. Where better one might say? Court is no place for my son at present.'

'If you will permit, my Lord. When does he plan to go?'

'The English party will set sail by September. From there the devout will journey to Vienna to meet my son, I gather he plans to be in Venice before Christmas. Such a pilgrimage is quite an undertaking, and should not be taken lightly. You are devout?' Gaunt eyed Argyle above the brim of the cup.

'Yes, my Lord.' Argyle prayed his lie was believable.

Gaunt surveyed Argyle's face. 'You look oddly familiar. I know, I have seen you somewhere before, although ... Ha! You are a Mowbray! Although you take after your lovely mother, I see. Now here is a wonder! Lockley, have you ever come across a more wondrous thing? A Mowbray freely seeking my company?'

Lockley appeared from the shadows shaking his head slowly in mocking wonder. Argyle felt his blood boil; Gaunt was harbouring a murderer. Argyle's throat went dry and his eyes burned, he cursed himself for not bringing his sword, for entering Gaunt's rooms completely unarmed. But if he had brought his sword, drawn it and attacked Lockley, the King himself would have to condemn Argyle for his folly.

'I distinctly remember another Mowbray spending much time denying any relation to my family. And now, his brother sits here, bold as brass, asking to go on my son's pilgrimage,' Gaunt's voice tore through Argyle's angry train of thought and brought him violently back to the present. 'Tell me - boy - who put you up to this?'

Before Argyle had a chance to answer, Lockley's voice crept in. 'I should think his brother, my Lord. Thomas de Mowbray was ever a slippery bastard. If he could tell the King anything he might believe would bring him favour, I'm sure de Mowbray would do whatever was required.'

Gaunt bellowed a laugh. 'Now, now, Lockley! I am sorry, Mowbray, but it is not among this man's virtues to trust anyone. Least of all your brother, although we must leave that tale to another day.'

Argyle was thrown at what tale Gaunt was referring to and for a moment he could only glare at Gaunt who leaned back, dangling the empty cup over the floor.

'My Lord, no one put me up to it.' Argyle was indignant. 'I simply desire to see more of the world. I should be a poor liar not to admit I also wish to be further from my brother, but for the most part I simply feel I have had no adventure in my life.'

Gaunt smirked. 'Very well. I can find many a poorer reason for leaving England before winter claims the lands and leaves us quite useless. Perhaps it will serve us well to have a Mowbray close at hand. What say you, Lockley?'

Lockley clearly struggled to stay calm and managed only a slight inclination of his head. Gaunt meanwhile was now grinning broadly, waving his cup-hand about. 'What fun you shall have, young Mowbray. I am sure of it. Now tell me, has my nephew knighted you yet?'

'Not yet, my Lord. But I feel certain his Grace will honour La Fontaine's will.'

Out of the corner of his eye, Argyle saw Lockley slip back into the shadows. There was something about this man that made his skin crawl.

'So too do I,' Gaunt's voice had cooled. 'La Fontaine was a close friend of our King, perhaps you seek to replace him in more than name?'

'I presume no such thing, my Lord.' Argyle leaned back a little. 'For the time being, I simply wish to go on a pilgrimage and I would be honoured to join your son, but I shall go all the same.'

'Peace, Mowbray, peace. Naturally, I will accept your joining Henry's pilgrimage. Be at the port in Dover this first coming Saturday, you can help survey the ships.'

Argyle agreed and made his excuses to leave. He had much to do before Saturday, including finding out exactly what to bring on a pilgrimage - and who.

ഇ ര ഇ ര

24 August 1392 — Dover

On the ride to the docks in Dover, Argyle pondered how to carry out his promise to the King once the pilgrimage was underway. Time and again suspicions surfaced that Lockley was more involved in La Fontaine's death than just being the lance-bearer. Each time Argyle decided to brush off the idea, certain he would gain but little if he decided on a guilty party too soon. To take his mind off things, Argyle scanned the road for a sign that Gaunt and his men were coming

'When'll they be here?' Stephen's voice stirred Argyle from his thoughts.

'He simply said Monday morning, but I should think they too would have arrived yesterday.' Facing the only road to the docks, Argyle was sure they could not miss Gaunt's retinue once it showed up.

'I've some news,' Stephen said as if to pass time. 'I've known for a while, but couldn't decide whether it was important. I didn't want to bother you if I didn't have to.'

'We have time, and now you have made me curious.' Argyle suppressed a sudden irritation that Stephen would not tell him everything he knew, after all he was in Argyle's service now.

'Remember how I told you, Coxcombe disappeared right after La Fontaine's accident?' Stephen asked.

'Yes.' Argyle felt a twinge of the familiar grief. 'What of it?'

'It seems he's reappeared. In France. Not far from Calais.'

'Now that is news!' Argyle was surprised. 'How did you hear of it? I cannot imagine he would write to you?'

Stephen's face split into a crooked smile. 'I've got friends at court too. Mayhap not the finest of people, but they're always around and no one ever really sees them. Most of them like to gossip.'

Argyle surveyed his friend. Dark ginger hair, blue eyes, slightly crooked teeth, but all of them still in place, his face could pass as handsome. Stephen was also tall, although no match to Argyle, and building a broad frame. Yes, why would a maid or two not find him a treat to the eye and a good confessor?

'Oh, I see.' Argyle smiled back. 'I think, I shall not ask such a question again any time soon - nor should I like details. If Coxcombe was seen in France what of it? That should only prove to set your mind at ease. He is not dead, as you often feared. What good news.'

'As to good news, it varies doesn't it? Who's to say, what truly good news is.' Stephen sniffled a little, a habit of his when more was to come. Argyle leaned back in the saddle and looked out over the harbour and held his tongue, waiting for Stephen to go on. 'It's said he surfaced there, 'cause Bolingbroke's got family in the area. Word is, Coxcombe's part of Bolingbroke's entourage, and ever has been. He was very skittish after Bolingbroke was accused of treason, some years ago - remember?'

Argyle did not, but he did remember La Fontaine in a rage and to this day, Thomas' involvement in the misdealing at court cast a dark shadow over his family.

'I never thought of it, the whole country was in uproar, but now …' Stephen paused. 'Who's to say Coxcombe wasn't involved back then as well? Just around that time, he went off on his own, followed only by a few men, and he left the rest of us behind. Still, a squire isn't supposed to ask questions, so I didn't.'

'Just as well, if he was involved, why would he make you privy to such information? And if he was not, there are many ways he could have punished you. Just because he shows up near Calais does not signify anything,' Argyle said. 'The same gossips might suggest I am keeping to Bolingbroke because of my brother. And that is as far from the case as may be.'

'They do, actually. I thought it'd make no difference, so I didn't say anything.' Stephen looked at Argyle.

Argyle felt uncomfortable, if the rumours were running wild at court; Thomas would surely stifle them. Unless …

'At any case, we shall see, shall we not? If Coxcombe joins the pilgrimage, it will be more proof that he is indeed part of Bolingbroke's retinue.' Argyle tried to make light of the situation.

Stephen pulled his cloak a little tighter as a gust of salty wind hit them square on. 'D'you think we'll set sails soon?'

Argyle looked out over the sea, the waves white-topped. 'I believe so. Gaunt was quite adamant. He does not want the party to linger in England and delay his son's pilgrimage.'

The sound of hooves on cobbles put an end to their conversation. Gaunt and a large troop of men turned the corner of a vast wooden building and came towards them. Gaunt held up his hand to stop the group, then saluted Argyle with the same hand. Argyle nodded in return and made to approach the newcomers.

Stephen tugged his sleeve lightly. 'I'd be careful, Lord Gaunt's steeped in turmoil wherever he goes.'

'I know, and yet we must make friends,' Argyle whispered and motioned his horse forward.

'Mowbray, what a fine morning, do you not think?' Gaunt was unabashed by the salty winds and seemed in very high spirits. Behind him the figure of Lockley loomed.

'My Lord. It certainly is fresh.'

Gaunt laughed and set the entourage in motion towards the moorings. 'I shall not rest until we have secured passing across the sea. There are so many crossing in summer; we must be quick if we are to secure appropriate ships. You seem to have been here some time, have any ships caught your eye?'

Argyle fell in with Gaunt. 'Not yet, my Lord, but I should not know what to look for. I am not of a seafaring family.'

At this, all the men laughed loudly, a few of them pounding him on the back for good measure. Even Lockley looked slightly amused. Stephen had drifted to the back of the group, joining a few squires some years younger than him.

'Now Lockley, let us pick out a ship vast enough to take men and horses alike. By this rate, this little expedition will have grown quite out of proportion before you even set foot on a ship. Mayhap we should charter two. That might be the way to do it. What do you say, Mowbray?'

'If we are all to take at least a few men and horses for all, I wonder if two would be enough, my Lord?'

'Fair point. We must make sure only the truly devout come aboard. All those seeking adventure can go another time.' At this, Gaunt turned slightly in the saddle to look directly at Argyle.

'Yes my Lord,' Argyle agreed. 'Surely only the devout will want to go. People of lesser faith may fear the sea.'

Lockley tightened his grip on the reins, his horse skidding a little on the wet cobbles.

'Right you are, Mowbray. We cannot send weaklings, only those who see the true purpose of this journey. Such as yourself no doubt,' Gaunt said. 'I shall look here. Lockley, you take Mowbray and find our second ship.'

Once left alone, the two did not exchange a single word.

CHAPTER 18

29 August 1392 — London

'Rise, Sir Argyle.' The King touched Argyle's shoulder lightly with the flat side of the blade, the sword hilt dull in the gloom of the room.

'Majesty.' Argyle got up, finally feeling the full weight and responsibility of being knighted and awarded a large household with many men much older than him. This was no trifling matter.

'Do not look so glum, Sir Argyle, you knew what was to happen - you have already taken over the household and sworn your men to your service,' the King said. 'Come, walk with me.'

The King turned and walked across the dais, down the stairs on the other side and out of a side door. Argyle followed him. As soon as the door closed, the King turned to Argyle. 'Now, you understand your assignment? And that no one must ever know you were here this night!'

'Yes, your Majesty,' said Argyle.

'Tomorrow I shall dispatch a royal decree that you are to take formal possession of La Fontaine's estates with my blessing. Mind you do not slip and tell your brother any more than that you are knighted.' The King stepped close, his majestic presence as overwhelming as ever.

'Only you and I can know what transpired here tonight,' the King half-whispered.

'As you wish, Majesty, I live to serve and obey.' Argyle forced the words out.

'Good. Now slip away and make sure not to be seen.' The King signalled for a guard to open a door at the back of the room and Argyle bowed low before walking briskly towards it. 'Oh, and Sir Argyle … There can be no communication between you and your family while you are away. If needs be, I may send a message to you, and if I do, you will read it and burn it. But whatever you do, you will not answer it!'

'Majesty.' Argyle swept a final bow, glad that the dark room concealed his face, and walked out of the room.

'Argyle Mowbray! I heard you had gone from court!' the Earl of Kent exclaimed, clasping a hand on Argyle's shoulder.

'My Lord,' Argyle mumbled.

'Have you been to see the King?' Kent tried to peer into the royal chambers before the door closed.

'No,' Argyle said.

'No?' Kent looked confused. 'And yet you just walked out of a door leading to the King's private apartments?'

Argyle forced a smile. 'Oh, well I was seeking his Majesty, but in vain, he was nowhere to be found. The guard at the door said he thought the King might have gone to Sheen Palace for the night.'

Kent laughed. 'It is his custom. The Queen seems to have cast a permanent spell over our King - we can have the rest of the women at court, as long as he has her.'

'Mayhap that is why you are prowling these corridors so late at night?' Argyle asked.

'You have me there. I was looking for this particularly fine German lady who has recently joined her Majesty's household. Long dark hair, fine white skin and emerald eyes.' Kent grinned.

'Then I shall detain you no longer,' Argyle said, briefly clasping hands with Kent.

'What of you? You could come with me, so fine a woman is sure to have fine companions,' Kent said.

Argyle shook his head. 'Not tonight, I must get back to my house.' He could have bitten of his tongue.

'Your house?' Kent looked curious.

'Well, you may as well know, the King has decided to grant La Fontaine his final request; that his household be turned over to me. But not a word to anyone, the King wishes to make the formal announcement himself.' Argyle stepped close, locking eyes with Kent.

'Ah yes, one for theatricals our King. Very well, your secret is safe with me,' Kent said. 'And well done! Not all of the King's court had imagined you would come into your own without the aid of a certain other Mowbray.'

Argyle smiled again. 'No, including the other Mowbray, I am sure.'

Kent laughed heartily and shook Argyle's hands before striding away into the dimly lit corridor.

'Would that I do not encounter more people and reveal more than I should,' Argyle muttered to himself.

With any luck Kent would find the lady he sought and forget he ever met Argyle, but Argyle was not accustomed to being lucky, and Kent was a close friend of Eleanor's husband the Baron de Welles.

The same night, an invitation issued by Eleanor reached Argyle, and he knew Kent had not kept his word. Sighing he wrote a swift reply that he would visit the following Friday.

30 August 1392 — Billingsgate, London

'You are telling me that Thomas was doing the King's bidding?!' Argyle shook from anger.

Eleanor blinked. 'Yes. He said so himself, and I have no cause to doubt him.' She stepped closer, tentatively reaching out to touch his sleeve. 'Please, Argyle, you know what the King is like. He is all about the show, theatrics are what he lives for.'

Argyle snapped back his arm. 'The King may love theatrics but staging a possible coup with his greatest enemies at court. Eleanor, even you cannot believe this to be true?!'

'Why not?!' The famous Mowbray temper was not lost on his sister, Argyle thought, as Eleanor pushed on. 'You have no idea what it was like at court! The King acted like a madman, decreeing the death and destruction of one family after the other. And to what end? So that his friends - who came from nothing - could play lords all over the land?' Eleanor's voice whipped Argyle's ears.

'What?' Argyle asked feeling his resolve waver. 'What are you talking about?'

'He would have had every last noble family living or dying in the gutter and his new fangled friends dressed in cloth of gold, showered in gemstones, all high and mighty!' Eleanor shook her beautiful golden hair in distress. 'He would have put us all out. And to what end, Argyle? So that La Fontaine and the likes of him could be Lords, Earls and Dukes?'

Argyle sighed. 'The King raised de Vere …' His voiced trailed off.

'Yes, he did,' Eleanor said, 'and he would have raised so many others after him. The King was … well, he needed the advice of those who understand how to run a country, how to master the public, how to rule.'

'La Fontaine was unsettled by the King's appointment of de Vere,' Argyle admitted.

'Really?' Eleanor asked in wide-eyed concern.

'Yes. He did not say in so many words, but it was clear to me that he felt the King had overstepped the mark. Of course, going on crusade to Scotland with the self same King, he could not outright admit the King was mistaken in his deeds …' Argyle said, pondering how to proceed.

In the end, Eleanor spoke again, softly this time. 'I was scared. When Thomas came to me and told me what the King had asked, I was scared for his life, for mine and my family's - and for yours.' She could not hold back the tears as she reached for Argyle's arm once more. 'When you wrote to me asking me for shelter, I did not know how to answer.'

Argyle looked at her curiously. 'But you invited me to come?'

'Only on the advice of my husband - and a promise from Thomas that …' Eleanor bit her lip and turned to stare into the gardens. 'That he would intercept you, if it came to that,' she confessed.

Argyle felt his knees give way, all the wind knocked out of him by Eleanor's words. He reached out blindly to find something to steady himself and felt Eleanor lock hands with him.

'I am sorry,' Eleanor whispered.

'Not as sorry as I am to hear this. I may have thought Thomas capable of anything, but not you.' Argyle let her lead him to a chair near the bay window, where he sat down heavily enough for the wood to creak under his weight.

Eleanor stepped away. 'I … I thought Thomas meant he would take you in, if necessary. It was only later that I learned what he had truly meant. That if he had to, he would have thrown you in jail - along with La Fontaine and every other man of his household.' She returned to the window facing the garden and fiddled with the ribbon around her neck. 'Even after all this time, I believe he was acting on the King's command. Why else would he be involved, Argyle?'

Argyle heard her pleading tone and kept his eyes shut. 'Because Thomas' vanity and ambition are greater even than his loyalty to the King.'

Eleanor smothered a whimper in her sleeve, new tears coursing down her flushed cheeks. In the gauzy light streaming through the narrow window, her hair seemed to turn silver, her skin chalk white.

'You do not believe him?'

'No, sister, I do not.' Argyle spread his hands. 'Not because I think he is evil, but because I know him now, truly know him to be only on his own side, not on anyone else's. Wherever there is an opportunity to further himself, I believe Thomas will take it.'

Eleanor pushed her back against the cold stonewall, the lace on her dress catching the stones. 'Why did he change his mind then?!' she demanded. 'When they were so close to toppling the King, why did he not go through with it?'

'I do not know. Perhaps he suddenly saw what his ambition was driving him to. Perhaps regicide was more than even Thomas' mind could bear. Or perhaps he simply decided to follow Bolingbroke's lead.'

'Bolingbroke,' Eleanor breathed, her voice shallow and thin.

'I mean to find out, you know.' Argyle got up slowly, testing to see if his legs were strong enough to carry him. 'That and much more, if I can.'

Eleanor came to him, reaching out to be consoled. 'So you will go?' Her voice was muffled against his shirt.

Argyle held her a moment longer, before gently detangling himself. 'Yes. And you cannot tell a living, breathing soul, not your husband, not our brother or sisters. No one must know, not your husband, not our sisters, not Thomas - no one.'

Eleanor nodded solemnly. 'If that is what you ask.'

'It is,' Argyle said, plastering on an unconvincing smile. 'I trust you.'

'What if I need to contact you?' Eleanor asked, walking with Argyle across the room to linger at the door.

'You cannot,' said Argyle, sadness welling up inside. 'Pray for me!'

He turned and walked out before Eleanor could reply, and Argyle waited until he heard the door close softly before he reached out to steady himself. The wall felt cold and unwelcoming beneath his hands, but it cooled his burning forehead, when he leaned heavily forward.

This was more than he could fathom. Either Thomas was the most foolish courtier in the whole of England, and the King had been playing with him - or Thomas was the most ruthless man Argyle had ever known. Somehow, Argyle would feel better if it was the latter than the first.

4 September 1392 — at sea outside Calais

It seemed God was on Gaunt's side when the ships set sail bound for France, tightly packed and heavy with horses and men. The journey was slow as there was little wind, but that only meant they would safely cross the sea and many took this fortune to be a sign that the journey was blessed. Argyle was less sure, but he enjoyed the clean sea-air and the steady roll of the ship, while some of his fellow travellers looked less comfortable.

Argyle passed the time speaking with the captain learning about navigation and hearing the old cook tell tall tales of mermaids, shipwrecks on distant shores and strange sea creatures. Many of the seasoned sailors knew what was happening in France and were willing to part with their knowledge for an extra cup of ale.

One bright morning, a young deckhand crabbed up next to Argyle pointing towards the horizon.

'There, Sire, there's France. You can just make out the coastline in the distance.'

Argyle squinted and saw nothing at first. Just as he was going to ask, what he was looking for, the coast came into sight. 'Is that Calais?'

'Aye, Calais. The best port for gamblers, whores and sailors alike!' The deckhand laughed, showing that he was missing a few teeth. 'Lost two of my teeth in a tavern near the docks, 'twas the best night of my life. My God the women were willing, the ale flowed and many o' the other sailors were so drunk it was almost like stealing when I played with them.'

'But you had to part with your teeth,' Argyle said.

'I grant you, losing my teeth wasn't my finest hour, but the way it happened was worth it!' The deckhand grinned and winked mischievously. 'If you ever meet a woman named Laura Longshanks, you tell 'er, she owes me a round on the house and a romp in the back room.'

A few of the other sailors roared with laughter, and one shouted. 'Aye, but first you go about your business, or you'll be missing that what makes women so much fun, lad!'

Argyle laughed along with the rest, finding a strange joy in the rough tone on deck.

Stephen sidled up next to Argyle, gripping the railing tight. 'I'll never be much of a sailor. But I'd sure like to meet that Laura.'

The deckhand slapped Stephen's back as he passed with an armful of rope. 'Aye, now there's a woman you'll never meet the likes of! But beware, she's a dangerous girl - when she found out, I couldn't pay for her services, she took a few of my teeth and all my winnings!'

Stephen ogled at the deckhand, who scuttled on, sailors shouting for the sails to be trimmed and the oarsmen to be ready.

'What'll happen once we reach Calais?' Stephen asked.

'We shall seek out the rest of the pilgrimage. Gaunt sent word to Bolingbroke to wait for two ships, but whether the message reached him in time, I do not know,' Argyle said, shielding his eyes against the sea spray. 'He may be in Calais, but it is far more likely, he will be waiting further south.'

'Why's Lord Bolingbroke decided to go on a pilgrimage?' Stephen asked.

'Gossip at court suggests he grew weary of being defeated near Vilnius. He lay siege to the city, but it turned into a stalemate.' Argyle looked around to see, if anyone was listening, but the sailors and the sea made so much noise that any curious ears would have to be standing very close to hear what was being said. 'Thomas said that Bolingbroke is going on his pilgrimage to avoid the King taunting him. Perhaps Bolingbroke too believes that offerings at the Holy Sepulchre and the Mount of Olives might bring both salvation and peace.'

'Makes sense,' Stephen agreed. 'Though I can't really believe the King'd tease his own cousin about defeat.'

Argyle smiled. 'Well, I know that if it was me and Thomas, he would never let me hear the end of it, if I failed in the one job, I am supposed to be good at.'

Stephen laughed and nearly choked on a spray of salty water. When he had recovered from his coughing fit, he pointed towards the coast, the Calais port now easy to distinguish. 'There awaits adventure, salvation and perhaps even redemption.'

'Aye, so it does, lad,' a sailor growled, his face lined from a life at sea. 'And there awaits Laura with her wicked ways.'

Once more, the sailors roared with laughter and Stephen blushed. 'Laura …' he said dreamily.

'That is all very well,' Argyle tried to sound stern. 'But we shall have to leave the infamous Laura for someone else!'

'What a shame that being with a woman isn't enough to get you into God's good graces,' Stephen said longingly, snorting when Argyle's elbow caught him in the ribs.

'Now that'd be my kind of worship,' Lockley said staring intently at Argyle. 'But there'll be no time, as Sir Argyle says. There'll be just enough time to get the horses off this bloody ship and provisions packed. Then we make for Vienna.'

Argyle returned the cold gaze. 'You have had word that Lord Bolingbroke is waiting for us there?'

'I don't think my Lord even knows you're coming, but he's waiting for Sir John Beaufort and me,' Lockley said. 'If your little horse can keep up, you'll be in Vienna soon enough and then we shall see what Bolingbroke makes of your showing up. But an earnest worshipper'll not be turned away, trust in that, Sir Argyle.' Lockley made a mock bow before retreating back below deck.

Argyle thought Lockley looked like an overgrown rat with his prickling eyes, he was certainly much more cunning than you might think. What if he knew the real reason Argyle was going on the pilgrimage? What if Bolingbroke knew?

Argyle bit his lip; although he had grown to like the idea of seeing the holy sites, he still could not shake the feeling of being a fraud. While most of the pilgrims longed in earnest to be close to God, he only longed to untangle the mystery of La Fontaine's death. But then Argyle did not think Lockley longed to be close to God either - so why was he going?

ꕥ ꕥ ꕥ ꕥ

Part 2
Pilgrimage

CHAPTER 19

4 November 1392 — Vienna

Lockley had been right. They stayed in Calais just long enough for the horses and provisions to be loaded off the ships. In the port, the pilgrimage grew by leaps and bounds as more men joined the entourage, either for adventure or true religious intent.

Spurring the pilgrims on, Lockley cursed all those who could not keep up, swearing that once the pilgrimage reached Vienna, Bolingbroke would leave at least half of the devout behind. But when the pilgrims reached the fortified city, Bolingbroke welcomed everyone with open arms, English or French, it made no difference.

Argyle was one to experience Bolingbroke's good will first hand. Lockley had loomed in the shadows as Bolingbroke welcomed Argyle to his pilgrimage giving him pride of place during the first night's banquet. Argyle suspected that his brother had something to do with his favourable treatment, not least because Bolingbroke kept mentioning Thomas in very amiable tones.

Bolingbroke was planning to leave Vienna three days later, which left ample time for Argyle and Stephen to explore the ancient city. Coming back from the marketplace just outside the massive Roman walls,

Stephen suddenly froze in place. Argyle had to sidestep to avoid hitting him square in the back, bumping into an old man, who was quick to strike him with a wooden cane. Argyle sent the man a regretful smile, which made no impression at all.

'Stephen! You must not stop in the gateway. We will be overcome by carriages and people.' Argyle pulled Stephen out of the way and into a small archway. 'Whatever is the matter with you?'

As if woken from a bad dream, Stephen wet his lips and swallowed several times before he could answer. 'I saw Coxcombe. But it can't be.'

'Why not?' Argyle asked. 'You knew he was on the continent. You told me as much yourself. I grant you, I had expected he would join us in Calais, but seeing him is far from a shock, surely?'

'Well, I'm shocked!' Stephen had gone white.

'You certainly look as if you have seen a ghost!' Argyle was confused. 'Do not worry; I shall explain to him that you have entered my service now. He cannot object, he took off and left most of his men in England. They have all found new retinues.'

Stephen smiled thinly. 'Thank you. You're right, he can't expect anything of me now.'

'No, why would he? You are a soldier in your own right.' Argyle patted his friend's shoulder. 'It has been almost a year, perhaps he will not even recognise you. Nonetheless I shall tell him, if you wish?'

'Only if he brings it up. You,re right, why'd he recognise me. I've changed much, haven't I? And I was just one in many squires after all.'

Argyle smiled at his friend. 'Changed you have - though how much I do not know. I have been right beside you all this time, I am not the right one to judge.'

At this comment, Stephen seemed to find his bearings once more, smiling brightly at Argyle and motioning to get on into the castle yard. 'Come on, you mustn't be late for the feast tonight.'

'For a pilgrimage, I think we feast too much. Are we not supposed to be devout and keep to church hours?' Argyle said without too much complaint. He knew he would go anyway; a good meal was not to be denied. Who knew how much longer they would eat this well?

That night Argyle went to the banquet hall with an uneasy feeling. He had not wanted to comment on it to Stephen, but Coxcombe's sudden arrival had stirred his doubts. The King's words weighed heavily on his mind, and he felt that something was not quite right. Had Bolingbroke paid off Coxcombe to reveal La Fontaine's weaknesses? And if so, why had one friend betrayed the other?

Deep in thought, he weaved his way through the maze of rooms, anterooms, corridors and galleries. He was quite lost to the world and almost barged straight into Lockley, who was loitering in a dimly lit niche.

'Sir Argyle.'

Argyle started. 'Lockley?'

'I wanted to catch you alone. Such luck you should appear just now,' Lockley said.

'And why might that be?' Argyle asked.

'Unlike Bolingbroke, who, for all his merits, falls easily for flattery, I believe you've come on a mission.'

'Is that so?' Argyle kept his voice level, his face calm.

'Yes!' Lockley snarled. 'That's exactly so. Let me tell you, boy, I've been asked to do much and more in the service of the great Lord Bolingbroke. And yet, what you might accuse me of, isn't one of those things.'

'What might I accuse you of, Sire?'

'You know of what I speak.' Lockley seemed overly tense. 'Come now, Sire. You can't be all that stupid with such a clever brother. By now you must know that Thomas too carries many secrets.'

'This is old news, Lockley,' Argyle said. 'Surely, you cannot believe, I should care what my brother is accused of. But since you ask, let me put you out of your misery. I do believe you had more to do with the death of La Fontaine than meets the eye. That being said, I know of no foul play, and should not be so stupid as to accuse you of anything without significant proof. My primary motive for being here is simple; I am on a pilgrimage to reach the Holy Land. What I encounter along the way has yet to reveal itself. Let us not get ahead of ourselves, it may all come to nothing.'

Argyle made for the doorway of the great hall, but Lockley's hand shot out and gripped his sleeve. 'We're not finished, Sir Argyle! You mark my words. It's one thing to carry out a deed, quite another to give the order. Don't confuse the two, there's a clever boy.'

Pulling away from the knight, Argyle offered a cold smile. 'I should think my days of being a boy are over. Do you not agree?'

Before Lockley could answer, Argyle slid into the steady stream of people heading for the feast and disappeared into the vast, warmly lit hall, out of sight of Lockley.

Yet Argyle could not shake off Lockely's final words. Do not confuse the two. It seemed too obvious that Lockley was the one to carry out the order, but that opened a passage to so many possibilities that his head felt as if it would split.

If there was truth to this, then who had given the order?

ഇ ര ഇ ര

CHAPTER 20

5 November 1392 — Vienna

The bells tolled for Compline. Soon the churches would fill with citizens, peasants, soldiers and knights in and around the city. It had been long since Argyle had last visited a church. Since La Fontaine's death he found he had little faith in a God that had abandoned him in his hour of need.

Tonight, Argyle brushed past the guards, skirting their glances and walked out into the increasing dark. Dusk had always been his favourite time of day, not quite the black night but dark enough to avoid prying eyes. He was on a mission that would send him close to one of the people he most believed to be responsible for the death of La Fontaine. The previous nights he had scoured the city, visiting taverns and brothels in the many narrow streets. Argyle had walked the battlements and slipped from tree to tree in many an orchard. Finally, in a stroke of sheer good fortune, he had overheard a whispered conversation when the pilgrims were breaking their fast that morning.

Now circling the battlements and slipping down a narrow alleyway, Argyle found himself close to the citadel gates. They were closed for the night, but poorly guarded. The entire city was a fortress; there was no need to guard every entry inside the city walls.

Argyle opened the small door to the side of the massive gates, quickly scouted the surroundings and, satisfied no one was nearby, he slid through the opening and made for one of the side buildings. Inside candles lit a beautifully decorated room. It played host to some of the most distinguished members of the pilgrimage. Including Bolingbroke.

Argyle peeked through the window and saw what he needed to see. Then he simply sat down on a stone under a window and waited, certain he was veiled in shadow. He did not have to wait long.

'Lockley, fetch me more wine! I want to toast our gracious hosts!' Bolingbroke roared.

Lockley opened the door only a few paces from the window, Argyle was hiding under, and made for the provisions chamber. Another shadow emerged and fell into step beside Lockley, who did not even turn his head at this. 'You have been avoiding me.'

'Not at all. We have nothing to say to one another,' Lockley said.

'I disagree.' The shadow's voice was low and hoarse. 'But not here. Meet me at midnight near the northern gate.'

'And if I do not?'

'My story will be very interesting to my Lord Bolingbroke, I believe,' the shadow said.

In a flash, the shadow had a glittering dagger at his throat. Lockley cocked his head and peered curiously into the man's hidden face. 'No one knows you're here. Mayhap I should keep it that way.'

'I have a mission for you. Another order.' The man's voice broke a little as Lockley slid the dagger closer to the hood.

Then Lockley tipped the knife and let the tip trace along the man's chin before he slipped the dagger back into his shirt and smiled. 'Very well. Midnight - by the northern gate. I will decide what to do with you once I have the order.'

Lockley pushed the man roughly aside, slung a small barrel of wine over his shoulder and snorted as he walked back towards the laughter and glowing lights of the citadel side building.

Argyle pushed himself further into the shadows and held his breath. As Lockley walked close by, he opened the door and then paused, hand on handle, while spying back into the darkness. He shrugged and closed the door behind him; Bolingbroke roaring what had taken him so long.

Argyle waited a while in the darkness wondering who the shadow might have been and what orders he had for Lockley. Somehow the voice sounded oddly familiar, but Argyle could not place it. When he felt sure that the other man had mysteriously disappeared as quietly as he had appeared, Argyle got up, stepping carefully on the grass near the building to avoid making a sound. He had to find a passable way to the northern gate before midnight.

On the battlements, he paused and surveyed the city. It was laid out in an overall grid but with so many alleys and passageways that he hardly knew where to begin.

Resolving to enlist a little assistance, Argyle turned and headed back to the camp.

Midnight, 5 November 1392 — Vienna

'How did you come by this?' Lockley's voice betrayed his presence in the darkness. Argyle could only make out the figure of a cloaked man, his face hidden in a hood, but Argyle did not think the cloaked man was Lockley; the figure was too slim.

It turned out the northern gate was the perfect place to meet if you were scheming and wanted privacy in Vienna. The gate was never used after sundown and the surrounding garrison buildings lay dark in disrepair. The Habsburg rulers must be very sure that no one would attack them in the heart of their own land.

'It is of no importance!' The hooded man sounded irritated.

'I will decide that,' Lockley's voice drifted up towards Argyle.

'Very well. It comes from the same hand that ordered the death of the Unicorn - and the others.'

'And you are sure?'

'It passed from his hand to mine.'

The hooded man's voice had a slight air of importance. Lockley must have moved with his snakelike speed because the man suddenly yelped.

'Shut up!' Lockley said in an unfeeling, cold voice.

Silence ensued. Argyle pushed forward on his stomach. He lay flat on top of the battlement above the gate. The gravel would reveal him in a heartbeat if he moved too quickly or had to make a run for it for some reason. He grabbed the hilt of his dagger closely and wriggled a little more. He could just make out the two shapes, his eyes now adjusted to the darkness from lying there so long.

Stephen had proved a great help in finding a way to the northern gate that would lead Argyle far away from the main streets. Stephen had also provided the idea of perching on top of the gate, although he had been offended when Argyle had refused to take Stephen with him.

Below, the two shapes moved a little. Paper rattled and then Lockley spoke again. 'You know what it says?'

'You broke the seal.' The man's voice seeped with equal amounts irritation and fear.

'Seals can be broken and remade. In this darkness how am I to see if the seal hasn't been broken before?' Lockley said icily.

'You will simply have to take my word for it.'

Lockley snorted quietly. It sounded like he crumbled the paper and pushed it into a pocket in his garments. The other moved restlessly. 'Well?'

'Do you know anything about the content?' Lockley asked.

'I was only privy to very little.'

'Tell me.'

Argyle could almost imagine the other man squirming under the knight's dead gaze. This was not a man to trifle with and yet, the other seemed to hold some kind of trump card. Lockley cracked his knuckles.

'There is a traitor in your midst,' the mystery man said. 'This paper gives you clemency to root out the unfortunate and disperse of him. Make sure it is achieved before you return. Sooner rather than later! You will be richly rewarded.'

Argyle was biting his lip so hard he could taste blood.

'Now I like the sound of that,' Lockley said. 'And the traitor's name is stated here?'

'You must discover who it is yourself. Get close to him and then disperse of him. I would look to some of those who joined the pilgrimage late.' The hooded man sounded as if he was explaining something difficult to a slow child.

'How the Hell am I supposed to carry out an order for a murder, if I don't know that I'm killing the right one?!' Lockley grumbled. 'Last time the order was clear and the name there for all to see. Well, for me to see.'

In the moonlight, Argyle saw the other man shrug; clearly this was not his problem but then Lockley's hand shot out and grabbed the man around the neck. He croaked as Lockley shook him violently.

'I suddenly find I've trouble believing you! Surely you can do better.'

Lockley released the man, who fell before him, grasping at his neck, his breath rattling. On his knees the man looked up at Lockley. His hood slid back revealing a greying mop of unruly hair. Argyle frowned. This was an old man, sent on a fool's errand, and why was his face so familiar?

Lockley dragged the old man roughly to his feet. 'Well?'

'There is a young soldier from your camp.' The man panted.

Lockley shook him once more. 'What is that to me?!'

'My men found him wandering aimlessly around an alley nearby.' Lockley loosened his grip on the man's shoulders as he continued. 'He claimed to be searching for a brothel, but that was clearly a lie. His pockets were empty - and everyone knows whores must be paid for their services!'

Argyle held his breath. Surely Stephen would not have been that foolish.

'You're saying this young man knows more than he's letting on?' Lockley asked.

'I am sure of it.' The man regained his footing. 'Maybe you could persuade him to tell the truth.'

Lockley laughed coldly. 'The truth?! Now that would be something! But let's put it to the test.'

'Us?' The man sounded frightened and Argyle could hardly blame him.

'Yes us!' Lockley smiled. 'Your men found him, surely they would have taken him with them - and how am I to find them, if you don't guide me?'

The man shivered. 'I could tell you …' His head snapped back when Lockley struck him hard on the jaw. The man fell backwards, knocked of his feet by the force of the blow.

Lockley towered above him. 'You will lead me to them, and you will stay until I have the truth from this soldier. You will not leave until I tell you, you can go!'

'You have no power …' The man doubled over when Lockley kicked him mercilessly in the ribs.

'Power is a strange thing,' Lockley snarled. 'Alone in a deserted part of town, just the two of us here - who is to know what might happen? I think you'll find that power lies with the one who seizes it.'

Lockley grabbed the man roughly by the arm and forced him to his feet, the man still out of breath wiped blood from his nose. Dragging the man along, Lockley was plunged into darkness, leaving Argyle pinned in his hiding place for what felt like an eternity before he dared move.

Finally deciding to risk all, he got up and ran along the rampart, sliding around corners and narrowly avoiding the guards and lookouts posted along the wall. It seemed the city was manning up as if they knew something was amiss, as if they knew there was a murderer at large.

Argyle had to get to the camp, his lungs burning hot from gasping breaths of cold air, his head spinning from what he had just heard and what he suspected but could not prove.

Eventually, he slipped into camp, meeting just one guard who was by some divine intervention one of Argyle's own soldiers. Argyle nodded at the soldier who let him pass without a single word. Thank God for small favours.

When Argyle found Stephen's bunk it was empty and cold and none of the other soldiers had seen him since Argyle had last spoken to him in the camp after nightfall. Argyle felt a ball of ice in the pit of his stomach, a frozen fear that Stephen had disobeyed his orders to stay in camp, to not go seeking out trouble - but to make sure that Argyle was not found sneaking about and either thrown in jail by the French or dragged before Bolingbroke by the English.

Damn the fool-hearted Stephen!

Argyle paced around Stephen's quarters for hours, striking up conversations with soldiers going to or coming from their shifts as watchmen. But to no avail - no one had seen Stephen.

Argyle left an order with the guard at the edge of camp to ensure that as soon as someone matching Stephen's description was seen entering the camp, Argyle was to be told immediately. There was nothing to do but to return to his own tent and wait for word of Stephen and for the sun to rise.

Argyle laid down, fully dressed, and when he finally fell asleep, his dreams were dark and full of terror.

6 November 1392 — Vienna

'M'lord, Smith is back.' A soldier appeared at daybreak to rouse Argyle.

'Bring him here!' Argyle blinked at the single flame from the soldier's torch. 'Squire! Light the candles and stir the fire!'

'M'lord,' Stephen's rasping voice crept through the air as Argyle was splashing water on his face.

'Stephen!' Argyle turned and stopped. 'What …?'

'Spot of trouble in a brothel, M'lord,' Stephen said. 'Please forgive me for bringing shame on …'

Argyle looked at the squire who was staring openly at Stephen's bruised face and torn clothes. 'You can go, boy. I will send for you, if I need you.' Argyle waved dismissively, though the boy lingered just long enough to earn a stern look. 'Out!'

Argyle turned back to Stephen. 'Enough with the nonsense, this was Lockley!'

Stephen swallowed hard and Argyle noticed black-blue marks around Stephen's neck. 'No M'lord - I think I may have stumbled on Laura

Longshank's sister in a brothel.' Stephen tried to laugh but grabbed his side and gasped instead.

'Sit down!' Argyle commanded, but Stephen stubbornly stayed on his feet, tottering ever so slightly at every painful breath.

'M'lord, I swear t'was my own fault.'

Argyle gave him a severe look. 'You will tell me the truth, you are sworn to my service and you swore an oath to be always loyal and truthful!'

'And I've just told you what happened. I got into a fight in one of the brothels, I know you told me not to go, but … Some wench or other thought I couldn't pay for her services and a few of her friends took it to heart to defend her rights.' Stephen took a shallow breath. 'That's all.'

Argyle pondered this for a while leaving Stephen to stew. 'M'lord, may I be excused?'

'NO! You will be excused when I am satisfied you are not lying to me!' Argyle closed the gap to Stephen, grabbing him roughly around the shoulders; Stephen's clothes were soaked with blood and he winced at the brutal grip. 'This is no brawl in a tavern. This is a proper beating. This must be …'

Stephen wrenched himself free, yammering when he bumped his elbow into a chair. He was sweating, his face a spattering of red and black from a night of abuse. 'M'lord, I've said all I have to say.'

'And I do not believe you!' Argyle retorted.

The two stared at each other, Stephen shaking from exertion, Argyle from anger. 'Stephen, whatever happened to you, I will not tell a living soul but I want the truth. You can trust me; you did with your tale of your father and you can trust me now to keep quiet whatever it is. Although I think I already know,' Argyle said darkly.

Stephen shook his head. 'It was a brawl gone out of control, M'lord. Nothing more.'

'It was Lockley!' Argyle snarled.

Stephen froze in place, fear plain on his battered face. 'No …' he whispered.

'Stephen, I heard Lockley and another man talk about a young soldier caught in an alley near the northern gate. No one knew I was going there but you! No one ever goes there. That part of the city is deserted in winter. Only you and I knew that something was going to happen there last night. It had to be you, it has to be Lockley who did this to you,' Argyle said. 'Do not lie to me again, I will not be able to forgive you if you do.'

Stephen swallowed hard. 'Then perhaps you'll see fit to release me, M'lord.'

'Release you?' Argyle was thrown by the request.

'Yes, M'lord. I would've waited to speak to you until later today, but …' Stephen looked away. 'I've been asked to join Lockley.'

Argyle felt his head go blank, the icy ball returning to his stomach. 'Lockley?'

Stephen nodded. 'Lockley asked me to join his service, and I … Well, I think it'd be better for all of us.' Stephen looked unhappily at Argyle.

'For all of us?' Argyle felt his temper rise. 'Or for Lockley?!'

'M'lord …' Stephen gulped. 'For … me.'

'Stephen, what did you tell him?' Argyle tried to coax Stephen, but it was pointless.

'Nothing! That's why I have to take his offer; that's why I have to change my loyalty and my service to him. 'Cause I said nothing,' Stephen said with eerie calm. 'I kept my word to you, but now you have to release me, or …'

'Or what?' Argyle asked, knowing full well Stephen could not be swayed.

'Or I'll have to desert you,' Stephen said.

'You will be Lockley's man. I cannot trust you anymore - we cannot be friends,' Argyle said feebly. 'You would desert me rather than tell me, what Lockley did, what you …'

'Yes.' Stephen cut across Argyle's stream of words. 'Yes, I would, knowing we can't be friends, knowing I've failed you and that you'll never trust me again. Knowing you can't trust me! I'd choose to desert you.'

Defeat and anger made Argyle's voice tremble. 'Fine! I release you to seek service elsewhere. If this is to be the end of it, then so be it. But be warned, Smith, I will be keeping an eye out for you! If I find you talking to my men, spying on my tent or find anything amiss, I will take it to Bolingbroke. I will name you a traitor and a spy before all, if I think you are turning on me!' Argyle felt his fingernails dig into his palms as he balled his fists to keep from attacking Stephen.

'I understand, M'lord,' Stephen said in a small voice. 'I'll do anything you ask save stay in your service. I can't, I have to go to Lockley.'

'Then go!' Argyle felt the finality claw at him, a friend lost and perhaps an enemy gained. Who knew what Lockley would do to Stephen, what he had already done?

Stephen bowed and turned to go. 'I've never been disloyal to you.'

No, Argyle thought, but that may yet come to an end. All he could do was hope that he had not revealed too much of his true purpose on the pilgrimage and that he might bring justice not only to La Fontaine, but to Stephen too before the journey was over.

The same afternoon, Bolingbroke announced that the camp would leave the city the following day to begin the pilgrimage in earnest. Argyle could not but feel relieved to leave a place that had brought a friendship to a close.

CHAPTER 21

19 November 1392 — En route to Treviso

Nearly two months later, just as the camp was making ready for the day's ride, Stephen pushed through the tent flap and bowed lightly to Argyle.

'Yes?' Argyle asked stiffly.

'I'm sent to ask that you join M'lord Bolingbroke in the main tent.'

Argyle slowly rose and grabbed his travelling cloak. 'Best not keep him waiting then.'

Weaving their way through the labyrinth of tents being dismantled, Argyle followed his one-time friend in silence.

Just as they came upon Bolingbroke's tent, Stephen turned and grabbed Argyle's arm. 'There's news from England. I fear you're walking into a trap. Be careful.' Stephen released his grip and trampled off, leaving Argyle to ponder what this all meant.

A soldier opened the heavy flap and let out a breath of warm air. The heat in the tent was palpable. Bolingbroke was famous for his desire to always be warm and many heaters were alight even as the sun was rising to another magnificently hot day.

'You requested my presence, my Lord?' Argyle bowed to Bolingbroke and nodded to the other knights gathered inside. It still felt a little strange that Argyle no longer had to lower his gaze or be overly polite to them.

Bolingbroke was seated comfortably, reclining on a pile of pillows, Lockley was bent over the makeshift table to one side of the tent. The rest of the knights were gathered around one of the heaters apparently pretending to be ornaments and not active participants.

'I did indeed. And look here all these curious people hoping for some titbits to take with them. Away with you!' Bolingbroke kept his voice perfectly level. Still, Argyle sensed something was amiss, although he could not say whether it was to the good or the bad. 'You too, Lockley!'

At this the knight shot Bolingbroke a cold glare and walked out, brushing close past Argyle with a grunt.

'You will forgive me, my Lord, if I do not know what those titbits may be?'

'Certainly. You are not on good terms with your brother, I gather?' Bolingbroke said. 'Otherwise you are the perfect fool and I applaud your ability to look astounded at old news. In any case, I shall make everything perfectly clear for you now. There is trouble brewing in England.'

'Trouble, my Lord?'

'Yes. And even with the fastest messengers in the kingdom, I was not informed until just at this moment.' Bolingbroke seemed very displeased and Argyle kept his silence, waiting for Bolingbroke to make his next move. It did not take long. 'Ah, well. Mayhap it will all come to nothing. Sufficing to say, I feel much more comfortable with you here than I have before.'

Argyle felt completely lost. 'My Lord, forgive me, but what trouble is brewing?'

'The King has once more taken to his old ways. It is a most unnerving situation. Nonetheless, I would rather be far away from court just now than close to it.'

Wily as a fox, Bolingbroke could smell problems from miles away. Something he had proven some years ago, when he had very nearly deposed the King. But this time, Bolingbroke could claim distance as his defence.

Argyle decided trust in honesty, he had not heard a thing from Thomas since he made off on the pilgrimage, and had not expected to. 'I believed the nation to be at peace.'

'So did the rest of the fools in England. It has made them quite reckless. I am grateful to your brother for sharing this information with me, true or not. At least, it proves the Mowbray loyalty to me.' Bolingbroke shook his head and laughed loudly. 'I only mean, once the King sees reason, I shall be one of his chief advisors alongside my father. Loyal servants and allies are in scarce demand even at the best of times. It is good to know whom to trust.'

'My Lord.' Argyle had to bite his tongue not to reveal his true purpose. So far he still could not shake the notion that Bolingbroke had more than a little to do with La Fontaine's untimely death. Rather than putting his concerns to rest, this new development brought more kindling to an already smouldering fire.

'I thought you would like to know, Sir Argyle. After all, you must have known I did not entirely trust you. However, I have had a change of heart. Today, you will join me in the van. Lockley will take the rear and you will not be troubled by his brooding.'

Bolingbroke smiled complacently. This ended the audience and sent Argyle out into a sunny morning he no longer paid any heed to.

ஐ ௐ ஐ ௐ

CHAPTER 22

27 November 1392 — near Portogruaro, Italy

'Sir Argyle!' Lockley appeared in a cloud of dust, shaking Argyle from his thoughts.

Lockley's dark grey cape was muddy and stained by the trip from Treviso to Portogruaro, and his brown steed kicked up more dirt as it danced nervously sideways. How he had ever bested La Fontaine in the joust and thrown him from his saddle was beyond Argyle's imagination.

'My Lord Bolingbroke requests your presence in the vanguard.' Lockley was clearly dissatisfied being a messenger.

'I see.'

'Now, Sire!' Lockley snapped. 'Or do you not recognise an order, when you hear one?'

'Naturally. You are riding back with me?' Argyle looked ahead towards the city of Treviso.

'No.' Lockley circled round and rode away and, for a moment, Argyle watched him go. For a knight loyal to his master, Lockley was acting very peculiarly, it almost seemed he no longer felt Bolingbroke was his superior. Just a few days ago, Argyle had heard Beaufort and Lockley exchange words, and not of a kind nature. Beaufort had stalked away to make his report to Bolingbroke no doubt and Lockley had not seemed the least bit concerned.

Was La Fontaine's death just an accident? Or had Lockley been ordered to kill the knight? The more time he spent with the man, the less he thought Lockley clever enough to be the instigator of the murder. Although not many died in tourneys anymore, it was known to happen; perhaps the King was mistaken. And yet Lockley had received a strange order in Vienna and he had mentioned La Fontaine to the grey-haired man.

Argyle kicked Noble into a canter and found Bolingbroke alone at the head of the van. His clothes were scarcely touched by the grime and dirt that the rest of the entourage had to move in. Argyle fell in alongside him.

'Sir Argyle, very good. How do you find the pilgrimage?'

'Very well, and you, my Lord?' Argyle asked.

'Good. Everyone should go on a pilgrimage. Nothing like it to cleanse a man's mind and soul!' Bolingbroke declared with satisfaction. 'I for one cannot wait to set my eyes on the Holy Land, although I have been told that the weather is not fit for sailing. I fear we may be stranded in Venice for some time,' Bolingbroke said. 'Why did Richard send you along?'

Argyle's heart nearly jumped into his throat. 'His Grace did not send me. I chose to go voluntarily as I wished to see the Holy Land,' he said hoping to feign indifference.

'I see, then my father is out of pocket to me, you see he wrote to tell me that you were just a little too eager to join my pilgrimage, but I replied that unlike your brother, you are an honest man. And while we speak of him, still no news from Thomas?' Bolingbroke's languid speech made Argyle shift uncomfortably in the saddle.

'My Lord?'

'In Vienna, you told me Thomas had not written to you. I simply wondered if perhaps, you had since heard from him,' Bolingbroke said. 'Even if we are making our way to the Holy Land, I should like to know of anything that might prompt me to change course. Knowing your brother, he is in the thick of things. And knowing your brother, he would not miss an opportunity to boast of his good fortunes. If the lay of the English land was to shift while we were away - and if you did know of it and told me nothing, I should be sorely disappointed, Sir Argyle.'

Bolingbroke's insinuation lingered in the air as he drew his hood up against the beginning drizzle. 'The grandeur of a man is easily perishable,' Bolingbroke said, before he forced his massive steed into a canter and rode ahead of Argyle.

3 December 1392 — Venice

A week later, while Bolingbroke was busy visiting with the doge who had declared that he would act as Bolingbroke's personal guide while he visited Venice, Argyle received an unexpected visitor. He had just sent his squire away for the evening and was preparing for the night when the door opened. Thinking it was his squire back to ask something, he did not turn. 'Yes?'

'Sir Argyle.'

A chill crept up Argyle's spine. 'Lockley?'

'Aye. It is time to have it out, isn't it?' Lockley asked, his voice cold and quiet.

Argyle turned slowly, considering if he was too far away to reach for his sword. Then his hand found the short, broad-bladed knife at the waist, concealed under his tunic and he relaxed a little. Not a sword, but it would have to do.

'Not to worry, boy, I haven't come to slit your throat. Far too many peeping eyes here,' Lockley said.

'Am I to take your word for it?' Argyle asked as he got up, feigning the need for something at the other end of the room.

'It'll have to do.' Lockley looked around the room and chose a low stool next to the fire to sit on. Argyle leaned on a windowsill keeping some distance between them all the same.

'You have been asking questions about me.' Lockley said.

'Is that so?'

'Come now, this is no time to be mysterious. If you want the truth, why not come straight to the source?' Lockley asked.

Argyle felt panic threaten to wash over him and forced it back. 'Perhaps it has occurred to you that I do not find you reliable?'

Lockley laughed softly, an unfamiliar and unnerving sound. 'Good. Better to be feared than found wanting I say. All the same, in a party such as this it's hard to keep secrets for long.'

In the dim light of the fire, Lockley's grey eyes glistened for once. Argyle decided to bide his time.

Lockley slapped his gloves together, folding them into one hand then looked up again. 'If it's the truth you seek, you need only ask.'

'Very well, tell me the truth then. Who hired you to murder La Fontaine?' Argyle asked.

In the silence that followed, they locked eyes until Argyle felt his burn, but it was Lockley who looked away. 'No one you know. Not first hand at any rate.'

'That is not quite the truth, I should think?'

'I will tell you more, but first I must know, what you plan to do, if I reveal my dirty little secret?' Lockley demanded.

'That would depend on the quality of your information.'

Argyle felt anger threaten to blind him to the King's mission and worked his hands to relieve some of the tension and keep his wits about him. This could prove to be an important conversation and Argyle could not afford to lose his temper and pounce at the man who killed La Fontaine. Not yet and not here at any rate.

'So you'd sell me to my own master? Do you think Bolingbroke is completely without knowledge of the things I've done? Or even why I did them?' Lockley asked. 'Because if you do, you aren't as clever as I had come to think you were.'

'I do not answer to Bolingbroke.' Argyle struggled not to let Lockley's words unnerve him. He had wondered if Bolingbroke knew anything of La Fontaine's death, but he had seemed genuinely surprised upon hearing that Argyle had inherited the estate. And besides, the King had ordered the tournament out of the blue while Bolingbroke was at sea, travelling towards Vilnius. He would hardly have received or sent word to the effect of killing La Fontaine, even if he wanted to. The sea journey around Denmark and through hostile waters was perilous enough without drawing attention to yourself.

'No, I should think not but still you've become fast friends I should think. Relax, it is naught to me.' Lockley stretched his legs and took a deep breath. 'I killed La Fontaine! Even if the lance had only grazed him, he wouldn't have lived long afterward. The order came from someone high at court. Not Bolingbroke, nor your brother. But they both know the person intimately.'

Argyle realised he had stopped breathing and exhaled slowly, the idea that someone in the heart of court had decreed La Fontaine's death all but choked him. Argyle wanted to ask a thousand questions but his mind had gone blank.

'What'd you think?' Lockley looked at Argyle. 'That I'd take such an order from just anyone? No, I may not be much in the way of chivalry, but even I have my standards. The order came from someone you can't touch. Someone for whom we'd all do anything.'

'You are pointing your finger at the King?' Argyle hardly recognised his own voice.

'I'm saying that even you'd be hard pressed to disobey this order,' Lockley smirked. 'I did what was requested and I did it not entirely without pleasure. That man always acted all high and mighty with his childish Unicorn and his high favour with the King. It felt good to finally meet him face to face on the list and know that I'd come out victorious.'

Argyle turned his back to Lockley, grabbing the hilt of his dagger so tight that he felt the intricate pattern bite into his palm. In his disbelief, Argyle clung to the King's words before his departure that nothing, absolutely nothing, could stand in the way of discovering what had happened to La Fontaine. Still, Argyle felt he would be able to defend himself, if he did attack Lockley and slit his throat. But it would have to wait until he was certain of what Lockley knew.

With a massive effort, Argyle reined in his temper and turned around to face Lockley. 'You are proud of your actions?'

'To be called and to obey? Yes, I'm proud. Killing a man who was undefeated was just a bonus.' Lockley got slowly to his feet but continued eying Argyle wearily. 'Keep that knife in its hilt. You may be a match to me, but you wouldn't survive killing another knight for paying a courteous call. I made sure to inform several of the soldiers about my plans, and Bolingbroke of course.'

Opening the door again, Lockley spoke loudly. 'Thank you for the drink, Sir Argyle! We may yet be good friends.'

Argyle loosened his tight grip on the silver hilt, his hand sweaty and trembling.

20 January 1393 — Rhodes

Argyle took the piece of crumbled paper and sent his squire away. Watching the boy drag his feet as he walked away, Argyle pushed the note into his sleeve and went in search of food and a quiet place to read. He still marvelled at the warmth of the islands that they had passed since sailing from Venice, it might only be January but you would not know from the warm sunshine and light breeze.

A nearby stall caught his attention and he bought a spit of roasted mutton, apple and onion. It had a sweet and slightly exotic smell of oranges making his mouth water. At the far side of the small town square, Argyle found a bench under a budding olive tree, where he unfolded the paper, smoothing it out on his knee.

- Beware! The whole court knows you are travelling with Bolingbroke. What is more, they believe you are doing your brother's dirty work for him. I have long suspected a faction at court and now I am certain. Remember your loyalties! -

Argyle did not need to read it again; he crumbled it and tucked it back into his sleeve. The first fire he could find, he would drop it there to burn, just as the King had commanded.

Looking out over a little, bustling square, Argyle contemplated the content of the note while chewing on the last bite of meat. These words were sent by a troubled man. Thinking back, Argyle could not remember when the King had not been troubled, and yet the message seemed more desperate than any he had received before.

Throwing away the wooden spit, Argyle considered what the King might be implying in relation to Thomas. Argyle had not heard from his brother since their row before his departure when Thomas had lashed out and accused Argyle of betraying his own family.

He was somewhat relieved that the English court seemed to think that he had left without the King's blessing. This would mean that Stephen really had not told Lockley anything of consequence, anything that might endanger the King's mission. This could even prove to make his task easier to …

The sound of someone clearing his throat behind him tore Argyle from his thoughts.

'Sir Argyle.' Sir Alan Coxcombe looked around in his customary nervous way.

'Sir Alan. Have you tried the spits from that little stall just there? I highly recommend them - very succulent.' Argyle rubbed his hands together trying to get rid of the last grease from the tender meat and gestured for Coxcombe to sit down.

Coxcombe's eyes darted around. 'No, I have little appetite.'

Argyle let the silence stretch between them until Coxcombe spoke again. 'I had hoped to catch you alone - though are we ever truly alone on this trip?'

'How can I help you?' Argyle said, surprised to hear Thomas' smooth tones ring in his own voice.

Coxcombe leaned in. 'I wanted to …'

'Yes?'

'Well, to offer my condolences on La Fontaine's untimely death,' Coxcombe said, but Argyle suspected there was more to this.

'Thank you, I know what great friends you were, it must have come as a shock for you,' Argyle said.

'I knew nothing about it!' Coxcombe whispered, a desperate note in his voice as he grabbed Argyle's sleeve.

'About what?'

'About La Fontaine being a target. Not that we were not all targets in our own right, but he was so high in favour with the King. I tried to warn him, after Lockley nearly killed me on the training course, but La Fontaine would not hear me out. Said I had disappointed him when I had come to him all that time ago. When de Vere was chased from England and we were all outlawed.' Coxcombe spoke fast, words tripping over themselves to get out, it seemed he was unable to stop. 'I did not know, I swear it, Sir Argyle! If I had, I would have told someone, you … anyone!'

Argyle slowly freed himself from Coxcombe's grasp and looked him in the eye. 'Now why would I think, you knew?'

Coxcombe shook all over, his voice thin and frail. 'Because … that is what they are all saying. That you think I am somehow responsible for his death and that you mean to kill me.'

'Kill you?' Argyle asked genuinely surprised and a little shocked that the camp would have so many wagging tongues. 'I can assure you, I have no such desire.'

'Good … that is good. I knew nothing. That I went to see Gaunt was on the old man's behest, he wanted to know if I would go to Calais and secure the harbour for the fleet. I have done so before and so …' Coxcombe's voice trailed away.

'And so you did?' Argyle said.

'Ah, yes … And then the order arrived that I was to join the pilgrimage and it seemed as good an opportunity as any; I did not feel like going back to England just then.' Coxcombe smiled sadly.

Turning his head towards the inn, Argyle saw a boy running away, his clothes nondescript and yet he seemed oddly familiar. 'He was in a hurry,' Argyle remarked to Coxcombe, whose face was suddenly white as chalk. 'Sir Alan?'

'I know him,' Coxcombe said, frowning as if to recall from where. 'I am sure, I know him.'

'I am sure, I do not,' Argyle said.

'No, perhaps I am mistaken. Maybe I just need to eat, and then I will be myself again.'

'Travelling by sea is hungry business, although many seem to lose their appetites on the water.' Argyle suddenly felt sure that Coxcombe was entirely right to be nervous. Wagging tongues and strangers lurking nearby - this was no ordinary pilgrimage to be sure.

'Was there more you wished to say to me?' Argyle asked.

'No, only that I knew nothing and have lamented my friend's untimely death ever since I heard of it,' Coxcombe said before abruptly getting up and walking away in the opposite direction of the inn and the food stall.

Argyle contemplated him as he vanished around a corner, he might be sorry for his friend's death, but then why did Coxcombe not attend the funeral? Certainly here was someone who might, in time, shed more light on what had happened shortly before and just after the tourney. Argyle increasingly felt that he needed to know not just who had ordered La Fontaine's death, but also the circumstances around the hastily arranged tournament. And Argyle knew he could not rely on anyone else for that information as long as he was on this pilgrimage, so he decided that once they reached Jerusalem, he would try to find another moment alone with Coxcombe.

CHAPTER 23

28 January 1393 — near Jerusalem

'He said WHAT?!' Wrath filled Bolingbroke's voice.

After deliberating long and hard, Argyle had decided to reveal some of his conversation with Lockley earlier that month. Now, Argyle was testing the waters to see how much Bolingbroke knew about Lockley's involvement in the murder of La Fontaine and he felt certain now that continuing his investigations without sanction from Bolingbroke would prove a fruitless endeavour.

Argyle delivered his carefully planned message one afternoon after Bolingbroke had visited Lydda and declared that they would camp on the outskirts for the night.

'It was my impression that Lockley named you, my Lord.' Argyle made himself breathe naturally.

'Outright? Or are you making assumptions?' Bolingbroke asked suspiciously.

'Not in so may words, but his message was clear. He is certain you will protect him, if anyone was to accuse him of La Fontaine's murder.'

'He was responsible for La Fontaine's death - that I will not deny. When you kill another knight, even unwontedly in front of the entire court the deed is hard to disguise, but it was an accident, and those do happen. This is old news, Sir Argyle. Why do you lay it at my door?' Bolingbroke was fuming but not ready to give up on the notion that this was a mistake.

'I only bring it to you, as I felt you should know. He said the order came from deep within the court,' Argyle said.

'How deep?' Bolingbroke had paled.

'Deep, my Lord.'

'I know what you will ask of me, and I cannot, Sir Argyle. This can go no further for the time being. If he was truly under orders to kill La Fontaine, I shall have it out of him in due course.'

'My Lord?' Argyle opened his mouth to continue.

'Quiet, Sire!' Bolingbroke snapped. 'You are not high in my favour right now either. Why would he suddenly confess to you?'

'Perhaps to goad me on for a fight, or to test my loyalties. Either way I shall do nothing, if you find it to be best.'

Bolingbroke closed his eyes and seemed to ponder this for a moment. 'Be off, Sire. If I have need of you, I expect you to be loyal to me first.'

Argyle bowed lightly and made to exit the tent when Bolingbroke spoke again. 'Sir Argyle.'

'My Lord?'

'Not a word to anyone. I trust you know how to keep your mouth shut. Once we reach Jerusalem, I shall have made a decision - one way or the other.'

As Argyle pushed the flap aside, out of the corner of his eye, he saw a small boy run from the side of the tent.

ജ ന ജ ന

'It is time we speak of what happened in Vienna.'

Stephen had joined Argyle in his tent for the evening, and was now lounging leisurely on a makeshift bed of pillows and furs. He propped himself up on one elbow and looked curiously at Argyle. 'Vienna? It's so long ago, I'd almost forgotten.'

'Forgotten or stored away?' Argyle probed.

Stephen nodded slowly. 'What'd you want to know?'

'Everything about the night I spied on Lockley and you disappeared. What truly made you decide to leave my service to join Lockley? I've turned it over and over in my head, and I can only reach one conclusion.' Argyle paused leaving plenty of time for Stephen to answer, but he merely waited. 'Lockley has some sort of hold over you.'

'Yes.'

'Will you tell me? It may save a life.'

Stephen smiled sadly and sat up, pushing away some of the pillows. 'I doubt it. And I don't know what difference it'll make.'

'Then why not share it with me. I will not do anything with my knowledge unless you let me; you know I am true to my word. I have never been disloyal to you, even when you disappointed me in Vienna,' Argyle pressed.

'Share the burden, you mean?' Stephen sat up. 'And how am I to prevent you taking what I say to anyone of your choosing? I'm but a soldier and you're a knight.'

It was spoken without a trace of spite or regret, merely stating facts. If Argyle chose to share his knowledge with others, Stephen would indeed be powerless to stop him.

Argyle thought for some time before replying. 'I could call on our friendship, but it has changed too much. I could call on chivalry or loyalty but I doubt that would make a difference to you. Instead, I will share something with you that you might use against me if I betray our agreement.'

Stephen narrowed his eyes for a moment considering the proposal and then he nodded. 'It seems fair. You first.'

'I know Lockley killed La Fontaine. Not in a clumsy jousting accident but on orders from a powerful magnate. The King has asked me to join the pilgrimage to find out what happened. That is why I asked for your help in Vienna, and why I would not let you come with me. I hoped to spare you and keep you innocent of my dealings.' Argyle watched Stephen intently. Nothing betrayed previous knowledge when his blue eyes bulged at the admittance. He had chosen wisely then.

'No one knows?' Stephen whispered.

'Bolingbroke knows that I am here to find out what happened at the tourney. He does not suspect I have come under orders from anyone. I have given him no explanation other than that I want to see justice done for La Fontaine. To be honest, he probably views me as a simple, naïve man in want of a brain.'

Stephen chuckled. 'Anyone who knows your brother as Bolingbroke does'd never think you in want of a brain. Wisdom and timing mayhap, but not wits.'

Argyle smiled complacently. He had shared enough. 'Your turn.'

Rising to fetch two cups of the lukewarm, sour local wine, Stephen turned away as if contemplating where to begin and how much to say. Argyle accepted the offered wine and waited.

'They found me in an alley, just as you said back then. I was concerned for you and wanted to help. Instead, I made it much worse,' Stephen said.

'Who found you?'

Stephen shrugged and sat down again; his back hunched he stared into the cup. 'I don't know. They didn't see fit to inform me. They just knocked me out and when I came to, I was in a dark room with Lockley and at least one other man though I never really saw him.'

Argyle motioned for him to go on, sipping the sour wine and longing for some English ale.

'He began asking questions. Who was the traitor? How'd I come to know him? When I told him I'd no idea, he … Well, he spoke with his hands for a while, repeating his questions between every blow. Eventually, I told him it might be Coxcombe.' Stephen took a swig of wine and winced at the sour taste. He kept staring into the cup rather than Argyle, crawling into his memories with an unhappy expression. 'Remember I told you that Coxcombe'd disappeared right after La Fontaine fell from his horse? I since discovered that he'd in fact left just before the last joust. Excused himself with some half-truth of troubles in his household.'

Stephen began pacing back and forth. 'From the tourney, Coxcombe went to his house. There he chose four trusted soldiers and made for Westminster. He was there for some hours before Gaunt returned from the tourney. They spoke briefly and then Coxcombe rode hard for Portsmouth, even as La Fontaine lay dying. Once in Portsmouth, Coxcombe consigned a ship and sailed for France. He knew what'd happen before it did. He did nothing to prevent it. He just went to Gaunt and declared the deed done.'

Stephen looked up defiantly, challenging Argyle to make his case. But Argyle said nothing. This would tie in with Lockley's mystery master ordering the death of another knight and Coxcombe's own story that he was sent to France on Gaunt's orders. Inward, Argyle admitted that he was relieved Lockley had not acted on the King's orders after all and worried that they might have come from Gaunt.

Stephen went on. 'Lockley's never going to be charged with murder.'

'Why not?' Argyle was surprised.

'He told me the order carried a seal that would protect him from any accusations. Your quest is entirely fruitless.'

Argyle felt anger rise and suppressed it. 'Why beat you senseless if you could reveal so little?'

'He convinced me to enter into his service that night - by the end of it all, I think I would've agreed to anything to stop the abuse. Lockley told me you wouldn't go back from Jerusalem. That it was wise to choose another master and that he'd protect me.' Stephen shivered, clutching himself as if to ward off a despicable memory. 'I believed him. I still believe him.'

Argyle felt cold despite the suffocating heat in the tent. 'You believe that I will not return from Jerusalem?'

'He has powerful friends,' Stephen said evasively and sat down.

'As do I.'

Stephen's face grew dark. 'I wonder if your friends're truly your friends.'

Argyle leaned in, fixing Stephens gaze. 'Which friends are we speaking of now?'

'All of them.' Stephen squirmed, uncomfortable to label himself an untrue friend.

'I see.' Argyle reached for the cup of wine. 'Well, I cannot really say I trust many on this pilgrimage as it is. I think I know Bolingbroke not to be a friend, but he has had no cause to distrust me.'

'Are you sure?' Stephen frowned.

'I am sure of very little in this world. For a time, I counted you a friend and you have done nothing to my disservice. Therefore, I chose to count you a friend and I still do.' Argyle looked intently at Stephen. 'What I will think in future is another matter.'

Silence descended on the tent for a while, before Argyle spoke again. 'Make me a promise?'

Stephen began to get up. 'If I can.'

'Be careful. Your journey in this world may not run parallel with mine, but I think we may yet be linked together for some time. Do nothing to attract attention to yourself.' Argyle took Stephen's cup. 'If Lockley asks, I invited you to drink a cup of wine with me, the drink was sour and the company likewise.'

Stephen left with a slight smile, neither agreeing nor denying the promise. Once alone, Argyle leaned back in his chair. If Coxcombe was named traitor and yet was such a friend of Bolingbroke, what would Lockley do? Who could hold such sway as to make a loyal man disloyal?

Any way he looked at it, Argyle could only come up with one answer. And he did not like it. He was unravelling much more than he cared for, and he kept coming back to the same two people - one he would like more than anything to name, and one he would not.

ཨ ཨ ཨ ཨ

CHAPTER 24

1 February 1393 — Jerusalem

The sounds and smells were so foreign and overwhelming that, for the first days, most of the entourage chose to stay in the camp just outside the city gates of Jerusalem. However, Bolingbroke was determined to go directly to the sacred mount to pay homage to the Son of God.

Bolingbroke had been in high spirits for several days, seemingly looking forward to his great religious act in earnest. Argyle did not share his enthusiasm, but still felt compelled to go with him when asked to.

It was in this capacity that the two unlikely companions now wound their way along the narrow passages of the bazaar. Men, women and children were peddling everything from food and clothes to exotic animals and even slaves. Bolingbroke lazily waved them away, parting the sea of people not unlike Moses in the Bible.

'How I wish I knew what they were saying.'

'My Lord?'

'We must acquire an interpreter. I have already said as much to several of the others, but none of them seem capable of carrying out a simple order any more. What of you, Sir Argyle, have you the capacity to secure an interpreter that might be trusted?' Bolingbroke looked at

Argyle and nearly overturned a small cart that came trundling out from a dark passageway.

Argyle quenched a smile. 'I am sure, I should hardly know where to begin.'

Bolingbroke grumbled.

'However, you are right, we do indeed need someone who knows both language and customs. I shall attend to it,' Argyle promised.

'Well done.' Bolingbroke stopped to prod at some peculiar fruit. The vendor glanced at the two strange men with some curiosity, then seemed to decide they were not worth his haggling and waved them on with a grin. Argyle made to go on, but Bolingbroke intervened and stared angrily at the vendor who did not seem startled but was already looking for customers elsewhere.

'How can they eat this? Oh, I long for proper food,' Bolingbroke complained.

'My Lord, I believe the natives feel this *is* proper food. They would not like our food I should warrant.'

Bolingbroke pretended not hear. 'I believe if we attempt at eating it, it will poison us.'

'What makes you say that, my Lord? The food may be foreign, but the people here eat it and they are fine, I suspect once we grow accustomed to the food, so will we be. Besides, they do not even know who we are, nor would they care, I think,' Argyle said, biting back laughter at Bolingbroke's suspicious thoughts of a city full of strangers.

'For now perhaps, but once we have an interpreter, we must make ourselves known to all the right people in town.' Bolingbroke looked around. 'Then these paupers will think twice before peddling their measly goods to me.' Bolingbroke sidestepped just in time to avoid a large pile of manure.

For a while the two made headway in silence, letting the bustle and strange sounds drown out any uneasy attempts of conversation. In the end, it was Argyle who spoke again. 'How strange all this seems. I wonder if my father ever saw Jerusalem.'

'Mine was much too busy in France.' Bolingbroke dabbled sweat from his brow.

Argyle dared a personal question. 'What is he like?'

'My father? You have met him, but I suppose that says very little. When I was young, he was a stranger to me. It was not until my mother died that he saw fit to return and make me part of his household. His was a life of always moving about, but now he is the master of peace in England.' Argyle looked at Bolingbroke, who smiled. 'What of it?'

'I never knew either of my parents. I simply wondered at what it must be to have a father, absent or otherwise,' Argyle said smoothly.

Bolingbroke looked up toward the pale blue sky, not a cloud in sight. 'Not much to envy. Most speak of their parents with reverence or even awe. Few have anything to be so very reverent about. However, my father is a great man, no doubt about it.'

Bolingbroke seemed happy enough to boast his father's achievements for all his faults.

'Look there, Sir Argyle. Is it not a sight worth travelling to the ends of the Earth for?' Argyle followed Bolingbroke's hand; they had come to the foot of a rolling hill. At the very top, a white church glistened in the sunshine, the sight made Argyle's eyes water.

'Today, we will be closer to God than ever before.' Bolingbroke's voice had taken on a dream-like quality.

'Yes, my Lord.'

'Now, now, do not take my word for it, Sir Argyle. This is what you came for after all,' Bolingbroke said.

Argyle turned his head from the sparkling white miracle on the hill and stared directly into two deep ponds of still black water. He stopped dead in his tracks. Barely aware that Bolingbroke had also stopped and was now eying him, Argyle could do nothing to move.

Directly before Argyle, a palanquin moved across the street. Behind the semi-closed shutters, the most extraordinary set of dark brown eyes were staring directly at him. It was all he could see; the rest of the woman's face was covered, above the eyes by layers of thin fabric in an array of colours, held tight to her forehead by a band of gold with small ringlets. Below, her nose and mouth were covered with red muslin. But her eyes - they were curious, dark and enchanting. Argyle quite simply lost his breath just at the sight of those eyes. And then in a moment, they were gone.

'Sir Argyle!' Argyle was called abruptly back to reality by Bolingbroke's forceful voice.

'My Lord. Do forgive me, I was almost …'

'Yes, you were. Now I believe, you have the proper incentive to find that interpreter, would you not say?' Bolingbroke said in a taunting voice.

Argyle nodded, then followed as Bolingbroke once more led the way towards their religious destination - the white church. But Argyle's thoughts were a jumble and he no longer found beauty in his surroundings.

3 February 1393 — Jerusalem

Bolingbroke had been right in his assumptions that the encounter in the marketplace was plenty of reason for Argyle to seek out an interpreter he thought could be trusted. Once Bolingbroke had approved of Argyle's choice, the pilgrimage began in earnest.

Bolingbroke brought those closest to him along to the Mount of Olives and Holy Sepulchre to pay homage and lay down offerings. The interpreter was put to hard work explaining the local customs, ensuring free passage through parts of the city that were mainly Muslim and securing invitations to visit important members of the Christian community in Jerusalem. Bolingbroke brought with him letters of recommendation, some even bearing the royal seal and even this far away from England, it seemed they could open the doors to the houses of a string of important people.

Although the area had long been the centre of religious fighting, the city itself seemed to be a pocket of peace, ready to invite in anyone who came to it with a pure heart. Bolingbroke had been travelling beneath a white flag adorned with an olive branch since they had left Vienna, and the pilgrimage had been welcomed with open arms wherever it set up camp. The same was true of Jerusalem, where Bolingbroke now enjoyed the hospitality of any man of means.

On one such an occasion, Bolingbroke brought Argyle along. 'This is a true honour. I am told the man we are to meet is one of the richest in the land. Though a Turk, I must believe he is cultured and refined.'

'Why now, my Lord?' Argyle hid a smile as Bolingbroke straightened his cloak for the third time.

'Apparently he has been away on business and has only just returned,' Bolingbroke said. 'Upon hearing of our visit, he made it his priority to see us immediately.'

'Then I am twice honoured to be invited.' Argyle inclined his head at Bolingbroke.

'Ah yes, Sir Argyle, and so you should be.'

Bolingbroke seemed in too high spirits. What did he know that Argyle did not? As neither had met the man before surely Bolingbroke did not have the advantage here, Argyle thought. The interpreter, riding a donkey in front of the small entourage of eight, waved enthusiastically and gestured towards a towering orange wall. Bathed in the sunlight of late afternoon, it loomed, casting a formidable shadow across their path.

'This is the place. I shall make the introductions and then leave you here.' The interpreter knocked on the door and gave brief instructions in that highly peculiar tongue that made no sense at all to Argyle.

'If only we could keep him with us. I feel much more at ease when I have someone that knows the language. French will do I suppose.' Bolingbroke motioned his horse forward as the massive wooden gates opened to reveal a Paradise within.

Everyone gasped at the sight and sound of babbling water and singing birds. The courtyard was crowded with colourful ceramic pots filled with beautiful, exotic plants and flowers. Hummingbirds and parrots flew about and water seemed present everywhere.

'They certainly know how to make an impression.' Bolingbroke dismounted and made to greet a man dressed in pure white garments who was speaking to the interpreter before smiling broadly at the visitors. The interpreter made the formal introductions, bowing low first before the man dressed in white and then equally low to Bolingbroke.

'This, my Lord, is Abbas, Murshid, Hajji, Sheik of Samaria,' the interpreter said, turning from Bolingbroke to Abbas. 'And this, Murshid, is the English Lord Bolingbroke, cousin to the King of England and here on a pilgrimage to visit the holy sights. He comes seeking solace and peace.'

Then the two mighty men bowed to each other and Abbas took Bolingbroke's hands into his own and led him to the spring, where they washed their hands together. Argyle observed the strange custom, caught between amusement and wonder, but Bolingbroke seemed to be in his element, readily accepting Abbas' gesture and shaking his hands before accepting a piece of linen adorned with fresh flowers to dry his hands in.

After a few pleasantries in French, Bolingbroke introduced Abbas to the rest of the party. Argyle bowed as the last and was greeted warmly by their host who turned and clapped his hands twice. At this, the doors flew open and dozens of servants carrying silver plates filled with refreshments filled the courtyard.

The horses were taken to the stables and everyone was invited to the inner courtyard where many low tables were laid out for them. Several guests were waiting there and soon the chatter rose to the skies.

'Sir Argyle, come here.' Bolingbroke was in a fine mood, gesturing with much enthusiasm.

'My Lord.'

'This, Abbas, is Sir Argyle, his brother is high in favour with the English King and with me.'

Argyle smiled politely and bowed low before their host. Abbas in return inclined his head and briefly held Argyle's hands in his own before signalling for all to take a seat. Next to Argyle a pillow lay unused. When someone made to sit there, Abbas would shake his head just once and whoever it was found seating elsewhere. After a while, Argyle could not resist the temptation.

'Are you expecting a guest who has not yet arrived?' Argyle asked.

Abbas smiled, his teeth regular and as white as his clothes. 'Ah yes. I am waiting for my favourite to join us.' Argyle was surprised to hear Abbas speaking English, his accent uncommon but pleasant.

Bolingbroke's eyes glistened. 'I see. Then it must be a very special person?'

'Indeed. A magnificent jewel that would adorn any great court.'

As Abbas spoke, a hidden door to the left of the tables opened to reveal a party of ten dancers who began the traditional belly dance that Argyle found to be very peculiar. Bolingbroke was immediately engulfed, marvelling at the dancers' skills and appearance to anyone nearby. Argyle settled back to enjoy the show when something familiar caught his eye. He stared completely mesmerised.

When the dancers had finished their display, one of them left the group and floated towards Abbas' table. In a fluent movement, she removed her veil and reclined on the pillow next to Argyle, who could not but stare. Those eyes.

Abbas smiled at the woman. 'This, my Lords, is my crowning jewel, Najeelah.'

She let her glistening eyes rest briefly on each man around the table, and then settled on Argyle, locking his eyes in a silent struggle, while the others praised her dance and her appearance. When at last Najeelah released his gaze, Argyle was enthralled. She smiled pleasantly at Bolingbroke and accepted the cup of honeyed wine he offered her.

Argyle's brain had gone quite blank. Gone as well were his good manners, his easy way of speaking with anyone. He was left with a tongue that seemed too big for his mouth and nothing intelligent to say. Luckily, Bolingbroke took the lead in the conversation, engaging Najeelah in a praise of Jerusalem and its surroundings.

She seemed happy to speak to him, but her eyes kept returning to Argyle. In the end, Argyle felt quite foolish for not speaking to this beautiful woman who clearly sought his attentions.

'You were splendid in the dance,' Argyle said hesitantly and Najeelah just smiled.

'What a wonderful home you have,' Argyle tried.

'It is not mine,' Najeelah said.

Argyle thought for a while. 'You danced much better than all the others.' He heard his clumsy words and cursed himself.

Najeelah shook her head, the golden ringlets on her headdress sang. 'You must do better.'

'Very well.' Argyle decided to follow a tactic that had often worked with his sisters' friends. 'Tell me about your interests.'

Najeelah smiled in earnest, her eyes shining. 'Oh, where to begin? I find inspiration in books, religion, culture, people …'

They spoke with great ease about many subjects. Argyle was taken aback when Bolingbroke shortly after declared the wonderful evening at an end. It was not until they were outside the gates that Argyle realised it was well past midnight, the moon fat and full above them and thousands of foreign stars sparkling in the black velvet skies.

6 February 1393 — Jerusalem

Bolingbroke was as devout a worshipper as God had ever seen and he insisted on visiting every holy site in Jerusalem over and over again during the day and visiting the richest inhabitants at night. The visit with Abbas had opened every door he could possibly desire. Whenever Bolingbroke was about to leave, Argyle made certain he was not nearby, this way he escaped having to participate in the seemingly never-ending string of visits and could get on with his own work.

Argyle had to admit that he often found himself thinking very little about La Fontaine and very much about all the adventure he was having. He was ashamed to admit it and ashamed that his inquiries were falling desperately short too. It had been hard to probe his fellow pilgrims during their arduous journey from Venice to the Holy Land, and since then there had scarce been a moment not taken up by prayer or dreaming of Najeelah's smouldering eyes burning their way into his mind.

To rid himself of the obsession, he had left camp early to visit Abbas' house, secretly hoping to meet Najeelah, but she was not there and he had to spend some time speaking with Abbas before being able to excuse himself without being impolite.

The same afternoon, after spending hours at the Sacred Mount alongside Bolingbroke, Argyle had finally managed to slip away as the party made its way back to camp. He made up a story of wanting to visit the bazaar to find trinkets to bring home to his sisters. Bolingbroke had given him a scrutinising look, and then released him, asking that Argyle found a few jewels for his wife and daughters too. Argyle had been quick to agree and accept some gold from Bolingbroke's purse.

Now, Argyle found himself weaving through the maze of the bazaar. He had never truly planned to go there, except that Bolingbroke would be even more suspicious if he came back with nothing. Fingering lockets and bracelets in the many stalls, Argyle finally decided on a few choice items and haggled a while to drive the price down. Money and items exchanged hands and when Argyle turned, while tying the little purse to his belt, he was startled to gaze into the eyes, he had been dreaming of for days.

'My Lord.' Najeelah's accent was strange and pleasant; Argyle felt his mouth go dry.

'Princess.'

She smiled at his choice of greeting. Many young women from wealthy families in Jerusalem styled themselves princess, even if they had not a drop of royal blood in their veins. Shaking her head, her hairpiece tinkling lightly, Najeelah denied the title once again. 'You know my name, and I yours.'

'Najeelah.' Argyle made a little bow and Najeelah laughed.

'Come, I shall invite you to tea.'

Argyle followed her, pondering how to tell her, he had tried their strange drink and did not like it. Her two handmaidens followed at some distance, all four of them weaving a way through the crowded bazaar. Najeelah grasped Argyle's sleeve lightly and drew him into a shady archway.

Argyle looked at the worn, wooden door with some concern. 'This does not look like a place serving tea.'

'It does … among other things.' Najeelah smiled at him. 'I know how you like to see women dance. You think it very exotic?' Argyle nodded. Najeelah's eyes sparkled as she pulled him past the intricately carved door. 'Then you must see these women. I have trained with some of them, but they far outdo my feeble attempts.'

Inside, a dusty rainbow of lights lit a high, domed room. In the middle was a stage made of marble, its sides clad in tiles, depicting strange beasts and plants. Around the high vaulted stage were several deep niches set with low tables and plump cushions. Men and women speaking quietly while drinking tea or smoking pipes already occupied many tables. Argyle stared around the room in wonder.

'You do not have these teahouses in England?' Najeelah's voice crept into his ear, her lips so close he could feel her breath.

'No.'

'My handmaidens cannot enter here; I have asked them to buy fabric and jewellery for myself and them. That should keep them occupied for some time.'

'Is this wise, my Lady?'

She clapped her hands and a servant appeared, ushering them to a small alcove, which was dressed in sparkling fabric and lavishly laid out with cushions, sweet treats and tea.

'You wish to know more of my culture, yes?' She sat down and patted the cushion next to her. 'This is a fundamental part of it. The teahouses are for men and women alike. If you look closely, you will see that you are not the only white man here.'

'So I see, though that was not my concern.'

'No, but it is my answer. You are about to experience first hand some of the most essential parts of my culture. Will you deny me the pleasure of indulging in your experience? I can fetch Abbas if you choose?' Najeelah was eying Argyle with equal amounts of amusement and defiance.

'If it is your pleasure to open my eyes to this, I would be loathe to argue.'

'Bravo! The next scene is about to play out now. Just wait and see, they are magnificent.' Najeelah reclined and looking at Argyle patted the pillow next to her once more. He sat down gingerly, already overwhelmed by the warmth, smell and sounds of the teahouse.

'Perhaps you would like a teahouse like this in England, once you have seen what it is about.'

Before he could answer, the musicians began playing and everyone looked to the stage.

ꕥ ꕥ

It was like experiencing life for the first time. The first heartbeat, the first breath of air, the first touch and Argyle had never felt more alive.

In the subdued light of the teahouse, all his senses felt heightened. The dancers were just as she had said, magnificent. They twirled and bent in ways he had never thought possible, their veils and flimsy garments flowing in the hot, scented air.

Najeelah watched him intently. Every time he risked a glance at her, she was openly looking at him and not the stage. At first, Argyle brushed this aside as merely coincidence and the fact that she had trained with some of the dancers, so she would know them and the dances. But as time passed, he could not help feeling that it was he who was her true entertainment.

At a natural pause in the show, she ordered more sweet mint tea brought for them and shook out her hair. It fell like a thick, black cascade down her back, shimmering in the soft orange light. Pouring tea in the tiny glasses, Najeelah smiled at him. 'How are you finding it all?'

'Where to begin? You were right; they are extraordinary. I should wonder what they would say at court, if I brought back a troupe of dancers such as these.' Argyle was infatuated.

'You do not dance in England?'

'We dance, yes, but not like this. The women do dance alone, but it is all much more … restrained.'

'Restrained?' Najeelah looked confused. 'I do not know this word?'

'Measured and planned out, I suppose would be another way of saying it.' Argyle gestured towards the musicians. 'And the music is much different too.'

Argyle felt overwhelmed by the music, the dancers, the tea - and her presence. 'I suppose we must be getting back soon,' he said for good measure.

Rather than agree, Najeelah turned watchful. 'You are bored?'

'No, not at all, but I should not keep you. This was a chance encounter, and one I will treasure always, but …'

Now Najeelah was all smiles again. 'I will treasure it too, but I cannot in truth believe you wish to go now. You have yet to see the dance of Yasmin.'

'Well, I should not like to offend your friend,' Argyle said.

'She is not a friend, it is a special dance.' Najeelah laughed and pushed him back in the pile of cushions. 'I have ordered it just for you. Do not go anywhere. I forbid it.'

He relented and watched her sway away from sight. He sipped the sweet tea and wondered if he would ever grow to like it. When the music began again, a tantalizing drumming sent the rest of his musings floating away. From a sliding door, five dancers emerged. Argyle looked around to find Najeelah but did not. Slightly concerned, he turned back towards the stage, and saw her standing in the middle of the group of dancers, wearing clothes that any English woman would never be seen wearing, not even in the privacy of her own rooms.

Argyle felt his throat go dry; he was powerless to keep his eyes off Najeelah, as she began swaying seductively to the pining tones of the sitars. Slowly, the rest of the dancers fell in, writhing and flirting with the spectators, gliding off the stage to move around the room, picking out men or women to dance before.

The hairs on his arms and neck rose as Najeelah broke free from the other dancers, trailing her way across the room, shedding one veil after another as she danced ever closer to Argyle. His breath caught in his throat as Najeelah stopped before him, slowly bending backwards, her hands and arms making intricate patterns in the air, the veils tied to her wrists and upper arms flowing and touching him lightly.

As the music stopped, the dancers held their poses, and Najeelah daringly fixed Argyle's gaze with a glittering look. She slowly stood up, her upper body covered only by a few strands of fabric, her pantaloons cut so low, Argyle could not help but stare at the golden bands around her waist, the thin chains that caressed her belly.

Najeelah smiled knowingly, and reached out a slender hand. Argyle grabbed it and clumsily helped her sit down, never taking his eyes off her. As the music began once more, afternoon slid into night.

CHAPTER 25

8 February 1393 — Jerusalem

The little teahouse became their private haven. They would meet as if by chance in the bazaar, and Najeelah would send her handmaidens away, asking them to buy cloth, gems or exotic food to bring home. Argyle asked whether her handmaidens could be trusted and Najeelah laughed and brushed the subject aside. He wondered if perhaps they were more loyal servants than any in England.

'They think you are slow to learn,' Najeelah would tease and he would leave it at that feeling colour rise on his neck and up his jaw. 'They also think, I am tasked a most boring job of showing you around the city, they are bored and like nothing more than to go home.'

When night claimed the city and cooled the air that night, she brought him to the rooftop of the tearoom, where she had showed him the stars and told him tales. He was spellbound and hoped she was too. Argyle knew that her dancing for him that afternoon in the tearoom was more than just a show of her skills. Najeelah's eyes had never left his, her enticing moves had been just for him, she must have known there and then that Argyle was hers, body and soul.

This night, Najeelah was toying with her plait underneath her colourful thin veils while she looked across the flat rooftops. Her back was turned slightly and he could freely enjoy her silhouette in the moonlight. A couple of times, Argyle made to reach for her then stopped. Najeelah had never indicated she was not interested and yet he still felt uncertain. It was a new feeling to him because in England, he knew what the girls expected. He knew how to dance with them, he knew how far he could go, and he certainly would never see an English woman in such a state of undress, as he had seen Najeelah. Argyle pondered where to go from here.

'You are very quiet,' Najeelah said.

'I am enjoying the view.'

'I hope so,' she teased.

'The moon and stars are so much brighter here than at home. Does the sky ever cloud over?' Argyle said feebly trying to keep the conversation going.

'Ask the astronomers.' There was laughter in Najeelah's reply as she turned around.

'Very well. What would you have me speak of?' Argyle did not want to be annoyed with her, but he was.

You have told me about your family and the English court, you have even told me about that knight and your journey here. Yet I feel you are leaving out something.' Najeelah's hand crept towards his and she intertwined her fingers with his. Argyle tensed a little and then relaxed when she simply sat before him, holding his hand.

'What might that be?' Resting on his knees, Argyle felt for her other hand. She gave it freely.

'I like to think myself clever,' Najeelah said. 'You are searching for something.'

'Very clever.'

She acknowledged this with a slight nod that sent a strand of hair grazing her cheek. For a while they sat quietly looking at each other.

'Tell me. I can keep a secret,' Najeelah whispered.

'I am sure.' Argyle leaned back a little and she followed his movement, her hair flowing forward as she leaned in, fixing his gaze.

'I like secrets,' Najeelah said. 'They make life worth living.'

'Some do. Perhaps this is not such a secret.' Argyle felt tongue-tied.

'Come now. We are alone, the moon may listen but it never speaks.' Najeelah smiled.

'This is …' Argyle paused, he felt completely at ease and entirely tense at the same time. He trusted Najeelah and yet something in the very back of his head told him to keep quiet.

She let go of his hands and sat back. 'You do not trust me.'

'Yes, I do. But I do not trust that you would be safe, if you knew. Much and more has happened already on this trip to warrant my concern in telling anyone,' Argyle said passionately.

Najeelah's lips tightened. 'I shall be the judge of that. Do you think me safe now?'

'Yes.'

'Then you are a fool! Do you think Abbas has sanctioned my many excursions? That my mother has?' Najeelah had leaned in but now she sat back, clearly furious. Perplexed, Argyle reached out for her hand trying to recapture the moment, the intimacy. She pulled it back.

'Najeelah … I did not think. I am sorry,' Argyle said. 'Let us look once more at the moon and be content to be here; now. See what secrets do?'

'Yes. But without secrets and adventures, what is left?' The sadness in her voice and eyes pierced Argyle's heart.

He tried to lift her spirits. 'Life.'

'For you, perhaps, but not for me. Mine is to be a life in seclusion. I was content it was so, and then there you were. You made me feel alive again. Now every day I fear the moment you leave.' Waving at his worried frown, Najeelah continued with a small smile. 'I give my heart freely. Take it without guilt, as I plan to take yours.'

Najeelah turned her back to him once more, her plaited hair falling to her waist. This time, Argyle reached for her. He slid his hand into her veils, the wispy cool silk embracing his wrist. He followed the veils to her intricate golden headpiece and then slowly began to unfasten the veils.

One by one they floated down to nestle on the rooftop tiles. Argyle placed the golden headpiece on top of the little pile. Najeelah sat perfectly still as Argyle began loosening her plait, his hands brushing lightly against her back as he worked his way up towards the nape of her neck.

She sighed quietly, tilting her head slightly to the side, her loose hair cascading down her left shoulder, the right one exposed but for a little sleeve. Argyle traced the line of her shoulder, reaching slowly around to her collarbone. He could feel her skin burn beneath his touch when he pushed her thin sleeve down. It gave way as if it had simply been waiting for this moment. Najeelah tensed for the tiniest moment, straightening her neck, her hair brushing along her back and over his hand. Her move made her dress fall down around the small of her back.

For a while Argyle sat behind her, not quite sure how to proceed. She was like a statue carved in precious golden wood. Najeelah's shoulders moved ever so slightly with every breath she took.

Once more, Argyle reached for her, feeling her give way under his hands. He turned her slowly, her hair spilling forward, momentarily hiding her face. Then Najeelah looked up and shook her hair back behind her shoulders. She truly was the most amazing creature Argyle had ever laid eyes on. His fingers seemed to get a life of their own as they traced along the lines of her face and down her neck.

Then her hands found their way inside his shirt, sending shivers through his body.

ꟷ

Back in the camp, Argyle stole from tent to tent, constantly watching to see if he was being followed.

For weeks he had had a knot in his stomach, a sensation that while all seemed well, it was not and tonight after he had returned Najeelah to her home, the sensation had overwhelmed him. Without knowing why he had threaded his way back to camp through the narrow alleyways of Jerusalem, even scaling low walls to make sure he was alone. Yet, even in the safety of the camp, Argyle felt uneasy.

'My Lord.'

Argyle almost jumped out of his own skin. 'Yes?' He turned to face a young boy dressed in Bolingbroke's colours. 'What is it?'

'You looked lost, can I help you?' the boy said boldly.

'No,' Argyle said. 'What are you doing here at this hour?'

'My Lord Bolingbroke asked us to keep an eye out in the camp - seems there have been pilfering going on of late. A little trinket going astray here and there, some food, other supplies.' The boy had an unnerving air about him.

'Ah well, I had best not keep you from your duties,' Argyle said. 'Be off with you.' The boy did not move. 'Unless you wish to turn out my pockets?' Argyle ventured and finally, the boy seemed to realise with whom he was speaking.

'My Lord, I do apologise, no of course I need not see …' The boy's voice trailed off and he bowed low.

'Sir Argyle.' Lockley's cold, smug voice announced him before Argyle could make him out.

'Hiding in the shadows, Lockley?'

'As much as any man at this hour,' Lockley said. 'Be off, boy! I would have a word with Sir Argyle here.'

The boy darted away, weaving his way through the camp and was soon swallowed up by the astounding dark that always coated Jerusalem at night.

'Out on a midnight stroll, Sire?' Lockley grabbed Argyle's arm and forced him along.

'I could ask the same of you, Lockley, but I think the answer would be equally disappointing to me, as mine would be to you,' Argyle said, wrenching free but walking along with Lockley. The two of them headed away from the main encampment.

'My Lord Bolingbroke was concerned for your wellbeing. He called on your tent earlier and was surprised to see you weren't there,' Lockley said.

Argyle brushed his hair back, the smell of Najeelah still lingered on his skin. 'Lord Bolingbroke has given us all free rein of the camp and Jerusalem. I was paying homage at the Holy Mount and lost track of time.'

'You were certainly paying homage at some mount … but I doubt its holiness very much.' Even though Argyle could not see Lockley's face, the man's smirk was plain in his voice. 'Beware the allure of the city, Sire, there will come a day when you shall have to depart. Best not to leave anything behind that cannot be easily forgotten.'

This time Argyle grabbed Lockley by the arm and pulled him in. 'What are you implying?'

'Only that what you desire most in the world is conflicting, I think, with what you came here to do.' Lockley's icy voice rattled Argyle. 'I suggest you let go of me.'

'And if I do not?' Argyle snarled.

'Perhaps it has escaped your notice, but we are far from the tents now - far enough that no one would know how you came to be here, with a dagger in your throat,' Lockley said quietly.

Argyle felt a cool blade graze his jaw and jerked his head back, but Lockley's hand followed suit. 'I told Bolingbroke from the beginning that you being here was a bad omen. You are as rotten as that meddling brother of yours and I intend to prove it!' In the moonlight, Lockley smiled viciously. 'And who would Bolingbroke believe, huh? His sworn ally - or a Mowbray brat?'

Argyle released Lockley's arm and felt for his own blade. As soon as his fingers closed around the hilt, Argyle sidestepped quickly, drawing the dagger just in time to fend off Lockley's lunge. The two short blades met at full force, the sharp encounter of metal ringing out into the dead of night.

Lockley circled Argyle, watchful and with his dagger stretched out before him. Argyle followed his movements but stayed still. Then Lockley spun around to his right and thrust forward again, narrowly missing Argyle's thigh. Despite the cool night air, Argyle felt beads of sweat work their way down his back. Lockley advanced again and Argyle grabbed for his attacker's left arm, whirling away from the sharp blade, spinning Lockley with him. When the two fell to the sandy ground, Argyle felt a sharp twinge as Lockley's dagger met the flesh just beneath his left elbow. Argyle pushed Lockley hard against the ground, Lockley spitting out curses and sand and wriggling to avoid Argyle's blade.

Argyle hit him square in the face, drawing blood as Lockley's nose cracked under the force of the blow. Lockley rolled away, wrenching free from Argyles grasp, Lockley's sleeve giving way in the struggle. The ripping sound was as loud as thunder in Argyle's ears.

In the distance, a few flickering dots appeared; someone in camp had heard their struggle. Argyle could hear muffled shouts coming in their direction. Lockley made his move, jumping at Argyle, dagger raised like a sword, and when Argyle spun aside, his wounded arm took the full blow of Lockley's body. Argyle bit down hard not to scream out loud.

Torches danced towards Argyle and Lockley, who seemed to decide it was time to stop. Holding up his left hand in a disarming gesture, Lockley slid his dagger back in its scabbard with his right hand before wiping his bloody nose. 'Enough for now.'

'Another time, and another place, I shall have my own revenge for what you did to La Fontaine. But not here,' Argyle sheathed his dagger.

'You can always try,' Lockley grinned, his face streaked with dirt, sand and blood. 'When they arrive, you and I were just out for a friendly walk when we were attacked by villains.'

'I certainly was attacked by a villain!' Argyle said.

9 February 1393 — Camp outside Jerusalem

Argyle heard voices outside his tent and sat up slowly, careful to spare his wounded elbow. He licked his lips, feeling the swelling from last night's exertions. As he was trying to get up, the tent flaps were pushed open. Argyle fell back clumsily and looked at his visitor.

'My Lord.' The man's olive skin, black hair and colourful clothes were so strange to see at camp that Argyle did not know what to make of it all.

'Who are you?'

'Abbas sent me,' the man said, waving at a young girl, who was carrying a big, lumpy bag. Her face shone with sweat from the effort of keeping up with the lean, long-legged man, and from the struggle of carrying her heavy burden. 'I am Marsal, physician to Abbas and his entire household.'

Marsal signalled to the girl to put down the bag. 'This is Shanta.' The girl stood completely still next to the bag, her eyes fixed on the sandy ground.

'Nice to meet you,' Argyle said suddenly acutely aware that he was naked but for his thin sheet, which was wrapped loosely around his midriff not really hiding anything. 'Please forgive my appearance …'

'Shanta must get used to it if she is to succeed me. Naked men are just the same as naked women … well almost.' Marsal smiled sardonically as Shanta blushed, her olive skin turning darker, and Argyle laughed shortly, his ribs protesting wildly.

'It was kind of Abbas, but how did he know …' Argyle cut his sentence short. How did Abbas know? Then it dawned on him. 'Bolingbroke.'

'Yes, the Lord Bolingbroke sent word that a physician was required in camp.' Marsal began rummaging around in the bag, sighing and muttering as he took up small glass bottles, little packages and strips of linen. 'Clearly, he was right to do so.'

Argyle winced when fresh pain shot through his arm. 'We have a physician in the camp.'

'Yes, an English one,' Marsal said simply as if that explained everything. He picked out two small cloth packages and unwrapped them carefully.

'Shanta, fetch me water - a big pitcher I think.' Marsal turned to Argyle. 'And now that the girl is out, you can get dressed - or undressed, whatever you desire.'

Argyle blushed a little, as he let the sheet drop and tried to pull up his breeches. He groaned at the effort, his bruises were acting up and he could feel the wound near his elbow threaten to burst.

'I shall examine you, as soon as Shanta is back.' Marsal sat down on the cot next to Argyle.

'She is to be a physician?' Argyle asked to pass the time and shake the feeling that Marsal's being here was about much more than a few bruises.

Marsal smiled, his teeth white in the olive face. 'Yes. She will be a fine physician in her own time. She is still young, but she has all the makings of a great healer.'

Argyle nodded. 'And you feel confident sending her into a camp full of English soldiers?'

'Yes, the whole camp knows she is here with me to treat you,' Marsal said simply, measuring out the herbs from the small packages and laying out some of the linen strips. 'If your elbow is not treated, the wound will fester in the heat and take your life.'

His matter-of-fact manners were a strange solace to Argyle, who let Marsal feel around the wound, gritting his teeth when Marsal prodded the wound with a thin needle. 'I may have to stitch this up.'

'Really?' Argyle cleared his throat.

Marsal nodded absentmindedly. 'Yes, we cannot have you dying at our doorstep.' He turned towards the opening in the tent, where Shanta appeared with a large pitcher of water. She tottered when her little slipper caught the rough spun carpet that covered most of the tent floor, and Argyle caught her by the elbow.

Shanta smiled shyly. 'I thank you.' Her accent was thick but pleasing and Argyle nodded briefly.

Marsal got up, pouring his measured herb-mixture into a pewter cup before sloshing water on it and stirring vigorously. 'This water is not sufficiently warm, silly girl,' he scolded, sending Shanta back into the blazing sun to heat up the cup. 'Learning she might be, but she is … Ah … I do not know the word.'

'Willing?' Argyle suggested, but Marsal just smiled at him a glimmer of humour in his eyes.

'Now, let us begin the examination. Shanta, tell me what is wrong with the man.' Shanta had slipped back into the tent so quietly that Argyle had not even noticed her.

Now she stepped forward slowly, her slender hands tentatively reaching for his arm, her fingers searching around the wound. Shanta muttered as she went, Marsal nodding or shaking his head here and there. Finally, she let go of Argyle's elbow and turned her big, light-brown eyes at Marsal.

The two of them quickly exchanged words in their language. Najeelah had tried to teach Argyle a few words, but they did not come out right and the only result was that Najeelah had laughed so hard that she was breathless. Since then, Argyle had given up his attempts, satisfied that he could communicate with anyone he needed to through the interpreter, Bolingbroke had hired. For the rest, he had to get by with gestures.

Shanta shook her head, her thick black braid swinging across her back, but Marsal seemed to get the last word, because she turned around to face Argyle.

'I must clean,' she said slowly. Argyle nodded; of course she had to clean the wound. Marsal waved her on, and Shanta summoned what seemed to be a considerable amount of courage. 'I … it will pain.'

'No matter, do what needs to be done,' Argyle said, and Shanta nodded sombrely before prowling through the big bag to find the tools she needed.

Once she had fetched the brew from a small fire outside Argyle's tent, Shanta sat tentatively on the cot next to Argyle, looking intently at the wound. Argyle reached for the cup, but Shanta pulled it away. 'Not for drink,' she said firmly.

'No, my Lord, it is not for drinking, this is for the wound.' Marsal smiled. 'If you need a drink, I shall send a boy to fetch wine?'

'No, there is no need,' Argyle said, looking at Shanta's hands that were now soaking strips of linen in the cup; she looked up briefly and blushed when she caught Argyle's eye. She looked at the wound again.

'Well, can it be saved?' Argyle asked to relieve the awkward situation.

'I am sure,' Shanta said and with much flourish, she produced out a long woollen cord from her sleeve.

Looking over at Marsal for his approval, she snapped the cord back before whipping it precisely across Argyle's wound. Argyle bit down so hard, he could taste blood from where his teeth had caught the inside of his cheek. Shanta glanced up before proceeding and Argyle could see the wound was open, lazily pulsing blood and pus.

'Good!' Marsal said from his safe distance at the other end of the cot. 'It is best if the wound cleans itself, after Shanta will bandage it. You should not …,' Marsal searched for the word, '… do too much these next days. No trouble.'

'No trouble,' Argyle agreed, gritting his teeth, when Shanta pushed the wound together to help the muddled stream of blood along.

Marsal got up and came to see, how Shanta was doing. He seemed pleased with her work, said a few words to her and then excused himself. 'I am to see another patient. Shanta will help you.'

Argyle smiled vaguely and Marsal left the tent. Shanta seemed engulfed by her work with the wound, and slowly Argyle felt the pressure in his elbow diminish. Her cool linen strips were a pleasure and Argyle was even more pleased when Shanta indicated that she at least did not seem to think there was any need for sowing.

'My Lord?' Shanta spoke so softly, Argyle hardly heard her. 'My Lord,' she tried again.

'Yes?' Argyle's eyes were still closed to the newfound joy of having a woman treat his wound.

'You must have care,' Shanta said. Argyle looked at her, but she was staring intently at the wound. 'You must have care when you meet.'

Argyle frowned. 'Meet?'

'When you meet her - you must have care. They know.' Shanta finally looked up, her light-brown eyes guarded. 'They know you meet Najeelah.'

Argyle felt his heart sink. 'Who knows?'

'They …' Shanta paused, trying to find the right words. 'Abbas, the Lord Bolingbroke. She think they know. And Marsal - he knows too.'

'Marsal?' Argyle asked in disbelief.

Shanta nodded, tying a neat knot on top of her bandage before leaning back. 'Marsal is physician to all Abbas' women.' Shanta dried her hands in a spare piece of linen. 'I … just have care.'

Argyle bit his lip, if Shanta was right, if they all knew then Najeelah was in far more danger than he was. Argyle grabbed Shanta's hand. 'Can you get a message to Najeelah? Can you tell her …' She stiffened at the grasp, turning her startling, light-brown eyes to his face.

Argyle felt a surge of passion that Shanta seemed to mistake for interest. She pinched his wrist and turned towards the opening in the tent just as Marsal entered. Argyle saw her neck was blushing.

'I am done,' Shanta said, throwing the small herb packages back into the big bag, closing it with a snap. She turned to Argyle. 'No trouble, my Lord.' Shanta stared at Argyle with great determination.

'No trouble,' Argyle agreed once more as Shanta left the tent.

Marsal lingered in the opening. 'Best to stay in camp while you heal. Then perhaps later, we shall speak again … perhaps,' Marsal said, tasting the word.

Argyle nodded and Marsal nodded at the cup with the warm herb mixture. 'Also good for bruises,' he said as way of farewell.

Good for bruises, Argyle thought, was that a hidden message or simply a physician's advice to his patient. He knew then and there that his promise to Shanta to stay out of trouble would be extremely hard to keep.

ꕥ ꕥ ꕥ ꕥ

10 February 1393 — Jerusalem

In the early hours of the morning, a dark shadow crept from tent to tent, head hidden in the depth of a cloak, soft leather boots not making a sound on the sandy surface. It kept looking over its shoulder from time to time as if expecting to be followed. But all was quiet in the camp.

As the sun spread its first warming rays over the tents, brushing away the damp of the night, the shadow was long since gone, horse and all.

The morning was broken by a booming voice demanding the attendance of Stephen Smith. A scurry of squires spread out through the tents and shortly after brought back Stephen, not quite awake yet.

In the presence of Bolingbroke, Stephen was asked to explain himself. 'M' … M'lord?'

'I said, explain yourself!' Bolingbroke was fuming with rage. For once no heaters were fired up, and yet the tent was thick with heat, no doubt most of it generated by the man himself.

'I … I don't know what to explain, M'lord?' Stephen said weakly.

'Is that so? Then allow me to make it clearer! Lockley is missing!' Bolingbroke's voice was icy and sharp. 'Now, what say you to that?'

It seemed like an eternity passed, before Stephen finally spoke. 'I didn't know, M'lord. Perhaps Lockley has the early watch, or saw something that made him want to investigate. He's left no word with me.' His voice gathering some strength, Stephen continued. 'M'lord, you yourself demanded a vigil watch while we camp here. Mayhap he took it to heart? Have you asked the other soldiers?'

'I should think not. I asked for watchmen, not knights to do it for them. Lockley is not so very stupid that he would risk his own neck for anyone - including his own men.' Bolingbroke had deflated somewhat, but was still extremely watchful.

At this moment, Argyle pushed open the tent-flaps. He had heard the exchange from outside the tent, faking a sudden urge to check his boots for holes. Now, Argyle strode straight to the centre of the tent, resting a hand on Stephen's shoulder. 'My Lord. If Smith says he knows nothing then I believe him.'

It was a gamble. While Bolingbroke had long acknowledged that he now trusted Argyle, he was still unsure what might happen if he ever stood up to Bolingbroke. Now, Argyle felt he had no option. Even without speaking to Stephen, Argyle felt sure he knew nothing.

'Perhaps I can ask my Lord to explain what this is about? I apologise for being late, I was attending the horses when word reached me. Otherwise I should have been here much sooner, and so I have missed the point, I am afraid.' Standing his ground, Argyle looked Bolingbroke in the eye.

'Very well. Under the veil of night - it is uncommonly dark here in God's own land, I have observed - it appears Lockley has seen fit to disappear. I am now enquiring whether this man knew. That is after all my prerogative in my own camp, would you not say, Sire?!' If Bolingbroke was looking for a fight he would not find it with Argyle who bowed his head as if in despair and grabbed Stephen by the arm.

'That is grievous news, my Lord. Did you know, Smith?'

'No, I swear it! I don't know nothing!' Stephen cried, concealing his relief to be saved.

'Perhaps I should make enquiries around the camp, my Lord? Someone must have seen something. We are strongly guarded and many boys are up early to feed the horse, tend the fires and such,' Argyle said to appease Bolingbroke's wrath.

Surprisingly, Bolingbroke relented. 'Very well - as long as you report all to me. Take this one with you, perhaps he is happy to share with a friend, if not with me.' Bolingbroke waved them out without another glance.

ꕤ ꕤ

Outside the tent, Argyle pulled Stephen aside and tightened his grasp. Stephen gasped, eyes wide at the sudden pain.

'If you do know anything, now is the time to confess! I shall not judge, you are in his service, but know that if you keep something from me that is discovered later, Bolingbroke will spare no efforts in punishing you.' To this Argyle added a fierce stare that made Stephen cringe.

'I'm innocent! I knew nothing.' Stephen's voice cracked. 'They woke me, for the love of God; I wasn't even awake when Lockley's disappearance was discovered! How would I know? He may've taken me on but he isn't one to confide in anyone, save perhaps Lord Bolingbroke. And they seem to've had a falling out a while back, which didn't lighten Lockley's mood.'

Argyle released his grasp and Stephen rubbed his bruised arm. So this was what it had come to. He had hoped that Lockley's startling speech in Argyle's tent before they reached Jerusalem had gone no further than to Bolingbroke. Now he had to wonder how many knew? Was Lockley truly gone or had someone got rid of him - in the failed belief of doing Bolingbroke a favour?

'You do believe me, don't you?' Stephen was shaking.

ꕤ ꕤ

CHAPTER 26

13 February 1393 — Jerusalem

In camp, enemies surrounded Argyle though he was blind to see them. He resumed his inquiries about La Fontaine's death, striking up conversations with pages, squires and knights alike. Lockley's disappearance had made Argyle's work much easier as many willingly declared their distrust and dislike for Lockley, happy to share all that they knew. And yet it seemed that Argyle could not get any further in his discoveries; it was as if Jerusalem had a strange spell over the entire camp, lulling everyone into a daze in the warm, dry sunlight and the pitch-black nights.

In the daytime, Argyle resumed his duties of escorting Bolingbroke around Jerusalem. Argyle excused his previous behaviour with an upset bowel, which many in the camp had experienced due to the strange food and perhaps drinking water straight from the wells in town.

At night, Argyle would meet Najeelah, exploring the hot baths of the hammam and visiting several other teahouses in and around the bazaar. Once he had asked her if they were being too carefree. Najeelah had laughed and thrown her arms around his neck, covering his face in kisses pressing her body against his. That was the end of such speculations.

Argyle began feeling safe and then late one afternoon as he was getting ready for his nightly excursion, Stephen slipped into his tent. 'I've news.'

'Go on.'

'Lockley. I'm sure, he was planning something.'

Argyle frowned; his friend had previously been reluctant to open up about Lockley's movements, Argyle had warned Stephen not to keep anything from him. Before he disappeared, Lockley had been mysteriously gone for days on end, only coming back at dusk and skirting Bolingbroke whenever he could. Actually, he had acted much as Argyle, leading him to think Lockley might also have found some comfort in the town.

Argyle shook out a shirt of thin linen. 'There are several brothels that many of the men frequent. Perhaps he is simply there? Hiding at the bosom of a friendly woman.'

Stephen shook his head. 'Lockley's shown no interest in women, not here. As a matter of fact, he hardly ever left to go through the city gates at all, unless under direct orders from Lord Bolingbroke.'

'Then where?' Argyle asked.

'The day before he disappeared, I tried to follow him. No easy feat, there's scarcely a bump or bush to hide behind,' Stephen gestured; the landscape was very flat just here, making it a good place for a camp, and a bad place to try and spy on someone. 'I managed without being seen, I think.'

Argyle tucked the shirt into his breeches. 'Why wait until now to tell me?'

'I was scared,' Stephen said. 'Lockley'd been acting very strange - ever since Constantinople. I began wondering at the things you told me, and what you'd found out in Venice, putting it all together. He was hiding something.'

Argyle forgot all about his plans to see Najeelah. This could be the answer to a million questions presenting itself to him, the King's mission perhaps solved as easily as snapping your fingers. But in order to discover if indeed Stephen was the key to solving the wider mystery of La Fontaine's death, Argyle would have to hear him out and leave no question unanswered. Argyle had doubted if his oath to the King, his loyalty to the country he loved held more sway than even Najeelah's alluring eyes and easy company, now he was about to find out.

Argyle settled in his chair, motioning for Stephen to continue. 'Lockley went to a small oasis. There he waited for the longest time. I swear; I lost the feeling in my legs from squatting behind the only bit of rock for miles around. At length, Coxcombe appeared.'

'Coxcombe?!' Argyle was dumbfounded.

'Threw me too. I couldn't hear all, being far away and I couldn't creep closer, but they clearly had words.' Stephen winced at the memory. 'Lockley was livid and Coxcombe looked terrified before they parted ways. I heard some bits and pieces, but they made no sense to me.'

'Go on, I have to know it all. Do you promise you will leave nothing out?' Argyle asked.

Stephen nodded grim-faced and poured down half a cup of wine in one go. 'Yes. I know things haven't gone right between us, and I'm sorry for the part I played in that. Well, you already know that Lockley didn't exactly give me any choice …' Stephen paused to reflect. 'But I suppose I should've trusted you more than I did at the time. I was scared and alone, in my mind I'd betrayed not only you, but all of England too.'

Argyle let Stephen get his bearings, best if he began his tale on his own, Argyle could always ask questions, if need be.

'It actually began in Calais.' Stephen cleared his throat. 'When we first arrived, I's approached by a mysterious man who wanted to know where I was in service. I was so proud to be part of your retinue that I readily answered, and I swear, he looked like he wanted to kill me there and then.'

Argyle scratched his cheek; this was worrying news. 'Is he part of the pilgrimage?'

'He was for a while, I think. At least as far as Vienna, but since then I don't remember seeing him anywhere. I suppose he found what he was looking for …' Stephens voice trailed off as Argyle's squire entered the tent, clearly surprised to see them sitting there.

'Thank you, I will not need you any more tonight,' Argyle said lightly to the boy, sending him off with a dismissing wave.

'Is he gone, d'you think?' Stephen asked, fear in his face.

'He is just a boy.' Argyle got up just the same and went to peer out the opening of the tent, his squire nowhere to be seen. 'He is gone.'

'Good. If anything, I've learned that the camp has both ears and eyes, and none are to be trusted.' Stephen's neck reddened a little. 'I mean, I trust you, of course, but hardly anything gets past Lord Bolingbroke's spies, or whoever else has sent spies along for the journey.'

'Spies?' Argyle asked contemplating how much Bolingbroke really knew about his nightly excursions.

Stephen seemed to have read his mind. 'Most of us know that you slip from camp at dusk and don't return until early in the morning. It's naught to me, but others've been worried to see you always skulking near Abbas' palace.' Stephen smiled widely. 'I, for one, think you're wooing some maid or other, but there are those who think Abbas is paying you to spy for him, to tell him what Bolingbroke's doing, and who he's meeting. While they play a good game of straight faces in this wretched town, everyone knows that the Christians and the Turks're only just rubbing along.'

'Well, I am no spy!' Argyle forced a laugh thinking about his mission for the King and his affair with Najeelah. 'Not for Abbas.'

Stephen nodded. 'I've never mentioned our agreement these many weeks since we made it. And I'll take it to the grave with me if needs be.'

'I am glad to hear it.' Argyle offered a little more wine, but Stephen declined.

'I long for ale. And I long for England, for people I know and understand, for a place to call my own - oh, I even long for the cold English maids!' Stephen added with emphasis. Argyle nodded along, although he did not long for any of it, save perhaps the ale.

'Ale I cannot produce, but hopefully you can tell your tale without it?' Argyle asked. 'I will be sure to have you always stocked with ale when we return to England.'

Stephen's smile faltered a little. 'Do you think, we will return?'

'Yes, why not?'

'Cause some nights I wake from a terrible nightmare. We're both of us in jail, here in this hellhole. We're starving and thirsting, and we know we'll die here. I don't know what our crimes are, but they'll never release us!' Despite the dry heat in the tent, Stephen trembled. 'The mind is a curious thing, ain't it? Always playing tricks.'

Argyle simply nodded not wanting Stephen to stop talking. 'But that's not what I came here to say. Now where was I … the man from Calais. He was old, his hair grey, and his clothes showed no signs of any house he might belong to. But when he spoke, he sounded like an English lord. I suppose that's why I didn't hesitate to tell him that I was in your service. Though afterwards, I wondered why he'd singled me out.'

Stephen kicked his heel in the sandy carpet on the floor of the tent, little clouds of dust swirled around. 'I remember seeing him again in Vienna, a day or so before you asked me for directions to the northern gate. A day or two before … well, yes.' Stephen rubbed his cheek absentmindedly, as if trying to rub away the pain of his old bruises. 'He came to speak with Lockley, but he wasn't in his rooms. When the man saw me, he almost fled from the inn. It wasn't till much later that I realised that it was the same man. There're always people coming and going, I never really bothered to look at their faces.'

Argyle half-smiled. This was true; there was never any shortage of strangers coming or going in the camp, not even now, so far away from England. Still, if this was the same man, Argyle had seen Lockley with in Vienna it stood to reason that he was more important than Argyle had previously thought.

'In the weeks after I joined Lockley's service, I'm sure I was being followed wherever I went.' Stephen pushed on. 'That's why I acted so distant to you. That and 'cause I thought I might keep you safe if I pretended we weren't friends no more. Lockley might not've liked the other travellers, but he loathed you.'

'Oh, I know,' Argyle said. 'When Lockley and I were attacked by villains, there was only one villain - and it was not me.'

Stephen looked puzzled for a moment and then he understood. 'Lockley?!'

'Yes, and if someone at camp had not heard us fighting, I think only one of us would have survived,' Argyle said. 'Truth be told, I could not tell you if it would have been me or him.'

'Thank God, I alerted the others then.' Stephen breathed, and seeing Argyle's confusion, he continued. 'I knew Lockley was out, so I was – well - spying a little myself. I'd gotten it into my head that perhaps Lockley was the spy. He disappeared almost every night, and I thought it was very strange. So, I took it upon myself to do a little nosing around.' Stephen coloured. 'Though I never found out where he went all those nights, at least I might've saved your life.'

'I am sure you did,' Argyle said. 'But were you the one to tell Bolingbroke of my injuries?'

Stephen looked shameful. 'No. I sent others looking to see what was making all that noise, but I didn't go myself. I was afraid. What if it was Lockley fighting off the Turks? Or some other unknown enemy? I could hardly go there and be found out to be spying on my own master! And I don't know who told Lord Bolingbroke of your injuries or Lockley's for that matter. I only know that, the very next day, that strange physician showed up with that pretty girl in tow and went straight to your tent.'

'Straight to my tent?' Argyle asked. 'He did not first visit Bolingbroke?'

'No, I would've known. I was waiting for Lockley at the outskirts of camp, on that mound just east of the city gates. You know the place where you can see everyone coming and going ?' Stephen wrung his hands. 'I'd gone to see Lockley, and he threw me out, shouting that I was cursed and that all his misfortunes're my fault. I was on the mound trying to find out where he might go in his state when that man arrived.'

'Marsal,' Argyle said. 'The physician's name is Marsal, and the young girl is Shanta.'

'Ah,' Stephen said. 'Well she's a fine girl, wasn't she?'

'You never miss a pretty face, do you?'

Stephen grinned. 'No, there're plenty of exotic women here, no doubt, but not many my age come willingly to a camp full of unwashed, unshaven and rugged Englishmen.' Argyle laughed heartily as Stephen continued. 'I wondered how they knew where your tent was. You don't have a banner or anything. It's not even that much bigger than a soldier's tent. The same goes for Lockley's and still, despite the two being as far apart as our camp can muster, this Marsal found them without asking any directions.'

'Are you quite sure he did not speak to anyone?' Argyle asked.

'Hardly anyone was up really. The heat makes the men sleep in, and the watch'd changed at sunrise. No, he just went straight to your tent,' Stephen insisted, finally succumbing to his thirst and accepting a cup of wine.

Argyle pondered this for a while. 'If he spoke to no one, and he went straight from my tent to Lockley's, Abbas must have spies in camp.'

'Probably. He's the means to pay off as many as he likes. I've heard several of the senior soldiers comparing experiences in Abbas' harem. Surely he can pay them any way they like,' Stephen added.

'Surely,' Argyle said, a terrible thought clutching at him. If Abbas could pay anyone any way he liked, with the women of his harem, what was to say that Najeelah was not simply payment for some service or other Argyle had unknowingly rendered. He balled his fist and breathed deeply.

'But my main concern's another,' Stephen said, resting his elbows on his knees. 'My main concern's a strange document that I saw in Lockley's possession, which is now missing.'

'What?' Argyle asked quickly.

Stephen looked up. 'A document.'

'Be more specific.'

'A document with a big seal on it. I never truly saw the seal, mind you, but I've only ever seen one of them before.' Stephen shrank back a little, as Argyle moved closer. 'I saw one once in Coxcombe's study back in England. Before the tourney, before La Fontaine …'

'La Fontaine died,' Argyle said harshly. 'Tell me what kind of document.'

'An order of some sort.' Stephen fiddled with his cup. 'I couldn't say for sure which seal was on this one, but the one in Coxcombe's was the King's.'

Argyle's breath caught, and he staggered backwards to his chair. 'The King's?'

'Aye, I remember asking what seal it was and one of Coxcombe's men speaking out of turn. He got such severe punishment afterwards that no one in the house ever spoke of it again,' Stephen said. 'But as I say, I can't swear that it's the same seal on Lockley's document.'

Argyle felt numb. All the cards had fallen into his lap, and now he found, he did not want to play his hand. He did not want any of this to be true. Considering for a very long while, Argyle tried to make out if Stephen too was a spy sent to muddy the waters, but Stephen just sat there, his honest gaze on Argyle.

'I know this is pointless, but I have to ask,' Argyle finally said. 'Who sent you tonight?'

Stephen frowned. 'No one. I wanted to tell you the truth. I didn't know Lockley would disappear, nor did anyone else, I think. But I thought the document might be important to your … yes, well, to you.' Stephen checked himself.

Argyle stared at his own cup of wine, swirling the content slowly as if the motion would set all his thoughts right. 'And I thank you. Truly, Stephen, I do. You have done the right thing, and I thank you.' Argyle looked at Stephen. 'Now I ask you never to speak of this to anyone ever again.'

Stephen simply nodded. Clearly no stranger to secrets, Stephen knew when to talk and when to keep his mouth shut. He had proven as much when Lockley tried to beat answers out of him in Vienna.

'Stay close, I have a feeling something will happen soon,' Argyle warned Stephen, as he stepped into the black of night.

Stephen turned around, his face lit in splinters by the weak new moon. 'I thought it was just me, but I'm glad it isn't.'

14 February 1393 — Jerusalem

Argyle had spent the day in camp mulling over Stephen's words from the night before, trying to find someone who might know a little more about Lockley's disappearance and coming up short. The boy who had finally admitted to readying Lockley's horse was taken sick and had since died from his malady. This was not the first time a pilgrim had died from the flux and dehydration, but Argyle could not help thinking that this particular death was a little too suspicious.

As dusk settled, Argyle was tired, grumpy and crestfallen. On a whim he decided to freshen up and go to Marsal, hoping he might shed some light on Lockley's behaviour. After all he had been tending to both Argyle and another patient, and Argyle felt sure the other patient could only be Lockley. No one else in camp had been ill or injured around the time that Argyle had fought Lockley.

Stephen found Argyle on his way to the makeshift stables. 'Going somewhere, M'lord?'

'Just into town,' Argyle said not quite certain how much to tell Stephen. Even though Stephen had told him about Lockley's meeting with Coxcombe, their friendship was still very fragile and he was reluctant to share too much.

'M'lord Bolingbroke's just returned from a visit to the Holy Mount,' Stephen said. 'Why he wants to keep going there, I'll never understand. It's a mountain like any other, once you've seen it, what more's there to do?'

'Perhaps Bolingbroke finds solace there,' Argyle suggested, happy to know that Bolingbroke was back in camp and probably would not return to the horse-pen tonight. 'There are those in the pilgrimage who are devout and have come for prayer - and salvation.'

'Salvation?' Stephen's mood pricked up. 'What would M'lord need salvation for?'

'War is a dirty business,' Argyle said, and signalled to a squire that he would need his horse. 'Bolingbroke has seen his fair share of war - and are any of us truly devoid mortal sin?'

Stephen thought on this for a while. 'I suppose not. Can you be forgiven your sins at the Mount?'

'Of course. There are any number of religious places in town that will provide forgiveness.' Argyle gave Stephen a quizzical glance. 'Why did you think we lingered here so long?'

'I thought pilgrimages were supposed to be long and tedious,' Stephen said defensively. 'I'm not well-versed in religion, and God's divine ways're often lost on me. But if I can be forgiven my sins, I'll go to the Holy Mount tomorrow!'

'Now that is a plan.' Argyle smiled, taking the reins from the squire. 'I will not be gone long should anyone ask.'

Stephen nodded. 'Someone's bound to. I hope you find what you're looking for - salvation or otherwise.'

Argyle swung into the saddle. 'So do I. Goodnight Stephen.'

Stephen turned back towards the camp, and Argyle spurred his horse into a canter, eager to get through the city gates before the sun set because then the city was barred and manned with grim-faced guards. Getting out of the city at night was difficult enough, as Argyle had experienced on more than one occasion, but getting in was virtually impossible.

It was only a short ride from the city gates to Marsal's house, but to get there Argyle would have to pass Abbas' massive estate, and tonight he could not afford to be diverted by his desire. To avoid temptation, Argyle took the long way around the centre of the city, stopping once or twice to ask for directions. He had learned just enough Arabic to get by and luckily gestures were easy to interpret when his vocabulary ran short.

Ducking to get through a low gate that opened up to a small square filled with the sweet smell of orange trees, Argyle turned right and rode around the circle of trees, stopping before a wall to tether his horse to a large brass ring. Argyle did not like leaving the beast alone in the square, but there was nothing to do about it, he would have to make the last part of the trip on foot to avoid calling too much attention to himself.

Argyle walked slowly along the narrow alley, stopping now and then to look around, adjust the hood of the cloak or to peer through lattice doors. He had been told that Marsal's house was the only one in the alley that had two doors and glass windows, and since Argyle could not read the strange letterings that announced who was living in the houses, he had to inspect every house to make sure he found the right one.

Nearly at the end of the alley, Argyle finally found the house he was searching for. Glass windows, two doors and a small yard behind the lattice doors. This had to be the place.

Argyle stepped into the yard, but something stopped him from announcing his presence. He heard muffled cries and angry voices from the door furthest away. Stealing along the painted, clay wall Argyle held his breath; something was amiss.

He stopped outside the door. It was quiet in the room, the voices had stopped but Argyle thought he heard sobbing. Once his eyes had adjusted to the dark of the room, he saw shelves filled with pots and baskets of herbs, vials of oils and other fluids, a fresh sheet of linen on a table. It looked as if whoever had been working in the room had been disturbed, a short bladed knife lay underneath the table and there were drag-marks in the sand on the floor.

Argyle moved slowly through the door, feeling his way along the cool wall, his eyes scanning the room. He was halfway along the wall, when it disappeared under his palm, his fingers knocking over a series of clay pots on a shelf built into the wall. Argyle bit his lip to keep from cursing out loud.

'What was that?' a familiar voice growled.

Argyle looked around and saw a trapdoor at the end of the room, a pinprick of light in the pitch-dark corner. There was a thump from the cellar followed by a muffled scream.

'I said, what was that?!' the voice repeated. 'You told me, you were alone!'

'I am, my Lord.' Marsal's voice was unmistakable although it sounded frightened and thick.

Argyle stole closer to the trapdoor, careful to avoid the wall, feeling his way with his feet rather than his hands, staring at the light in the corner.

There was a grunt and a wail, which was immediately muffled. Argyle heard cloth ripping and a series of quick punches probably administered to warn Marsal to be quiet. Heavy breathing ensued, some pottery fell to the floor; the light flickered unsteadily.

Argyle held his breath, licking his dry lips, his eyes stinging from staring into the semi-darkness. He felt for the hilt of his sword and cursed inwardly as he remembered that he had chosen not to bring it. Getting into town in broad daylight with a sword was possible, but bringing weapons into the city at night was sure to get you thrown in jail or worse.

He slid his hand around the back and breathed out quietly when he felt the cool metal hilt of his dagger. He got slowly to his knees wondering briefly whether to …

A scream pierced the air and made Argyle's hair stand on end. There was a brief struggle in the basement, and then Argyle heard a blade being slid from a scabbard.

'Shut your mouth!' the hoarse voice snarled and, finally, Argyle recognised it. Lockley! Argyle's body made the decision for him, he scrambled to his feet, lunging for the trapdoor - his dagger drawn.

'No …' Marsal whimpered as he looked up to meet Argyle's eyes. Lockley looked up too, smiling viciously. He slowly released Marsal's throat, but kept one hand on Marsal's back.

Argyle choked at the scene in the cellar. Marsal was bent over, his tunic torn and flung from his backside, Lockley standing behind him, sword in one hand, his breeches open, his cock hard and his dead eyes alight for once.

'Please, no …,' Marsal whispered again, turning his head shamefully away from Argyle's stare.

'Just in time to see the fugitive and the spy together,' Lockley's voice was icy and triumphant.

Lockley thrust one last time half-closing his eyes letting sweet relief wash over him. Marsal choked back a scream, hanging his head while his body convulsed under the abuse. Argyle felt sick, he wanted to save Marsal, he wanted to kill Lockley - but all he did was stand above the scene stunned and disgusted. His cold hand lost the grip on the dagger and it fell to the floor.

'Better than a sweet maid!' Lockley licked his lips and stepped back, pulling up his breeches, he grinned widely at Argyle. 'Oh so much sweeter. You should try it, Sir Argyle - you'd never go back to that vixen of yours.'

Argyle gulped, he grasped blindly for his dagger, but his fumbling hands pushed it over the edge and it clattered to the cellar floor, ringing on the tiles.

'What luck! Not that you should come and cut my amusement short - oh no, Sire, I'll never forgive you for that. But that you should see this!' Lockley bent to pick up Argyle's dagger, shoving Marsal sideways. The physician fell to the floor, his face hitting the tiles, his backside bloody and exposed.

Argyle looked around in desperation, his mind screaming to find another weapon. The only thing he could think of was Marsal's little blade, and he lunged for it, sliding through the sand on the floor. His shoulder impacted with the massive wooden table in the centre of the room and the fresh linen flapped aside as Argyle reached out and grabbed the knife.

He rolled around, landing on one knee just in time to see Lockley leap from the hole in the floor, sword in one hand and Argyle's dagger in the other. The two eyed each other as Argyle slowly got to his feet.

'Come now, Sir Argyle, that little knife will help you no more than it did Marsal.' Lockley's voice had a sick dreamy quality when he spoke Marsal's name.

Argyle gripped the handle harder, his head swimming. 'You filthy bastard! SODOMITE!'

'Oh, I am so much more than that,' Lockley said softly.

Argyle felt powerless; his mind was blank, his eyes burning with the image of Marsal and Lockley.

'No words this time, Sire? You certainly are no match for your brother - you will be no match for Bolingbroke. You will be no match at all for the King,' Lockley smirked. 'Tell you what we do - you let me go.'

Argyle shook his head violently. How could Lockley think he would let him go now? Lockley who had killed La Fontaine, who had received a secret order to kill again on the pilgrimage, who had just abused another man. But no words came.

Lockley gave him a cold, dead stare. 'You will let me go! You may be a match to me when you have a sword in your hand, but with that childish little knife? You have no chance of besting me. I've got the upper hand here. Why don't you run back to camp, tell Bolingbroke what you saw - and that you had to let me go because you were foolish enough to let a little romping shock you?' Lockley laughed. 'And see if he believes you!'

Marsal came slowly up the stairs from the cellar, his face bloody, his body bruised, clutching his tattered tunic close. 'No …,' he whispered.

Argyle felt lost. Why would Marsal not - and then reality dawned on him. Marsal would be thrown in jail, tortured, publicly shamed and most likely stoned to death. Lockley was right. If Argyle went back to camp and told Bolingbroke he had let Lockley go, he too would be a prisoner, his mission failed, and his last friend would abandon him. Stephen's nightmares would come true, for Argyle at any rate - he too would be thrown in jail in Jerusalem, and there he would rot to death.

The realisation stunned Argyle, just as it fuelled Lockley, who advanced, sword and dagger held at waist height, ready to attack if Argyle moved.

'You understand, I think, the trouble you're in.' Lockley's voice was slick and exultant. 'You know now that I've won. That I told you everything about La Fontaine's death, because I was safe to do so.'

'Bolingbroke …' Argyle croaked.

'Bolingbroke knows nothing!' Lockley hissed, holding the tip of his sword to Argyle's chest, moving it around in tiny, slow circles, the touch almost a caress. Argyle took a step back and felt his thighs bump into the table. He swallowed hard.

'What will you do now, Sir Argyle?' Lockley taunted. 'Live or die? If you choose life, I will be long gone before you ever get back to Bolingbroke. If you choose to fight, you will die here, in this filthy place, and everyone will think you were Marsal's lover.'

Marsal whimpered at Lockley's words. 'They'll think this was a lovers' spat. That Marsal would not share you with anyone - especially not a woman. They will parade your corpse in the streets, they will punish Marsal for your folly and Bolingbroke will have to leave in disgrace.'

Lockley rested lightly on the table, the dagger lying beneath his palm, his sword still moving slowly on Argyle's chest. Argyle thought he saw true desire in Lockley's eyes and felt defeat mingle with disgust.

'What do you suggest?' Argyle asked.

'Let me go.' A cruel smile crawled slowly across Lockley's face. 'No one needs ever know what happened here tonight.'

Lockley turned a little to face Marsal who was cowering in a corner, his bruised and bloody face tearstained, his body shaking.

'This delicious man will certainly say nothing - and if you do …' Lockley looked back at Argyle. '… you will both die. Choose life and let me go. Or choose death and I shall give it to you tonight.'

Argyle could not think, his mind was screaming that it would be his undoing if he let Lockley go, his body was disgusted and wanted to turn and run, his eyes were burning from what he had just witnessed, his ears thrumming from the blood boiling in his veins. Lockley moved closer, the point of his sword piercing Argyle's chest.

'But before I give you the sweet relief of death, I shall teach you the sweet pain of love,' he whispered.

Argyle gulped, his throat dry as the desert. 'No!'

Lockley peered at him. 'No?'

'You can go,' Argyle said, his voice hoarse and low.

'Oh …' Lockley looked disappointed. 'I thought you would fight for honour and valour. I thought I would have you tonight. But wait … I still can.' He pushed the point of the sword a little further into Argyle's chest, making him flinch. 'I have the upper hand, would not you say, Sire?'

Finally, Argyle's brain began working again. 'Perhaps, but I will not go quietly, I will not be subdued by a beating. I will sound the alarm, if it is the last thing I do, and there will be nowhere for you to go!'

Lockley eased his hold, the tip of the sword retracted from Argyle's skin, a little trickle of blood trailing slowly down his shirt. Lockley considered the threat for a moment longer.

'Your fight would be magnificent, I am sure of it, but not worth the bother.' Stepping quickly away from Argyle and the table, Lockley kept his sword up. 'Wise choice, Sir Argyle. Tiresome - but wise. Mayhap we will meet again. If we do, I will make good on my promises,' Lockley mocked.

'When we meet again, you will be in chains,' Argyle promised.

Lockley barked a laugh and threw Argyle's dagger at the floor in front of Marsal. The knife bounced of Marsal's leg and skidded into the cellar, its hilt once more clattering on the tiles.

'Throw the knife into the hole, Sir Argyle,' Lockley said. 'Just for good measure.'

Argyle did as he was commanded, Marsal wincing when the knife flew past his face and disappeared into the cellar.

Lockley backed towards the door. 'I'll have your horse too.'

Argyle lunged for the cellar the moment Lockley turned and fled. Stumbling down the stairs, Argyle heard the lattice snap shut and Marsal's uneven breathing. When he returned with dagger and knife, Marsal had hoisted himself onto the table, wincing at the pain.

'You saved my life,' Marsal said quietly. 'Why did you save my life?'

'I saved my own!' Argyle said brusquely, skirting Marsal and peering out the door into the darkness. 'Where is Shanta?'

Marsal shook his head. 'She is not here.' His voice was sad.

Argyle grabbed Marsal by the shoulder, making the gangly man wince in pain. 'Where is she?!'

'She is gone to Abbas' house with healing herbs for the master,' Marsal said unhappily. 'But she will be home soon. Please, you must leave. You have my eternal gratitude, but you must go. If Shanta sees you here …' His voice trailed off.

'If she sees me here, she will think I did this.' Argyle finished the sentence without emotion and Marsal nodded, fresh tears coursing down his cheeks.

'And you would not protect me.' Argyle continued, and once more Marsal nodded. Argyle stuck his dagger back in its place beneath his tunic. 'I cannot say that I blame you. If it were me, I would not protect you either. But I must have your word you will not name me if you are called to question.'

'I will never speak of this night again, I will never think of it, I will never … never get into the kingdom of Heaven, but I will NEVER name you,' Marsal said emphatically while getting up, his torn tunic bloody and dirty and his face swollen from Lockley's abuse. 'You must go now!'

Argyle had to get back to camp, and he too had to forget this ever happened, though how he would manage, he would never know. He had to keep this, as he had kept so much else, from Stephen and Bolingbroke - and the King.

Stealing from the house, he saw Shanta's slight frame lit by the flame of an oil-lamp, shadows contorting her face. She looked so innocent, and Argyle mourned the sight she was about to see.

All the way back to camp Argyle wondered what Marsal would say to Shanta and how she would react - if he would be safe. Argyle hoped he could trust the physician - only time would tell.

15 February 1393 — Jerusalem

In the bazaar, Najeelah waited until the new moon sent a sliver of silver light across the alley. As she made her way back through the narrow streets, a figure detached itself from the shadows and followed her.

Argyle had watched Najeelah from across the alley, pining for her and yet not going to her. His fear of spies and concerns for her safety had kept him in the dark, his body silently crying out for hers. Now, he followed Najeelah and the figure, weaving their way through the dark maze of the bazaar.

When the two slipped around a corner, Argyle had to step into the street to follow them, momentarily exposing himself.

'Stop!' The sharp voice whipped across the street making Argyle turn to face a couple of English soldiers.

Relieved to see fellow men, Argyle took a step towards them, but stopped, when one of the soldiers drew his sword, his face a stone mask, his bald head glistening in the moonlight. The other soldier kept his hand on the hilt of his sword, clearly considering the best approach.

'Can I help you?' Argyle asked trying to keep his voice level but feeling panic wrap its cold arms around his chest. He could not afford to leave Najeelah for too long alone with a stranger following her.

'What're you doing here?' The soldier who had yet to draw his sword asked.

Argyle made a disarming gesture trying to buy time. 'The same as you, I suspect.'

The soldier with the sword snorted. 'I doubt it. If you were, 'cause you'd be spying on yourself!'

'Now would that not be a wonder,' Argyle said, smiling at the both of them while sliding a hand around the back to grab the dagger beneath his tunic; tonight nothing would make him drop it. He held out his right hand out to appear friendly.

'We're ordered to keep an eye on you,' the bald soldier said and the other chimed in. 'We knew you'd be going into town, not wanting to keep the lady waitin' no doubt.'

'Except tonight you didn't do nothing. Just stood there like a fool.' The bald soldier grinned savagely. 'What's the problem? Not good enough for you anymore?'

Argyle bit the inside of his cheek to check his temper. 'Not so. I saw the lady was being followed and decided to go too, to prevent that something might happen to her.'

The bald soldier grabbed his sword tighter while the other soldier stroked his thin, brown beard. 'No. I don't believe you. The way you've been carrying on with her for weeks, something's amiss. What'd she do? Found her in the arms of another man? Say that you weren't enough for her? I hear these women are so wanting, they'll have anyone who looks at them.'

The bald soldier barked a laugh. 'That'd be it, judging from his face. What's the matter, your pretty face wasn't enough for her?'

Both soldiers stepped back, as Argyle advanced, sliding his dagger from its hiding place in a fluent motion.

'What say you we call it a night?' Argyle hissed. 'You can go back to camp like good little soldiers and leave me to see the lady gets home safely.'

The bearded soldier gritted his teeth. 'Afraid not. You see, there's a reward for information 'bout you and we could use the money.' The bald soldier nodded, wheeling his sword aimlessly, and to Argyle, a little clumsily too.

'Money?' Argyle asked and saw the greed plain on the two soldiers' faces. 'We can come to an arrangement, if money is all you want.'

The bald soldier squinted. 'And if money's not all we'd be wanting?'

'We probably should not waste any more time!' Argyle replied, attacking the bearded soldier first, his dagger sailing effortlessly into the man's throat. A life taken with a single flick of the wrist.

The bald soldier paused just long enough to see his comrade fall down, blood gushing from the wound behind his ear, and Argyle took advantage of the moment to charge while drawing his own sword. Argyle's sword grazed the soldier's left arm as he sidestepped, but not enough to do serious damage. Argyle cursed under his breath. Twisting away, he quickly scanned the street. There was nowhere to go but around the corner after Najeelah, which would leave the bald soldier free to go back to camp and sound the alarm, or to defeat the soldier, clearing the path back to the city gate. Argyle did not like either option, but the soldier made the choice for him when he leapt at Argyle, sword held at shoulder height. Argyle spun away, throwing his shoulder into the soldier's wounded left arm. The man grunted and fell back only to attack again at full force.

Argyle parried the blow with vigour; the energy of the blades engaging sent a jolt through the soldier's arm. Rather than trying to get away, Argyle committed to the battle, overtaken by the rage and anger surging through his body. The surprised soldier scrambled backwards, his boot caught his dead friend's hand and he fell over, his elbow smashing the side of the dead man's face with a sickening crunch.

The bald soldier tried to crab away, making it easy for Argyle to drive the hilt of his sword into the fleeing man's temple, and he yelped as it burst open, blood gushing into his right eye blurring his vision. He slashed his sword aimlessly, striking Argyle across the calf by sheer luck.

Argyle felt his flesh give way, and warm, sticky blood coursing down his leg. He had accepted the fight; now he would have to finish it. The bald soldier was trying to get up, suddenly desperate to get away when Argyle struck the final blow; he wielded his sword and plunged it into the fleeing soldier's back, driving it up between two ribs. The man tried to cry out but only managed a gurgling sound as the sword cut through bones and lungs.

Standing over one of his own countrymen, Argyle wrenched his sword free and dried it on the dead soldier's tunic, before drawing free his dagger from the other soldier's neck. He looked around in the street to see if there were any more enemies waiting in the shadows and was baffled that no one had come to the windows at the sound of a swordfight. But the street was quiet and the windows black.

As he turned away, Argyle noticed the searing pain in his calf. He gritted his teeth and pushed his legs into a half run, turning around the corner to pursue Najeelah, to warn her of dangers, to …

Argyle smashed into a small shadow that gave off a startled, high-pitched cry. Stumbling back, Argyle looked at the person lying in the street, a pair of light brown eyes staring into his, an olive face twisted in fear and agony.

'Shanta?' Argyle whispered.

'My Lord,' Shanta muttered, trying to get up and falling back, clutching her ankle.

Argyle looked at her in utter confusion. 'What are you doing here? Are you hurt? Where is …' His voice trailed off when Shanta turned a shameful face from his gaze.

'She is safe,' Shanta whispered. 'We not stay here. Come.'

She tried to get up once more, but had to bite back a scream when she put weight on her hurt ankle. Large tears rolled down her face as she looked around, her eyes betraying her fear.

Argyle stepped back; she would not be able to follow him, if he walked away. He wanted more than anything to go to Najeelah, to find her and comfort her, perhaps even persuade her to go with him. If

Lockley could steal away in the night, surely the two of them could do the same. As long as they were together, they could make a life for themselves, he did not even care if she had spied on him, he would forgive her.

'Please,' Shanta whimpered. Argyle looked down at her again and saw for the first time that she was just a scared girl, probably younger than Argyle had thought when he had first met her in the camp. 'Please!'

'She is safe?' Argyle asked softly and Shanta nodded. 'But we are not?' Again Shanta nodded, looking around wearily.

'Very well, if you can vouch for her safety …' Argyle reached down and scooped Shanta up into his arms. She was as light as a bird, trembling from pain, her face wet with tears and her hair dirty and tangled. 'Where to?'

Shanta guided him by pointing and pulling his sleeves; they weaved through alleys and streets, Argyle careful to keep to the shadows, the both of them keeping a watchful eye out for any movement. At length, they arrived at the smooth, clay wall that was far too familiar to Argyle, the latticed door slightly ajar. He swallowed hard and pushed the lattice open, he kept blinking trying to clear his mind from the haunting memory of the night before. Shanta's face was white with pain; her slick hands clung to Argyle's shirt leaving wet marks on it.

'Is he here?' Argyle whispered and saw a single flame flicker to life in one of the windows.

Seconds later, Marsal peered out of a door, an oil lamp in his hand. 'Shanta!'

Marsal was at Argyle's side in two strides, his walk strained and his face twisted in agony. Shanta cried out in pain when Marsal's hands reached her bruised ankle, and he looked accusingly at Argyle.

'Inside now!'

Marsal led the way across the small, dark courtyard to the second door. Once inside, he lit another oil lamp before handing over his own to Argyle and gesturing for him to light the rest of the oil lamps standing on small shelves or hanging from colourful weaved cords on the walls. Looking around the room, Argyle could see no evidence of last night's horrid events. Only Marsal's bruised face and the black marks on his neck bore witness to the image that had burned into Argyle's mind. He shook to clear his head.

'Foolish girl! I told you to be careful,' Marsal scolded, his voice a mixture of anger and concern.

Shanta whimpered and tried to put on a brave face when she saw her twisted ankle. Even Argyle could tell that it was broken, the foot sticking out from her leg at a strange angle.

'I must put it right!' Marsal turned to Argyle. 'You will help.'

'Shanta, bite down on this.' Marsal handed Argyle a strip of leather, riddled with teeth marks and he passed it on to Shanta, who reached out a shaking hand to grab the strip. She bit down hard on the leather, her scared eyes seeking Argyle's for comfort.

'Hold her arms tight, she will fight, but it must be done now.' Marsal pushed Argyle around the table, and he grabbed Shanta's arms softly, feeling the girl tremble.

'Hold hard!' Marsal dictated, and Shanta gasped as Argyle tightened his grip. 'Good, hold her down.'

Marsal gritted his teeth, slid his hands down either side of Shanta's fractured ankle and twisted it, the bones cracking loudly at the violent treatment. Shanta screamed piercingly before collapsing in Argyle's arms, her limp body slumping against his chest.

'Good,' Marsal said. 'She is passed out. Now I work and you let go.'

'I did not know she would be there. I did not expect anyone to be there,' Argyle said defensively.

'Then you have learned nothing from last night!' Marsal said. 'Do you think Lockley was the only one watching you - watching us?'

'No, but he is gone,' Argyle said bitterly. 'He said he would go, there is nothing left for him here …'

Marsal hunched at the words, working Shanta's ankle with his hands, his bruised cheeks flushing. 'He is gone - I am sure of it! But since your first visit to Abbas, you have never been alone. Lockley was not the only one to watch you, I warned you it was so.'

'Who else?' Argyle asked.

The soldiers that now lay dead in the dark street somewhere in the bazaar were testament to the fact that he had not been alone, but that others had been watching him for all this time still made his blood boil. He had been a bloody fool, a bloody besotted fool.

'Handmaidens, servants, boys, guards - perhaps even your own men,' Marsal said as Shanta moaned in agony. 'Hold her again, it is best if she does not wake, but she must stay still.'

Argyle grabbed Shanta roughly and feeling her thin arms give way in his grasp, he relaxed his grip not wanting the cause of more harm. 'So we were never alone, not once?'

'No.' Marsal eyed him wearily before rummaging through a few boxes, picking out thin boards and strips of clean linen. 'Never.'

'Why did Abbas allow it?' Argyle asked.

He had never wanted Najeelah to take any chances, to put herself in harms way, and yet he had gone willingly with her everywhere, exposing her to danger and not even being clever enough to realise it. Argyle tried to direct his resentment towards someone else, but it kept pointing back to his own childish behaviour. Of course they would never have been allowed to spend so much time together without anyone knowing of it. His believing that Najeelah's handmaidens were completely loyal suddenly seemed so stupid. He cringed at the thought.

Marsal measured a few thin boards and chose the ones best suited for Shanta's tiny ankle. He worked so efficiently that Argyle thought he had not heard him. Just as he was about to ask again, Marsal looked up.

'Who knows? Perhaps he wanted her to have an adventure. Or perhaps he asked her to spy on you thinking you were a fool who would tell her anything if she led you on. No matter - he will not do so again.'

Argyle felt his legs give way and he slid to the floor, the painted clay wall cool against his sweaty back. Abbas had been spying on his own spy, and now she was back in his house, under his rule, helpless to his will. Argyle grunted at the searing pain from his calf when the wound began pulsing again.

'You are wounded,' Marsal said without feeling.

Argyle let Marsal examine his calf without complaint; uneasy to be touched by a man he had seen abused. Argyle scolded himself for being so petty, but he could not forget the sight he had seen last night, Lockley triumphant, Marsal defeated, the degradation, the molestation. Argyle bit his lip, when Marsal scrubbed the wound, wondering if he was trying to scrub away the memory of last night, the filthy secret they had together.

Marsal was done stitching up Argyle's wound, when Shanta came to, her olive skin had a strange ashen quality, and her eyes were bloodshot from pain and tears. Stealing glances at Argyle, who still sat on the floor, his calf bound with linen, Shanta fumbled with her skirt suddenly acutely aware of her state of disarray.

'You are hurt too?' she asked quietly.

'More than you can imagine.' Argyle hung his head again. He had risked everything for Najeelah, for love of her - or lust? He could not say.

Marsal sat down next to Shanta, letting thinned wine drip slowly from a spoon into her mouth. Once he was satisfied she was not in too much pain, he turned to Argyle with a strained face.

'You must go. The sun will be up soon, and you cannot be here. I will take you to the camp,' Marsal said shaking off Shanta's pawing hand. 'No! He must go!'

Argyle thought Shanta pleaded his case, but could understand nothing of their heated debate. Argyle's mind was whirling with incoherent thoughts of Najeelah, spies and secrets when Marsal suddenly slammed his hand into the table Shanta was lying on.

'NO!'

Argyle looked up. 'No need, Shanta. I am sure you speak to my defence, but I must go back.'

Shanta shook her head, tears welling in her eyes once more. 'No, there is danger.'

'I know, but there will be more danger, if I do not go back.' Argyle smiled softly at her and took her hand in his. 'You must recover and become a great healer, so that I might some day return and boast that I knew you when you were just an apprentice. And above all else, you must stay safe. No more stealing through the streets in the dead of night. I have put you and Najeelah in danger, and I cannot do so any more.'

Shanta blushed but fixed his gaze. 'I shall. I shall be great.'

'I have no doubt.' Argyle hid a sad smile. 'Now we must say farewell.'

As he turned to go, Shanta grabbed his arm and Argyle turned around. She pulled herself up by his sleeve and kissed his cheek, breathless at her own daring.

'Shanta!' Marsal was shocked.

'Now you go,' Shanta said, a mischievous smile lighting up her face. 'Now I have kissed a white man!'

Argyle laughed despite the dire situation and so did Marsal. Shanta lay back on the table, closing her eyes, a soft smile on her full lips, as she passed into what Argyle hoped would be a dreamless sleep.

'She will be a fine woman,' Argyle said, as Marsal led the way out of the small courtyard.

'Yes, and I shall keep her safe, she will never experience what I have!' Marsal said staunchly. 'I will keep her safe and when she is ready, I will make a good match for her. She will marry in her own faith and she will be a great healer, greater than me, I think, and I will say that I trained her.'

Marsal looked at Argyle. 'This is another night we can never speak of again. I give you my word, and you will give me yours.'

'Yes. There are too many secrets already, but you have my word.' Argyle bent his head, finally understanding the severity of his actions with Najeelah, how much grief he had caused and would never be able to right again. 'Marsal, will Najeelah be safe?'

'Perhaps. Abbas decides for her,' Marsal sighed. 'Love is dangerous and powerful and so is lust. Without danger there will never be power. But she cannot be yours - and you cannot be hers, it is the law. She was never free to choose. If she did not say so, she should have.'

Argyle felt so defeated that he simply followed Marsal through the dark town, out of a side-gate that had them skirting the camp. The long, silent walk left Argyle with ample time to contemplate his own folly, his careless behaviour and all the trouble he would now have to face. He began wondering what would happen when the city guard informed Bolingbroke that two of his soldiers had been killed in the bazaar. Who would Bolingbroke suspect? Who had sent them spying on him in the first place? Argyle had an idea about that, but he did not want to dwell on it.

When Marsal left without a word of farewell, Argyle could no longer feel the pain in his calf, only the gaping, jagged void where his heart had been.

ഇ ഏ ഇ ഏ

CHAPTER 27

16 February 1393 — Jerusalem

The message came with the first rays of sunlight. Argyle heard the hooves as he lay awake and in pain, although if it was his wounded calf or his broken heart that had kept him from sleep, he could not say. He got up and pulled a loose tunic over his head; he winced in pain when he pulled on his breeches, and then he made his way towards the camp centre.

In front of Bolingbroke's tent, an olive skinned man sat atop a beautiful Arab steed; its neck shone with sweat as if from a long gallop through the night and early morning. Bolingbroke emerged from his tent and his squire handed him a crumbled piece of paper.

Argyle was whipped back to one of his earliest memories, of falling on the hard wooden floor of a great room and no one caring to pick him up. He shook his head to clear the image.

Bolingbroke glared at the message and then seemed to find his bearings, as he paid the messenger. 'Summon the others, send them to my tent immediately!' Bolingbroke growled at the squire.

The boy ran quickly from sight, and Bolingbroke turned to Argyle. 'Sir Argyle, you come with me!'

His calf was white-hot with pain, and he struggled to walk normally as he followed Bolingbroke into the tent. Bolingbroke was alone and in a foul mood.

'My Lord, what news?'

'You tell me!' Bolingbrooke seethed and Argyle blinked at the realisation that the message must have come from the town. Bolingbroke rounded on Argyle. 'Two English soldiers have been murdered in town last night!'

'I do not …'

'Before you think to lie to me, a word of caution. I know you have been visiting the city at all hours of the night - and I know whom you have been seeing. What I do not yet know is what you have been saying!' A vein on Bolingbroke's temple bulged.

Argyle cringed. 'Nothing, my Lord. Nothing of any consequence.'

'DO NOT LIE TO ME!' Bolingbroke roared. 'If you ever lie to me, I shall make you pine for the Devil himself to relieve you and send you to HELL! I should have known you would be just like your brother, always turning your coat, for sale at the highest bid. Tell me true, Sire, what have you been peddling?!'

'Nothing, my Lord,' Argyle insisted and Bolingbroke lost his temper, hitting Argyle hard across the cheek.

'NOTHING! The two soldiers who died last night, they were nothing to you?' Bolingbroke seethed.

'What soldiers?' Argyle asked, rubbing his cheek. He knew that he had crossed a dangerous threshold and would have to keep to his story that he knew nothing of the two men he had killed last night in a fight for what he thought was love.

Bolingbroke advanced again; the impact of his fists knocked the wind out of Argyle. 'ARE YOU MAD!? How big a fool do you take me for?'

Argyle caught his breath. 'I do not …'

'Oh, I think you do!' Bolingbroke interrupted, angrily dismissing his squire who had returned. 'Get out boy! Tell the others to wait outside until I say different!'

The boy scrambled back into the heat of early dawn, mumbling the order to the waiting officers and noblemen. Argyle cringed at the knowledge that all his peers were right outside and would hear every word spoken in the tent if Bolingbroke kept shouting.

Argyle decided on a new approach. 'My Lord, where did the men die?'

Bolingbroke seemed thrown by the question. 'What do you mean?'

'I was in the city last night, I admit that freely, but I saw no English soldiers. Where were they found?' Argyle asked.

'In the bazaar. Your favourite haunt I gather.' Bolingbroke's eyes glinted with malice. 'You have some woman or other, you visit - they say you are generous with your visits and the lady is generous too.'

'But last night I was not in the bazaar,' Argyle said, a scant plan forming in his mind.

Bolingbroke looked suspicious. 'No?'

'No, my Lord. I was visiting the physician Marsal to thank him for treating my wounds after I was attacked by villains,' Argyle said. 'We talked late into the night, and I stayed in his house until dawn.'

Bolingbroke considered this for a while. 'Oh really? A physician you say? And he will attest to this?'

'I should think so, I drank too much of his honeyed wine and he offered me a makeshift cot for the night,' Argyle said, wondering at how easy lying came to him, feeling more and more like Thomas.

Bolingbroke seemed to arrive at the same thought. 'You tell a smooth tale, but I cannot help feeling something is amiss. If only I had the time to find out what is truth and what is not.'

'And if I may, my Lord, if the dead men were following me, who ordered it?' Argyle asked.

'None of your business,' Bolingbroke sneered, suspicious once more. 'I keep tabs on all my men, I like to know who I can trust - and I cannot shake the feeling you might not be one of them. Meeting with a woman from Abbas' house, you do know that he is a dangerous man?'

Argyle played the fool. 'I had no idea, my Lord. We were treated so kindly on our visit?'

'Indeed, but he was too quick to invite us in, and too eager to please by half,' Bolingbroke said. 'Which usually means a man has something to hide. I have since learned that nothing happens in Jerusalem that Abbas has not sanctioned or instigated. Which begs the question; what did you tell that woman of yours?'

'Nothing of consequence,' Argyle said. 'She asked about my family and England, but I never told her anything that would compromise …'

Bolingbroke smiled coldly. 'Compromise your true purpose on this journey?'

'Compromise you or the King,' Argyle said feeling his inadequate plan crumble.

'And what could you possibly know about me or my cousin that could be compromising this far away from England?' Bolingbroke asked in a low voice, stepping close to avoid the crowd outside the tent should hear too much of what was being said.

'I … Who knows what information these savage people look for? What they use to inspire hatred? Is this not why we wage wars on them, lay sieges to their cities and join crusades?' Argyle wavered.

Bolingbroke grabbed Argyle's collar. 'If I find out, you have been feeding Abbas with information that could compromise me, the men here in camp or indeed England, I will kill you myself. I care not what it might be, but if anything is reported back to me that I can pin to you, I shall.'

'You will make no such discoveries, my Lord.'

'We shall see about that, Sir Argyle. Squire! Let the men in!' Bolingbroke commanded. 'Oh, and I hope you said your goodbyes the last time you met your lady, for today we ride for England.'

'My Lord?' Argyle croaked as the flap went up again and the knights filed in, including a clearly uncomfortable Coxcombe who cowered at the back of the tent. Many of the men gave Argyle filthy, curious looks before turning their attention to Bolingbroke.

'I have decided that my pilgrimage is at an end,' Bolingbroke announced. 'It is my command that we break camp today and ride for port! We shall return to Venice and my gracious hosts, as I have promised them. I long to once more be among likeminded men. Sir Argyle, Coxcombe, Beaufort, prepare to leave at midday!'

Several knights sounded their surprise, while others looked round in bewilderment. Bolingbroke barked an order to disperse and make ready, and Argyle half ran through the camp ignoring the pain in his leg. He called for one of his squires to round up Argyle's ten best soldiers and have them rally by the western side of the camp within the hour. Another squire was sent to request provisions and make arrangements for any purchases to be made as soon as possible. Bolingbroke would expect to ride before midday. Argyle had to be ready.

Once back in his tent, reality hit hard - he was going back. Argyle had come close to solving his mission, but he was not satisfied with his results. More to the point, he was about to leave the one person who had opened his eyes to all that life could be - and fool that he was, he had risked everything including her life - because of what? Love? Desire? Did she even really care for him?

Shaking his head angrily, Argyle grabbed his travel clothes and began dressing, barking a command to his squire. The boy left the tent in confusion to fetch Argyle's horse.

If he was quick about it, he might just have time to do one last thing.

༄ ༄

They never said goodbye. Argyle went to Abbas' house and was met by a handmaiden, saying her mistress was indisposed. Then she pressed a small velvet pouch into his hands and pushed him gently out of the door.

Argyle did not open the pouch until he was back at camp overseeing the packing of his tent and other vital supplies. Satisfied that all would be done in time, Argyle searched for a place to be alone. Leaning against his horse, he loosened the purse strings and poured the content into his hand.

A thin gold chain twinkled in the sunlight. Adorning it was a gold pendant carrying a small diamond within. Argyle swallowed hard. Najeelah had been with him in the bazaar, they had been walking through the area where the goldsmiths had their stalls when Argyle had seen the pendant. He had told Najeelah that he wanted to buy it for his sister, believing that Eleanor would love it, and Najeelah had smiled at him, explaining that this was a gift given only by a woman to a man for a very special occasion, when a couple's union was blessed with new life.

Argyle slowly pulled the chain over his head and hid the pendant under his tunic. His hands were cold despite the burning heat, his stomach was in turmoil and his head was spinning. Najeelah had sent him away - or Abbas had. Argyle would never know if Najeelah had truly had feelings for him or if she had been a spy for her master, luring him in with her body, letting him taste the forbidden fruit so many times he had lost count - and almost lost his mind. He had been angry and distraught last night, when Marsal had put forward the idea that Najeelah was an emissary of Abbas, sent to extract information from a young, foolish Englishman.

Rage and regret once more tore through his body, his mind blurred from memories of holding Najeelah close, her silky skin warm to his touch, her eager mouth seeking his. If all of that was just an act, she had to be the greatest actress the world had ever seen. Perhaps she had never loved or even liked him, but he loved her, longed for her, it was as simple as that. For the first time, he did not regret that he had kept his true purpose from her. It might be exactly what saved him in the end.

The noise in the camp called Argyle back to the painful present. He looked back only once, finding that the piercing sun was blotting out Jerusalem; he decided that this was perhaps the best way to remember the place - a black mark in his memory.

Argyle fell in behind Bolingbroke who was ready to go.

ഗ്രെ ഗ്രെ

Part 3
Deceit

CHAPTER 28

21 March 1393 — Venice

'You will go in my place!'

'But brother …' Beaufort looked bewildered.

'I must return to England and no one can know!' Bolingbroke pointed towards Argyle who sat hunched on a cot at the far side of the room. 'This vile creature must be returned to England, and I must go too.'

'If you would just …'

Bolingbroke gave Beaufort a sharp glance. 'The less you know the better!'

'How do you propose we get away with this?'

'You will not return to any of the cities we visited on our way here,' Bolingbroke said. 'You will go by way of Milan, Macon and Troyes. I shall rejoin the retinue before you reach Paris. It will be your task to ensure the journey home takes as long as possible. Linger wherever you get the chance, spend lavishly; I give you free reign. I trust you, brother!'

Beaufort did not seem nearly as convinced that the plan would work as Bolingbroke did. Argyle had to acknowledge that it was a daring plan, and that it just might work. Beaufort and Bolingbroke were of an age, and both were dark haired and of similar build.

'You will be wearing my clothes, travelling in a style befitting a prince of England,' Bolingbroke continued. 'I shall ensure that no one in your retinue gives you away. They are all sworn to me and will be to you before the day is over.'

'I could return Sir Argyle,' Beaufort suggested.

'No! It must be I. I shall have to speak to my father too, and I cannot see how else to achieve what I want - for no one but a few men to know who is truly where.'

'You would go as me?' Beaufort looked aghast and confused.

'I had not thought that far but perhaps I should,' Bolingbroke said. 'Most would believe that my father could have use of you in England, and all would believe that I was in no hurry to return home.'

Beaufort shook his head slowly. 'I … Even if it were possible, how will I know when you are at Troyes? How will we communicate if no one is to know that you are travelling in secret, making for England while the whole kingdom believes you leagues away?'

'I have my ways,' Bolingbroke said glancing at Argyle. 'Would you not agree, Mowbray?'

Argyle was tired, irritated and more than a little annoyed that Bolingbroke always addressed him by his family name, as if to spite him. Any other knight would be addressed as Beaufort did, but Bolingbroke refused to call him Sir. However, Bolingbroke had little reason to do as Argyle wanted.

'Yes, my Lord.'

'There Beaufort, our visitor agrees,' Bolingbroke offered a cold smile.

'Why is he here?' Beaufort asked.

'Mowbray?'

Argyle shrugged. 'I can only assume that my Lord Bolingbroke is testing me to see if I am a spy. If someone were to catch wind of him returning in an untimely fashion to England, who would be better to blame than me?' He was angry with himself even more than he was with Bolingbroke and his heart was still bleeding from the sudden departure from Jerusalem.

'Exactly!' Bolingbroke slapped Beaufort on the back. 'You will do well, brother, you know me as well as I do myself, and you are loyal to a fault. You have studied me in my ways and can mimic me without effort.'

Beaufort silently agreed and rubbed his forehead. 'How do you propose to go about it?'

'We will leave on the morrow. I have already requested horses, carriages and the like,' Bolingbroke said. 'I have also made sure the doge knows that I am making for Verona and Milan, no doubt he has sent word ahead of my journey.'

'They will know you are coming?' Beaufort's face turned white.

'They know some English prince is coming. You or I, it does not matter. I know no one in either city, and you and I are very alike.' Bolingbroke poured a glass of wine. 'You will be wearing my clothes and rings, be riding my horse and commanding my men, what more could they ask for as proof that you are me? They will have no reason to ask questions.'

Argyle was almost certain Beaufort thought as he did that no one would ask, and although he did not want to admit it, the plan was well made, but it had one massive flaw.

'And when you return to England?' Beaufort asked what Argyle had been wondering.

Bolingbroke downed the wine. 'I will make directly for Pontefract.' He looked at Argyle. 'If needs be, I will go in shackles along with our friend here. My father's soldiers escorting a couple of prisoners to Pontefract would raise little suspicion, now that England is rumbling with much more serious threats once more.'

'Serious threats?' Beaufort reached for the pitcher of wine and looked disappointed when only a few ruby red droplets ran into his glass. 'What threats?'

'The King,' Bolingbroke said indifferently. 'What else is new? He is up in arms and ready to make trouble for us all. He has to be stopped!'

'And him?' Beaufort pointed once more at Argyle who was seething in the corner. 'What of him?'

'He is to go to the King.'

Beaufort staggered. 'You will bring him back to England yourself, and you do not think the moment he stands before the King, he will not give you away?! Are you mad?!'

Bolingbroke laughed. 'Perhaps! But I feel Mowbray here will keep my secret safe. After all, he has more pressing matters to lay before the King than how he came to be in England months before I returned. It was the King that sent him on my pilgrimage - the fool!'

Argyle bit his lip so hard that the taste of iron filled his mouth. He had decided to keep quiet and simply let matters unfold, but then he had thought that Bolingbroke would send Beaufort ahead, and Argyle was pretty convinced he could outwit Beaufort. He could not dream to outwit Bolingbroke and knew that was why he was sending Beaufort to impersonate him.

'It is a royal offence …' Beaufort started.

'Are you ignoring my command?!' Bolingbroke's voice was thick with threat. 'That would be unwise.'

Beaufort had the courtesy to look abashed and ask forgiveness, which Bolingbroke waved off.

'Gather the men!' Bolingbroke turned to Argyle as Beaufort slid out of the room. 'As for you … You will not breathe a word of this to anyone! You and Smith will come with me.'

'What do you hope to achieve?'

One of Bolingbroke's men entered the room and whispered in his ear. Bolingbroke nodded. 'Justice - just like you. Except perhaps we strive for different men to be redeemed." He turned to one of the soldiers: 'Keep him here!'

Argyle's sword hand itched, but he had no blade to draw. Bolingbroke had made sure to take both sword and dagger before letting Argyle enter his rooms. The soldier stared at him, probably trying to scare him into submission but the moment Bolingbroke left the room, Argyle stood and walked to the narrow window. Beneath him in the courtyard, Bolingbroke's men were jumbled together standing shoulder by shoulder. Argyle opened the window a little and heard the soldier clear his throat, but he did not come closer; fortunately he had earned quite a reputation along the way of being both dangerous and unreliable.

Bolingbroke's voice drifted through the window. 'We make for England tomorrow! I request that each of you come to my rooms for instructions - one by one!'

A few moments later, Bolingbroke walked into the room and dismissed the soldier. 'Do you still think my plan foolish?'

'Daring, yes, but perhaps not foolish,' Argyle said. 'Not until we reach England. Not even you can hope to travel to Lancashire unnoticed.'

'Time will tell,' Bolingbroke said as the first knight entered the room. 'Sir Thomas, I demand your allegiance! I am leaving it up to you to ensure that my brother Beaufort is presented and passed off as me on the journey home. You will address him my Lord Bolingbroke and do his bidding. He is in command, and he must be believed to be me! You will be rewarded handsomely when you return to England - if you succeed …'

If Sir Thomas Erpingham was shocked by Bolingbroke's order, he hid it well. 'Yes, my Lord.'

Bolingbroke smiled at Argyle as Sir Thomas left and the next man entered.

By nightfall every knight, soldier and squire in Bolingbroke's retinue were sworn to secrecy. No one had complained, asked or even voiced concern at this plot to pass off Thomas Beaufort as Bolingbroke. Argyle marvelled quietly at the fierce loyalty Bolingbroke enjoyed.

At midnight, Bolingbroke assembled 10 soldiers and ordered them to saddle the horses and make ready to depart as soon as possible. He also told his personal squire to fetch Beaufort and make sure he was not seen entering the room.

By tomorrow, Beaufort would wake to be Bolingbroke - and Bolingbroke would be gone.

CHAPTER 29

6 May 1393 — at sea

Argyle shook his head violently, fighting to open his eyes, to clear the image of her dark, smouldering eyes. He felt his cheeks burn, streaks of wet coursing down either side. Peering around carefully, his eyes small painful slits, Argyle fought to push back the memory of her touch, and he relaxed a little when he discovered he was alone.

Letting the mingled pleasure and pain of the dream subside, Argyle got slowly to his feet, staggering a little at the tumbling motion of the ship and went in search of the barrel of drinking water. It was stale, but he drank greedily anyway trying to flood away the vivid vision of her half-naked body.

Argyle climbed the narrow stairs and relished the sudden gush of sharp sea air while he leaned heavily on the railing. Beneath him, the ship creaked and moaned at the roaring sea. The same day that Coxcombe's burned body was discovered, Bolingbroke had chartered a ship to take them back to England now that the storm had died down.

Squinting against the spray, Argyle saw nothing but leaden skies and foaming waves. It was unnerving to think that soon they would be back in England. How would Bolingbroke proceed then? He might be able to travel mostly unnoticed in France, but to expect the same in England was in every way ridiculous.

'Mowbray!'

Argyle turned to see Bolingbroke standing, legs set firmly apart to stay afoot on the slippery rocking deck.

'My Lord!'

Both had to yell to be heard over the increasing wind that had kicked up in the early hours of the morning.

'Join me in the captain's quarters!' Bolingbroke turned and Argyle followed musing briefly on how strange they must look both shuffling along the deck, hunched against the wind, pulling their cloaks tight.

Inside, heaters ensured a steaming warmth that still left the walls clammy and the portholes damp.

'Sit. You missed breakfast, although it was not much to bother with, but there is bread if you want it.'

Argyle gratefully grabbed a piece of stale bread and dunked it in a tankard of small ale. He wondered what had inspired Bolingbroke's sudden generosity.

'It is miserable but it will have to do. The captain has promised me the first sight of English soil today; we will be in Dover before nightfall. The wind is favourable, blowing us towards shore. But I must settle something before we land,' Bolingbroke began.

Argyle looked up from his meal.

'I cannot help but marvel at how many men, somehow tied to you, have died and disappeared. Or what your role in Coxcombe's untimely death was.' Bolingbroke leaned back, the sound of his cloak dripping on the boards beside the cabin door seemed to grow louder the longer Argyle held his tongue.

'I found him with you,' Argyle finally said. 'We neither of us knew he was missing before the fire was lit.'

'Well now, I see it differently! You prowled the rampart that night. Both before and after our little talk.' Bolingbroke held up his hand as if to silence any outbursts. 'Of course, I know this because you were not the only one on the rampart.'

'And you trust the one, who spied on me?'

'To a fault.'

Argyle chewed the soggy bread attempting to recall who else had been on the rampart that night. Inwardly, he also admitted he could not fully account for his own whereabouts. Once he had finished his discussion with Bolingbroke, he had indeed prowled the rampart, deep in thought. At one point he had looked up to find himself descending turret stairs he could not recall climbing. Could he have seen Coxcombe - and whoever did the deed?

Bolingbroke continued. 'You vanished for almost an hour just before dawn. Where did you go?'

Argyle shook his head trying to recover a fleeting memory. It slipped away once more.

'Well?'

'Perhaps the church?' Argyle said reluctantly.

'You are asking me? You do not remember?' A smug undertone crept into Bolingbroke's voice. He laced his fingers together, the tips of his thumbs forming a small pyramid under his chin.

'I was deep in thought,' Argyle said. 'I wandered aimlessly.'

Argyle tried desperately to shake Bolingbroke's suggestion. He clearly remembered the two soldiers he had fought and killed in Jerusalem, surely he would remember fighting Coxcombe?

'You had discovered that Coxcombe knew about the tourney. Perhaps you felt angry. Perhaps you wanted revenge?' Bolingbroke's honeyed words cut him deep.

'I had known for months,' Argyle said with regret. 'And for revenge? Would I chase a murderer halfway across the known world only to turn murderer myself? And kill a knight right before a garrison of English soldiers? Do you really think so little of me?'

'Better men have lost their wits at less,' Bolingbroke said. 'There have been far too many lies and secrets for me to ever trust your word.'

'Someone in your retinue is a murderer, and I suggest you try to find out whom before we reach London. And if you decide that I did the deed, do not hesitate in reporting it to the King,' Argyle continued with greater conviction. 'Would a guilty man ask this of another? Or would he steal away in the night like a thief?'

'Perhaps he would, if he felt sure, he could get away with murder. If he was vain enough to believe himself safe and beyond punishment.' Bolingbroke narrowed his eyes. 'I do hope you are not protecting anyone out of misguided loyalty or mindless chivalry. Either way, what little trust I held out for you has vanished beneath the roaring sea, Mowbray.'

Bolingbroke waved Argyle away. As he reached the door, he was stopped by Bolingbroke's hoarse voice. 'Let us part with a piece of advice though. Ask your brother about the death of La Fontaine! Whatever you might think of him, very little gets past Thomas in the end. As for the other matter, I reserve the right to judge as I see fit once we reach England.'

For the rest of the crossing, Bolingbroke did not speak to Argyle. Neither did anyone else, even Stephen kept away.

8 May 1393 — England

Once the party set foot on English soil, Bolingbroke ordered one of his loyal soldiers to secure horses for the final ride. While riding across the continent, Bolingbroke had been calm and even a little amused at Beaufort's success in imposing as an English prince.

Now that they were in England, Bolingbroke was grim and quick tempered, biting the head off anyone who dared suggest that his presence could not possibly go unnoticed. Before they left Dover, he ordered extra guards for Argyle and finally decided to let himself be guarded as a prisoner too.

'You must act as if I am to be brought before my father for theft, and that you have been hunting me across the land before finally finding me here, boarding a ship,' Bolingbroke commanded of his men. 'It will be an inconvenience for me to be sure, but safer for all of us.'

'My Lord,' the captain said. 'Should we warn your father?'

'No, better he does not know; then he shall not have to choose whether to tell my cousin or not.'

Bolingbroke's soldiers looked doubtful but did not argue with him, nor did they complain, when they were ordered to keep treating Argyle and Stephen as prisoners; rather all of them looked happy at the prospect.

The ride left plenty of time for Argyle to ponder his findings, Bolingbroke's mistrust, the bodies that littered his pilgrimage and the feeling of impending doom. Argyle was disheartened that Thomas might know something that could potentially ruin his family, and it was not easy for him to admit that he was still torn between loyalty to the King and to his own blood. Argyle decided it was best that his brother did not know he was returning to London just yet.

Bolingbroke pressed the horses and riders hard, spending only a few hours every night in an inn along the way. They ate in the saddle and enjoyed the first tingling summer days slowly burning away the spring rain and floods.

Stephen rode up alongside him three days into the journey. Since Coxcombe's death, his looks had become haggard with premature white streaks in his ginger hair and beard.

'Every day I wake up and hope it's all a strange dream,' Stephen said without preamble.

Argyle had felt the same ever since they left Jerusalem.

'In some ways it has been a strange dream. And I fear not the adventure, you sought, nor the salvation I dreamed of. It was a dream that turned into a nightmare, just as you predicted,' Argyle said.

Stephen looked down as he rubbed his aching knee. 'I wish I hadn't told you.'

'Told me what?'

'I don't know. About the night in Vienna when Lockley beat me,' Stephen said. 'That he met with Coxcombe 'cause I'd said I thought he was a traitor. What I knew about the connection between Lockley and Coxcombe.'

'Lockley could not have known you told me.'

'By now, we both know that a camp has ears and eyes everywhere. Even Bolingbroke said he was spying on you, surely Lockley would've been too,' Stephen said. 'He wanted me to spy on you, but I flat-out refused. Told him I'd do many things but not that. He didn't take kindly to that.'

They rode for some time in silence.

'This morning I thought, what if you hadn't brought me? I'd be back in Hampshire, perhaps courting a maid and finding life worth living,' Stephen said wryly.

'You will,' Argyle smiled. 'Regardless of our current troubles, you have done me a great favour. I shall not forget - and sometime I might even tell you the whole story. Once we reach London, I want you to go straight to my house and stay there. Come only if I summon you and speak to no one, not even your former friends. This time, do not disobey my command!' Argyle added with emphasis.

Stephen nodded submissively. 'Yes, M'lord.'

Argyle squashed a sudden desire to scream at Stephen that he was no Lord and prayed he never would be.

ഇ ഌ ഇ ഌ

15 May 1393 — Pontefract Castle

'If a man commits suicide by flinging himself off a turret, would he scream?' Argyle asked.

'Why do you ask?' Bolingbroke stood and closed the gap between them. Argyle could tell he was tired after a long night with Gaunt who was furious that Bolingbroke had come back to England. The two had yelled and screamed at each other for hours before Gaunt had flung open the door to the study and stormed out calling for a horse and escort.

Bolingbroke was now alone in Pontefract with his men, Argyle and Stephen, who had been locked up in the castle prison. Argyle had been brought before Bolingbroke in the early hours of the day to answer a myriad of questions. It was obvious to all present that Bolingbroke desired nothing more than to be on his way back to France. The latest reports placed Beaufort close to Troyes - Bolingbroke was tied for time to return and resume his rightful place.

'I remember a shrill noise that night in Calais. It was almost drowned out by the wind screaming around the turrets. I thought I was alone on the battlement, so I did not think anything of it. But whoever was there might have seen who did away with Coxcombe,' Argyle said.

Bolingbroke looked thrown. 'He saw nothing.'

'Who?' Argyle asked.

'You must have been three on the rampart, not counting Coxcombe. If I am to take your word for it, you did not do it and neither did my man. Which means that one more man defied the storm - besides Coxcombe, if you are right that he did not kill himself.'

'I feel certain he did not, although I cannot prove it. And yes, whoever it was, besides me and your spy, he pushed Coxcombe to his death, and set his body on fire,' Argyle said.

Bolingbroke knew that Argyle had been at the top of the turret when the fire was lit that morning, There was no way he could have made it down to the body and back without being noticed by at least a dozen soldiers.

Bolingbroke narrowed his eyes. 'You know who?'

'No. I have my suspicions though.'

'Do share them with me. Perchance I can make something of them that you cannot.'

Argyle breathed deeply. 'Lockley.'

'Lockley?' Bolingbroke almost laughed at the name. 'Are you to pin all the misfortunes of the world on one man?'

'No, but he does stand to gain most by Coxcombe's death.'

'How so?'

'Lockley and Coxcombe had a falling-out in Jerusalem. Stephen told me of it at the time, but before I could report back to you, the letter arrived that took us here.' Argyle forced a stark image of the last time he had seen Lockley out of his mind.

'You knew and said nothing?' Bolingbroke replied.

'Lockley had already disappeared and Coxcombe was still in the retinue. It seemed to have resolved itself.' Argyle felt the vision from Marsal's cellar creep back again and blinked it away.

'And what was this falling out about?' Bolingbroke sat down heavily on a chair near the only window in the room. Argyle decided then and there to share what he knew with the one man, the King would never have taken into his trust.

Argyle began. 'They met a few days before Lockley disappeared …'

When Argyle finished Bolingbroke was shaking with anger. 'I should have locked him UP!'

'He must have decided that it was too big a risk to stay.' Argyle knew what Lockley was capable of, how much he was willing to risk and yet, he had not simply killed Coxcombe in Jerusalem. But perhaps he would have, if Argyle had not disturbed him that fateful night.

'The FOOL!' Spit flew from Bolingbroke's mouth as his fury burned. He was a magnificent sight when in a rage, and Argyle fully understood all those who shrank before him.

'Do you believe Lockley's tale?' Argyle asked.

'How can I not? I have known him for years; he does not know how to lie. How to keep silent? Yes. He can even endure torture without saying a word if sworn to secrecy. But lie? No!' Bolingbroke looked weary. 'I must say; this pilgrimage has been marred by too many secrets.'

'For my part, I am sorry,' Argyle said. 'What I set out to do was not intended to affect your journey. I was clumsy and foolish, and I let Lockley slip away.'

Bolingbroke waved dismissively. 'Trust Richard to ruin my one solemn act in life.'

Silence ensued. Argyle pondered if Bolingbroke believed him. He could offer no proof but what he had spied himself and what Stephen had told him. Would the King believe him, if Argyle told him that the order to kill his great friend bore the royal seal? Argyle wondered if Bolingbroke would let him go to the King, would trust him not to betray his secret.

'England is a broken land,' Bolingbroke said. 'She cries and wails, and no one comes to her aid.'

'My Lord?'

'So much could have been avoided if only my cousin had the courage and sound mind to follow advice, rather than discard it, because it does not suit him,' Bolingbroke said.

Argyle shook his head. This old grudge again.

'Yes, I know what you think. That I am discouraged because I am jealous of Richard's favourites. That I want to be part of his glittering court and I have exiled myself with my previous actions.' Bolingbroke looked tired. The journey had taken its toll on everyone, not least him.

'Can you blame me?' Argyle asked.

'For Lockley's undue departure and Coxcombe's death? Yes.' Bolingbroke's voice was free of any emotion. 'And I do, never doubt that. As for the rest, I only wish you could see it from your brother's perspective. I know you all but grew up in the household of a royal favourite, but you have a family too. Blood relatives who only wanted what was best for the country. For the people.'

This was it then. Everything Argyle had discovered was reverted back to this one point in time when Thomas had chosen to turn his cloak and side with those who opposed the King.

'It is so long ago,' Argyle said. 'The country has been at peace since then.'

'A frail peace. And mark my word; it will not last. Richard will not let it last.' Bolingbroke seemed sombre almost at the point of giving up. His shoulders hung as he leaned forward and rested his elbows on his knees. Then he looked up at Argyle.

'It will never be over. Make your report to the King, say what you like. It is all the same to me. But if you are right, and Lockley stepped foot on English soil around the time we did, then hunt him down and bring him to justice. He has unsettled the peace of the realm, and I cannot let him live on for that,' Bolingbroke said. 'If you are clever, you will not go to court and to the King before you know Lockley is in your keep. And you will not tell my cousin that I was here, when he thought I was far away in France.'

Argyle nodded grimly, however tired he was, he would not rest until Lockley was in the Tower. Argyle would see justice for all the men Lockley had killed and maimed. He would have retribution and redemption - even if he would never have salvation. And he would hunt Lockley to the ends of the earth if he had to.

ꙮ ꙮ

'In two days, you are to release the prisoners! No more or less. They are to be given horses and escorted to London.' Bolingbroke looked at Argyle. 'Present them to the King, then seek out my father and he will give you new orders.'

'And you M'lord?'

Bolingbroke paused. 'I was never here!'

CHAPTER 30

3 June 1393 — London

'Brother, whatever are you doing here?' Margaret's voice rang out across the room. Argyle spun around, quickly securing a smile to his face and hoping she would not notice how tense it was.

'Margaret, I am so pleased …' Argyle said.

'Yes, yes, but that does not answer my question, now does it?' Margaret said, taking hold of Argyle's outstretched hands. 'What are you doing here? I thought you were halfway around the world - on your pilgrimage.' The last few words came out as a discerning whisper.

Argyle pulled her towards a window bay hoping the thick stonewalls would provide a little cover and privacy. He cursed his own foolishness at walking out into the waiting rooms outside the King's chambers and not returning to the back corridors from where he had come. 'Margaret this is neither the time, nor the place …'

Once more Margaret cut him short. 'I do not care what time it is! You will answer my question because I ask it of you. Just yesterday, Thomas was telling me that Bolingbroke had returned from his pilgrimage, and he said not a word about you being with him!'

This was his eldest sister in full effect. Margaret had never let go of her feeling of responsibility for all her brothers and sisters - nor her inherent dissatisfaction, when one of them displeased her.

Argyle glanced around before answering her. 'I cannot speak with you here, I should not be seen here. I was a fool to come into this room. But I shall visit you tonight and explain.'

For a moment, Margaret seemed to consider his proposal then she nodded. 'Very well, but you had better have a very good explanation ready - oh and remember, I always know when you are lying. You are no match for Thomas on that score.'

Argyle made to leave, but Margaret pulled him back into the half-gloom of the window bay.

'Stay here for a while. I shall go to my ladies and make sure you are not seen.' When Argyle gave her a curious look, she half-smiled. 'Do you really think you are the only Mowbray who can keep a secret?'

Argyle wondered why her husband, Sir Reginald, was not around, he never usually let Margaret out of his sight for very long. Whatever his sister was up to, she had been curiously quick to accept that they could not be seen together. Bustling from the room amidst her ladies, Margaret half-turned for just a moment and discreetly waved her left hand. Argyle slipped from the window bay and made for a low wooden side door, which would take him into the servants' corridors.

After closing the door as quietly as possible, Argyle stole a moment to rest his forehead on the doorframe, taking in the mingled scent of wood, dust, old rushes and grease from the kitchens. He had to keep out of sight until nightfall, and he could not go to his own house because no one knew he was in London and no one could know.

ꕥ ꕥ

Once darkness descended upon the city, Argyle slipped into Margaret's house by the backdoor, startling the scullery maids. He sent one of them to announce his arrival and then settled down in the corridor connecting the scullery and the kitchen. Margaret's evening meal must soon be over, Argyle could see the cook preparing the sweetmeats that always concluded the Mowbray meals. When he was fairly certain no one was watching, Argyle slid into the kitchen and helped himself to some leftovers. Chances were that once he had told Margaret why he had returned without informing anyone, all she would offer him was a scolding.

Argyle was licking duck-fat from his fingers when the scullery maid arrived with a lady in tow who Argyle did not know. She curtsied and Argyle inclined his head to her. 'My Lord, please follow me, my Lady is just finishing her supper,' the lady said.

'She is entertaining company tonight?' Argyle asked.

The lady hooked up her skirt and began walking briskly down a corridor leading off the kitchen. 'It may interest you to know that she is eating with your brother.'

Argyle grabbed her gently by the arm. 'My brother?'

The lady pursed her lips at his touch. 'Yes, Lord Mowbray is bound to go soon. My Lady has already said she wishes to retire to her rooms, and my Lord is not in London at the moment.'

'Margaret is here alone?' Argyle asked.

'I should say no more, my Lord, please wait in here.' The lady opened a door to what was clearly Margaret's private room, lush fabrics and thick furs strewn on chairs and fresh rushes on the floor. While his sister took great care to appear thrifty in the eyes of the public, she had had a weakness for all things comfortable since childhood. Margaret simply chose to stow her indulgences away in her private quarters and let the world see only what she wished it to see.

Argyle went to one of the narrow windows and opened the shutters to try and change the stale air in the room. London in summer was almost too much to bear.

'Close that window immediately, would you let all the bad humours into my room?' Margaret brushed past him, snapping the shutters close.

'Margaret, I did not hear you come in.'

Argyle stepped away from the window and offered Margaret his arm, leading her to a comfortable chair near the empty hearth. She took it willingly enough, but her squeeze turned into a pinch before she let go of Argyle's arm. Rubbing the place her fingernails had dug into his flesh,

Argyle sat down opposite her. Just to the right of her, he could clearly see the door - just in case.

'Now, tell me why you had not told Thomas of your return,' Margaret said, pushing aside the deerskin on the armrest. 'Do not worry yourself, I was hardly going to tell him, I was seeing you tonight - he would have been livid!'

'I …'

Argyle got no further before Margaret spoke again. 'I confess when you wrote to tell me you were going on a pilgrimage, I was shocked! You, who had always refused to take holy orders. When you were a child, I had to drag you hand and foot to church. What was going on, Argyle?' Margaret was not asking, she was demanding.

'Margaret, let me explain …' Argyle said.

'Let you explain?! Oh, you will explain, dear brother, and then you will go to Thomas and beg his forgiveness!'

'Beg Thomas' forgiveness?' Argyle asked.

Margaret worked her hands to keep her temper. 'Yes. I should think that would not be too much to ask. After all if he had not happened upon you here in London before you left, he would not even have known you were going away. Honestly Argyle, I am so disappointed in you! What were you thinking? You leave to go with Bolingbroke, a sworn enemy of the King - and of your beloved La Fontaine - and you send no word. No word! For months on end I have been worried sick, my husband will attest to that. And now, I find you at court?!'

'Margaret, please …'

'Margaret, please!' Margaret sneered. 'Very well, I did ask you here to explain yourself, and so you shall.'

She leaned back, releasing the top of the deerskin that she had crushed in her fists. 'Well?'

'The King sent me,' Argyle said.

'The King?' Margaret's laugh startled Argyle.

'This is no laughing matter, Margaret.' Argyle suddenly felt his own temper rise, clawing at his throat like a bear woken from its deep winter sleep. 'No laughing matter at all!'

'I am sure it is not. Only when you said that, I could so clearly see Thomas in you, back when he told me that the King had asked him to …' Margaret looked away. 'Never mind, go on.'

Argyle paused to wonder if Margaret might be suggesting what Eleanor had told him before he left for Jerusalem. But Margaret had not asked him here to be interrogated herself.

'Very well, but what I am about to tell you can go no further than this room. You can never speak of it to anyone, including Thomas.' When Margaret made to protest, Argyle silenced her. 'I must have your word, Margaret. I am betraying the King's orders for you!'

'You have my word,' Margaret said in a toneless voice.

'The King believed Bolingbroke was responsible for La Fontaine's death, so he sent me on the pilgrimage to find out what had happened.'

Margaret cut in at once. 'This old grievance? La Fontaine's death was tragic to be sure, but …'

This time, Argyle interrupted Margaret. 'No, it was not tragic, it was murder.'

In the silence that ensued, Margaret stared blankly into the air. Argyle got up and began pacing the room. They would be here for some time if he were to convince her that she could not send word to Thomas, or to anyone else.

'Margaret, before I go on, I must ask you, why you are here alone? Where is Sir Reginald?'

'He is at our home. Thomas asked me to come, and though I do not normally travel unattended it seemed his matter could not wait. So I asked Sir Reginald if I could go alone,' Margaret said. 'He was uncommonly willing to part with me.'

For the second time, Argyle felt as if his sister was keeping secrets and, for the second time, he brushed it aside; they had more important matters to discuss. 'I shall tell you as much, as I dare. I must keep you safe if anyone finds out I was here and asks you questions, do you understand?'

Margaret just sat there.

'Margaret, do you understand?' Argyle repeated, finally breaking his sister's spell.

'Yes, Argyle, I understand.' Margaret looked as though she would say more, then changed her mind and motioned Argyle to go on.

'The King suspected Bolingbroke's involvement in La Fontaine's death, as did I at the time I set out for France, but I quickly discovered that it was much more than that.' Argyle began, finding it easier to tell his tale to his sister than he had thought possible.

ꕥ ꕥ

'So what are you saying?' Margaret asked once Argyle had finished.

He had been careful to leave out several pieces of information that he was saving for the King's ears only. It was better for Margaret if she did not know. When the King had not been at court earlier that day, Argyle had cursed his bad luck, but now he found that meeting Margaret had been a blessing in disguise. Telling her the story had even provided a few more revelations, none of which he had passed on to Margaret.

'I am saying that someone at court is determined to create a rift between the King and his friends.'

'And this someone … you know who it is?' Margaret asked.

'I have a fair notion.' In fact, he had no idea. Lockley was in the wind, Bolingbroke was most assuredly innocent and the proverbial herd was thinning.

'Really?' Margaret stopped his half-hearted reply with a gesture. 'Because if you do not - I would advise you to speak to Thomas.'

'What could Thomas …'

'No, hear me out. At dinner tonight, Thomas was concerned, worried even. You and I know him best; he does not worry for nothing. Argyle, Thomas is frightened! Though he tries to hide it,' Margaret said, sighing. 'Since you have been away much has happened at court, I believe the Lords Appellant are up to their old tricks again. Now, Thomas would never confide in me unless he had no other option, and I do believe he does not.'

Argyle knelt before Margaret, bringing them at eyelevel. 'What are you not telling me?'

Margaret reached out to muss his hair. 'Oh, where to begin my dear little brother?'

'Anywhere would do. You say that much has happened in my absence. Let us begin there.'

'I hardly …' Margaret said, stifling a yawn.

Argyle looked out the window into the dead of night, a thin sliver of moonlight being the only light outside Margaret's windows. It seemed London had gone to bed while he had been speaking with her.

'It is late, I know, but you must be honest with me - as I have just been with you. Anything you can tell me, especially about the Lords. I must know if the King is in danger.' Argyle grabbed Margaret's hands and squeezed them.

Margaret relented. 'Very well, I will tell you what I can, but it may not be enough.'

'Now I am truly worried,' Argyle said.

'And you had better be, because the mighty Lords of the land are up against the King once more, and he hardly even knows it. The King has reverted to his old ways, Argyle.' Margaret's voice broke slightly. 'He is seeing ghosts, and now they are giving him ghosts to see. If he is not careful, it will be as it was once before. Thomas felt sure that was why Bolingbroke had returned home before time, and why Woodstock and Warwick have been visiting Gaunt's rooms at all hours of the day - and night.'

It was Margaret's turn to squeeze Argyle's hands. 'Thomas says it is not so, but I fear that England is on the brink of war - with itself!'

Argyle patted Margaret's hands before letting them go and settling back into his chair. 'Are you quite certain?'

'That Warwick and Woodstock are plotting? I believe they are always plotting, but after Thomas' visit tonight, I am sure,' Margaret said.

'And Thomas?'

Argyle hated to ask, but Margaret just shrugged. 'Not this time, he is quite adamant that he is loyal to the King. And what is more, I believe him, Argyle; I believe Thomas has chosen the right path this time. Bolingbroke's return has rattled him.'

'If Bolingbroke has returned to join Warwick and Woodstock, then it is certainly news to me,' Argyle admitted. 'Not that we are friends, or even allies, but I do not think Bolingbroke even knows of any plots against the King. We returned because Bolingbroke had a worrying message. And now I understand his concerns.'

'What did the message say?' Margaret asked.

'That the King is building an army,' Argyle said.

'The Cheshire archers?' Margaret asked. 'Because we all know he has those.'

'Not just them - the news was that the King is recruiting soldiers and knights across the land. He is arming for battle.'

Margaret slumped in her chair, suddenly looking years older. 'Oh God! If this is true, Argyle, you must speak to Thomas. You must make sure the King hears your story, and then we must hope that it is enough to set the King's mind at ease. Once and for all.'

'Yes, Margaret, we must,' Argyle agreed.

But he knew that his story - the whole story - was more likely to drive an even bigger wedge between the King and the Lords. Suddenly, Argyle hated his task and what he knew must come next.

'I shall speak to Thomas on the morrow,' Argyle promised with a smile before he bent to kiss his sister's hand.

Margaret inclined her head to him, gratefulness glittering in her eyes. 'Thank you, Argyle. For telling me what you have, and for understanding that in these trying times, we must unite as a family.'

Leaving Margaret's house, Argyle looked to the east to see the first feeble rays of sun struggling to push the night, and he hoped this was a sign that there was still time to set things right.

4 June 1393 — London

'You are back, without a word to me?! To anyone?' Thomas demanded angrily.

'I am here now, am I not?' Argyle was tired and irritated from a long night of first speaking with Margaret and then prowling the streets of London until he felt sure he could visit Thomas without anyone from the King's household finding out. 'Margaret knows, she spied me yesterday at court, and so would you have, had you been there.'

'Well, I was not!' Thomas' temper was rising. 'And how did you get here?'

'I got tired of travelling as slowly as Bolingbroke, I am sure he was quite happy to let me go,' Argyle said careful to choose neutral words for Bolingbroke's actions.

'Oh I see. You go away and come home blessed with a new friend!' Thomas hissed.

'No brother, but my Lord Bolingbroke …' Argyle tried.

'My Lord Bolingbroke! Now he is your lord?!' Thomas spat pacing furiously around the room. 'And you would have me believe, you are not friends? What of your allegiance to the King, or have you quite forgotten what your precious La Fontaine brought you up to believe?'

'No Thomas. But Bolingbroke …'

'Bolingbroke what?' Thomas closed the gap between himself and Argyle with a few, angry steps, panting in Argyle's face. 'I once believed Bolingbroke to be my friend and look where it got me, where it got all of our family!'

Argyle pushed Thomas away. 'Yes, look where it got you! I have not forgotten where my loyalties lie, nor am I likely to. All I am saying is that Bolingbroke is not part of this.'

'How can he not be part of this?' Thomas demanded.

'Because he did not even know I was to come on the pilgrimage. And, undoubtedly, he only welcomed me because of our affinity - your old friendship with him,' Argyle said.

'Then why did you go? And do not try to wrangle me with another tall tale about your sudden desire for piety or wanting to see where our father died!' Thomas said.

'The King ordered me.' Argyle let the words hang in the air.

Thomas staggered. 'The King?'

'Yes. He wanted to know the truth about La Fontaine's death.'

'And did you unearth it?' All Thomas' anger seemed to have evaporated, his face a white mask.

Argyle nodded. 'Yes.'

'So?' Thomas sat down heavily on the edge of his table, pushing a pile of paper aside.

'It was decreed by the King himself,' Argyle said, testing what his brother knew.

'What?' Thomas whispered.

'I cannot explain here, brother. These very walls have ears - you of all people should know that. If you can set aside your dislike for Bolingbroke and your disdain of me, I need your help,' Argyle said.

Thomas looked rattled. 'My help?'

'I should like to visit our aunt Blanche's grave. It has been too long since I have last paid my respects, and my newfound Christianity moves me to go and beg her forgiveness,' Argyle said, motioning to the door. 'Will you come with me tomorrow, Thomas?'

CHAPTER 31

5 June 1393 — Outside London

Argyle rested his hand on the massive white marble stone. It felt oddly cold to the touch even though sun was burning his neck. He turned his face to the startling blue sky.

'Have you quite finished?' Thomas' sharp voice whipped Argyle back to the present.

He shook his head sadly and turned towards the massive carriage. Argyle sent his brother a warning look that made him close the shutter with a snap. Taking a deep breath, Argyle knelt in front of the massive cover-stone, which was adorned with beautifully carved roses.

Argyle smiled. 'I am sorry I have not been here more often, aunt. Much has happened, but that you must already know, as you are surely in Heaven and privy to all that we do here on earth. I only hope, you can forgive me.'

He patted the stone and closed his eyes for a moment, remembering his aunt's sharp features and keen eyes. He had never been able to lie to her and had but seldom tried. Returning to the carriage, Argyle could feel Thomas seething within. For a moment, Argyle regretted leaving his horse behind and accepting to travel in style, as his brother had put it, to Blanche of Lancaster's final earthly resting place.

'Do be sure you do not bring in too much dirt. And shut the door quickly.' Thomas' forehead shone with sweat, Argyle was sure you could roast chickens in the carriage. 'Why did you insist on coming here?'

'You already know that I wanted to get away from London and from the spies that lurk at court,' Argyle said. ' And I need your help, as I told you yesterday - as you agreed to give me, when you went with me this morning.'

Argyle had contemplated his options. It was Margaret's words the other night that had swung the balance in favour of confiding in Thomas, which would serve two purposes.

First, to have an ally once he told the King who was behind La Fontaine's death. Second, to test Thomas' self-professed belief in the principle of family first. If word of Argyle's findings reached court before he did, he would know for sure that Thomas could never be trusted again. He hoped this was not to be the case. Settling back across from his brother, Argyle began his tale.

'The King sent me on the pilgrimage to investigate the real reason behind La Fontaine's untimely death,' Argyle said. 'The King had prayed long for a sign from God and received it just in time to knight me and order me to join Bolingbroke and secure a place in the party leaving for France. It was the King's opinion that Lockley was not alone in his actions. I agreed.'

As the carriage rumbled along the uneven road, Argyle told Thomas as much as he dared, careful to keep a few key elements to himself. He did not like to keep his brother in the dark, and yet he felt it necessary as long as the King had not yet had the news himself.

Once Argyle had finished, Thomas sat gaping at him. For the first time, Argyle saw a glimpse of the bright boy that had turned into this cold, cunning man. It took some time for Thomas to recover enough to clear his throat and begin asking questions.

How did Argyle know that Lockley was not dead in the Holy Land? Why did he suspect a link to the inner circle at court? How much did Bolingbroke know?

Argyle answered to the best of his abilities, emphasising that Lockley had confessed to his part of the affair before they reached Jerusalem, probably as he had secured allies there. He was careful not to mention his last encounter with Lockley and vague about why he was sure Lockley was still alive, and possibly in England once more. Instead, Argyle emphasised that Bolingbroke had sanctioned the search for Lockley, and that the King could not but condone.

At length, Thomas leaned back, apparently satisfied with the information Argyle had unearthed. 'I must say you surprise me. I should give you more credit than I do. Suffice to say I shall not make the mistake of underestimating you again. And yet, you are missing a final piece of information, am I right?'

'Yes. I cannot find the direct link to the court. I know for certain that Bolingbroke had nothing to do with the affair. And I know that the orders carried the royal seal. If they were not signed by the King himself, then who?'

'Well now, I might be able to assist you in unravelling this final little conundrum,' Thomas allowed.

Argyle smiled slightly, he had hoped as much. Never put it past Thomas to have all manner of information that he might find useful at some point. No doubt he had not known what to do with it until just now.

'I know that, some years ago, when Woodstock was in control, he made out several decrees in the King's name. Decrees he kept to himself as a kind of security in case the King should prove troublesome,' Thomas said. 'The decrees were marked by the King's own seal.'

Argyle drew breath, his mind whirling with this new information. 'Is that so? Woodstock was concealing them from the King?'

'Of course. Woodstock knew that his time in control was limited and he felt sure the King would revert to his old ways once he reclaimed power. I believe we can all agree that Woodstock was right.' Thomas actually smirked.

Argyle curled his hand into a fist then unclenched. 'What of it? The decrees must have been rooted out once the King took back power.'

'Or were they?' Thomas asked. 'Very few knew of them. I can as much as guarantee that he did not think I knew. And I am certain he did not share this information with many. Warwick and Arundel perhaps, they were both old allies, but no one else. Probably not even Bolingbroke'

Argyle leaned back. 'A wise move. Though I do wonder how you came about this information?'

'Ah brother, let us not pick at the wrong bone. I have my ways. In any case, some of these decrees made out in the King's name and bearing his royal seal, were death warrants for his 'former friends'. Including La Fontaine, I have no doubt after your tale. Do you not see?' Thomas' eyes shone. 'Woodstock never felt safe as long as any of the King's friends were still alive. While many were sentenced to death in absentia, your knight was left to roam free in England. Woodstock was furious when he heard the King had called La Fontaine back to court. Apparently, Woodstock had dictated that the King should not let back his former friends when he resumed power. And what does the young buck do? He welcomes his most seasoned comrade, soldier and counsellor back. The King's actions made La Fontaine powerful enemies.'

Argyle sat frozen in his seat, his head spinning. If Woodstock had indeed acted on this and sent the decree to someone like Lockley, who would end up being pinned to the murder? If the King's seal was on the decree, it would be a battle of wills beyond belief. The King would be livid and yet many would probably rally to Woodstock's side, claiming his innocence.

Thomas surveyed his brother with a cool gaze. Thomas looked as if he thought he now knew as much as Argyle did. Best leave it at that.

'Thomas, you must tell no one,' Argyle pleaded.

'This was your investigation, I am only happy to be of assistance.' Thomas looked concerned. 'Though I do implore you, the King and his uncle are balancing a fragile peace. It would be a bad idea to break it.'

Argyle was confused. 'What?'

'The King asked you to find the man responsible. Well, Lockley thrust the lance into La Fontaine's body. We all saw it, and he has freely admitted to it. Is it impossible he was acting alone? He might have received a royal decree, but in the end he was the one executing it.' Thomas rubbed his sweaty hands on his gown.

Argyle was torn. 'The King wanted the whole truth. Who am I to deny him?'

'I am not saying you should deny him,' Thomas said quickly. 'Only that it might be wise to weigh your words carefully and only point fingers where it is absolutely necessary.'

'Or else?'

'The old council is not without power. The King may be in command, but he needs good counsellors who are not afraid to give sound advice. If you shake the tree too hard, more may fall than one bad apple.'

Argyle sighed in despair. 'Thomas, I am not a good courtier. You have played the game much longer than I, and no doubt much more deftly. Yet at times I wonder where your allegiance lies?'

Rather than taking offence, Thomas laughed. 'All you need know is that I have indeed played the game both longer and more skilfully than most. So you would do well to heed my advice: leave well enough alone! The King wants a scapegoat; give him Lockley. You can hint vaguely that the man probably had incentive of some kind but that you cannot find any real evidence of that being the case. As Lockley is missing he will not step forward to name names, especially when he knows he will most likely hang for his crimes.'

Argyle nodded. Was La Fontaine's death worth risking the peace of the kingdom for?

The rest of the way they spoke of trivialities, exchanged news from their family and friends, Thomas in a fine mood and Argyle concealing a troubled mind. Once they reached London, he stepped off the carriage and sent Thomas along with a nod. As soon as the carriage turned the first corner, Argyle made directly for the stables calling for a horse.

5 June 1393 — Eltham Palace

Argyle knelt before the throne. High above, the King stared coldly at him, the room deserted but for the two of them. 'Rise! You have taken much time, Sir Argyle, I assume you have found the culprit?'

'Yes, your Majesty. He also claimed the life of an English knight in Calais.' Argyle had prepared his speech for some time, practicing it over and over again in his head. Still, standing here in front of the King, it was another matter entirely.

'Continue.'

'I have no doubt Lockley is the one guilty of carrying out the deed. He may even have coated his lance with some kind of poison to ensure La Fontaine would not survive even a superficial wound.'

'The physician suspected as much when the wound would not heal. There is more, I am sure?' the King said impatiently.

'Lockley is not a cunning man. He had no obvious grudge against La Fontaine as the two hardly ever met outside the jousting ring, and even there he, more often than not, lost before ever coming against La Fontaine. One thing I am certain of though,' Argyle paused, 'I do not believe Bolingbroke had any knowledge of the crime.'

'WHAT!' the King exploded.

'I have thought long about the matter and cannot see how Bolingbroke would even have known of La Fontaine's death until after the fact,' Argyle said quickly. 'He had left Lockley in England as a safety precaution but was himself at sea for the long voyage to Vilnius at the time, as you are well aware. Your Majesty kept the idea of the tourney a secret until two weeks before it took place. Even if Bolingbroke had known, he would surely not have had time to make arrangements.'

Argyle had come to this conclusion when he had himself experienced how long it had taken for a messenger to get from England to Jerusalem. Although this required two journeys at sea, even with just one sea voyage and subsequent hard riding across Northern Europe, there was no way a message could have been dispatched, delivered, answered, sent back and put into the hands of Lockley before the tourney. It took Bolingbroke out of play all together.

'Really?!' The King seemed less convinced, but his temper had subsided a little. 'Who then? You say this Lockely is not a cunning man, are you quite sure?'

'Beyond a doubt, your Grace. He is driven by three things - battles, lands and riches. But he has made little progress in the latter two, which suggests he is not good at playing the games of court.'

The King nodded gravely, motioning Argyle to continue. 'I asked Lockley's soldiers and squires, knights he had previously fought alongside with and those who were part of his retinue during the joust. They all confirmed my suspicions; Lockley was an angry man but not likely to act purely on dislike. He simply lacked cause.'

'How lucky, or he would have overturned us all,' the King said, leaning back in his mighty throne.

'I am sure he harboured no ill will towards La Fontaine outside the obvious; that he was a better knight,' Argyle said. 'Not something that would stir Lockley to a personal vendetta. He freely admitted as much to me before we reached Jerusalem.'

A page in the royal livery turned up at the King's side to whisper a brief message. He was waved away once the King had heard it. 'Go on, Sir Argyle. And make sure you leave nothing out.'

'Yes, Majesty. Lockley was the one to do the deed, but he was not the one to instigate it. When the pilgrimage reached Vienna, Coxcombe, who disappeared just after La Fontaine's death, showed up. I had always thought him a friend of La Fontaine and was shocked to learn he had long been in Bolingbroke's retinue.'

'Bolingbroke again!' the King growled, his face darkening.

'Naturally, Bolingbroke would welcome an ally to the pilgrimage, he had no reason to do otherwise. He welcomed me too - that does not mean I had anything to do with La Fontaine's death.'

The King waved impatiently.

'One of Coxcombe's former squires - Stephen Smith - is a friend of mine. Upon finding Coxcombe gone the night of the joust, he came to me and asked if I knew anything about it. I dismissed Stephen at the time, as I was deep in grief, yet his words stayed with me. Before setting off, I accepted Stephen into my service and made him a soldier. I brought him along for the pilgrimage, wanting a friend close by. In Vienna, Stephen was swayed to take a place in Lockley's retinue for reasons that do not matter now. After a while, I asked him to keep his eyes open for anything unusual.'

The King leaned forward, resting his elbows on his knees, as he stared at Argyle. 'What did he find?'

'Not much at first. I was sure that Lockley held some sway over Stephen and as he was eager not to anger his new master, Stephen kept his mouth shut for some time. However, when Lockley disappeared in the dead of night in Jerusalem, Stephen came to me. What he had seen and heard was very disturbing,' Argyle said.

The King got up and began pacing the dais. At every turn, he would kick up dust that danced lazily in the firelight.

'Coxcombe was no true ally to Bolingbroke.'

The King stopped dead in his tracks and whipped his head around. 'Then who?'

Argyle took a deep breath. 'Warwick.'

The silence in the room seemed to reach out cold fingers that slid up Argyles neck and made his hairs stand on end. He bowed his head and waited.

'Go on.' A threatening chill had crept into the King's voice.

'When the Lords sent away your friends, Coxcombe wrote to La Fontaine, who turned him away. At the time, I wondered why La Fontaine did not open his doors to his friend. Everyone close to you was at risk, and La Fontaine was one of the few not banished openly and who had not fled to France or Scotland.'

'Loyal to a fault,' the King said. 'I suppose you believe this turned Coxcombe against La Fontaine?'

'That was my original idea,' Argyle said. 'Yet something about it all bothered me. When Stephen let slip that Coxcombe had dwelled in Warwickshire for a while, I thought nothing much of it at the time. But when Bolingbroke's innocence was evident, it surfaced again.'

'And Coxcombe knew Lockley?' The King asked.

'Yes. Before Lockley became a sworn man to Bolingbroke, he served as squire and then soldier in Warwick's household.'

Argyle had asked Thomas if he knew about any connection between Lockley and Warwick, but if he did, Thomas had kept it to himself.

Fortunately there were some previously employed in Lockley's household who did not have any qualms giving up their old master.

'I have little doubt that it was Warwick who presented Bolingbroke with the idea of taking on Lockley,' Argyle said. 'As Warwick rarely went on crusade or into battle at all, Lockley would be rearing to go to war with someone that would let him fight. He was a warrior at heart - at that time at least, I think. He was of an age with Coxcombe, suggesting the two of them would perhaps have been trained together.'

'Warwick.' The King's fists were clenched so hard his knuckles had turned white. His lips formed a thin line and in his eyes a fire burned. 'It all comes back to the old guard then; the men who have never seized viewing me as a boy. Is there more?'

'Yes, your Majesty,' Argyle said. 'I have reason to believe Lockley thought he acted on your orders.'

The King threw a fit that sent most of the things on the dais flying in all directions. His roaring and bellowing made the doors to the room fly open as guards and courtiers came running in to see what was happening. Shaking with fury, he pointed blindly at them and sent them scuttling back out the doors in a shower of curses.

After visibly restraining himself, the King sat back down on the massive throne. A trembling page brought a cup of wine and barely managed to deliver it without spilling all the contents. The poor boy's relief was obvious when he was sent from the room.

'On my orders?' The King drank deep from the cup. 'Such a fool! Why would he think so?'

'The order for La Fontaine's death came by way of a document bearing your royal seal,' Argyle said.

'And you have seen this document with your own eyes?' the King asked icily.

'No, Majesty, not that document. I have had Lockley's house turned upside down, but to no avail. This leads me to think he was asked to destroy it once he had read the content.'

'That hardly proves that such a document ever existed,' the King said. 'It is a grave accusation to lay before me, Sir Argyle! You are trying my patience and slandering my court. How would you have me react? I could throw you in the Tower for your claims!' The King jumped down the steps from the dais and stopped only when his face was inches from Argyle's. 'You are saying that my dear friend was killed at my command?'

'No Majesty. I am saying that Lockley might have thought, it was your command, but …' Argyle said.

'But what, Sir Argyle?' the King's voice was thick with anger. 'Speak carefully.'

Argyle steeled himself. 'But the document hails from a time when your Majesty was not fully in control of the country.'

The King stared Argyle down. 'You are saying …'

'I am saying that, at one time or another, someone else had access to your seal. I cannot know who might have made out the document or even who might have kept it once you were restored to power. But I saw a document like it in Vienna, so I know such documents exist.'

'And did that too bear my seal?' the King asked, his cheeks flushed red but beneath his face had gone white.

'Yes. I saw it only once, but it did bear the royal seal,' Argyle said.

The King slowly mounted the steps and sat down on his throne. 'And who do you suspect is behind this treason?'

'I should hesitate to guess, your Majesty.'

'A guess will do.' The King leaned forward, resting his elbows on the knees and fixed Argyle with a frantic glare.

'A remnant from that horrible time could have survived somewhere,' Argyle fidgeted with the lining of his cloak.

'I think you are too quick to acquit Bolingbroke! Lockley was his man for the longest time, could not my troublesome cousin have left such a document in England and instructed Lockley to make use of it, in case he stumbled on a good opportunity?' the King asked.

'That is an uncertain possibility at best. There is no clear cause for such actions, and I am not entirely certain Bolingbroke ever really trusted Lockley that much,' Argyle admitted. 'I was further affirmed of Bolingbroke's innocence, when Lockley received another document in Vienna from an unknown messenger. It was clear to me that the order came from someone still in England.'

The King nodded slowly, seemingly lost in thought.

'This is as far as my investigation can go, Majesty,' Argyle concluded. 'I feel certain Lockley did not act alone, and just as certain he will never reveal where the order came from, not even under duress.'

'That may be so, and yet I order you to find Lockley!' the King commanded. 'Once you have done so and brought him here, I shall release you from further service. I have others who are keen to prove their loyalty to me; perhaps they can get Lockley to sing, even if you think he will not. When Lockley is in the Tower, you are free to do as you please. Including to marry, which your brother has spoken of often and loudly of late.' The King smiled wanly. 'I believe he has found a suitable bride for you. When I am satisfied you have done all you can, I will sanction the match.'

Argyle bowed deeply fighting back an insolent reply that he would never marry any woman Thomas picked out - that he would never marry at all, and that the King was mad to think that he would so easily forget that Lockley killed La Fontaine - that it would all be settled with a wife to warm his bed.

'I must ask you something, Sir Argyle.' Clearly the audience was not over, as Argyle had thought and hoped.

'Your brother was one of the Appellants. He is not, by any chance, either the source of your information or the cause of La Fontaine's death? I should hate to think you would feel more loyalty towards your family than your King.' The King's threat was clear.

'Thomas was helpful in unveiling the possible source, Majesty,' Argyle said. 'He had seen such documents being dictated in the past, but he was adamant that none had passed to him. I must believe that my brother did not lie to me when he knows what is at stake.'

'I hope you are right,' the King said sourly. 'Find Lockley and you will have my unending gratitude. Now go, Sir Argyle. And send those eavesdropping courtiers behind the door packing. I have no need for their counsel today.'

The King rose and Argyle knew the audience was finally over. Backing away from the throne, Argyle felt a mix of relief and concern.

His men were already hunting for Lockley, and Argyle had no doubt they would find him.

CHAPTER 32

27 July 1393 — Beauworth

Argyle looked up from the pile of papers as the door opened and his young page George entered the study. The boy stood at some distance from the table, looking at his own feet. Argyle felt tired to the bone and years older than he was, and looking at the boy, Argyle tried to remember a time when he was that age and found he could not. The pilgrimage, the spying, the secrets, the haunting memories and the troubles at court were enough to make any man old before his time.

Of late Argyle had barely slept; he had spent far too much time on reports and worrying and too little time attending to his squires and soldiers on the training grounds, not to mention his lands and tenants. Argyle resolved to spend the following day outside to do both, perhaps bringing George with him.

'Yes?' Argyle smiled at the boy.

'A message for you, M'lord.' The boy tentatively came forward. He shot Argyle a brief look of utter terror, clearly mistaking the smile for a grimace, Argyle thought, as he took the message from the boy's trembling hands.

'How would you like to accompany me on my rounds tomorrow, George?'

George's eyes widened 'Me, M'lord?'

'Yes, I am asking you. You look in need of fresh air, much as I do.'

George stuttered a thank you and darted out the door. Argyle leaned back in his chair and studied the paper. The characteristic lettering revealed the writer before he had even bothered to read the content. Thomas.

Sighing, Argyle brought the message to the window and rested there while he read. In an instant, the idea of a pleasant ride around the spring countryside was thrown from his mind. Argyle ran out the door, roaring in anger, one of his servants narrowly escaping a trampling as Argyle took the stairs two steps at a time.

By the front door, Argyle came upon Edward Warden, by now a greying man, who had come in search of his master. 'M'lord?'

'Gather eight of my best men. We ride before midday!' Argyle commanded.

Warden was clearly taken aback. 'Where to?'

'London! Inform the kitchens and my squires. I need two of them to go too and a full set of provisions gathered this instant. You can send more men later if you choose, I leave that up to you.'

'Yes, M'lord.' Warden turned to do as he was bid, but Argyle called him back. 'Warden, I need the fastest horses. Time is of the essence.'

2 August 1393 — London, Westminster

The horses clopped across the drawbridge and into the cobbled courtyard. Argyle swung down from his mount and strode straight for the King's audience chamber. Almost forgetting his manners, he brushed past the courtiers in the antechamber and only waited to be announced to the King in a sudden realisation that he too must adhere to court etiquette.

Argyle entered the grand room and knelt before the throne. The other men gathered there stared haughtily at him, but the King acknowledged his presence at once and motioned for him to come closer. 'Sir Argyle. Have you brought my culprit?'

'My men apprehended him before he made it across the border to Scotland,' Argyle said stiffly.

The King spread his hands. 'Let us praise the unpredictable summer and sudden floods in the North.'

The King sat brooding on the throne, several feet above the crowd. Each time his gaze fell on someone, the man immediately fell to the floor, puffing up rushes.

'You could simply have sent a messenger.' The King's voice was low and dangerous. 'I assume that is not why you are here?'

'Your Majesty is correct. I have come to plead on behalf of my brother,' Argyle said and a murmur rose in the crowd. The King silenced it with a single glance and stood up. Everyone fell to their knees, except Argyle. He had decided to stand his ground. While he still harboured doubts about his brother, this latest allegation was madness.

'I see. Is that wise, Sir Argyle?' the King said in an undertone.

'I could not say, Majesty. Nonetheless, here I am.'

'Your brother is quick to react. It was only yesterday I called him here to lay before him my belief that he ordered the death my beloved la Fontaine.'

'I believe he is innocent, Majesty - and I believe I have already proven this,' Argyle said.

'You are trying my patience, Sire!'

'Thomas helped me in my enquiries on your behalf, Majesty.' Argyle struggled to stay calm. 'Thomas comes from a long line of servants loyal to the Crown. I cannot help but feel he is being wrongly accused because others refrain from owning up to their responsibility. I warrant he has, in the past, no doubt been led astray, but in the end he proved his loyalty and was acquitted all charges - by you.'

The King did not like to be reminded of his own actions in the gruelling days of the Lords Appellant. He had indeed acquitted Thomas and even raised him higher by appointing him another title, although Argyle felt certain that the same man, who had in the end ordered the death of La Fontaine, had forced the King's hand where Thomas' title was concerned. The King's sudden spur of ill will was most likely exactly as Argyle suspected; a lashing out at the one who stayed at court while others had dispersed and claimed sanctuary behind their thick castle walls.

'Retrieve Lord Mowbray!'

The King's command was carried out instantly by a couple of guards who soon returned with Thomas in tow. He looked crestfallen but relieved at the sight of Argyle in front of the throne.

Thomas threw himself to the floor. 'Your Majesty.'

The King surveyed the room. 'See here, this is how it should be - my loyal servant showing me due humility. Rise Lord Mowbray, let me look upon you.'

Thomas did as he was bid, quickly glancing at Argyle, who had done nothing to acknowledge his presence.

'Now, is this a man who has done nothing wrong, Sir Argyle?'

When the King looked directly at Argyle, he felt Thomas' attitude change. He was not content to be passed over for his younger brother by the King.

'I believe so, your Majesty,' Argyle said. 'He knew nothing of the death of La Fontaine before it happened. Nor did I or anyone else here. If he is guilty, we all are.'

Argyle chanced a look around the room, but no one looked up to meet his defiant gaze.

However, the King laughed, a shrill and unnerving sound. 'Well spoken, Sir Argyle. I suppose I will have to acquit your brother - for the time being. The rest of you can leave me with the two Mowbrays.'

The room emptied slowly, many trying to find a reason to lag behind or even plead for the opportunity to stay. The King waited until the room was empty and then sat down slowly, his movements seemed to suck all the air out of the room.

'Now that we are alone, I would have the truth, Sir Argyle,' the King hissed his name and Argyle felt some of his nerve evaporate; this was not a King content.

'My men are returning with Lockley, Majesty,' Argyle said. 'He has denied any contact with my brother.'

'I am to believe a liar and a murderer?'

'He is most certainly a murderer, Majesty, but …'

The King turned a darkened face towards Argyle. 'How do you know he is not lying? That he has not been paid off by Lord Mowbray here?'

Thomas made to speak, but the King silenced him with a gesture, his eyes never wandering from Argyle's face. 'Well?'

Argyle would rather have the King yell and scream at him than this sinister, low voice that wormed its way into his stomach. But he had gone too far.

'I know he had his orders from someone at court, your Majesty, I also know the document was not sealed with the Mowbray crest. I will vouch for my brother's innocence.'

Next to him, Thomas took in breath as the King stood and closed the gap between them in three long strides. 'Are you certain?'

'Yes, Majesty.'

The King's breath was sour and warm, and Argyle had to fight an instinct to step backwards. If he did, the King would most certainly consider it an admission of Thomas' guilt.

'I should let a jury decide,' the King said, turning slowly towards Thomas. 'That is what you are hoping for, Lord Mowbray, is it not?'

Thomas balled his fist but kept quiet, so did Argyle.

'If a jury should decide that you were involved, it would not just affect you, it would tear down your brother too.' The King's threat was plain and cruel. 'Which leaves with me a difficult situation. If I hand you over, Sir Argyle will be at risk, and he has done nothing but what I ordered. If I do not, how will the court see me?'

'As a benevolent King,' Argyle said, and Thomas nodded. 'They will know that you would not judge rashly.'

The King scratched his chin thoughtfully. 'Very well. For now, Lord Mowbray, you are free to go. But I warn you that if I find anything to suggest otherwise, you will be arrested! You are to remain here in London and speak to no one without my permission! I am sure we can easily accommodate you in the Tower if needs be.'

'Your Majesty is too kind,' Thomas said with a trembling voice.

'Perhaps. You just see you do not find me questioning my decision. Now go!'

Argyle made to leave with Thomas, but was stayed by the King. 'Sir Argyle, I would bend your ear.'

Thomas creased his brow for a second before exiting the room by a plain side-door to the left of the dais.

'Your Majesty?'

'You say Lockley is apprehended? Is this true?'

Argyle was relieved. 'Yes. My men found him a few days ago cowering in a barn close to the Tyne. The flood had made it impossible for him to escape to Scotland and so he was biding his time there. They arrested him in your name and are heading directly for London this very moment. The terrain is hard but I expect them to make good time.'

'Well done. And you are quite certain of your brother's innocence?'

'Yes, Majesty, quite certain. He would have little to gain from La Fontaine's death, as your Majesty had already forgiven him any past misdeeds. To risk his own fortune is not the way of my brother.'

The King nodded thoughtfully. 'That is so. But I am never sure if he is working for me or to further himself.'

'Surely most courtiers do both.'

A loud laugh let Argyle know the King thought as he did. 'That is as true as it was in the days of my ancestors. I wonder if King Arthur ever had the same troubles as I do.'

Still smiling the King released Argyle. 'You must come back when Lockley reaches London. We will have the truth, one way or the other.'

CHAPTER 33

19 August 1393 — Tower of London

The return of Lockley to London took longer than Argyle expected, as the fickle late summer weather turned for the worse, pelting hail and rain relentlessly down on the land, flooding the roads, and churning the fields and roads to mud.

On a wet Thursday afternoon, Argyle's men marched Lockley into the heart of the city and straight to the Tower. Here, Argyle waited to personally escort him into the King's apartments, hoping to steal a moment alone with Lockley who looked haggard but resolute.

'Lockley!'

'Sir Argyle.' Lockley sized him up. 'I knew you weren't the devout kind. Just as slippery as your brother, finding favour with Bolingbroke and then the King in equal measure. How can any man trust you?'

'I am not such a traitor as you, nor a sodomite.' Argyle's anger rose in his chest. 'If you are lucky, you will still be alive when the King is done with you.'

'Lucky? I will tell the King that I wanted to be rid of that pathetic unicorn once and for all. I wanted to win. No one told me to do it - I did it on my own.' Lockley paused and licked his lips. 'And as for being a sodomite, I believe that can stay between us.'

Argyle grabbed Lockley by the arm and pushed him into a dimly lit corridor. 'I will be the judge of that. And rest assured, it *will* be a short audience if you are going to tell lies, but it will be a long stay in the Tower! We will go by the back way to the King's chambers,' Argyle said and forced Lockley ahead down the corridor.

'Tell me, Sir Argyle, who do you think orchestrated it?' Lockley asked. 'Now that you seem determined I couldn't have acted on my own.'

'I take you to be more of a knight than you might think. That is the only reason I did not just proclaim you the murderer,' Argyle said. 'I could have stayed in England and known nothing of your disgusting ways!'

Lockley stopped and eyed Argyle suspiciously.

'No, I believe you received a royal command,' Argyle said and Lockley swallowed. 'You truly thought it came direct from the King? But why would he kill his old friend?'

'A King is a King. Who am I to question his motives?' Lockley asked.

'Who handed you the decree? Was it the same man who you met in Vienna?' Argyle stepped close to Lockley who did not back down.

'I forget,' Lockley said in a strained voice. 'It might've been the same - all spies look alike to me. And I wouldn't know one hand from the other. The paper bore the royal seal; I took it for what it appeared to be - a royal decree to dispense with an enemy.'

Argyle hesitated. He wanted nothing more than to rid himself of Lockley by delivering him to the King, and yet he decided to push Lockley once more. 'Tell me the truth this once; who arranged the joust?'

'A man can't have a golden day on the field?' Lockley looked away.

'A man can - but not you,' Argyle said. 'You were a soldier first and never very lucky on the lists.'

'That is true, but that particular day I was. Leave it at that, Sir Argyle. Your brother wasn't involved if you must know. I never liked him much, but he had nothing to do with it.' Lockley pressed his chest against Argyle who cringed at the touch.

Argyle resumed the progress towards the King's chambers. In front of the doors to the King's chambers, he paused once more.

'Last chance, Lockley. Perhaps you could persuade me to plead your case - if you tell me who it was.'

Lockley just hung his head, and the doors swung open. The King rose from his throne on the dais and everyone in the room fell to their knees. Argyle turned his back to Lockley and walked him past the kneeling crowd.

22 August 1393 — Tower of London

Bolingbroke had been welcomed back to court in early July, the King all smiles and pleasantries. He had embraced his cousin and immediately made him a trusted diplomat, much to the surprise of all - none more than Bolingbroke. Argyle hoped, rather than believed, that this act proved the King had decided that Bolingbroke was in truth innocent. But Argyle had long since learned not to put his faith in either God or King.

The King's men came to fetch what evidence Argyle had gathered and he handed over a carefully written statement about his findings. In it, he mentioned neither Warwick nor Coxcombe. The evidence against the former was speculation and the latter had suffered a grisly death in Calais. Since Argyle had never mentioned Woodstock, even to the King, he also left him out. As Lockley was determined to stick to his story, it did not seem to matter much what Argyle thought.

Thomas had proven quite useless in the attempt to find any documents dictated by Woodstock and Argyle could not find out if his brother was trying to sabotage further discoveries or if Thomas had indeed tried and simply could find no more proof.

Argyle had to settle with Lockley taking the fall for La Fontaine's death and Coxcombe's too, both of whom Lockley had readily admitted to killing. The trial was a show and nothing more. Once Lockley admitted his crimes he sealed his own death sentence. Argyle could not suppress the feeling that someone much more powerful had gone free, and that had a bitter taste.

Word reached Argyle's London house that Bolingbroke had retired to his father's estate. Thomas told Argyle that Warwick came but briefly to court by direct royal request and went back to his estates before Lockley was tried. The Earl of Arundel ignored his royal summons and stayed in Surrey far away from court. If the King was irritated by this blatant display of disrespect he did not show it.

26 August 1393 — Tower of London

Argyle paused outside the heavy door while the jailor found the right key. After delivering Lockley to the King, Argyle had thought long and hard on whether to go and see Lockley or not. Now here he was standing before Lockley's cell - and still he was not sure why he was here.

The door screamed on its hinges as the jailor opened it. A single torch lit the small cell, casting dancing shadows on the slimy walls of the Tower cell and onto the prisoner on the low cot. Lockley turned slowly towards the door, the skin on his face taut, his hair matted and caked. His nose had an odd shape and his one eye was a closed, bloody mess.

'Leave us,' Argyle said, pressing a few coins into the jailor's hand. 'I shall call for you, when I am ready.'

The jailor simply nodded and closed the door behind him, leaving Argyle and Lockley alone.

'Come to say goodbye?' Lockley's voice was tired and rusty.

Argyle settled his own torch into a wall holder and then went to sit on the table left of the cot. 'No.'

'What else is there?' Lockley asked.

'I once promised you, I would have my own revenge for what you did to La Fontaine.'

Lockley barked a rough laugh that turned into a coughing fit. 'You would kill me before the King can? He will not like that!'

'No, he will not. And so I shall not have revenge by my own hand.'

'Learn to live with it,' Lockley said. 'So many things you could revenge, if only you had the time.'

Argyle leaned in. 'Like what?'

'That little bird of yours in Jerusalem,' Lockley sneered.

'What?' Argyle recoiled.

'She was a pretty thing. That soft hair, those dark eyes - and that mouth!' Lockley rasped. 'Made to enchant men, I should wager. Had you wrapped around her little finger, didn't she? How many times did you have her?' Lockley licked his lips.

Argyle shook his head. 'No ...'

'No? Not even once? Then I'm one up on you - just as I was with the physician.' Lockley's laugh was silenced when Argyle threw his fist in Lockley's face. Recoiling, Lockley spat out blood and a tooth. 'She screamed for you - in the beginning.'

Argyle's nails dug into his palms and drew blood. 'I do not believe you! You are a sodomite; you lie with men - unwilling men - but not women! You are a vile, evil creature, what you did was blasphemy, it was ungodly - it is sickening and DISGUSTING!'

'Why would I lie to you now? Do you think your words can harm me? Do you think I don't already know what I am?' Lockley licked blood from his split lip. 'When they slip the noose around my neck, I shall see her face before my eyes. Remember her shocked eyes, tearstained cheeks and begging words. Her vile, writhing body - a foul thing to touch.'

Argyle rounded on Lockley, grabbing him by the hair and pulling his face close. 'YOU ARE SICK!'

'If so, she was not a cure. She was no match to men - although towards the end, she tried to entice me, I think she even liked it. She must be the most disgusting thing I ever touched, but I had to see what you saw in her. Too bad all I thought about while she screamed was you!' Lockley laughed.

He did not even duck when Argyle swung for him again; Lockley took the blow straight to his jaw, his head bouncing to the side.

'Had to have insurance, you see,' Lockley choked on some blood.

'Insurance?' Argyle fought back the blinding rage, the images of Najeelah beneath Lockley. 'What insurance?'

'In case you came running back for her. I had to make sure, Abbas would not let you - or any other Englishman - inside the city walls again.' Lockley worked his jaw, which was already turning a sickly blue. 'You all thought I left before you - but I did not. I left after you.'

Argyle felt the room spinning. Najeelah … After … 'How?'

'What do you mean how? Following your tracks was easy once I knew Beaufort had taken Bolingbroke's place. Getting a ship to England was the hard part.' Lockley gave Argyle a curious stare. 'You know, I thought you cared more for the little bird, than you seem to …'

'I am sorry to disappoint you,' Argyle said feeling the rage return like a thousand horses thundering down a single path. He turned to avoid Lockley's gaze.

'Don't be. I don't care anymore. She was nothing to me, except a means to be close to you,' Lockley observed.

Argyle breathed in deep, exhaling slowly to cool his anger. 'How did you return to England?'

'I got on your ship,' Lockley offered.

'You are telling me, you were on the same ship as us?' Argyle asked.

'Imagine what Bolingbroke would say if he knew. Only by then I was certain that he would no longer believe me, he would side with you. That business with Coxcombe in Calais - that was foolish of me, although for a while it got you into trouble. To be honest, I'm not even sure, I killed the right man.'

'What?' Argyle felt his throat go dry. 'What are you saying?'

'I climbed on board just before you set sail. Easy to do considering that you had other things on your mind. I stowed away in the lower deck and stayed there until you were well on your way. You can always count on Bolingbroke to make short business of anything, he's one of the most impatient men in England after all,' Lockley said.

'No - what do you mean that Coxcombe might not have been the right man?' Argyle asked, his mind whirling.

Lockley leaned back, his eyes wary. 'Hard to tell who the order was for, there was no name this time.'

'This time?'

'Still haven't caught up, Sir Argyle? Then I believe it's time you call for that guard and get out - you have many people to speak to. Why not begin with your brother and work up the nerve to visit our good old friend Bolingbroke?' Lockley winced when Argyle lunged for him, grabbing his filthy collar and pulling it tight.

'I do not care what you have kept from the King - or anyone else - but you will be honest with me, Lockley! Who gave you the order?' Argyle whispered, ignoring Lockley's dead gaze.

Finally, Lockley broke eye contact. 'Don't know.'

Argyle let images of Najeelah screaming in pain and fear flood his mind. If Lockley wanted to get really close to him, Argyle was here to grant him his wish. Seizing Lockley by the throat, Argyle slowly applied pressure.

'Better speak up now, or I will disobey a royal command and kill you with my own, bare hands. And I will relish every single second of it,' Argyle sneered.

'Be the last thing you do,' Lockley croaked, his face first turning white then slowly red going on purple.

Argyle bore down on him. 'Tell me!'

Lockley closed his eyes, veins popping at his temples, his breath shallow. Then he nodded, and Argyle reluctantly released him - in truth he wanted to kill Lockley, even if the King would condemn Argyle to death for it.

'It bore the royal seal,' Lockley coughed, his voice rasping. Argyle shook his head violently, but Lockley persisted. 'It was even signed by the King.'

'You are wrong!'

'I may not know much, but I do know that. The royal seal was on all those documents.' Lockley bit his split lip, fresh blood running from the wound.

Argyle turned abruptly. 'All those documents?'

'The one for La Fontaine and the one I got in France,' Lockley said evasively.

'There were more.' Argyle moved towards Lockley once more, and this time Lockley winced and pushed himself up against the wall behind the cot. 'Who else?'

'No, there were two. Not good with numbers, me,' Lockley said, but Argyle persisted. 'Who else?'

'Guard!'

Argyle stepped away from Lockley just in time to see Bolingbroke standing behind the jailor. Bolingbroke quickly took in the scene before stepping forward, stopping the jailor before he could leave. 'Sir Argyle will be going with you.'

Argyle made to protest, but Bolingbroke stopped him. 'Goodbye, Sire. I do hope you have said a fond farewell to your prisoner. I doubt you will get another chance to be alone with this poor devil again.'

Argyle could do little but bow stiffly and leave with the jailor. As the door closed, Argyle heard Bolingbroke say. 'What did you tell him?'

But he did not hear Lockley's reply. Walking away from the cell, Argyle felt he was being torn apart on the inside, his mind whirling with broken, contorted images of Najeelah writhing and screaming beneath Lockley.

1 September 1393 — Tower of London

The prisoner was dragged along between two large guards, his feet shuffling to keep up, his arms turned an odd angle from his body, one of his hands bloody and mangled. To Argyle, it looked as if several fingers were missing. Just as the guards passed Argyle, Lockley looked up, a defiant glimmer in his otherwise dead grey eyes.

'They say he did not speak.' Thomas was rubbing his hands together trying to keep the unseasonable cold, wet wind at bay, but Argyle could not refrain from thinking that Thomas looked smug too.

'Really?' Argyle asked, looking after Lockley and the guards.

'Well, he may have said something, but nothing that could incriminate anyone.'

'To whom?' Argyle asked.

'They say Bolingbroke visited his cell a few days ago,' Thomas said as the crowd began to move, pushing Argyle towards the gallows on Smithfield. He walked along, powerless to stop himself.

Thomas kept pace. 'He is a fool.'

Argyle nodded bitterly. 'Soon he will be a dead fool.'

'Where is his Majesty?' Thomas looked around at the men and women. 'He is not one to miss a good hanging.'

Argyle rolled his head on his neck, the muscles taught and stiff. 'Perhaps he does not feel for going out into such miserable weather. Or perhaps he will not give Lockley the satisfaction of having a royal execution.'

'You look disgusted,' Thomas said.

'I am. If Lockley was not my prisoner, brought here to be tried and punished for his crimes, I would not be here today,' Argyle replied, anger seeping into his words.

Thomas shrugged. 'Sometimes I think you should have been born a girl.'

'That may well be, but I have no desire to see a man lose his life!' Argyle stared at the gallows and the guards trying to get Lockley to stand long enough to slip the noose around his neck. 'What is the matter with him?'

'I hear the King had one more go at getting the truth from the wretched man,' Thomas said. 'Perhaps the questioning was taken too far. It happens, you know? When the prisoner is not happy to comply and answer readily, one has to take certain measures.'

Argyle stared at his brother. 'Measures? For certainly that would be torture.'

'Some would say so. But if everyone always told the truth, there would be no need for applying instruments.' Thomas sounded bitter. 'The thing is that the truth is an elusive creature. Always subjective and almost never what the person asking the questions is looking for.'

'I suppose there is truth in your uncommon philosophic words, brother.' Argyle heard the crowd around them take in breath, as the guards finally managed to get Lockley positioned on the gallows, one guard holding him up. The priest stepped forward, saying a short prayer and asking Lockley, if he had something to say.

Lockley looked out over the crowd, his eyes resting on Argyle who stared back. Lockley was some distance away, standing on the old wooden construction, the noose around his neck, and yet Argyle felt that, at this moment, the two of them were alone on Smithfield. Then Lockley slowly shook his head.

'I give this prisoner unto God!' the priest announced, crossing himself before stepping back.

The executioner stepped forward, his dark hood pulled down low over his face, only a greying beard visible. He rested his hand on the whinge controlling the trapdoor and he nodded briefly to the guard holding Lockley.

The trapdoor gave way just as the guard stepped back and Lockley fell through the hole, the noose drawing tight. The crack of Lockley's neck breaking sounded like a tree being hit by lightning and Argyle involuntarily recoiled a little.

Thomas gave him a curious look. 'I could have sworn you would be used to death by now, brother.'

'Not this kind.' Argyle stared at Lockleys dangling legs and bulging eyes.

'Oh,' Thomas breathed. 'That is why he had nothing to say towards the end.'

'What?' Argyle asked.

'Looks like someone got his tongue,' Thomas said, and Argyle felt his breakfast surging up when he saw the gaping, bloody hole that used to be Lockley's mouth.

ഈ ഇ ഈ ഇ

CHAPTER 34

13 September 1393 — Westminster

On a warm Friday, the King finally summoned Argyle. He had waited impatiently in London since his final encounter with Lockley and the following execution. He was tired, angry and frustrated and he wanted nothing more than to leave London behind forever. But he could not leave before the King had formally dismissed him. When a page in royal livery had arrived, it was a sweet relief.

Argyle immediately boarded a barge and sailed along the Thames relieved at the opportunity to avoid riding through the streets of London. The stench had been building along with the sunny weather, making the city smell foul and malodorous from midday till dusk.

Argyle stepped off the barge and followed a royal guard across one of the small royal gardens facing the river. Before long he was outside the royal chambers in a dimly lit corridor.

'Brother.'

Argyle started at the whisper. 'Thomas?'

'I have been hoping to meet you for some time now. Matters have kept me at court, but I had thought you would come for one of the dinners, though I know Lockley's execution troubled you.' Thomas sounded disappointed.

'I have been much preoccupied with other things,' Argyle lied.

'Yes, well here you are. Now that Lockley is no longer a threat, the King seems appeased. He is about to accept the bride I have proposed for you. You will not disappoint me, I am sure?' Thomas looked expectantly at Argyle. 'Brother, I need your word.'

Just then the door opened and a guard gestured for Argyle to enter, and he was happy to escape Thomas' stern look. How could he possibly explain why he would never marry? Why not even the King could make him? That he would happily live the rest of his days in a Tower cell to avoid ever being with a woman again, knowing how much pain they could inflict - and how much pain another man could inflict upon a woman?

'I must go in.' Argyle left Thomas seething in the corridor.

He could feel Thomas' piercing eyes through the door and stepped aside as if to escape his brother's glare. Then Argyle knelt before the King, who was sitting at his desk.

'Sir Argyle! I forgive you for being right about Lockley, he did not own up to anyone else being involved. At that I suppose we must simply be satisfied to wonder and speculate. It is hard for a hanged man to speak, though mind you, before he got to the gallows, I had tried other things, but to no avail.' The King seemed in high spirits, and Argyle smiled out of duty.

'Now to the matter of my gratitude to you. You have served me well, and I am pleased to reward you for the effort. I know it has not been completely without risk.'

'Your Majesty is too kind,' Argyle said ruefully.

'Nonsense. I am a man of my word. Marriage can be bliss, Sir Argyle, I can warrant that much. I should not be half the man I am without my beloved Queen.' The King came around the table and put a knowing arm around Argyle's shoulder. 'Now, I know you avoided the subject before leaving for the Holy Land. And again last I mentioned it, but you have nothing to fear. Your brother has found a very suitable girl for you and I am happy to give my blessing for the match, if you wish it?'

Under the King's intense gaze, Argyle summoned his courage. 'Your Majesty, it is not marriage or women I fear, it is my brother's personal agenda. I should like to marry, but I would prefer to find the woman myself. She may not be from the right family or even of noble birth, but she must be the kind of woman who I can see myself sharing a life with. Preferably one my brother cannot meddle in.'

The King let go of Argyle and laughed. 'I know what you mean, Sir Argyle. My own marriage was made for politics, and yet as soon as I set eyes on my sweet Anne, I knew a kindred spirit. She is my port in high seas, and I should like nothing better than for you to find the same.'

'Nor I, your Majesty. I do not know the girl Thomas has picked for me, nor do I feel a need to. I am sure she is amiable and kind, but …'

'But that is not what you seek?'

'Well, no. I cannot yet say what I do seek, only that I should like to find her myself.'

'If you are quite sure. You risk your brother's wrath.' The King's eyes sparkled with amusement at the thought.

'I shall have to brave it,' Argyle said.

'Sir Argyle, you are not looking for me to refuse the poor girl, are you? I should not like to, she is very excited about the match, although for my part, I would have picked someone else for you,' the King said. 'And there are conventions that must be adhered to. It will be an advantageous match for both your families, and it will give you a title.'

'I am not complaining about the match or indeed the prospects, Majesty. And I shall give her the news myself; we have never met so I think, she will recover easily,' Argyle replied. 'However, I hope you will trust me to make my own decision when it comes to marriage - regardless of society's rules. I hope you will not take offense, your Majesty?'

The King nodded. 'Very well, you are free to make your own choice. I will make your brother give her the bad tidings. He has been eager to prove his loyalty to me and would you know it, here is his chance.'

At this, the King gave Argyle a jovial pat on the back, indicating that the matter was settled and the meeting was over. When Argyle took his leave, Thomas was motioned into the room by one of the King's servants, leaving them no time to exchange anything but a single glance.

Before Argyle was out of the corridor he could hear his brother's indignant outburst. Smiling, Argyle decided not to linger and went straight for the barge and the sanctuary of his own house.

The next day, Argyle's entire retinue left for Beauworth. Thomas sent no word of farewell.

ഗ്ര ഗ്ര

CHAPTER 35

3 May 1394 — Beauworth

Argyle stood by the side of his training grounds, surveying the boys and young men hard at work. He had spent much of his time restoring peace in his own household, visiting the tenants and sorting out a whole array of matters, acutely aware that everything had been left too long while he had been away.

Edward Warden was handing over his work to Stephen, who had returned to Beauworth while Argyle had been in London awaiting the result of Lockley's imprisonment and trial. Listening to Warden and Stephen discuss the progress of each apprentice, Argyle was pleased with his decision to take Stephen on and give him a position with some measure of independence. Argyle had no doubt he and Stephen would work well together.

'I shall leave the training in your capable hands.' Argyle nodded at Warden and Stephen then headed towards the stables.

George was waiting by the pen, whiling away time by rubbing the nose of a red gelding.

'George, what news from the house?'

The boy lit up in a smile of crooked teeth, then began to chatter away about what was going on in the kitchens and scullery. Eventually, Argyle stopped him and asked if there was any particular reason for his staying near the horses.

The boy's face grew solemn. 'I'd very much like to work in the stables, M'lord.'

Argyle gave the boy a quizzical look.

'I'd like it better to fetch the horses water, than wait on tables at feasts. The horses don't shout if you spill a little.'

Argyle laughed. 'That much is true. However, I believe we can find a middle ground. You can help in the stables when I have no need of you, and you will still train to be a squire.'

'Yes, M'lord.'

Grabbing George softly by the shoulder, they turned towards the house. Argyle noticed some commotion in the courtyard and saw one of his servants run from the main hall towards the stables.

'M'lord, a messenger has just arrived!' the servant gasped when he reached Argyle and George.

The messenger's horse had been brought to the water trough nearby and was drinking deeply, its neck covered in sweat. Argyle sent George to the kitchens to fetch drink and food for the messenger, and then took a scrap of paper from the man's outstretched hand.

The message was from Bolingbroke. Briefly and to the point, he accused Argyle of foul play and reminding the King of matters of old. It was clear that Thomas had not taken kindly to Argyle's rejection of his chosen bride and had been quick to forge his revenge.

Bolingbroke demanded that Argyle leave immediately for Pontefract Castle to explain himself. The message did not specify what Bolingbroke wanted, only that he expected to be satisfied in his order.

Argyle spent several minutes calming down before writing a note for Thomas. It still took three attempts before Argyle had stopped shaking with anger enough for the writing to be legible. He put the letter directly in the messenger's hands along with a purse of silver to ensure a speedy delivery.

Then Argyle summoned Stephen and Warden to have them gather four soldiers and prepare horses for departure that afternoon.

12 May 1394 — Pontefract Castle

Bolingbroke made him wait for hours in the draughty hallway. Pages, servants and knights came and went, not one of them sparing even a single glance in his direction. As evening closed in, Argyle had sent his men to a nearby inn, believing that he would be kept in the hall until the next morning.

Just when the summer sun began to melt into the horizon, a page finally approached Argyle. He was led to Bolingbroke's study and the door closed quietly behind him. Bolingbroke was standing by the open window apparently taking in the view of his father's estate.

'Sir Argyle. How good of you to come.'

Argyle let the biting tone slip past without a word.

'Your brother was here just a few days ago,' Bolingbroke continued. 'He came to give me the King's orders for a diplomatic journey. One night, after a little too much wine, he told me a very worrying tale.'

Bolingbroke turned from the window and sat behind his desk. No chair was offered so Argyle remained standing in the middle of the room.

'You believed the King responsible for La Fontaine's death,' Bolingbroke said. 'That could be considered treason.'

'The King and I have already covered the subject, and here I stand before you,' Argyle answered. 'Clearly he did not think it treasonous.'

'My cousin is a man of great temper. When Thomas spoke to you in that carriage, he did so at his own discretion - and he believed you would not take it to the King. Do you realise how much your account has affected the ruling of this land?'

Argyle held his ground. 'I gave his Majesty a full account. Only a fool would have left more out than I did. Suffice to say I only mentioned you to testify to your innocence, and I never mentioned Woodstock at all.

The King knows you had nothing to do with La Fontaine's murder. The deed is done; Lockley was caught, tried and hung for his crimes.'

'Be that as it may, when you mentioned Warwick and the foolish idea of a royal decree, you as much as said Woodstock's name,' Bolingbroke said.

'I was under royal orders. I hardly owed equal allegiance to you,' Argyle protested. 'And Thomas helped prove that there were indeed royal decrees floating around from the time Woodstock held power. Even you cannot deny this. Mentioning Warwick hardly made any difference.'

'FOOL!' Bolingbroke worked hard to control his temper. 'The King is brewing a cunning plan. He may have called a truce with the nobles of this land, but he will not be satisfied until every one of the Lords Appellant are either dead or under lock and key.'

Argyle kept quiet. Bolingbroke shuffled some papers about angrily. 'You have made trouble for us all! Why I ever thought you could be trusted …'

'And yet Thomas can be, my Lord?'

'Leave your brother out of this,' Bolingbroke said. 'Thomas has worked tirelessly to assure the King of his loyalty, as have I. It was I who ensured the other Lords did not dethrone Richard in the past; I should do so again in a heartbeat. But my cousin is fickle and resentful. Even presented with the truth, he will twist it to fit his own cause.'

Just like you, Argyle thought and said, 'Last I heard, the King was content to keep Warwick and Arundel away from court. Woodstock is still his advisor and you an honoured diplomat. If the King is serving up punishment, he has a strange way of doing so.'

'Beware what you say. I too am honour bound to tell the King if I hcar anyonc spcak ill of him,' Bolingbrokc said maliciously.

'Then surely you will know I am bound by the same honour, my Lord.' Argyle returned the threat.

'Nothing comes from this! Tell me true, Sir, were you or were you not my ally?' Bolingbroke demanded.

'I may have gone on the pilgrimage suspecting your involvement in La Fontaine's death. After all you stood to gain most from it, and

Lockley was your man.' Argyle drew breath before continuing in a calmer tone. 'Yet I was first to name you innocent! The King knows this to be true. I have not caused trouble for you, my Lord.'

Bolingbroke seemed a little appeased at this. He rose and motioned for Argyle to sit by the empty hearth, relieving some of the tension in the room. In the warm summer night there was no need to bank a fire. For a while they sat in silence, Bolingbroke brooding and Argyle wondering what might happen next.

'You may have kept Woodstock's name firmly from your story and with good cause. None of us know if a royal decree in his name with the King's seal ever existed that demanded the death of La Fontaine,' Bolingbroke finally conceded. 'And you are right, I might have stood to gain most, but the King already believed me an enemy.' Bolingbroke laced his fingers behind his neck and looked Argyle straight in the eye. 'Consider this. You have named Warwick a likely candidate for delivering the message to Lockley by way of Coxcombe. It is well-known that Warwick and indeed even Arundel does nothing without the sanction of my uncle Woodstock. Now how is that not making trouble?'

'I have been too little at court to play your games,' Argyle said. 'My assignment was clear, name La Fontaine's true killer, with evidence that can hold in court. In the end, the only one who was responsible without any doubt was Lockley. I named him.'

'Lockley, who just happened to be a former soldier in Warwick's household? Who happened to have trained with Coxcombe before their knighthood? Lockley who happened to be in my service when La Fontaine died by his lance right in front of the King?' Bolingbroke shook his head sadly. 'Sir Argyle, even I would think myself involved and, at that, anyone who has ever been my ally. The King would be a fool if he did not think so too. From now on it will be every man for himself, I fear.'

When Argyle left Pontefract at sunrise the next day, he found himself haunted by Bolingbroke's last words. If Bolingbroke was right, the country might be teetering on the brink of chaos, all because Argyle had chosen to tell the King nearly all he knew. And at the same time, not mentioning his suspicions that Woodstock was ultimately responsible for La Fontaine's death might be exactly what would keep the fragile peace between the King and the nobles.

Still, Argyle felt sure he had averted a crisis by leaving out Woodstock. But to leave out Warwick would have been too much of a risk, too disloyal to the King. It could hardly be Argyle's fault that Lockley had proved too hard a man to break, although the King had tried with all his might to get Lockley to speak before he was taken to the gallows.

No, if Bolingbroke felt so insecure, it was his own fault for ever rising against the King. Argyle had too long been wrapped up in a play for power that he had never asked to be part of. The King had released him from his oath - he resolved that if Bolingbroke sent another order for Argyle to go anywhere or do anything, he would ignore it. And he would certainly ignore any message Thomas might send.

Sick and tired of being hounded, Argyle spurred his horse, desiring nothing more than to put miles and miles between himself and Pontefract.

CHAPTER 36

27 May 1394 — Beauworth

England prospered in this time of peace. Although the King had taken measures to ensure more power for himself the people of England felt safe. Rumblings in Wales subsided, the northern border to Scotland appeared calm and France had other troubles to contend with than the old threat of English summer raids, something that had not taken place since the time of King Edward III.

Back at Beauworth, Argyle laid his worries to rest as nothing had happened since his return from Pontefract to prove Bolingbroke had been right in his concerns and threats. Argyle was satisfied to be free of court at last and turned to the business of running his estate and drilling his soldiers.

One bright morning as the dew dressed the grass and gardens in diamonds, hooves clopped on the cobbled courtyard. Argyle was reclining beside the hearth in his study, enjoying a mix of the fresh breeze through an open window and the last heat from a few glowing embers when voices and scuffle caught his attention. A few moments later, a servant knocked on the door to let in a messenger. Argyle placed a few pieces of silver in the hands of the messenger for the note he brought.

Alone again, Argyle rested on his desk and broke a wax seal with the familiar Mowbray crest. As always, Thomas wasted no time with pleasantries.

- This is to give you warning. Warwick has betrayed Woodstock to the King. Somehow Warwick has found out he was named in relation to La Fontaine's death, and he turned his cloak in an instance. From his safe haven in Warwickshire, he sent word to the King that he was only a messenger to Woodstock.

The King is livid. He sees enemies everywhere. Woodstock is stubbornly staying at court under the protection of Gaunt, but he knows his situation is uncertain at best. Woodstock is determined not to lose what little power he still holds and fears if he does leave London, it will be a testament to his guilt.

Also, the Queen is ill. It has thrown the King into a fit of rage and impotence. He is beyond council. I beg of you brother, come to London as soon as you can. - Thomas -

Argyle put down the note and stared blindly at the door for just a moment. Then he stalked into the corridor and down the stairs, shouting for a servant to stop the messenger before he rode off.

1 June 1394 — London

Argyle reached London with a small retinue just as May turned to June. Stopping only to pay his respects at his brother John's grave in White Friars, Argyle reached his London house before noon. It had been an exhausting ride and the horses were as tired and sweaty as their riders.

Argyle only paused long enough to change out of his travel-stained clothes and find a fresh horse. Trotting through the narrow streets of London, he reminisced about the first time he had seen the capital with La Fontaine. It seemed a lifetime ago. Tearing himself away from the memories, Argyle headed straight for his brother's house in Dowgate.

'Brother.'

Thomas turned from his desk, where piles of papers tottered. 'Thank God you are here!'

'I know not what difference it will make; I have not the King's ear as La Fontaine did.' Argyle was tired, weary and not in the mood to beat about the bush.

Thomas waved dismissively. 'It makes little difference. He spends day and night outside the Queen's chambers at Sheen. When he does leave, he goes straight to his own rooms only to return a few hours later, ordering all but the physicians and priests from her rooms.'

Argyle accepted a cup of wine. Joining his brother by the narrow window, he looked gravely at Thomas. 'What has happened?'

'I know you have already spoken to Bolingbroke. I am not sorry I told him of our conversation.' Thomas gritted his teeth, but Argyle simply nodded for him to go on. 'A few weeks ago, I had word from Pontefract that Warwick had sought amnesty there. Bolingbroke had turned him away and now feared where Warwick would go and to whom he might speak. Warwick was quite beside himself.'

'I should imagine,' Argyle said, 'although I am a little surprised he has not been troubled before.'

'It seems the King had not mentioned your suspicions before then. Now, Warwick feels like a fox in the hunt. The King has been restless and eager to redeem himself ever since you returned from Jerusalem. The more power he steals from Woodstock the more he reverts to his old ways.'

Argyle was annoyed. Why was Thomas so determined to paint a bleak picture before they knew anything for certain? 'England is at peace. Are you sure you are not simply being paranoid?'

Thomas turned abruptly away from Argyle, spilling most of what was left in his cup. 'Paranoid! You sit the lord of your little house in the countryside and think you know what goes on here?'

'No, Thomas, I do not. Since you have stopped sending reports, and our sisters are so little at court, I hardly know anything. Except what I can see from my trips around the countryside.'

'The King does not forget.' Thomas sounded weary. 'He is sure that if Warwick was involved, so was Arundel, Bolingbroke and I. And if we knew of anything, Woodstock must have been heading the affair. I have tried in vain to make the King understand that I knew nothing …'

'He does not believe you?' Argyle asked.

Thomas snorted. 'He believes only himself and God. Some days, I think he does not know the two are not one and the same.'

Argyle was baffled. 'Thomas!'

'At any rate, the Queen had him calm and now she lies wasting away. It would not surprise me if he thinks the old league responsible for her illness too.' Thomas slumped in a chair near an empty hearth.

Argyle threw open a window to let out the toxic air and the papers on Thomas' desk fluttered a little in the summer breeze. 'But you are not?'

'No!' Thomas half-shouted. 'What insanity. Would we take the life of the one who has always compelled the King to be merciful and kind?'

'I should hope not. I imagine that life at court is intricate, though I have little political understanding,' Argyle said.

'No one who met you would ever think you capable of scheming. Even if you are my brother.' Thomas gave a weary smile and continued. 'I know full well I have a reputation, and I warrant to some degree it is well earned.'

'Too true, and yet you had nothing to do with either La Fontaine's death, or the death of any other favourites while Woodstock was in power?' Argyle asked though he knew the answer.

'No.' Thomas put his head in his hands.

'I cannot ask the King to see me. I have not the influence, and so I cannot see what purpose I have being here. Yet if you wish it, I shall stay for now.' Argyle looked at Thomas with concern, this was very unlike his brother. Thomas nodded and had the grace to at least feign gratitude when Argyle put a hand on his shoulder. 'Maybe nothing with come of it once the Queen is well again.'

'I hope so, for if she does not recover, the King will be beyond control,' Thomas said. 'She is the one keeping him sane and the country safe. Whatever we thought of her when she first came here, the Queen has been a solace to us all, a beacon of good will and grace, and the only one to ever fully master the King.'

'He loves her,' Argyle said simply.

Thomas looked serenely at Argyle. 'And what do you know of love, Argyle?'

More than you know, Argyle thought, but he simply smiled a little at Thomas. 'You are the married one, Thomas, does Elizabeth do for you, what the Queen does for the King?'

Thomas shook his head slowly. 'If only … Oh well, perhaps you are right, the Queen will rise from her bed, the King will smile again and the country will be safe.'

Thomas saw Argyle to the small courtyard before going back inside. Argyle spent the ride back to his own house, deep in thought. That night for the first time in over a year, Argyle went to church and prayed for God to spare the Queen's life, to keep the King sane and to keep England safe.

ꕤ ꕤ ꕤ ꕤ

Six days later, the Queen drew her last breath.

Bolingbroke had been by the King's side in the Queen's final hours and when she died, he shared the King's bereavement and sorrow. Even Warwick summoned his courage and came to court to pay his respects. The only one remarkably absent was Thomas' father in law, the Earl of Arundel.

The King was crippled by grief. He had lost half his soul, the one person who could calm his temper and whom he viewed as utterly flawless. The Queen had been his safe haven and now his ship was adrift on a roaring sea. In his madness, the King decreed that Sheen Castle was to be torn down; he wanted nothing to remind him of the place the Queen had died.

Argyle briefly visited court to pay his respects and was acknowledged by the King with a heavy pat on the shoulder as he passed from his own rooms to the church. Other than that, Argyle stayed away, having no desire to be at the now grief-stricken court.

ꕤ ꕤ ꕤ ꕤ

24 June 1394 — London

At length, Argyle was summoned by Thomas' servant and led straight to his brother's house. 'Brother, how good of you to come.'

Argyle began to reply then stopped. By the hearth, he saw the looming shape of Bolingbroke.

'Thomas. My Lord.' Argyle was taken aback.

'Ah, Sir Argyle. It has been long,' Bolingbroke mumbled.

Argyle nodded his assent, and Thomas offered both his visitors refreshments. The atmosphere in the room was tense, and Argyle felt a bead of sweat trickle down his spine.

'I did not know you had company, brother. I should be happy to wait outside.'

'Bolingbroke here asked for your presence.'

'I wanted to discuss a matter with you, Sir Argyle.' Bolingbroke settled in a large wooden chair and motioned for Argyle to take a stool nearby, leaving Thomas standing at his desk. He looked oddly out of place and was clearly uncomfortable in his own home.

'You will attend the funeral of our beloved Queen, I am sure?' Bolingbroke enquired.

'Of course, my Lord.' Argyle cleared his throat. 'Has a date been settled yet?'

The King's grief was such that he had thus far avoided naming a date for the funeral, as if he half expected the Queen to rise from her lie in state and come to him all smiles and life.

'Yes, the 29th of July, the King's herald announced it just this morning. All the nobles will attend and many of the King's personal favourites too - I should count you as one of the latter, and myself as one of the former,' Bolingbroke said. 'My cousin is devastated. I knew he loved her, yet even I am surprised at the all-consuming grief that has descended upon him. I fear what might happen once the Queen is buried.'

'My Lord?' Argyle had an idea of what would come next.

Bolingbroke wasted no time. 'Richard has long been volatile. Now that the one who could broker peace has gone, I think he may lash out at anyone.'

'Perhaps it would be wise to find the King a new wife,' Thomas interfered and then shrank back, as Bolingbroke glared at him.

'He will never agree to take another wife. His heart is broken, you fool!'

Thomas cringed. When his first wife, the little Elizabeth le Strange, had died only months after their wedding, Thomas had immediately sought out another wife. But then she had been a nine-year-old girl, the Queen had been a loyal and loving wife for 14 years and the King had worshipped her.

The King cannot afford to be alone,' Thomas said defensively. 'The Queen failed to produce an heir. We all know what that means.'

'Since my father long ago swore never to succeed Richard that leaves me his heir, yes,' Bolingbroke agreed.

'I have heard talk that the King plans to find an Heir Presumptive,' Thomas continued, but Bolingbroke shook his head and Thomas stifled his next sentence, gulping down wine instead.

'Best you forget this,' Bolingbroke said to Argyle.

'My Lord,' Argyle agreed curtly.

Bolingbroke continued. 'I called you here for a favour. Once the King is back in usual form, I am all but certain he will not rest until he has found a scapegoat for the Queen's death and many other faults. I should hate to have him look my way.' Argyle frowned as Bolingbroke pressed on. 'The King believes himself invulnerable. Now that the Queen is dead, he cannot believe God would be so cruel as to take her from him. Thus, he is looking for someone else on whom to pin the blame. He needs not look far; there are several at court who have wronged him in the past. He remembers fault better than favour.'

'He will look to the old Lords Appellant,' Thomas said.

'It is the easy conclusion,' Bolingbroke agreed. 'And I cannot entirely say that I fault him for it. Yet in the end, we have helped the King govern England wisely and together we have introduced peace. I worry that he may resort to extremes in future. Woodstock has lost almost all his power, Warwick fears for himself first and cannot be trusted, Arundel is spectacularly absent and Thomas here, well, while he may have redeemed himself, no one is safe.'

'And you, my Lord?' Argyle asked.

'I am close to the throne, and I have several male heirs. I am the greatest thorn in his paw.' Bolingbroke shrugged.

'I still do not see what I can do?' Argyle said as much to himself as to Bolingbroke.

'Stay close to the King and be his friend,' Bolingbroke said. 'He will remember you as the heir to La Fontaine and be fond of you simply because you solved a little conundrum for him.'

Thomas threw his arms out in despair. 'Do you see, my Lord, what I have to contend with?'

Bolingbroke ignored Thomas and fixed Argyles gaze. 'Be a good friend - that is all I ask.'

Argyle nodded but said nothing. Better not to be overheard agreeing to be a friend when the one asking the favour was the King's enemy.

As Argyle left Thomas' house, he felt a sudden chill that the summer sun seemed unable to burn away.

ꟗ ꟗ

CHAPTER 37

29 July 1394 — London

The devastated King laid his wife to rest in a glorious ceremony at Westminster Abbey. The King had spared no expense in the preparations and execution of the magnificent burial, even surpassing their lavish wedding some twelve years earlier. It seemed that the King believed he could only express his undying devotion and love for the Queen through pomp and ceremony. Rather than curb his theatrical whims, the Queen had always supported her husband in his pageantry and show of riches. It seemed only natural for the King to give his beloved Queen one last, illustrious spectacle.

Just as the Bishop of London was about to appear, the choir already singing a slow, melancholy song, the boys' crisp and clear voices mingling with the tones of the bells ringing to the Queen's memory, the large church doors creaked open and the Earl of Arundel slipped in.

The King whipped his head around and glared at the tardy guest.

'He should have stayed away,' Thomas whispered to Argyle, the two of them sitting a few rows behind the King.

'Why?' Argyle asked, careful to keep his eyes down and his voice low.

But before Thomas could answer, the King jumped up and half-ran up the aisle towards Arundel, who shrank back. The King snatched a cane from one of the mourners and lashed it through the air, striking Arundel across the face. The old man went down grasping his bloody face, his eyes wild with fear and anger.

Thomas started but Argyle held him down, gripping Thomas' arm hard enough for him to give a muffled cry. 'What …?'

'Sit still, brother. This is not our quarrel,' Argyle hissed.

Woodstock and Gaunt were making their way up the aisle, brushing aside many other nobles all of whom were in uproar. The Bishop tried to calm down the masses but to no avail.

'WHERE THE HELL HAVE YOU BEEN??' The King roared at Arundel, who wisely stayed on the floor, blood dripping on the stone slabs beneath his crouching figure. 'THE QUEEN DIES AND YOU LEAVE NO WORD!!'

Gaunt was first to reach the King. 'Majesty, I implore you, do not …'

'Not WHAT?!' The King rounded on Gaunt, but his voice had dropped several octaves. 'Not make a spectacle? Well, I think we can agree that if Arundel truly felt it beneath him to show his Queen the proper respect, she deserves, he should simply have stayed away!'

'Certainly, Majesty, but the ceremony must go on,' Gaunt said in a soothing tone.

'Yes, Majesty. Certainly the Lord Arundel is devastated that he is tardy for this most aggrieving ceremony, and he will apologise to your Majesty, but is this the time or place?' Woodstock chimed in.

Gaunt shot him an irritated look before turning to the King once more. 'Majesty, I will make sure the Lord Arundel feels the full wrath of the court for his delay,' Gaunt said, his hand resting lightly on the King's shaking arm. 'But I feel we should honour the Queen's memory and not let her ceremony be desecrated by acts of violence and anger.'

The King's face went white. 'Anne …' he whispered, cringing away from the mass of staring faces. 'Uncle, you will see to …?'

'Naturally, Majesty, I shall take measure,' Gaunt said quickly, nodding to two guards who hard-handed gripped Arundel and dragged him from the aisle.

Leaning on Gaunt, the King walked back to his place before the altar, his beloved Queen resting in her coffin, her effigy waiting for her once the ceremony was over.

'This will not be the end of it,' Thomas said, rubbing his arm where Argyle had dug his fingers in.

'Surely this was grief …,' Argyle said but did not really believe it.

Thomas glanced sideways. 'No, this is the King we all must obey. This is who he is, and you are simply lucky that this is the first time you see him for what he truly is.'

Argyle stared at the Bishop as he commenced the ceremony, the choir drowning out the murmur of enraged and troubled nobles and knights alike. If this was who the King truly was, he was a stranger to Argyle.

☙ ❧ ☙ ❧

The same afternoon, Thomas once more summoned Argyle. Before leaving, Argyle instructed the household to pack for departure the following day. He had had quite enough of the scheming court and longed for the simple country life that Beauworth afforded him.

This time, the servant did not lead Argyle to Dowgate but to Westminster. Within, he found his brother, Bolingbroke and the aging Gaunt.

'I hoped you had not left.' Thomas sounded almost desperate.

Argyle stared angrily at his brother. 'You were just in time, I plan to leave at daybreak tomorrow.'

'What did you think of the King's display today?' Thomas asked.

'Arundel should have chosen a faster horse,' Argyle said, earning a half-smile from Bolingbroke.

'It was ungraceful.' Thomas' voice almost broke, and Argyle gave his brother a curious look.

'Surely you only care because Arundel is your father-in-law?' Argyle examined Thomas carefully. What was this truly about?

'Let us leave it for now, boys!' At Gaunt's comment, the room went quiet. Bolingbroke turned his back to Argyle to face his father, so whatever transpired between the two, Argyle could not tell.

'Suffice to say, we now know that no one is safe at court,' Gaunt said. 'I have asked Arundel to leave at once before he finds himself in even more trouble, and I will issue the same request to Warwick. The King is not himself, we should not taunt him.' Thomas huffed but said nothing as Gaunt continued. 'Woodstock stays! I cannot do without him, but I will rein him in. Furthermore, I will plead for the King to reconcile with Arundel. The peace of the land is paramount.'

Argyle wondered why he had been asked to join a discussion about the ruling of the land. Argyle had no place offering either council or advice to anyone, he was a knight and solider first and foremost. His eyes sought his brother, who looked away.

'My Lord, what is all this to me?' Argyle asked Gaunt.

'I merely needed you to bear witness that my son and I are doing all we can to secure peace in the land. In case the King should ever find himself wondering what happened in those most distressful days when he was unable to rule himself.' Gaunt looked coolly at Argyle.

'And he should ask me?'

Gaunt sighed, clearly displeased. 'Perhaps - or I might ask you to relay this debate, Sir Argyle. Thomas, I do believe you are right, he is most certainly not court material.'

The two laughed and Argyle smiled, let them think what they wanted. As long as he could leave London tomorrow, he would gladly be the butt of their little joke.

'Do not be fooled, father,' Bolingbroke said. 'I should remind you that he got you to send him to me and tricked me into thinking he was a truehearted pilgrim right till the very end.'

'Right you are, Henry. I almost forgot he is not Thomas!' Gaunt said sardonically.

Thomas shirked then seemed to get his bearings once more. 'Thank you, brother, you are free to return to your home. If we need you, we will know where to find you.'

Argyle left the room hoping in earnest never to be at court again.

ဢ ဢ

Epilogue

3 June 1395 — Beauworth

Late at night, Argyle woke in a sweat, haunted by a pair of glittering dark eyes. The sensation of silk and warm skin lingered on his fingertips. He could even make out the smell of sweet mint.

Knowing he would not sleep again that night, he sat instead on the windowsill of his bedchamber. Deep in thought, he absently fingered the thin chain around his neck. Argyle never took it off, but would sometimes forget it was there when it was hidden beneath his clothes. Now it seemed to cling to his skin, burning with a strange fire.

He breathed deeply taking in the familiar smell of summer in the country. In the shimmering moonlight, he could make out trees and fields as far as the eye could see. Looking at the moon, he was jolted back to a time that seemed all but a dream.

1393 — Jerusalem

'One day I would like to experience your land.' Najeelah turned her glittering eyes at him; his stomach was free falling. Her exotic voice and the strange way she pronounced some words still tickled him.

'You would be disappointed,' Argyle ventured.

'How can you know?'

'Because it is a cold, dark and hard place. The complete opposite of here.'

'And I could not possibly like something that is not like here?'

Argyle shrugged. He would choose Jerusalem - and Najeelah any day. Almost. Najeelah slowly got up and worked her way around the shaded room, her fingers tracing the walls, stopping at every window to peer out between the ornate carvings. No one knew they were here, no one could see them.

'What would you do in England?' Argyle asked.

'Visit all the places that mean something to you. Your home, the place you were born. Meet the King.'

He watched her moving around the room. 'He would fall in love. It would not be fair to his Queen.'

'He would be nothing to me.' When Najeelah smiled, her eyes would squint a little giving her a mischievous look. 'Or perhaps meet your family?'

'My sisters would dote on you. Joan especially.'

'She is your favourite?'

'I have never thought of it before, but yes, I suppose so. Although I think you would like Eleanor best. She looks like me.'

'Then I will like her very much.'

He gave a warm smile and reached for her as she passed but she kept walking, fingers tracing the room as if she was memorizing every stone with her touch. 'And your brother?'

Argyle pondered this for a long time. She kept moving round and round. He closed his eyes, how would Thomas react? 'He might take to you, but he would not like the idea of us.'

Najeelah looked at him. 'There is an 'us'?'

'Is there not?' Argyle had not thought she would disagree.

'Right now, yes there is. But if I were to go to England, I would have to travel with Abbas.'

There was that sadness again, seeping through her voice and wandering into her eyes. Najeelah finally chose a chair across the room from him. Between them stood a low ornate silver table on spindly legs. It felt like an insurmountable wall.

'What if you left him?' Argyle said hopefully.

'I cannot.'

'Why not? I would care for you, keep you safe, give you a home, children perhaps.'

She laughed quietly, unlike her melodic voice it was a husky sound. 'They would have your eyes and my hair. What a sight they would be.'

Argyle liked toying with the idea. Secretly he had done so ever since he first met Najeelah, even before he knew her name. What would a future be with someone like her? How would they live and where? What would their children look like? Little girls just like her, boys with fair hair and blue eyes but with her deep olive skin.

'They would be beautiful.'

'They would be different,' Najeelah said and smiled her sad smile. 'They would not belong here or in England. You must see this. It is a wonderful dream, but it is just a dream. I can never leave Abbas. Not because of my mother, although I think of her too, but because I am bound to his house. That is my life.'

They had spoken of this before. In the beginning, Najeelah had been reluctant to explain the arrangement in detail. When she finally did, Argyle had not believed her; he had not wanted to believe. Her story was so strange that he still struggled to understand it.

Her mother was part of Abbas' harem. Argyle had consequently thought her the daughter of Abbas. Why else give her a seat of honour at the high table for the feast? Why call her his jewel?

It had turned out she was not his daughter. Her mother had been married before to a man who had left them ruined when he fled Jerusalem. Abbas had been kind to take in the mother and daughter, but at a price. Struggling to make a life for herself and her child, Najeelah's mother had accepted.

'You think too much. It makes you look old.' Najeelah was sitting before him, her hands resting on his chest.

Argyle had not even noticed her move. Every time he thought of her situation, he felt a little sick. As he looked at her, she stood once more and began circling the room. There would always be this distance between them.

Argyle reached for her. 'Then teach me not to think.'

ꕥ ꕥ ꕥ ꕥ

12 June 1395 — Beauworth

She haunted his days and nights. Sometimes he blamed the memory of her for his inability to take a wife, to get on with his life.

Thomas had pressed the matter of marriage a few times since Argyle had returned from Jerusalem. He had even found other suitable candidates, when Argyle had turned down Thomas' first choice, but in the end, he had given up.

Even Argyle's sisters had pleaded with him not to wait too long, they themselves happy wives with children and wishing the same bliss for their beloved brother. To himself, Argyle conceded he had given the matter little effort.

In Beauworth, he settled contentedly to the work of being a good landlord and loyal knight. He successfully amassed a large retinue of skilled soldiers. He paid his dues to the crown every year in barley, oats and venison from his woods.

Yet despite it all, he felt a thirst no drink could ever quench.

ꕥ ꕥ ꕥ ꕥ

Argyle slid the gold chain inside his shirt to once more rest against his chest.

While he broke his fast, Stephen informed him about progress in the training, equipment that needed repairs or replacement and ideas for the expansion of the stables. Argyle smiled absently and nodded occasionally.

'So you agree, we need to purchase more horses, M'lord?'

Argyle snapped back into the present. The noise in the hall pressed into his ears, pushing away a faint exotic tune. 'What?'

'More horses to be sure we're ready if the King summons us?' Stephen gave Argyle a curious look.

'How many?' Argyle felt a twinge of shame. 'I am sorry. I was miles away.'

'At least a dozen horses,' Stephen repeated.

'Very well, if you think this is necessary.'

'How many miles away were you?'

'Far enough that you could have said a hundred horses and I probably would have agreed,' Argyle said.

Stephen laughed heartily. 'Next time, I'll do that.'

'After breakfast, join me in my study, I have a matter to discuss with you.'

ꕤ ꕤ ꕤ ꕤ

'You're quite sure?'

Stephen was hovering over the map on the table, looking back and forth between it and Argyle with a concerned crease on his forehead. Argyle nodded, leaning on the cool stonewall. Outside another dry, sunny summer day was on its way.

'Yes. I have to do this.'

'The King'll let you go?' Stephen asked curiously.

'The King released me once Lockley was hanged for his crimes. What does he care what a lowly knight does?'

'You aren't a lowly knight.'

'Trust me, he has forgotten all about me,' Argyle said. 'There are matters much more pressing for a King to deal with than what I do. If he enquires after me, simply send word that I have gone on another pilgrimage. He can scarcely say anything to that; after all he sent me on my first one.'

Stephen shuddered. 'And what an adventure that was, M'lord! I shouldn't wonder if he finds it a great mystery that you'd brave the journey a second time.'

'Perhaps I have grown fond of travelling and become more godly.'

'Perhaps I'll see a pig fly someday,' Stephen said, 'but I doubt it, M'lord.'

Argyle laughed. 'Surely you cannot imagine, he would argue against a desire to visit Jerusalem once more?'

'If he knew why, he'd call you back before you ever set foot in Calais.'

Argyle rested on the windowsill, looking out over the open fields and beyond to the green woodlands. There were rumours that the King was in a difficult mood, but when was he not? The Queen's death had sent him into a rage that had lasted for months, and Gaunt had encouraged him to go on progress far and wide to take his mind of his beloved wife. The King had returned in a much better state than when he left, and yet there were rumblings.

'I do not intend to tell him why, but for your sake, I shall leave behind a message in my own hand explaining why I went abroad without consulting the King,' Argyle said. 'Will that set your mind at ease?'

Stephen stretched, his back cracking loudly, and turned to look at Argyle. 'I suppose. But I still think you'd be better off asking permission than pleading forgiveness.'

Argyle smiled and tapped his cup. 'And I say we toast the decision! After all it leaves you in charge.'

'I know - and I like that even less!' Stephen poured ale into Argyle's cup and then his own, raising it. 'To new journeys and old friends.'

'New journeys, old friends and England at peace,' Argyle added and the two of them drank deep.

'When'll you go?'

'Well before the winter storms - September if I can.' Argyle patted Stephen on the shoulder. 'I will return by God's grace and my own good fortune.'

'What do you hope to achieve?' Stephen asked. 'You must know that nothing good can come from this journey. Maybe I should come with you?'

'No, you are needed here. I only ask that you do not buy a hundred horses while I am away.'

It was Stephen's turn to laugh. 'If that's what you want. But you didn't answer my question, M'lord.'

'Because I do not know. Maybe I hope for closure? Maybe matters have changed since I was there last? Maybe I can impress on Abbas to relent? Maybe just to know there is no hope?'

'Too many maybes, if you ask me.'

'I need a change of air. Will that do?' Argyle ventured.

'You're free to do whatever you choose, M'lord.' Stephen agreed. 'I'm free to think what I like. But if this is your wish, I'll make the preparations, and personally pick out the men to take with you.'

Argyle inclined his head, Stephen knew the men as well as he did, he would choose wisely.

'And choose a few of the new horses too,' Argyle added as an afterthought.

7 September 1396 — at sea

Argyle had secured a crossing for ten men, horses and provisions. He had inspected the ship and talked to the captain when the ship was last moored at Dover. Completely satisfied that everything was in order, he had instructed Stephen on what to do while he was away - and what to do if they had no news from him.

'After all, I will be far away, and you know yourself how hard it is to get messages across from England,' Argyle had said to Stephen. 'Just make sure everything is taken care of.'

Stephen had agreed, plainly relieved Argyle had not changed his mind and asked him to come too. Now that Argyle stood at the bow of the ship looking towards Calais, he did wonder if perhaps he was wrong not to ask Stephen to go. Granted, he had found a servant girl who he was courting, but if Argyle had asked, Stephen would have agreed, although reluctantly, he was sure.

'How long before we can see the port?' he asked Hobbs, the captain, a burly, weather-beaten man with an honest face and tightly cropped, greying hair.

'The Titan'll know!' Hobbs said, pointing to the crow's nest atop the tallest mast. 'Why not climb up and ask him?'

Argyle smiled. 'I ask too often?'

'Third time today, Sire.'

'Forgive me,' Argyle said, 'I have been looking forward to this journey for a long time!'

'Aye, and Calais we'll see, when we see it,' Hobbs said before going back to the helm.

Argyle leaned on the railing, rejoicing in the fresh sea-air, his mind once more turned to Jerusalem. He wondered what it would be like to return, if Lockley had indeed made it impossible for Argyle - or any other Englishman to set foot in the city. At the thought of Lockley, the sodomite and murderer, Argyle strengthened his grip on the railing.

Even now, with his sights set on the horizon, Argyle could not shake the feeling that the light he had shed on La Fontaine's death was not enough. There were so many unanswered questions, so many loose ends. Thomas had begged him to let it go and the King had thanked him for bringing in Lockley and said the mystery was solved. Then why did Argyle not think so?

Lockley had swung on the gallows, the hideous black hole where his tongue had been a permanent image burned into Argyle's mind. If only he had had more time with Lockley in the Tower before Bolingbroke had interrupted him. Argyle snorted, then Lockley would most likely had died by his hand, and he would have swung from the gallows in his place for ignoring a royal order.

But still … the memory of La Fontaine falling from his horse, unsaddled by the least likely opponent gave Argyle pause. There was something not right about it. He had wondered for weeks before leaving, waking in the night to pace the halls of Beauworth, his mind and heart battling to win the silent argument. Loyalty or love? Love or loyalty? He could not see that he could have both and still be in one piece.

In the end, his heart had won and now he almost felt, he could see Najeelah's black eyes gazing for him from the city walls of Jerusalem, silently begging him to return for her. He had wondered what La Fontaine would have done, but since he had never thought to ask, when his master was still alive, how could he think, he would know what advice La Fontaine would have given, now that he was dead.

Dead and buried, Argyle thought, let him rest now in his grave and know that I did all I could, that forces larger than I sought to stop me and prevailed. If I could have wrestled more from Thomas or Lockley, I would have, if I had the power to make Bolingbroke speak, I would have. The King himself ...

'What's that behind us?' a sailor called, but Argyle did not turn.

'Could be sails, Captain!'

The crew sprung to life, the deck suddenly alive with men rushing to the stern of the ship to spy what was looming in the horizon.

'It'll be fog!' Hobbs ruled after looking briefly behind. He turned his gaze once more towards the French coastline. 'This time of year, it always is.'

'Damn quick fog then!' the Titan called from his crow's nest.

Argyle turned around, he could only see something white in the horizon but not make out what it was.

'PORT AHOY!' the Titan cried. Argyle turned back and at first saw nothing, he strained his eyes and suddenly little knobs came into view on the French coastline. He marvelled at the Titan's magnificent sight, Argyle could only make out a few dots on the horizon.

It felt as if he could almost smell the dry air of Jerusalem riding in on the waves, the sea's salty spatter felt like the warm sand of the bazaar. Argyle closed his eyes and saw Najeelah dance before him.

The captain corrected his course and let the ship's mate take the helm.

'Won't be long now, Sire,' Hobbs said as he joined Argyle at the bow. 'You'll see the big pillars in the water soon, and make out the garrison. You'll be in by nightfall and on your horse by daybreak.'

'CAPTAIN!'

'WHAT?' Hobbs turned his gaze to the crow's nest. 'That damned Titan, what's all this yelling for?'

Argyle too gazed up and saw the Titan climbing deftly down the rigging.

'GET BACK UP THERE!' Hobbs shouted. 'I don't recall asking you to come down!'

The Titan landed on the deck and ran to the bow. 'It's a ship, Captain, and no mistake! It's a ship coming for us, and they're calling to us.'

'What'd make you say that, you mongrel?!' Hobbs demanded and the Titan paused to give his captain a weary look, his eyes gleaming white in a face as dark as tar.

''Cause they be calling Sir Argyle's name.'

'Mine?' Argyle blinked. 'You must be mistaken.'

'Pro'bly too much time alone in that nest of yours,' Hobbs agreed, 'and I'd advise you climb back up there, 'fore I find someone else to do it and you'll be out of a job!'

'Captain, I don't make mistakes. I've the best ears and the keenest eyes on this ship, and I say, they're yelling for Sir Argyle,' the Titan insisted.

'Gulls,' Hobbs said and the Titan frowned. 'It'll be gulls screaming, we're near land now.'

'Unless the gulls have learned to speak like you white men do,' the Titan grumbled, 'it's men calling.'

Argyle and Hobbs made for the stern, one of the seamen joining them to light the signalling lantern. If it was a ship hailing them, maybe the crew were in trouble.

'I can't hear a thing!' Hobbs declared when they reached the stern. 'Light the lantern!'

Argyle felt his heart plummet, he could hear some of the words, and one of them did sound like his name, but it could not be so, he had left Stephen in charge of Beauworth, surely nothing could have happened there already? It must be a mistake … Argyle turned to spy the harbour of Calais now in full view, seagulls floating above them, crying and screaming.

'It's making good speed,' the seaman with the lantern said.

'IT'S ENGLISH!' the Titan had reclaimed his nest and was now looking not ahead to Calais but behind towards England.

'WHAT COLOURS?' Hobbs called back. 'If it's a crew in need they'll be flying a signal of distress. If it's not …'

Hobbs' unspoken words drifted away on the sea breeze. Argyle gritted his teeth, he had an ominous feeling that he knew what colours they would fly. 'How long before we are at port? Can we get there before nightfall?'

'Aye, the wind's picked up a fair bit, we could set the headsail and prob'bly get you there sooner,' Hobbs said, his eyes showing what concern his face did not. 'But if the ship …'

'If it is in need, naturally we must turn around and aid them,' Argyle said quickly. 'But if it is not, I will pay you more to keep sailing to Calais and as fast as you can. Hoist any sail you must to get me there before the ship catches up.'

'You know who'd might be?'

Argyle did not answer but simply stared into the misty air until his eyes burned from all the spray of the keel. All he needed to do was land in Calais, get the horses and men off the ship and slip out of the city. Once outside, he would have several choices for his route and he would choose the wisest, if not the quickest. Without a large pilgrimage to contend with, Argyle knew that he could make the journey to Jerusalem in just three months. He would not have to stop at every castle or city; he had brought enough coin to make such tactics unnecessary.

But what if it is important? his mind whispered. What if something has happened that cannot be ignored?

'They're flying the royal banners!' Argyle jumped at the Titan's voice, he was standing right next to him. How did such a big man move so swiftly and silently? 'They don't do that for no merchant ship!'

Hobbs looked at Argyle. 'The choice is yours, Sire. You have paid for the passing.'

Argyle licked his lips, tasting the salt of the sea. His cloak billowed around him. If he asked the captain to hoist the headsail and get him to Calais, he would. But could they outrun the other ship? Since it was first sighted, it had grown substantially in size. 'Can we make it?'

'It'll be tight, but I think so,' Hobbs said.

The Titan looked from Hobbs to Argyle, his black face never revealing his feelings.

'What say you?' Argyle asked.

'I'm just the lookout,' the Titan said. 'But you'd be a brave man to try.'

I can be brave! Argyle thought, I can brave anything for the love of my life. She is waiting for me; I know she is! She will be my salvation …

and my undoing. His mind was a jumble of incoherent thoughts, he felt as if he was being pulled apart by the ship behind and the port ahead.

The seaman with the lantern turned around. 'It's a message for you, Sire. From the King!'

Forget them all! his heart screamed. Let them know they cannot command you - only one soul in the world commands you and she is ahead, she is the future. Leave it behind - let it go!

'What does it say?' Argyle heard himself ask, his heart thumping so loudly he could hardly hear the seaman's voice over it.

'It's your family.'

Argyle's vision blurred, he had to steady himself on the railing, the Titan giving him a worried look. Hobbs was squinting against the increasing spatter of saltwater, trying to make out the rapid flashing from the approaching ship. Argyle could see the people on the deck now, tiny little figures, but growing bigger by the minute. He had to decide, set sails and try to outrun the fast ship, or turn about.

Hobbs glanced at him. 'What's your order, Sire?'

HISTORICAL NOTE

The reign of Richard II Plantagenet is perhaps best known for the Peasants Revolt in 1381, and yet, it plays only a very small role in this book. It does, however, prove beyond a doubt what kind of King, Richard was to become.

In his defence, Richard II was not raised to be a King, his father the Black Prince was. It was always believed that there would be plenty of time to teach Richard all he needed to know to be a good King. When the Black Prince predeceased his own father, Edward III, there was but little to be done. Edward III was close to death himself and by many historical accounts his mind was fragmented at best. The latter years of his reign, Edward III was seen only on rare occasions and preferred to be in the company of his mistress rather than at court.

When Richard II was crowned King of England, he was surrounded by his uncles who sought to protect the child King and govern the country. But Richard was strong-willed and following the heroic act on Smithfield where he singlehandedly saved England from civil war, he grabbed power from those more experienced at wielding it. Richard's notion that he was chosen by God to serve as King was fed by his lucky escape that day and fuelled his entire reign.

Most historians agree that Richard and his cousin Henry of Bolingbroke - later to be Henry IV - were by all accounts never close. Though of the same age and made equal in many ways by their royal blood, the two seemed never to find a common foothold. Perhaps because Richard was crowned and anointed at an early age, perhaps because Henry grew up to be all that Richard never was; skilled in combat and often called one of the finest jousters in all of England. Richard was pious and favoured peace rather than war, much to the dismay of many of his contemporaries. He was a far cry from his grandfather and father, both of whom had won their reputations on the battlefield.

In 1387 when the Lords Appellant tried to dethrone Richard, they probably believed they were acting to ensure stability and continuity in England. But it is fair to assume that much of the hatred between the King and the nobles were born out of jealousy and a lust for power. Despite being a firm friend from childhood and having grown up with the King, Argyle's brother Thomas was in the thick of things and would by all accounts have helped unseat Richard, had not Henry changed his mind.

It is worth noting that while Henry joined the Lords Appellant, his father John of Gaunt never wavered in his loyalty to his royal nephew King Richard. Did Gaunt interfere and persuade Henry that toppling Richard was a bad idea? Perhaps, no one knows for sure. But the Lords' failed attempt certainly created a rift between the King and the nobles that would never be mended.

Many reasons could be stated for Henry deciding not to return to England from his trip to the Baltic region in 1392. Some historians believe he was trying to avoid a public humiliation at Richard's court, while others claim that it was Henry's godly nature that drew him to Jerusalem. Whatever the reason, by the time he reached Jerusalem, Richard was rattling his sabre, amassing his own private army. No King before him had ever had cause to or need for a private army, but Richard was allegedly so terrified that the English nobility would not answer his call in a time of war that he felt compelled to establish his White Harts.

It is fair to assume that when word reached Henry in Jerusalem, he may well have feared for his father's life and his inheritance in equal measure. Certainly, he must have been keen to return home, and yet, his return to England took several months. In this book, I have used this rather strange behaviour to excuse a little charade. While Henry rides hard to get to England, his half-brother pretends to be Henry and visits many great courts around Europe. Historians agree that the brothers went on the pilgrimage together. They were of similar looks and build and it is possible that Thomas Beaufort could have impersonated Henry to ensure that he could travel quickly to England to take orders from their father John of Gaunt.

While the Mowbray family is a real noble family with strong ties to the royal court, Argyle is entirely fictional. According to several historians, his older brother Thomas was indeed a troublemaker often finding himself on the outs with the King. And yet he always seemed to return to positions of ever increasing power and importance. Why the King decided again and again to trust him, we will never know.

Most of the knights in the book, including La Fontaine, are dreamt up for this particular occasion. However, the close relationship between the likes of La Fontaine and the King would have existed. Like his ancestor, Edward II, Richard has been accused of being too close to the young men at court who were not of noble birth. He seemed to prefer their company to that of his family, perhaps another reason why Richard and Henry were never close.

All the characters that the pilgrimage meets while in Jerusalem are fictional. It is safe to assume that there would have been many powerful men in Jerusalem interested in knowing all that went on in Henry's camp, and that some might even have tried to strike up friendships to find out more. At the time, the region was often a place of strife between religions and peoples.

ABOUT THE AUTHOR

Mette Holm is a writer of historical fiction focusing on last of the Plantagenet rulers beginning with Richard II. The Mowbray family caught her eye when she was first researching the age and especially Thomas Mowbray was so fascinating, she simply had to write about him and the Mowbray family. The decision led to her first book: At the King's Command.

Mette Holm has been telling stories all her life, be it in school, at university or even in her day-job as an independent business owner and copywriter. While historical fiction holds a special place in her heart, a yet unfinished fantasy manuscript occupies her top drawer and rumour has it that it will in time be dug out and finished. As a quirk despite her Danish heritage, she knows more about medieval England than she does about Danish medieval history.

For more information please visit: metteholmbooks.com or follow Mette Holm on Facebook: @MetteHolmBooks and on Instagram: @authormetteholm

If you want to make absolutely certain, you don't miss a beat – sign up for her newsletter at this address: www.metteholmbooks.com

FOLLOW ARGYLE MOWBRAY ON HIS NEXT QUEST IN BOOK 2: COURT OF DEADLY WHISPERS

'There were things to be done, masters to serve and orders to carry out.'

Two women of great importance. One can save a kingdom, the other can topple it. Only a knight stands between peace or war – but is he willing to pay the ultimate price?

Argyle Mowbray, knight and nobleman, has fallen into disgrace, the suspect of treason and fraternising with the enemy.

When the King takes a child bride, Argyle glimpses the opportunity to return to favour and secure a peaceful existence at the outskirts of courtly life. But when a ghost returns from the grave, Argyle knows what he desires most can never be his.

As the vengeful King of England throws down his gauntlet and challenges his past demons, the destiny of thousands shifts. As the heads roll and blood spills, a traitor slips between the royal sheets.

Argyle is forced to realise that, sometimes, chivalry can lead to only one destination; death.

Court of Deadly Whispers is based on historical events and is the second volume of the Mowbray Chronicles. The book is set in and around the medieval English court in the late 14th century.

ALSO BY METTE HOLM

Court of Deadly Whispers

Web of Lies

Printed in Great Britain
by Amazon

28151693R00216